SPECIAL

THE ULVERSCROFT FOUNDATION
(registered UK charity)
was established to provide funds for
research, diagnosis and treatment of eye diseases.
Examples of major projects funded by
the Ulverscroft Foundation are:-

- The Children's Eye Unit at Moorfields Eye Hospital, London
- The Ulverscroft Children's Eye Unit at Great Ormond Street Hospital for Sick Children
- Funding research into eye diseases and treatment at the Department of Ophthalmology, University of Leicester
- The Ulverscroft Vision Research Group, Institute of Child Health
- Twin operating theatres at the Western Ophthalmic Hospital, London
- The Chair of Ophthalmology at the Royal Australian College of Ophthalmologists

You can help further the work of the Foundation by making a donation or leaving a legacy.
Every contribution is gratefully received. If you would like to help support the Foundation or require further information, please contact:

THE ULVERSCROFT FOUNDATION
The Green, Bradgate Road, Anstey
Leicester LE7 7FU, England
Tel: (0116) 236 4325

website: www.ulverscroft-foundation.org.uk

30130505647198

THE RETURN

Trevor Benson never intended to move back to New Bern, North Carolina. But when a mortar blast outside the hospital where he worked sent him home from Afghanistan with devastating injuries, the dilapidated cabin he'd inherited from his grandfather seemed as good a place to regroup as any. From their very first encounter, Trevor feels a connection with deputy sheriff Natalie Masterson that he can't ignore. But even as she seems to reciprocate his feelings, she remains frustratingly distant. Further complicating his stay in New Bern is the presence of a sullen teenage girl, Callie, who lives in the trailer park down the road. Trevor hopes Callie can shed light on the mysterious circumstances of his grandfather's death, but she offers few clues. Trevor will learn the true meaning of love and forgiveness.

NICHOLAS SPARKS

◆

THE RETURN

Complete and Unabridged

CHARNWOOD
Leicester

First published in Great Britain in 2020 by
Sphere
An imprint of Little, Brown Book Group
London

First Charnwood Edition
published 2021
by arrangement with
Little, Brown Book Group
An Hachette UK Company
London

A catalogue record for this book is available
from the British Library.

ISBN 978–1–4448–4643–0

Published by
Ulverscroft Limited
Anstey, Leicestershire

Set by Words & Graphics Ltd.
Anstey, Leicestershire
Printed and bound in Great Britain by
TJ Books Ltd., Padstow, Cornwall

This book is printed on acid-free paper

To the Van Wie family
Jeff, Torri, Anna, Audrey, and Ava

Acknowledgements

It's hard to believe that twenty-four years have passed since my first novel, *The Notebook*, was published . . . and even more remarkable to think that so many of my initial collaborators, advisors, and friends remain the same after all this time. It is impossible to adequately express how grateful I am to the multifaceted team that has supported my long career, but I'll give it a try once again:

First, to my literary agent Theresa Park, of Park & Fine Literary and Media: we were just kids when we started on this journey, and here we are in middle age, twenty-two books later. To say we share a brain, a heart, and the same wellspring of determination only begins to scratch the surface. Thank you for being my creative partner and unwavering supporter through all the stages of our adventurous lives.

The team at Park & Fine is the most sophisticated, proactive, and effective literary representation in the business. To Abigail Koons, Emily Sweet, Andrea Mai, Alex Greene, Ema Barnes, and Marie Michels: you are the savviest folks in publishing and a joy to work with. To the new members of Park & Fine, Celeste Fine, John Maas, Sarah Passick, Anna Petkovich, Jaidree Braddix, and Amanda Orozco — welcome! I'm thrilled to see the agency expand and avail myself of your wider expertise.

At Grand Central Publishing (formerly Warner Books, back when I first got into the biz), President Michael Pietsch has continued to champion my publishing career and has shown me only unflagging support. Working with publisher Ben Sevier and Editor-in-Chief Karen Kosztolnyik has been a true pleasure — they are steadfast, insightful, and above all, kind. Brian McLendon continues to be a creative marketing force for my books, and Matthew Ballast and Staci Burt manage to orchestrate my publicity campaigns with first-rate care and skill. Flag and Art Director Albert Tang, thank you for coming up with such signature looks for my covers, each more striking than the last. Amanda Pritzker, you are a wonder at keeping all the pieces of my campaigns in sync and working hand in hand with my team at PFLM.

Catherine Olim at PMK-BNC remains my hyper-responsive and super-experienced outside publicist, whom I have leaned on so heavily over the years — Catherine, how could I have survived the shark-infested world of publicity without you? Mollie Smith and LaQuishe Wright are always, always ahead of the curve when it comes to social media outreach; you know me better than I know myself, and have never stumbled in your efforts to bring out the best in me.

My Hollywood representation is justifiably the envy of every creator: Howie Sanders at Anonymous Content, ardent advocate and loyal friend beyond reproach; Keya Khayatian, savvy dealmaker and longtime supporter; and of course, Scott Schwimer, the most dogged, conscientious, and tireless lawyer anyone in Hollywood could ask for. Scottie, they broke the mold after you were born!

However, home is truly where my heart is, and I'd be remiss not to mention the people who safeguard and warm the place from which I draw greatest comfort: my children Miles, Ryan, Landon, Lexie, and Savannah, who all add joy to my life; Jeannie Armentrout and Tia Scott, who help keep my daily life running smoothly; Pam Pope & Oscara Stevick, my wonderful accountants; Victoria Vodar, Michael Smith, Christie Bonacci, Britt & Missy Blackerby, Pat & Bill Mills, Todd & Gretchen Lanman, Lee & Sandy Minshull, Kim & Eric Belcher, Peter & Tonye-Marie, David & Morgan Shara, Dr. Dwight Carlblom, and David Wang, all of them fantastic friends. And of course, I'd like to thank my extended family as well: Mike & Parnell, Matt & Christie, Dan & Kira, Amanda & Nick, Chuck & Dianne, Todd, Elizabeth, Monty & Gail, Sean, Adam, Sandy, Nathan, Josh, and finally, Cody and Cole — who always keep the doors and phone lines open.

Prologue

2019

The church resembles an alpine chapel, the kind you might find in the mountains outside Salzburg, and inside the cool air is welcoming. Because it's August in the South, the temperature is sweltering, made worse by the suit and tie I'm wearing. In my daily life, I generally don't wear suits. They're uncomfortable and as a physician, I've learned that my patients respond better to me when I'm dressed more casually, as they tend to be.

I'm here to attend a wedding. I've known the bride for more than five years now, though I'm not sure that she would consider us friends. Though we'd spoken regularly for more than a year after she left New Bern, our relationship since then has been limited to a couple of texts every now and then, sometimes instigated by her, sometimes by me. We do, however, have an undeniable bond, one that has its roots in events that occurred years ago. Sometimes it's hard for me to remember the man I was when our paths first crossed, but isn't that normal? Life endlessly offers us chances to set new directions and in the process we grow and change; when we look in the rearview mirror, we catch a glimpse of

1

former selves who sometimes seem unrecognizable.

Some things haven't changed — my name, for instance — but I'm thirty-seven now and in the early stages of a new career, one I'd never considered in the first three decades of my life. While I'd once loved the piano, I no longer play the instrument; where I'd grown up with a loving family, it's been a long time since I've seen any of them. There are reasons for that, but I'll get to those parts later.

Today, I'm simply glad to be here, and to have made it on time. My flight from Baltimore had been delayed and the line to pick up my rental car was long. Though I'm not the last to arrive, the church is more than half full and I find a seat in the third row from the back, doing my best to slip in unobserved. The pews in front of me are filled with women wearing the kind of hats you expect to find at the Kentucky Derby, extravagant confections of bows and flowers that goats might enjoy eating. The sight makes me smile, a reminder that in the South, there are always moments when it's possible to slip into a world that seems to exist nowhere else.

As I continue to take in my surroundings, the sight of flowers also makes me think about bees. Bees have been part of my life for most of my living memory. They are remarkable and wonderful creatures, endlessly interesting to me. These days, I tend to more than a dozen beehives — it's much less work than you might imagine — and I've come to believe that the bees take care of me in the same way they take care of everyone.

2

Without them, human life would nearly be impossible, since we rely on bees for a large part of our entire food supply.

There's something impossibly wonderful about that concept, that life as we know it can come down to something as simple as a bee making its way from one plant to another. It makes me believe my part-time hobby is important in the grand scheme of things, and yet, I further understand that tending beehives also led me here, to this small-town church, far from the landmarks of home. Of course, my story — like any good story — is also the story of events and circumstances and other people as well, including a pair of old-timers who liked to sit in rocking chairs in front of an old mercantile store in North Carolina. Most important, it's the story of two different women, though one was really just a girl at the time.

I'm the first to notice that when others tell their stories, they tend to frame them in ways that make them the star. I'll probably fall into the same trap, but I'd like to offer the caveat that most of the events still strike me as accidental — throughout my telling, please remember that I regard myself as no kind of hero.

As for the ending of this story, I suppose this wedding is a coda of sorts. Five years ago, I would have been hard-pressed to say whether the conclusion of these intertwining tales was a happy, tragic, or bittersweet one. And now? Frankly, I'm even less certain, as I've come here wondering whether the story might in some winding fashion pick up exactly where it left off.

3

To understand what I mean, you'll have to travel back in time with me, to revisit a world that despite all that has happened in the intervening years, still feels close enough to touch.

1

2014

I first noticed the girl walking past my house the day after I'd moved in. Over the next month and a half, I saw her shuffle by a few times a week, head down and shoulders hunched. For a long time, neither of us said a word to each other.

I suspected she was in her teens — something about the way she carried herself suggested she was struggling beneath the twin burdens of low self-esteem and irritation at the world — but at thirty-two I'd reached the age where it was almost impossible for me to tell. Aside from noting her long brown hair and wide-set eyes, the only thing I knew for sure about her was that she lived in the trailer park up the road and that she liked to walk. Or more likely, she had to walk, because she didn't own a car.

The April skies were clear, the temperature hovering in the low seventies, with just enough breeze to carry the perfumed aroma of flowers. The dogwoods and azaleas in the yard had roared into bloom almost overnight, framing the gravel road that wound past my grandfather's house just outside New Bern, North Carolina, a place I'd recently inherited.

And I, Trevor Benson, convalescing physician and disabled veteran by profession, was shaking mothballs from a box along the base of the front porch, lamenting that it wasn't how I'd planned to spend my morning. The problem with doing chores around the house was never knowing quite when you might be finished, since there was always something else that needed to be done . . . or whether fixing up the old place was even worthwhile at all.

The house — and I used the term loosely — wasn't much by way of appearance and the years had taken their toll. My grandfather built it himself after returning from World War II, and though he could build things to last, he didn't have a lot of talent when it came to design. The house was a rectangle with porches on the front and back — two bedrooms, kitchen, family room, and two bathrooms; the cedar siding had faded to a grayish silver over the years, mimicking my grandfather's hair. The roof had been patched, air seeped through the windows, and the kitchen floor slanted to the point that if liquid spilled, it became a tiny river that flowed to the door that led to the back porch. I like to think it made cleaning up easier for my grandfather, who'd lived by himself the last thirty years of his life.

The property, however, was special. It was a shade over six acres, with an aging, slightly tilting barn and a honey shed — where my grandfather harvested his honey — and dotted with seemingly every flowering plant known to mankind, including clover patches and wildflowers. From

6

now until the end of summer, the property would resemble a ground-level fireworks display. It was also situated on Brices Creek, where dark, brackish water flowed so slowly that it often reflected the sky like a mirror. Sunsets turned the creek into a cacophony of burgundy and red and orange and yellow, while the slowly fading rays pierced the curtain of Spanish moss draped over the tree branches.

The honey bees loved the place, which had been my grandfather's intent, since I'm pretty sure he loved bees more than people. There were about twenty beehives on the property; he'd been a part-time apiarist all his life, and it often struck me that the hives were in better condition than either the house or the barn. I'd checked on the hives a few times from a distance since my arrival here, and though it was still early in the season, I could tell the colonies were healthy.

The bee population was growing rapidly, as it always did in spring — I could actually hear them buzzing if I listened — and I'd left them to their own devices. Instead, I'd spent most of my time rendering the house livable again. I cleaned out the cupboards, setting aside a few jars of honey to keep, and tossing the remainder — a box of stale crackers, nearly empty jars of peanut butter and jelly, and a bag of dried-out apples. The drawers were crammed with junk — out-of-date coupons, half-used candles, magnets, and pens that didn't work, all of which went into the garbage. The refrigerator was mostly empty and oddly clean, without any of the moldy items or disgusting smells I'd expected. I purged a ton of junk from the house — most of the furniture was half a century old, and my grandfather had a minor hoarding issue — and then hired various crews to do the more difficult work. I had had a contractor do a cosmetic remodel on one of the bathrooms; a plumber fixed the leak in the kitchen faucet; I had the floors sanded and stained, the interior painted; and last but not least, I had the back door replaced. It was cracked near the jamb and had been boarded over. Then, after bringing in a crew to clean the place from top to bottom, I got my laptop set up with Wi-Fi and picked up some furniture for the living room and bedroom, as well as a new television for the family room. The original television had rabbit ears antennae and was the size of a treasure chest. Goodwill declined the donation of my grandfather's used furniture, despite my argument that it could all be regarded as antiques, so it ended up at the dump.

The porches were in relatively good shape, though, and I spent most of my mornings and evenings there. Which is how and why I'd started with the mothballs. Spring in the South isn't only about flowers and honey bees and pretty sunsets, especially when you live adjacent to a creek in what seemed like the wilderness. Because it had been warmer than usual recently, snakes had begun to wake from their winter slumber. I'd spotted a big one on the back porch when I'd wandered outside that morning with my coffee. After having the bejesus scared out of me and spilling half the coffee down the front of my shirt, I quickly ducked back inside the house.

I had no idea whether the snake was poisonous or what kind it was. I'm not a snake expert. But unlike some people — my grandfather, for instance — I didn't want to kill it, either. I just wanted it to stay away from my house and live *over there*. I knew that snakes did useful things — like killing mice, which I'd heard scurrying in the walls at night. The sound creeped me out; despite spending every summer here when I was a kid, I'm not used to country living. I'd always considered myself more of a condo-in-the-city guy, which is what I had been, right up until the explosion that blew up not only my entire world, but me as well. Which was why I was convalescing in the first place, but more on that later.

For now, though, let's get back to the snake. After changing shirts, I vaguely remembered that my grandfather used mothballs to keep snakes away. He was convinced that mothballs had magic powers to repel all kinds of things — bats, mice, bugs, and snakes — and he would buy the stuff by the case. I'd spotted plenty of them in the barn, and figuring my grandfather must have known something, I seized a box and began to scatter them liberally around the house, first in the back and along the sides, then finally in the front.

That was when I again spied the girl trudging down the road that led past the house. She was dressed in jeans and a T-shirt, and when I lifted my gaze, she must have felt my eyes on her because she glanced in my direction. She didn't

9

smile or wave; instead, she ducked her head as if hoping to avoid acknowledging my presence.

I shrugged and went back to work, if dropping mothballs could actually be considered work. For whatever reason, though, I found myself thinking about the trailer park where she lived. It was at the end of the road, about a mile away. Out of curiosity, I'd walked down there shortly after I'd arrived. It had sprung up since the last time I'd visited, and I suppose I wanted to know who the new neighbors were. My first thought upon seeing it was that it made my grandfather's place look like the Taj Mahal. Six or seven ancient and decrepit trailers appeared to have been dropped haphazardly on a dirt lot; in the far corner were the remains of another trailer that had caught fire, leaving only a black, partially melted husk that had never been cleared away. In between the trailers, clotheslines drooped between slanting poles. Scrawny chickens pecked an obstacle course of cars on blocks and rusting appliances, avoiding only a feral pit bull chained to an old discarded bumper. The dog had teeth the size of bacon and barked so ferociously at my presence that spittle flew from its foaming mouth. *Not a nice doggy,* I remembered thinking. Part of me wondered why anyone would choose to live in a place like this, but then again, I already knew the answer. On my walk back home, I felt pity for the tenants and then chastised myself for being a snob because I knew I'd been luckier than most, at least when it came to money.

'Do you live here?' I heard a voice ask.

Glancing up, I saw the girl. She'd doubled back and was standing a few yards away, clearly keeping her distance, but close enough for me to notice a spray of light freckles on cheeks that were so pale as to seem almost translucent. On her arms I noted a couple of bruises, like she'd bumped into something. She wasn't particularly pretty and there was something unfinished about her, which made me think again that she was a teenager. Her wary gaze suggested that she was prepared to run if I made the smallest move toward her.

'I do now,' I said, offering a smile. 'But I don't know how long I'll be staying.'

'The old man died. The one who used to live here. His name was Carl.'

'I know. He was my grandfather.'

'Oh.' She slipped a hand into her back pocket. 'He gave me honey.'

'That sounds like something he'd do.' I wasn't sure if that was true, but it struck me as the right thing to say.

'He used to eat at the Trading Post,' she said. 'He was always nice.'

Slow Jim's Trading Post was one of those ramshackle stores so ubiquitous in the South and had been around longer than I'd been alive. My grandfather used to bring me there whenever I visited. It was the size of a three-car garage with a covered porch out front, and it sold everything from gas to milk and eggs, to fishing equipment, live bait, and auto parts. There were old-fashioned gas pumps out front — no credit or debit accepted — and a grill that served hot

11

food. Once, I remember finding a bag of plastic toy soldiers wedged between a bag of marshmallows and a box of fishing hooks. There was little rhyme or reason to the offerings on the shelves or displayed on the walls, but I always thought it was one of the coolest stores ever.

'Do you work there?'

She nodded before pointing at the box in my hand. 'Why are you putting mothballs around the house?'

I stared at the box in my hand, realizing that I'd forgotten I was holding it.

'There was a snake on my porch this morning. I've heard that mothballs will keep them away.'

She pursed her lips before taking a step backward. 'Okay, then. I just wanted to know if you were living here now.'

'I'm Trevor Benson, by the way.'

At the sound of my name, she stared at me. Working up the courage to ask the obvious.

'What happened to your face?'

I knew she was referring to the thin scar that ran from my hairline to my jaw, which reinforced the impression of her youth. Adults usually wouldn't bring it up. Instead, they'd pretend they hadn't noticed. 'Mortar round in Afghanistan. A few years back.'

'Oh.' She rubbed her nose with the back of her hand. 'Did it hurt?'

'Yes.'

'Oh,' she said again. 'I guess I'll get going now.'

'All right,' I said.

She started back toward the road before

suddenly turning around again. 'It won't work,' she called out.

'What won't work?'

'The mothballs. Snakes don't give a lick about mothballs.'

'You know that for sure?'

'Everyone knows it.'

Tell that to my grandfather, I thought. 'Then what should I do? If I don't want snakes on my porch?'

She seemed to consider her answer. 'Maybe you should live in a place where there aren't any snakes.'

I laughed. She was an odd one, for sure, but I realized that it was the first time I'd laughed since I'd moved here, maybe my first laugh in months.

'Nice meeting you.'

I watched her go, surprised when she slowly pirouetted. 'I'm Callie,' she called out.

'Nice to meet you, Callie.'

When she finally vanished from view, blocked by the azaleas, I debated whether to continue putting out mothballs. I had no idea whether she was right or wrong, but in the end, I chose to call it a day. I was in the mood for some lemonade and wanted to sit on the back porch and relax, if only because my psychiatrist recommended that I take time to relax while I still had time.

He said it would help me keep *The Darkness* away.

13

My psychiatrist sometimes used flowery language like *The Darkness* to describe PTSD, also known as post-traumatic stress disorder. When I asked him why, he explained that every patient was different and that part of his job was to find words that accurately reflected the mood and feelings of the patient in a way that would lead the patient along the slow path toward recovery. Since he'd been working with me, he'd referred to my PTSD as *turmoil, issues, struggle, the butterfly effect, emotion dysregulation, trigger sensitivity*, and of course, *The Darkness*. It kept our sessions interesting, and I had to admit that darkness was about as accurate a description of the way I'd been feeling as any of them. For a long time after the explosion, my mood *was* dark, as black as the night sky without stars or a moon, even if I didn't fully realize why. Early on, I was stubbornly in denial about PTSD, but then again, I'd always been stubborn.

In all candor, my anger, depression, and insomnia made perfect sense to me at the time. Whenever I glanced in the mirror, I was reminded of what had happened at Kandahar Airfield on September 9, 2011, when a rocket aimed at the hospital where I was working impacted near the entrance, only seconds after I'd exited the building. There is a bit of irony in my choice of words, since glancing in the mirror isn't the same as it once was. I was blinded in my right eye, which means I have no depth perception. Staring at a reflection of myself feels a little like watching swimming fish on an old computer screen saver — almost real, but not

14

quite — and even if I were able to get past that, my other wounds are as obvious as a lone flag planted atop Mount Everest. I've already mentioned the scar on my face, but shrapnel left my torso pockmarked like the moon. The pinkie and ring finger on my left hand were blown off — particularly unfortunate since I'm a lefty — and I lost my left ear as well. Believe it or not, that was the wound that bothered me the most about my appearance. A human head doesn't look natural without an ear. I looked strangely lopsided and it wasn't until that moment that I'd ever really appreciated my ear at all. In the rare times I thought about my ears, it was always in the context of hearing things. But try wearing sunglasses with just one ear and you'll understand why I felt the loss acutely.

I haven't yet mentioned the spinal injuries, which meant having to learn how to walk again, or the thrumming headaches that lingered for months, all of which left me a physical wreck. But the good doctors at Walter Reed fixed me up. Well, most of me, anyway. As soon as I was upright again, my care shifted to my old alma mater Johns Hopkins, where the cosmetic surgeries were performed. I now have a prosthetic ear — so well done I can hardly tell it's fake — and my eye appears normal, even if it's completely useless. They couldn't do much about the fingers — they were fertilizer in Afghanistan by then — but a plastic surgeon was able to diminish the size of my facial scar to the thin, white line that it now is. It's noticeable, but it's not as though little kids scream at the sight of me. I like to tell myself that it adds character, that beneath the surface of the suave and debonair man before you exists a man of intensity and courage, who has experienced and survived real danger. Or something like that.

Still, along with my body, my entire life was blown up as well, including my career. I didn't know what to do with myself or my future; I didn't know how to handle the flashbacks or insomnia or my hair-trigger anger, or any of the other crazy symptoms associated with PTSD. Things went from bad to worse until I hit rock bottom — think a four-day bender, where I woke covered in vomit — and I finally realized that I needed help. I found a psychiatrist named Eric Bowen, who was an expert in CBT and DBT, or cognitive and dialectical behavioral therapies. In essence, both CBT and DBT focus on *behaviors* as a way to help control or manage what you're thinking or feeling. If you're feeling put-upon, force yourself to stand up straight; if you're feeling overwhelmed because you're faced with a complex task, try to lessen that sensation with simple tasks of things you *can* do, like starting with the first easy step, and then, after that, doing the next simple thing.

It takes a lot of work to modify behavior — and there are a lot of other aspects to CBT and DBT — but slowly but surely I started to get my act back together. With that came thoughts of the future. Dr. Bowen and I discussed all sorts of career options, but in the end, I realized that I missed the practice of medicine. I contacted Johns Hopkins and applied for another residency. This time, in psychiatry. I think Bowen was flattered by that. Long story short, strings were pulled — maybe because I'd been there before, maybe because I was a disabled vet — and exceptions were granted. I was accepted as a psychiatric resident, with a start date in July. Not long after I'd received the congratulatory notification from Johns Hopkins, I learned that my grandfather had had a stroke. It occurred in Easley, South Carolina, a town I'd never heard him mention before. I was urged to come to the hospital quickly, as he didn't have much time left.

I couldn't fathom why he was there. As far as I knew, he hadn't left New Bern in years. By the time I got there and found him in the hospital, he could barely speak; it was all he could do to choke out a single word at a time. Even those were hard to understand. He said some odd things to me, things that hurt me even if they made no sense, but I couldn't shake the feeling that he was trying to communicate something important before he finally passed away.

As his only remaining family, it was up to me to make the funeral arrangements. I was certain he wanted to be buried in New Bern. I had him transported back to his hometown, set up a small graveside service, which had more attendees than I'd imagined there would be, and spent a lot of time at his house, wandering the property and wrestling with my grief and guilt. Because my parents were so busy with their own lives, I'd spent most of my summers growing up in New Bern, and I missed my grandfather with an ache that felt like a physical vise. He was funny, he

17

was wise and kind, and he always made me feel older and smarter than I really was. When I was eight, he let me take a puff from his corncob pipe; he taught me how to fly-fish and let me help whenever he repaired an engine. He taught me everything about bees and beekeeping, and when I was a teenager, he told me that one day, I would meet a woman who would change my life forever. When I asked how I would know if I'd met the right one, he winked and told me that if I wasn't sure, then I'd better just keep on looking.

Somehow, with all that had happened since Kandahar, I hadn't made time to visit him during the past few years. I know he worried about my condition, but I hadn't wanted to share with him the demons I was battling. Hell, it was hard enough to talk about my life with Dr. Bowen, and even though I knew my grandfather wouldn't judge me, it felt easier to keep my distance. It crushed me that he was taken before I had the chance to really reconnect with him. To top it off, a local attorney contacted me right after the funeral to let me know that I'd inherited my grandfather's property, so I found myself the owner of the very home where I'd spent so many formative summers as a kid. In the weeks following the funeral, I spent a lot of time reflecting on all the words I'd left unspoken to the man who had loved me so unconditionally.

My mind also kept returning to the odd things my grandfather had said to me on his deathbed, and I wondered why he'd been in Easley, South Carolina, in the first place. Did it have something to do with the bees? Was he visiting an old friend? Dating a woman? The questions continued to gnaw at me. I spoke to Dr. Bowen about it, and he suggested that I try to find the answers. The holidays passed without notice, and with the arrival of the new year I listed my condo with a realtor, thinking it might take a few months to sell. Lo and behold, I had an offer within days, and closed in February. Since I'd soon be moving to Baltimore for residency, it didn't make sense to find a place to rent temporarily. I thought about my grandfather's place in New Bern and figured, why not?

I could get out of Pensacola, maybe get the old place ready to sell. If I was lucky, I might even be able to figure out why my grandfather had been in Easley, and what on earth he'd been trying to tell me.

Which is how and why I found myself scattering mothballs outside his rattletrap old cabin.

I didn't really have lemonade on the back porch. That's how my grandfather used to refer to beer, and when I was little, one of the great thrills of my young life was getting him a lemonade from the icebox. Strangely, it always came in a bottle labeled Budweiser.

I prefer Yuengling, from America's oldest brewery. When I attended the Naval Academy, an upperclassman named Ray Kowalski introduced me to it. He was from Pottsville, Pennsylvania — home of the Yuengling Brewery

— and he convinced me there was no finer beer. Interestingly, Ray was also the son of a coal miner and last I heard, he was serving on the *USS Hawaii*, a nuclear submarine. I guess he learned from his dad that when you're working, sunlight and fresh air are overrated.

I wonder what my mom and dad would have thought about my life these days. After all, I haven't worked in more than two years. I'm pretty sure my dad would have been appalled; he was the kind of father who would sit me down for a lecture if I received an A — on an exam and was disappointed when I chose the Naval Academy over Georgetown, his alma mater, or Yale, where he'd received his law degree. He woke at five in the morning every day of the week, read both the *Washington Post* and the *New York Times* while having his coffee, then would head to DC, where he worked as a lobbyist for whatever company or industry group had hired him. A sharp mind and an aggressive negotiator, he lived to make a deal and could quote large sections of the tax code from memory. He was one of six partners who oversaw more than two hundred attorneys, and his walls were decorated with photographs of him with three different presidents, half a dozen senators, and too many congressmen to count.

My dad didn't simply work; his hobby was work. He spent seventy hours a week at the office and golfed with clients and politicians on the weekends. Once a month, he hosted a cocktail party at our home, with still more clients and politicians. In the evenings, he often secluded himself in his office, where there was always a pressing phone call to make, a brief to be written, a plan to be made. The idea of him kicking back on the porch and having a beer in the middle of the afternoon on a workday would have struck him as absurd, something a slacker might do, but never a *Benson*. There was nothing worse than being a slacker, in my father's eyes.

Though he wasn't the nurturing type, he wasn't a bad father. To be fair, my mother wasn't exactly a cookie-baking, hands-on PTA member, either. A neurosurgeon trained at Johns Hopkins, she was frequently on call and was a good match for my father in her drive and passion for work. My grandfather always said she came out of the wrapper that way, belying her small-town background and the fact that neither of her parents went to college. But I never doubted her or my father's love for me, even if we ate takeout for dinner every night and I attended more cocktail parties as a teenager than family camping trips.

In any case, my family was hardly unusual for Alexandria. Everyone at my elite private school had high-powered and prosperous parents, and the culture of excellence and career success filtered down to their children. Stellar grades were the norm, but even that wasn't enough. Kids were also expected to excel at sports or music or both and be popular to boot. I'll admit I got sucked into all of it; by the time I was in high school, I felt the need to be . . . *just like them*. I dated popular girls, finished second in my class, made all-state soccer in my junior and senior years, and was proficient on the piano. At the

Naval Academy, I started on the soccer team all four years, double majored in chemistry and mathematics, and did well enough on my MCATs to be accepted to Johns Hopkins for medical school, making my mother proud.

Sadly, my parents weren't around to watch me receive my diploma. The accident was something I don't like to think about, nor do I like to tell others what happened. Most people don't know what to say, conversation falters, and I'm usually left feeling even worse than had I said nothing about them at all.

Then again, I sometimes wondered whether I just hadn't told the story to the right person, or if that person was even out there. Someone should be able to empathize, right? What I can say, however, is that I've come to accept that life never turns out quite like one expects.

2

I know what you might be thinking: How can a guy who considered himself a mental and emotional basket case for the last two and a half years even think about becoming a psychiatrist? How can I help anyone if I've barely figured out my own life?

Good questions. As for the answers . . . hell, I didn't know. Maybe I'd never be able to help anyone. What I did know was that my options were somewhat limited. Anything surgical was out — what with the partial blindness and missing fingers and all — and I wasn't interested in either family practice or internal medicine.

I'd be lying if I said I didn't miss surgery, though. I missed the raw way my hands felt after scrubbing, and the sound of the gloves snapping in place; I loved repairing bones and ligaments and tendons and feeling like I always knew exactly what I was doing. There was a kid in Kandahar about twelve years old who'd shattered his knee-cap falling off a roof a couple of years earlier, and the local physicians had botched the operation so badly that he could barely walk. I had to rebuild the knee from scratch and six months later, when he returned for a checkup, he jogged toward me. I liked the way it made me feel — that I'd fixed him, allowing him to lead a normal life — and wondered whether psychiatry would ever give me that same satisfaction.

Because who is ever really fixed when it comes to mental or emotional health? Life takes radical twists and turns, and hopes and dreams shift as people enter different phases of their lives. Yesterday, via Skype — we speak every Monday — Dr. Bowen reminded me that we're all continual works in progress.

I was musing about all of this as I stood over my grill later in the evening with the radio playing in the background. The sun was going down, illuminating a kaleidoscope sky as I flipped the NY strip I'd picked up from the Village Butcher on the far side of town. In the kitchen, I had a salad and baked potato ready to go, but if you're thinking I'm some kind of chef, I'm not. I have a simple palate and I'm decent with the grill, but that's about it. Since moving to New Bern, I'd been shoving charcoal into my grandfather's old Weber three or four times a week and setting the coals ablaze. It made me nostalgic for all those summers of my childhood, when my grandfather and I grilled our suppers almost every night.

When the steak was ready, I added it to my plate and sat at the table on the back porch. It was dark by then, the house lights glowing from within, and moonlight reflected off the still waters of Brices Creek. The steak was perfect, but my baked potato was a bit cold. I would have popped it in the microwave, except for the fact that the kitchen didn't have a microwave.

Though I'd made the house livable, I hadn't yet decided on whether to renovate the kitchen, or put on a new roof, or seal the windows, or even fix the slant in the kitchen floor. If I decided to sell the place, I suspected that whoever bought it would tear down the old house, so they could put a custom home on the property. You didn't need to be a real estate whiz to figure out that any value to the property was in the land, not the structure.

After finishing my dinner, I brought the plate inside and set it in the sink. Opening a beer, I returned to the porch to do some reading. I had a stack of psychiatric books and textbooks I wanted to finish perusing before I moved to Baltimore, on subjects ranging from psychopharmaceuticals to the value and drawbacks associated with hypnosis. The more I'd been reading, the more I felt I had to learn. I had to admit my study skills were rusty; I sometimes felt like I was an old dog and these were new tricks. When I'd said as much to Dr. Bowen, he'd essentially told me to quit whining. Or that's how I took it, anyway.

I'd settled into the rocking chair, turned on the lamp, and had just started reading when I thought I heard a voice calling out from around the corner of the house. I turned down the radio, waited a beat, and heard the sound again.

'Hello?'

Rising from my seat, I grabbed my beer and moved to the porch railing. Peeking into the darkness, I called back. 'Is someone there?'

A moment later, a woman in uniform stepped into the light. Specifically, the uniform of a deputy

25

sheriff. The sight caught me off guard. My experience with law enforcement to that point in my life was limited to highway patrolmen, two of whom had pulled me over for speeding in my younger years. Though I'd been apologetic and polite, each of them nonetheless gave me a ticket, and dealing with law enforcement ever since made me nervous. Even if I hadn't done anything wrong.

I didn't say anything; I was too busy trying to figure out why a deputy sheriff was paying me a visit, while the other part of my brain was processing the fact that the uniformed officer was female. Call me a sexist, but I hadn't interacted with many women in law enforcement, especially down here.

'I'm sorry for coming around the side of the house,' she finally said. 'I knocked, but I guess you didn't hear me.' Her demeanor was friendly but professional. 'I'm with the sheriff's department.'

'Can I help you?'

Her eyes flickered to the grill, then back to me. 'I hope I'm not interrupting your dinner.'

'Not at all.' I shook my head. 'I just finished.'

'Oh, good. And again, I apologize for intruding, Mr . . . '

'Benson,' I said. 'Trevor Benson.'

'I just came by to ask whether you're a legal resident of this property.'

I nodded, though I was a little surprised by the phrasing. 'I guess so. It used to be my grandfather's, but he passed away and left it to me.'

'You mean Carl?'

'You knew him?'

26

'A little. And I'm sorry for your loss. He was a good man.'

'Yes, he was. I'm sorry, but I didn't catch your name.'

'Masterson,' she said. 'Natalie Masterson.' She was quiet then, and I had a sense that she was studying me. 'You said Carl was your grandfather?'

'On my mother's side.'

'I think he mentioned you. You're a surgeon, right? With the Navy?'

'I was, but not anymore.' I hesitated. 'I'm sorry — I'm still not exactly sure why you've come by.'

'Oh.' She motioned toward the house. 'I was finishing up my shift but I was out this way, and when I saw the lights on, I thought I'd check it out.'

'Am I not allowed to turn on lights?'

'No, it's not that.' She smiled. 'Obviously, everything is okay and I shouldn't have bothered you. It's just that a few months ago, after your grandfather had died, there were reports of lights in the windows. I knew the house was supposed to be empty, so I swung by to check it out. And though I couldn't be certain, I had the impression that someone *had* been staying here. Not that there was any damage except for the back door, but combined with the lights being seen in the windows, I felt that I should keep an eye on the place. So I've made it a point to swing by every now and then, just to make sure there's no one here that shouldn't be. Vagrants or squatters, teens using the place to party, tweakers working a meth lab. Whatever.'

'Is there a lot of that around here?'

'No more than other places, I guess. But enough to keep us busy.'

'Just so you know, I don't do drugs.'

She motioned toward the bottle I was holding. 'Alcohol is a drug.'

'Even beer?'

When she smiled, I guessed she was a few years younger than me, with blond hair tacked up into a messy bun, and her eyes were so aqua colored that they could have been bottled and sold as mouthwash. That she was attractive went without saying, and better yet, she wasn't wearing a wedding ring.

'No comment,' she finally offered.

'Would you like to come in and check out the house?'

'No, that's all right. I'm just glad I don't have to worry anymore. I was fond of Carl. Whenever he was selling honey at the farmers' market, we'd visit for a while.'

I remembered sitting with my grandfather at a roadside stand every Saturday during my visits, but I had no recollection of a farmers' market. Then again, New Bern had a lot more of everything now than it had in the past — restaurants, stores, businesses — even if it still remained a small town at heart. Alexandria, which was just a suburb in the DC area and one of many, had five or six times the population. Even there, I suspect Natalie Masterson would have turned heads.

'What can you tell me about the possible squatter?' I asked.

28

I didn't really care about the squatter, but somehow I was reluctant to see her go.

'Not much more than I already told you,' she said.

'Do you think you might come up here?' I pleaded, pointing to my ear. 'So I can hear you better? I was caught up in a mortar attack in Afghanistan.'

I could hear her fine, by the way; the inner workings of my ear weren't damaged in the blast, even if the outer part had been torn from my head. It's just that I'm not above playing the sympathy card when I need to. I retreated to my rocker, hoping she hadn't wondered why I seemed to be able to hear her without trouble only moments before. In the porch light, I saw her eyeing my scar before she finally started up the steps. When she reached the other rocker, she angled it toward me, while also sliding it back.

'I appreciate this,' I said.

She smiled, not overly warm, but enough for me to realize she did indeed have suspicions about my hearing and was still debating whether to stay. It was also a wide enough smile to notice her white and perfectly straight teeth.

'As I was saying . . . '

'Are you comfortable?' I asked. 'Can I offer you something to drink?'

'I'm fine, thank you. I'm on duty, Mr. Benson.'

'Call me Trevor. And please — start at the beginning.'

She sighed, and I could have sworn I saw the trace of an eye roll.

'There was a series of electrical storms last November, after Carl passed away. A lot of lightning, and at the trailer park down the road, one of the trailers caught fire. The fire department responded, so did I, and not long after the fire was out, one of the guys mentioned that he likes to go hunting on the far side of the creek. It was just small talk, you know?'

I nodded, remembering the burned-out husk I'd noticed my first week here.

'Anyway, I happened to bump into him a couple of weeks later, and he mentioned that he'd noticed lights in your grandfather's house, not just once, but two or three times. Like a candle being carried past the windows. He was kind of far away and I wondered if it had been his imagination, but since it kept happening and he knew that Carl had died, he thought he should mention it.'

'When would this have been?'

'Last December, maybe midmonth? There was a week or two there when it was really cold, so it wouldn't have surprised me if someone broke in just to stay warm. The next time I was in the area I stopped by and saw that the back door was broken and the knob had almost fallen off. I went inside and did a quick search, but the place was empty. Aside from the broken door, I didn't find evidence that anyone had been inside. There was no trash, and the beds were made; as far as I could tell, nothing appeared to be missing. But . . . '

She paused, frowning at the recollection. I took a sip of beer, waiting for her to go on.

'There were a pair of used candles on the counter with blackened wicks, and a half-empty box of candles as well. I also noticed that some of the dust had been wiped away at the kitchen table, like someone had eaten there. It also seemed like someone had been using one of the recliners in the family room because there was cleared space on the neighboring side table and it was the only piece of furniture in the living room that wasn't dusty. It wasn't anything I could prove, but just in case, I found some extra boards in the barn and sealed the back door.'

'Thanks for that,' I said.

Though she nodded, I could tell something about those memories was still bothering her. She went on. 'Did you happen to notice whether anything was missing when you moved in?'

I thought about it before shaking my head. 'Not that I could tell. Except for the funeral in October, I hadn't been down here in a few years. And that week is a bit hazy in my memory.'

'Was the back door intact then?'

'I went in through the front, but I'm sure I checked all the locks when I left. I think I would have noticed if the back door was damaged. I know I spent time on the back porch.'

'When did you move in?'

'End of February.'

She digested that, her eyes flashing to the back door.

'You believe someone did break in, don't you?' I finally asked.

'I don't know,' she admitted. 'Usually, when something like that occurs, things are broken

31

and there's trash strewn about. Bottles, food wrappers, detritus. And vagrants don't usually make the bed before they leave.' She thrummed her fingers on the rocker. 'Are you sure nothing was missing? Guns? Electronics? Did your grandfather keep cash around?'

'My grandfather didn't have much in the way of electronics or cash, as far as I know. And his gun was in the closet when I moved in. It's still there, by the way. It's a small shotgun to keep the varmints away.'

'That makes it even stranger because usually, guns are the first things stolen.'

'What do you make of it?'

'I don't know,' she said. 'Either no one was there or you were visited by the tidiest and most honest vagrant in history.'

'Should I be worried?'

'Have you seen or heard anyone creeping around the property since you've moved in?'

'No. And I'm frequently awake during the night.'

'Insomnia?'

'Some. But it's getting better.'

'Good,' she said, adding nothing more. She smoothed the pants of her uniform. 'But I've taken enough of your time. That's all I can really tell you.'

'I appreciate you swinging by and telling me about all this. And for fixing the door.'

'It wasn't much of a fix.'

'It did the job,' I said. 'It was still boarded up when I got here. How much longer is your shift?'

She glanced at her watch. 'Actually, believe it or not, it's over now.'

'Then are you sure I can't get you a drink?'

'I don't think that would be a good idea. I still have to drive home.'

'Fair enough,' I said, 'but before you go — and since you're off, and I'm new in town — tell me what I need to know about New Bern these days. I haven't been here in a while.'

She paused, arching an eyebrow. 'Why would I do that?'

'Aren't you supposed to protect and serve? Think of this as the serve part. Like fixing my door.' I tried out my most winning smile.

'I don't think that being a welcoming committee is part of my job description,' she deadpanned.

Maybe not, I thought, *but you haven't left yet.*

'All right,' I said. 'Tell me what made you want to become a sheriff.'

With my question, she looked at me. Maybe, truly, for the first time, and again I found myself transfixed by the color of her eyes. They were like the waters of the Caribbean in an upscale travel magazine.

'I'm not the sheriff. That's an elected position. I'm a deputy.'

'Are you avoiding my question?'

'I'm wondering why you want to know.'

'I'm a curious person. And since you helped me out, I feel like I should know at least a little about the person who did the helping.'

'Why do I get the impression you have an ulterior motive?'

Because you're not only pretty, you're obviously smart as well, I thought. I shrugged, feigning innocence.

33

She studied me before finally responding. 'Why don't you tell me about yourself first.'

'Fair enough. Ask away.'

'I'm guessing that the mortar round is the reason you're no longer in the Navy or a doctor?'

'Yes,' I said. 'I was hit by a mortar just as I was leaving the hospital where I worked. Lucky shot. Or, for me, unlucky. Fairly serious injuries. In the end, the Navy put me on disability and let me go.'

'Tough break.'

'It was,' I admitted.

'And you're in New Bern because . . . ?'

'It's only a temporary stay,' I said. 'I'm moving to Baltimore this summer. I'm starting a new residency in psychiatry.'

'Really?' she asked.

'Is there something wrong with psychiatry?'

'Not at all. It's just not what I expected you to say.'

'I can be a good listener.'

'It's not that,' she said. 'I'm sure you are. But why psychiatry?'

'I want to work with veterans with PTSD,' I said. 'I think there's a need for it these days, especially with soldiers and marines doing four or five rotations. As I mentioned, it can stay with a person after they're back.'

She seemed to be attempting to read me. 'Is that what happened with you?'

'Yes.'

She hesitated and I had the sense she continued to really see me. 'Was it bad?'

'No question,' I said. 'Terrible. And it still is,

every now and then. But that's probably a story for another time.'

'Fair enough,' she offered. 'But now that I know, I'll admit that I was wrong. It sounds like it's exactly what you should do. How long is a psychiatric residency?'

'Five years.'

'I've heard residencies are hard.'

'It's no worse than being dragged by a car down the highway.'

For the first time, she laughed. 'I'm sure you'll do fine. But I do hope you find some time to enjoy our town while you're here. It's a beautiful place to live, and there are a lot of good people here.'

'Did you grow up in New Bern?'

'No,' she answered. 'I grew up in a *small* town.'

'That's funny.'

'But true,' she said. 'Can I ask what you intend to do with the place? When you leave?'

'Why? Are you interested in buying?'

'No,' she said. 'And I doubt I could afford it.' She brushed a strand of hair from her eyes. 'Where are you from, by the way? Give me a quick sketch of who you are.'

Pleased that she was interested, I gave her a brief history: my youth in Alexandria, my parents, my regular summertime visits to New Bern when I was younger. High school, college, medical school and residency. My time with the Navy. All with a touch of the modest hyperbole men use when trying to impress an attractive woman. As she listened, her eyebrows twitched more than once, but I couldn't tell whether she was fascinated or amused.

'So you're a city boy.'

'I beg to differ,' I protested. 'I'm from the suburbs.'

Her lips turned up slightly at the corners, but I couldn't read the intent behind it.

'What I don't understand is why you went to the Naval Academy. If you were such a brilliant student, I mean, and were accepted at Yale and Georgetown?'

Brilliant? Did I actually use that word earlier?

'I wanted to prove to myself that I could make it without my parents' help. Financially, I mean.'

'But didn't you say they were rich?'

Oh, yeah. I vaguely remember saying that, too.

'Well-to-do, I should have said.'

'So it was a pride thing?'

'And service to our country.'

She nodded slightly, her eyes never leaving mine. 'Good.' Almost as an afterthought, she added, 'There are a lot of active duty military in the area, as you probably know. Cherry Point, Camp Lejeune . . . many of them have spent time in Afghanistan and Iraq.'

I nodded. 'When I was posted overseas, I worked with doctors and nurses from every region of the country, in all sorts of specialties, and I learned a ton from them. While it lasted, anyway. And we did a lot of good, too. Most of our work was with locals — many of them had never been seen by a doctor before the hospital opened.'

36

She seemed to consider my words. A chorus of crickets sounded in the silence before I heard her voice again.

'I don't know that I could have done what you did.'

I tilted my head. 'I'm not sure what you mean.'

'Experiencing the horrors of war every single day. And knowing there are some people who are beyond your power to help. I don't think I would be able to handle something like that. Not in the long run, anyway.'

As she spoke, I had the impression she was sharing something personal, though I'd heard the same thing from others before, in regard to both the military and medicine in general. 'I'm sure you've seen some terrible things as a deputy.'

'I have.'

'And yet you still do it.'

'Yes,' she said. 'And sometimes I wonder how long I'll be able to continue. There are times when I fantasize about opening a flower shop or something like that.'

'Why don't you?'

'Who knows? Maybe one day I will.'

Again, she grew quiet. Sensing her distraction, I broke her reverie with a lighthearted prompt.

'Since you won't give me a rundown of what's new in town, at least tell me what your favorite place is?'

'Oh . . . I don't go out that much,' she demurred. 'Except for the farmers' market downtown. It's open Saturday mornings. But if you're trying to find some excellent honey, you'll probably be out of luck.'

'I'm sure my grandfather still has plenty.'

'You don't know for sure?'

'There are a few jars in the cupboard, but I haven't checked the honey shed yet. I've been too busy fixing up the place. I mean, a palace like this doesn't just happen by accident.'

This time she smiled, if a tad reluctantly. She nodded toward the dock. 'Have you gone out in the boat yet?'

I haven't yet mentioned the boat, but suffice it to say that it was a lot like the house, only in worse condition. Even calling it a boat was somewhat generous, because it looked less like a boat than an outhouse and two vinyl recliners, all bolted to a floating platform. My grandfather built it using discarded oil drums and lumber of varying sizes — along with whatever else he could find — and when he wasn't checking on the bees, he was always tinkering with it.

'Not yet. I'm not sure the engine even works.'

'I know it was working last summer, because Carl told me. It's kind of a hard boat to miss and your grandfather loved to take it out. People take photos of it whenever they see it.'

'It is a bit eccentric, isn't it?'

'It suited him, though.'

'Yes,' I admitted. 'It did.'

She sighed and stood. 'I really should be going. I've got some things to do at home. It was a pleasure meeting you, Mr. Benson.'

Mr. Benson? I had hoped we'd moved beyond that, but I guess not. She started down the steps, reaching the bottom in the same instant my brain finally kicked back into gear.

'You don't have to walk around the back and side of the house. You can go through to the front door if it's easier.'

'Thank you, but I'll just retrace my steps. Have a good evening.'

'You too. And it was nice meeting you, Natalie.'

She raised an eyebrow before turning away; with a couple of quick steps, she vanished from sight. After a few beats, I heard a door slam in the driveway and her vehicle start up. All of which left me contemplating the intriguing Natalie Masterson. That she was beautiful, anyone would notice, but what I found interesting about her was how little she'd told me about herself.

It's been said that women are the mysterious sex, and even now, my first inclination is to laugh when a guy I'm talking to says he understands what makes women tick. I was flummoxed by the one-sided nature of the conversation. I'd told her a lot about myself but had learned almost nothing about her.

I did, however, have a hunch that I would see her again, if only because I knew just where I might find her.

3

In the morning I went for a run, something I hadn't been consistent about since arriving in town. I would tell myself that I had more important things to do — like spreading mothballs to keep snakes away — but the simple truth is that I don't always enjoy exercising. I know all the benefits — I'm a doctor, remember? — but unless I was chasing or dribbling a soccer ball, running always seemed kind of silly to me.

But I did it. Six miles at a steady pace; when I finished, I did a hundred push-ups and sit-ups. After a quick shower and a bite to eat, I was ready to face the day. Of course, since I technically had no real responsibilities, I decided on another quick survey of the house to check if anything was missing. Which was something of an impossible task, since I hadn't known what had been in the house when he'd left town, and I'd already cleaned out the place. In the closet, I spotted the shotgun again and found the shells; there was no other ammunition, which led me to believe there'd been no other weapons. In a box under the bed in the guest room, however, I discovered a wad of cash wrapped in a rubber band, beneath a thick envelope that held various documents and photographs of my grandmother's — social security card, medical records concerning her epilepsy, things like that. It wasn't a lot of money — enough for a couple of fancy dinners maybe — but definitely enough to entice someone who might want money for drugs or booze. Had someone been there, it would have been stolen, right? Which meant that the place had likely remained unoccupied.

And yet the door had been broken . . .

I shook my head. Either way, even if someone had been there, they were long gone by now, so I put it out of my mind and decided to hit the books on the back porch for a while. Unfortunately they weren't exactly page-turners, and after a couple of hours, I'd had enough. On the plus side, no snakes appeared, which made me wonder whether Callie had known what she was talking about.

I'll admit that my mind wandered at times toward the lovely Natalie Masterson. She was an enigma, and I kept picturing the amused flicker I saw in her eyes as I related my slightly embellished history. But thinking about my conversation with Natalie also reminded me of the bees and the boat, which turned my thoughts to my grandfather, and it brought to mind my last visit here. At the time, I'd been a resident and while others were heading off to the Caribbean or Cancun for well-deserved respites, I made the drive from Baltimore to New Bern, seeking the comfort and abiding love that I had always sought from him as a child. He was his own cup of tea — the boat was a good example of his quirkiness — but he had limitless room in his heart for unsheltered souls. He was the kind of guy who'd feed whatever strays happened to drift onto his property; he'd set out a line of bowls near the barn, and various dogs from God knows where would begin showing up. He named the ones that stuck around after cars . . . As a kid, I played fetch with dogs named Cadillac, Edsel, or Ford, Chevy and Pinto. Oddly, he also named one Winnebago — it was a tiny thing, some sort of terrier — and when I asked him why, he winked and declared, 'Look at the size of him!'

In his working life, he'd been employed at the mill, turning logs into usable lumber. Like me, he finished his life with fewer fingers than when he started; unlike me, it didn't cause his career to come crashing to an end. He used to tell me that unless a man has lost a finger on the job, it wasn't a real job, which makes the idea that he raised my mother — a sophisticated, ambitious, cerebral woman if there ever was one — rather astounding. When I was younger, I used to suspect my mother had been adopted, but as I matured I eventually came to recognize that they shared an innate optimism and decency that informed everything they did.

My grandfather hadn't had an easy time after my grandmother had died. I don't remember her at all, as I was still toddling around in diapers the only time we met. But I can recall my mom emphasizing that it was important to visit him, so that he wasn't always alone. For my grandfather, there was only one woman; he'd loved once and for all, right up until an epileptic seizure took her life. There's still a photograph of her on the wall of the bedroom, and after moving in, I couldn't imagine taking it down, even though I never knew her. That she was my grandfather's North Star was more than enough reason to keep it hanging exactly where it was

But it was odd being at the house. It felt empty without my grandfather and wandering into the barn deepened the feeling of loss. It had the same cluttered atmosphere as the house I'd inherited. Inside were not only mothballs and a wide assortment of tools, but an old tractor, numerous engine parts, bags of sand, pickaxes, shovels, a rusting bicycle, an Army helmet, a cot and blanket that looked as though someone had actually slept there, and countless remnants of a lifetime of collecting things. I sometimes wondered whether my grandfather had ever thrown anything away, but close inspection revealed no trash, ancient magazines, newspapers, or debris that belonged in a garbage can; there were only items that he felt he might one day need for whatever project he was working on.

On the night I received the call from the hospital, I wasn't doing much of anything. There was no reason I couldn't have visited him that week, or a month or even a year earlier. Or even, I knew, when I'd been at my very worst. He'd never been a man to judge, and even less likely when it came to the effects of war on a person. At twenty he'd been shipped to North Africa; in the years that followed he'd fought in Italy, France, and then Germany. He'd been wounded at the Battle of the Bulge, only to return to his unit not long after the Army crossed the Rhine. I

43

knew nothing about any of it from him, since he never spoke about the war. My mom mentioned it, though, and a few days after my arrival here, I discovered the records, along with his Purple Heart and various service medals.

According to my mom, he got interested in bees not long after he built the house. Back then, there'd been a farm up the road and my grandfather had worked there, before getting a job at the mill. The farmer had beehives but didn't like tending to them. My grandfather was put on the task. Since he knew nothing about beekeeping, he checked out a book from the library and eventually learned the rest on his own. To him, they represented an almost perfect species, and he'd hold forth on the subject to anyone who would listen.

I'm sure he would have told the doctors and nurses at the hospital in Easley about them if he'd had the chance. But he didn't. As soon as I got the call, I booked a flight to Greenville, South Carolina, via Charlotte. There, I rented a car and sped down the highway; despite all that, I arrived nearly eighteen hours after I'd heard what happened. By then, he'd been in the ICU for more than three days. It had taken that long to learn my name; the stroke first left him unconscious, and then largely unable to speak. The entire right side of his body was paralyzed, the left side only slightly better. As soon as I entered the ICU, I took note of the readings on the various monitors and after scanning the chart, I knew he didn't have much longer to live.

The bed seemed to dwarf him. I know it's a

cliché — that this is something that practically everyone says — but in his case, it was true. He'd lost a lot of weight since I'd seen him last, and the slack, lopsided expression on his face, even as he slept, nearly broke my heart. I took a seat near the bed and reached for his hand; it felt bony and brittle, birdlike, and I felt my throat lock up. All at once, I hated myself for not getting there sooner; I hated myself for staying away for so long. For a long time, the only movement I saw was the labored rise and fall of his chest.

I talked to him, even though I wasn't sure if he heard me. Quite a bit, if I remember correctly — making up for all the intervening years when I'd been too wrapped up in my own struggles to visit him. I told him about the explosion in Kandahar, and the trauma I experienced in the aftermath. I told him about Sandra — my most recent girlfriend — and our breakup. I told him that I was planning to begin another residency. And I thanked him, once again, for simply being there — as my real family, even if I'd taken him for granted at times — both before and after the death of my parents.

One of the nurses informed me that since his arrival, the only words he'd spoken were my name and Pensacola, which was how they were finally able to track me down. They told me that he'd been able to open his eyes and had tried to speak on occasion, only to rasp out unintelligible sounds. Still other times, he'd stared at them in bewilderment, as though he hadn't known where or even who he was.

I was upset and worried, but also confused. Why was he here, in Easley, South Carolina? How had he gotten here? In all the time I'd known him, he'd never traveled as far west as Raleigh, and he'd come to Alexandria only once. After the war, and until just a few days earlier, I was fairly certain he hadn't left the county in years. But Easley was a long way from New Bern. Six or seven hours on the interstate, maybe more, depending on traffic. At the time, my grandfather was ninety-one years old; where had he been going?

I would have suspected Alzheimer's, except for the fact that in his letters, he'd seemed as lucid and thoughtful as ever. He'd always been good at that — writing letters to me — and while I answered a few of them, I usually ended up phoning him after receiving one of his missives. It was easier for me, and I can be lazy about some things, like putting pen to paper; I'm not proud of it, but that's who I am. On the phone he was as clearheaded as ever. Older, of course, and maybe taking a bit longer to find the word he wanted, but certainly nothing that would indicate dementia severe enough to prompt a journey to a place he'd never mentioned before.

But staring at him as he lay unconscious made me wonder whether I was wrong about all of it. In the late-afternoon light, his skin took on a grayish pallor; by the evening, his breathing sounded painful. Though visiting hours were over, the staff at the hospital didn't kick me out. I'm not sure why — perhaps because I was a physician, or because they could tell how much I

46

cared for him. As nightfall came and went, I continued to sit with him, holding his hand and talking to him the entire time.

By morning, I was exhausted. One of the nurses brought me coffee, reminding me despite my exhaustion that there are good people everywhere. My grandfather's physician came by on his rounds; I could tell by his expression after checking my grandfather that he was thinking the same thing I was: The kind, old man was entering the final stages of his life. Maybe hours left, maybe a day, but not much more than that.

It was around noon on that last day that my grandfather shifted slightly in his bed, his eyes fluttering halfway open. As he attempted to focus, I noticed the same confusion the nurses had described, and I leaned closer to his bed, squeezing his hand.

'Hey, Grandpa, I'm here. Can you hear me?'

He turned his head, only a little, but as much as he could.

'It's me, Trevor. You're in the hospital.'

He blinked slowly. 'Tre . . . vor.'

'Yeah, Grandpa, it's me. I came as soon as I heard. Where were you going?'

I felt him squeeze my hand.

'Help . . . care . . . and . . .'

'Of course,' I said. 'They're taking good care of you.'

'If . . . you . . . can . . .'

Each word croaked out between ragged breaths.

'Collapsed . . .'

'Yes, Grandpa. You had a stroke.' As I said it, I

47

wondered if he'd been more ill than I suspected; in that same instant, I recalled that his wife had had epilepsy.

'*Sick.*'

'You'll be okay,' I lied. 'And we'll go take care of the bees and take the boat out, okay? Just you and me. It'll be like old times.'

'*Like . . . Rose . . .*'

I squeezed his hand again, hating his confusion, hating that he didn't know what had happened to him. 'Your beautiful bride.'

'*Find . . . family . . .*'

I didn't have the heart to remind him that his wife and daughter had long since passed away, that I was the only family he had left.

'You'll see Rose soon,' I promised. 'I know how much she loved you. And how much you loved her. She'll be waiting for you.'

'*Go . . . to . . . hell . . .*'

I froze, wondering if I'd heard him right. If he was attempting some kind of joke, it was one that would be out of character for him. 'It's okay, I'm here,' I repeated.

'*And . . . run . . . away.*'

'I'm not leaving you,' I said. 'I'm staying right here. I love you,' I said, bringing his wizened hand to my face. His expression softened.

'*Love . . . you . . .*'

I could feel the wellspring of tears beginning to form and tried to keep them at bay. 'You're the best man I've ever known.'

'*You . . . came . . .*'

'Of course I came.'

'*Now go . . .*'

48

'No,' I said. 'I'm going to stay right here. For as long as it takes, I'm staying with you.'

'*Please*,' he whispered, and then his eyes closed. That was the last thing he said to me. Less than two hours later, he took his final breath.

On the night he died, as I lay awake in a nearby hotel, I relived those last moments with my grandfather. I puzzled over the things he'd said, finally sitting up in bed to write them down on the notepad next to the phone, combining some of the words into phrases that I thought made the most sense.

> *Trevor . . . help care . . . and . . . if you can . . . collapsed . . . sick . . . like Rose . . . find family . . . go to hell . . . and run away . . . love you . . . you came . . . now go . . . please*

There'd been a bit of rambling, some disassociation, but at least he'd recognized me. He'd told me that he loved me, and for that I was grateful. I'd told him that I wouldn't leave, and I was glad I hadn't. The thought that he might have died alone was nearly enough to break my heart.

After I'd finished the note, I folded the paper and stuck it in my wallet, continuing to ponder it. Of all that he'd said, telling me to *go to hell* was the one thing I couldn't quite understand. Although I'd assured him he'd see Rose again soon, my grandfather had never been particularly religious. I wasn't sure what he believed with regard to the afterlife, but I was glad I'd said it. Whether he believed it or not, it was what I think he wanted to hear.

Rising from my seat on the porch, I descended the steps, heading for the dock. Like the boat, the dock wasn't much, yet somehow it had survived countless hurricanes since it was built. As I approached, I caught sight of the dry rot and stepped cautiously onto the ancient boards, wary that I might crash through to the water any second. But the boards held, and I eventually hopped onto the boat.

It was a boat that no one but my grandfather could have built. The outhouse portion, which my grandfather called 'the cockpit,' was located near the bow and had three walls, a crooked window, and an old wooden wheel he'd likely found at a thrift shop somewhere. Because he hadn't known much about boat design, the act of getting anywhere on the boat was more art than science. The wheel and rudder were connected, but only loosely; turning left or right usually required three or four rotations of the wheel, and how he was able to get it officially registered as legal watercraft was beyond me. Behind the cockpit were the two vinyl rockers, a small table he'd bolted to the deck, as well as a pair of secured metal stools. A railing made of two-by-fours prevented passengers from falling off, and the stern was decorated with a set of Texas long-horns mounted on a galvanized pole that he claimed a friend from the war had sent him.

The engine was as ancient as the rest of the boat; to start it, you pulled a cord, much like a lawn mower. When I was a kid, my grandfather had let me give it a try, and after numerous failed attempts, I could barely move my arm. With my good hand, I gave the cord a couple of sharp jerks now, and when the engine didn't catch, I guessed the problem was something as simple as spark plugs. My grandfather was a whiz at anything mechanical and I had no doubt he'd been able to keep the engine in good condition right up until he'd made the trip to Easley.

Which made me wonder again why he'd been there.

After ransacking the barn to find a wrench, I removed the spark plugs and got in my SUV. I'll admit my vehicle isn't good for the environment, but because it's stylish, I like to think that it adds beauty to the world, which makes up for it.

I drove a mile down the road to Slow Jim's Trading Post, finding that the place hadn't changed a bit. Inside, I asked the cashier where I might find spark plugs, and sure enough, the store had the exact ones I needed. My stomach gurgled as I paid for them, reminding me that I hadn't eaten since breakfast. Overcome with nostalgia, I wandered toward the grill. The six small tables were taken — the place had always drawn a crowd — but there were a few empty stools at the counter and I took a seat. Above the grill was a chalkboard highlighting the menu. There were more choices than I anticipated, though few were remotely healthy. But I'd run that morning, so what the heck? I ordered a cheeseburger and fries from Claude, a man I recognized from previous visits. Despite the apron he was wearing, he looked more like a banker than a cook, with dark hair turning silver at the temples and blue eyes that matched the polo shirt he was wearing beneath his apron. His father had originally founded the store — probably around the time my grandfather built his house — but Claude had been running the place for more than a decade.

I also ordered an iced tea, which was as sweet as I remembered. The South is famous for sweet tea, and I savored every drop. Claude then slid a bowl of small, brown soggy things toward me.

'What's this?'

'Boiled peanuts. It comes with every order,' Claude explained. 'I started that a couple of years ago. It's my wife's recipe, and there's a pot going near the register. You can buy some before you go. Most people do.'

I cautiously tried one, surprised by its salty goodness. Claude turned away and dumped some frozen fries from a bag into hot oil, before slapping a burger on the grill. Off to the side, Callie was stocking some shelves, but if she'd noticed me, she hadn't let on.

'Don't I know you?' Claude asked. 'I think I recognize you.'

'I haven't been here in years, but I used to come all the time with my grandfather, Carl Haverson.'

'Oh, that's right,' he said, brightening. 'You're the Navy doctor, right?'

'Not anymore. But that's a story for another time.'

'I'm Claude,' he said.

'I remember,' I said. 'I'm Trevor.'

'Wow,' he said. 'A Navy doctor.' Claude whistled. 'Your pappy sure was proud of you.'

'I was proud of him, too.'

'I'm sorry for your loss. I sure did like him.'

I shelled another peanut. 'Me too.'

'Do you live around here now?'

'I'm staying at his place until June or so.'

'Great property,' Claude said. 'Your pappy planted some fantastic trees. Really pretty this time of year. My wife has been making me slow the car whenever we pass by. Lots of flowers. Are the beehives still there?'

'Of course.' I nodded. 'They're doing well.'

'Your pappy used to let me buy and sell some of his honey every year. Folks love it. If there's any left from either of last year's harvests, I'd be happy to take it off your hands.'

'How many jars would you want?'

'All of them,' he chortled.

'That good?'

'Best in the state, or so they say.'

'There's a ranking?'

'I don't know. But that's what I tell people when they ask. And they keep buying it.'

I smiled. 'Why are you at the grill? If I

remember right, aren't you usually working the register?'

'Almost always. It's cooler and a whole lot easier, and I'm not covered in grease by the end of the day. But Frank is my regular grill man and he's out this week. His daughter is getting married.'

'Good reason to miss work.'

'Not so good for me. I'm out of practice on the grill. I'll do my best to make sure your burger isn't burned.'

'I'd appreciate that.'

He eyed the sizzling grill over his shoulder. 'Carl used to come here two or three times a week, you know. Always ordered a BLT on white toast, with French fries, and a pickle on the side.'

I remembered ordering the same thing when I was with him. For some reason, BLTs never tasted quite as good anywhere else.

'I'm sure he loved the peanuts, too. These are great.'

'Nope,' Claude declared. 'Allergic.'

'To peanuts?' I squinted in disbelief.

'So he always told me. Said his throat would swell like a balloon.'

'The things you don't know about a man,' I mused before recalling that Claude's father, Jim, and my grandfather had always been close. 'How's your dad doing?' I suspected that Jim had gone the way of my grandfather, as they were close in age, but Claude only shrugged.

'Same as always, I guess. He still likes to come by the store a couple times a week and sit in the

54

rockers out front while he has lunch.'

'Yeah?'

'As a matter of fact, your grandfather used to join him when he came by,' Claude said. 'They were a regular pair. I guess Jerrold has sort of taken your grandfather's place since your grandpa passed. Have you met Jerrold?'

'No.'

'He used to drive a truck for Pepsi. His wife passed on a few years back. Nice guy, but he's an odd duck. And frankly, I'm not sure what either of them gets out of it. My pa's deaf as a doornail and definitely slipping mentally. Makes it tough to have a conversation.'

'He must be almost ninety now.'

'Ninety-one. My guess is he'll live to a hundred and ten. Other than his hearing, he's healthier than I am.' Claude turned around and flipped the burger, then dropped the bun in a toaster. When the bun was ready, he added lettuce, tomato, and onion before facing me again.

'Can I ask you a question?' he said.

'Shoot.'

'What was Carl doing in South Carolina?'

'I have no idea. I still haven't figured that out. I was hoping you could tell me.'

Claude shook his head. 'He talked to my dad more than he talked to me, but after he passed, there was a lot of curiosity about it.'

'Why?'

He put his hands on the counter and regarded me. 'Well, for starters, he usually didn't go anywhere. He hasn't left town in years. And then there was that truck of his — you remember it?'

55

I nodded. It was a Chevy C/K from the early 1960s. It might have been called a classic, except for the fact the body was a faded, rusting wreck.

'It was all that Carl could do to keep that thing running. He was really good with engines, but even he said the truck was on its last legs. I doubt it could top forty-five miles an hour. It was fine for getting around town, but I can't imagine Carl taking it on the interstate.'

Nor could I. Clearly I wasn't the only person wondering what had come over him.

Claude turned back to the grill and added fries to the paper plate. He set my meal in front of me.

'Ketchup and mustard, right?'

'Sure.'

He slid the bottles toward me.

'Carl liked ketchup, too. I sure do miss him. He was a good man.'

'Yes, he was,' I said absently, but my mind became fixated on the sudden certainty that Natalie had been correct when she'd told me that someone had been staying in my grandfather's house. 'I think I'll bring this outside and eat out front. It was good talking to you, Claude.'

'That's why the chairs are there. Nice seeing you again.'

Taking my plate and drink, I walked toward the doors. After using my hip to push open the door, I made my way to the rockers and took a seat. I set my plate on the small wooden table beside me, thinking again about the possible vagrant in my house and suddenly wondering whether it was somehow connected to the other

56

mysteries surrounding my grandfather in the last few days of his life.

It was as I was finishing up my lunch that I saw Callie walk out of the store, carrying what looked to be her own lunch in a brown paper bag.

'Hey there, Callie,' I offered.

She glanced in my direction, looking suspicious. 'Do I know you?'

'We met the other day,' I said. 'When you were walking by my house. You told me the mothballs wouldn't keep snakes away.'

'They won't.'

'I haven't seen any snakes since then.'

'They're still there.' Surprising me, she squatted down and stretched out her arm, holding a paper plate with a glob of what looked to be tuna on it. 'Come on, Termite. Time for lunch.'

She set the plate on the ground, and a moment later, a cat popped out from behind the ice machine.

'Is that your cat?' I asked.

'No. He's the store cat. Claude lets me feed him.'

'He lives at the store?'

'I'm not sure where he lives during the day, but Claude lets him inside at night. He's a good mouser.'

'Why is he named Termite?'

'I don't know.'

'And you don't know where he goes during the day?'

Callie didn't respond until Termite was eating. Then, without looking at me, she spoke again. 'You sure ask a lot of questions, don't you?'

'When I'm interested in something, I do.'

'You're interested in the cat?'

'It reminds me of my grandfather. He used to like strays, too.'

Once the cat had finished, Callie picked up the plate. Termite, meanwhile, sauntered in my direction, ignored me completely as he passed, then disappeared around the corner of the store.

Callie still hadn't responded. With a sigh, however, she tossed the paper plate into the garbage and, with her back turned to me as she started walking away, said something that surprised me. 'I know.'

4

Both CBT and DBT emphasize common-sense living, or *things your mother taught you*, as a way to help improve mental and emotional health. While everyone can benefit from behavioral therapy, for those people like me, who suffer from PTSD, common-sense living is critical to ensuring the quality of life. In real terms — how I behaved, in other words — it meant frequent exercise, regular sleep, healthy eating, and the avoidance of mood-altering substances as ways to make things better. Therapy, I've come to learn, is less about navel-gazing conversation than it is about learning habits for successful living, and then, most importantly, putting them into practice.

Despite the cheeseburger and fries I'd had for lunch earlier in the week, I generally tried to stick to those guidelines. Experience had taught me that when I was overtired, or if I hadn't exercised for a while or if I ate too much unhealthy food, I was more sensitive to various triggers, like loud noises or irritating people. I could dislike running all I wanted, but the simple truth of the matter was that I hadn't been awakened by a nightmare in over five months and my hands hadn't trembled since I'd arrived in New Bern. All of which meant another workout on Saturday morning, followed by a better-than-usual cup of coffee.

Afterward, I changed the boat's spark plugs. Sure enough, the engine coughed to life, then began to purr. I let it idle for a while, thinking my grandfather would have been proud, especially since — compared to him — I'm not an engine guy. As I waited, I remembered a joke my grandfather had told me on my last visit. *A lady pulls her car into the mechanic's shop because her car is running poorly. A little while later, the mechanic comes out and she asks him, 'What's the story with my car?' The mechanic replies, 'Just crap in the carburetor.' 'Oh,' she says. 'How often do I need to do that?'*

My grandfather loved to tell jokes, which was yet another reason I always enjoyed my visits with him. He would tell them with a mischievous glint in his eye, usually beginning to chuckle even before he reached the punch line. In this and countless other ways, he was the opposite of my own earnest, achievement-oriented parents. I often wondered how I would have turned out without his easygoing presence in my life.

After I shut down the engine, I went back to the house and cleaned up. I threw on khakis, a polo, and loafers, then made the ten-minute drive to downtown New Bern.

I'd always liked the downtown area, especially the historic district. There were a lot of ancient, majestic houses there, some of them dating back to the eighteenth century, which was a bit amazing since the town was prone to flooding during hurricanes, which should have wiped them all out by now. When I first began visiting, many of the historic homes were in terrible condition, but one by one they'd been bought up by investors over the years and gradually restored to their former glory. Streets were canopied by massive oak and magnolia trees, and there were a bunch of official markers testifying to important historical events: a famous duel here, an important person born there, some roots of a Supreme Court decision the next block over. Before the revolution, New Bern had been the colonial capital for the British, and after he'd become president, George Washington visited the town briefly. What I liked most, however, was that compared to those in small towns in other parts of the country, the businesses in the downtown were thriving, despite the big-box stores only a few miles away.

I parked the car in front of Christ Episcopal Church and climbed out into bright sunshine. Given the blue skies and warmer-than-usual temperatures, I wasn't surprised at the number of people thronging the sidewalks. I strolled past the Pepsi museum — the soft drink was invented here by Caleb Bradham — and then Baker's Kitchen, a popular breakfast spot. It was already crowded, with people waiting on the benches outside for tables. A quick internet search before I left made the farmers' market easy to find, located as it was near the North Carolina History Center. Since Natalie had recommended the place and I had nothing better to do, I figured why not?

A few minutes later, I reached my destination. It wasn't the bustling agricultural horn of plenty

61

I'd pictured, with overflowing bins of fruit and vegetables typical of roadside stands. Instead, the market was mainly dominated by vendors selling trinkets, baked goods, and all sorts of craft items out of garage-type stalls. Which made sense once I thought about it, considering it was only April and the summer crops had yet to come in.

Still, it wasn't bereft of fresh produce, and I made a circuit of the market, getting a feel for the place and deciding what I needed for my own cupboards. As I looked, I bought a cup of apple cider and continued to wander around. In addition to food, I saw dolls made of straw, birdhouses, wind chimes made from seashells, and jars of apple butter, none of which I needed. It was getting crowded, though, and by the time I got back to my starting point I spotted Natalie Masterson hovering over a table of sweet potatoes.

Even from a distance, she stood out. She was holding a basket and wearing faded jeans, a white T-shirt, and sandals, all of which did a lot more for her figure than the boring uniform had. A pair of sunglasses was propped on her head and aside from lipstick, she wore little makeup. Her hair swept the top of her shoulders in untamed glory. If I could picture Ms. Masterson earlier that morning, I thought she must have dressed, run her fingers through her hair, and applied a quick coat of lipstick before skipping out the door, the whole process taking less than five minutes.

She appeared to be alone and after a moment's hesitation, I started toward her, almost colliding with an older lady who'd been examining a bird-house. When I was getting close, Natalie turned in my direction. She did a quick double take, but by then, I was already by her side.

'Good morning,' I chirped.

I could feel her eyes on me, gleaming with amusement. 'Good morning,' she responded.

'I don't know if you remember, but I'm Trevor Benson. We met the other night.'

'I remember,' she said.

'What are the odds I'd bump into you here?'

'Pretty high, I'd say,' she remarked, 'since I mentioned that I come here regularly.'

'After your recommendation, I thought I'd check it out,' I said. 'And I needed to get some things anyway.'

'But you haven't found anything to buy yet?'

'I had cider earlier. And there's a doll made of straw I'm thinking about.'

'You don't seem like the kind of guy who collects dolls.'

'I'm hoping it will give me someone to talk to while I'm having coffee in the mornings.'

'That's a troubling thought,' she said, her eyes lingering on mine for a beat too long. I wondered if it was her way of flirting, or if she scrutinized everyone this way.

'I'm actually here to pick up some potatoes.'

'Feel free,' she said, waving a hand at the table. 'There's plenty.'

She turned her attention to the table, chewing on her lip as she studied the produce. Moving closer, I stole a peek at her profile, thinking that her unguarded expression revealed a surprising innocence, as though she still puzzled over why bad things happened in the world. I wondered if it had something to do with her job, or whether I was simply imagining it. Or whether, God forbid, it had something to do with me.

She chose a few medium-sized potatoes, sliding them into the basket; I opted for two of the larger ones. After counting how many she'd already selected, she added a few more.

'That's a lot of potatoes,' I observed.

'I'm making pies.' At my questioning expression, she said, 'Not for me. For a neighbor.'

'You bake?'

'I live in the South. Of course I bake.'

'But your neighbor doesn't?'

'She's elderly, and her kids and grandkids are coming to visit later this week. She loves my recipe.'

'Very nice of you,' I commended her. 'How did the rest of your week go?'

She rearranged the potatoes in her basket. 'It was fine.'

'Anything exciting happen? Shoot-outs, manhunts? Anything like that?'

'No,' she said. 'Just the usual. A handful of domestic disturbances, a couple of drivers under the influence. And transfers, of course.'

'Transfers?'

'Prisoner transfers. To and from court appearances.'

'You do that?'

'All deputies do.'

'Is that scary?'

'Not usually. They're in handcuffs, and most

of them are pretty agreeable. Court is a lot more pleasant than jail. But every now and then, one of them will make me nervous, the rare psychopath, I suppose. It's like something elemental is missing in their personality and you get the feeling that right after killing you, they could wolf down a couple of tacos without a care in the world.' Peering into her basket, she made a count before turning to the vendor. 'How much?'

At the vendor's response, she pulled a few bills from her handbag and handed them over. I held mine up as well and fished the cash from my wallet. As I waited, a brown-eyed brunette in her thirties waved at Natalie and began to approach, all smiles. As the woman weaved through the customers, Natalie stiffened. When she was close, the woman leaned in, offering Natalie a hug.

'Hey, Natalie,' the woman said, her voice almost solicitous. Like she knew that Natalie was struggling with something I knew nothing about. 'How are you? I haven't seen you in a while.'

'I'm sorry,' Natalie responded as the woman pulled back. 'There's a lot going on.'

The woman nodded, her gaze flicking in my direction, then back to Natalie again, her curiosity evident.

'I'm Trevor Benson,' I offered, holding out my hand.

'Julie Richards,' she said.

'My dentist,' Natalie explained. She turned to Julie again. 'I know I need to call your office and set up an appointment . . . '

'Whenever,' Julie said, waving her hand. 'You know I'll work around your schedule.'

'Thank you,' Natalie murmured. 'How's Steve doing?'

Julie shrugged. 'Super busy,' she said. 'They're still trying to find another doctor for the practice, so he's booked solid all week. He's on the golf course right now, which I know he needs, but thankfully, he promised to bring the kids to a movie later so Mom can have a break, too.'

Natalie smiled. 'Cooperation and compromise.'

'He's a good guy,' Julie said. Again, her eyes flashed momentarily to me, then back to Natalie again. 'Soooo . . . How do you two know each other?'

'We're not here together,' Natalie said. 'I just happened to bump into him. He just moved to town and there was an issue at his house. Legal stuff.'

I could hear the discomfort in Natalie's voice, so I held up my purchase. 'I'm here to buy potatoes.'

Julie turned her attention to me. 'You just moved here? Where are you from?'

'Most recently, Florida. But I grew up in Virginia.'

'Where in Virginia? I'm originally from Richmond.'

'Alexandria,' I said.

'How do you like it here so far?'

'I like it. But I'm still settling in.'

'You'll get used to it. There are a lot of great people here,' she said, before focusing on Natalie again. I half listened while Natalie and Julie continued with a bit of additional small talk before their conversation finally wound down.

Toward the end, Julie leaned in for another hug.

'I'm sorry, but I'm going to have to scoot,' Julie said. 'The kids are with my neighbor, and I told her that I wouldn't be gone long.'

'It was good seeing you.'

'You too. And remember that you can call me anytime. I've been thinking about you.'

'Thank you,' Natalie answered.

As Julie wandered off, I noted a trace of weariness in Natalie's expression.

'Everything okay?'

'Yeah,' Natalie said. 'It's fine.'

I waited, but Natalie added nothing else.

'I was hoping to pick up some strawberries,' she finally said in a distracted voice.

'Are they any good?'

'I don't know,' she said, beginning to come back to me. 'This is the first weekend they're being offered, but last year, they were delicious.'

She moved ahead toward a table filled with strawberries, sandwiched between the table with birdhouses and the one displaying straw dolls. Farther up, I saw Julie the dentist speaking with another young couple; I figured Natalie must have noticed her as well, though she gave no indication. Instead, she sidled up to the table of strawberries. When I came to a stop beside her, Natalie suddenly stood straighter. 'Oh, I forgot I needed to get some broccoli, too, before it's all gone.' She took a step backward. 'It was nice chatting with you, Mr. Benson.'

Though she smiled, it was clear she wanted to extricate herself from my presence, the sooner the better. I could feel others' eyes on us as she continued to back away.

'You too, deputy.'

She turned around, heading back the same way we'd just come, leaving me alone in front of the table. The vendor, a young lady, was making change for another customer, and I wasn't quite sure what to do. Stay here? Follow her? Following her would probably come across as both irritating and creepy, so I remained at the strawberry table, thinking they resembled the ones I could find in the supermarket, except less ripe. Deciding to support the local farmers, I purchased a container and made my way back slowly through the crowds. From the corner of my eye, I saw Natalie browsing near a stall selling apple butter; there was no broccoli in her basket.

I debated heading home before noting again the beauty of the morning, and decided that a cup of coffee would hit the spot.

Leaving the market, I walked to the Trent River Coffee Company. It was a few blocks away, but given the pleasant weather, it felt good to be out and about. Inside, I listened to customers ahead of me order their half-decaf mocha chai lattes, or whatever it was people ordered these days. When it was my turn, I ordered a black coffee, and the young lady at the counter — sporting an eyebrow piercing and a tattoo of a spider on the back of her hand — looked at me as though I were still living in the 1980s, the decade in which I'd been born.

'That's it? Just . . . coffee?'

'Yes, please.'

'Name?'

'Johann Sebastian Bach.'

'Is that with a 'Y'?'

'Yes,' I answered.

I watched as she wrote *Yohan* on the cup and handed it to the ponytailed male behind her. It was clear the name didn't ring the faintest bell.

Taking my cup outside, I wandered over to Union Point, a park at the confluence of the Neuse and Trent Rivers. It was also, according to the appropriately located historical marker, the site at which a group of Swiss and Palatine settlers founded the town in 1710. The way I figured it, they were likely heading for warmer climates — South Beach, maybe, or Disney World — and got lost, thus ending up here, the captain being male and unwilling to ask for directions and all.

Not that it was a bad location. In fact, it's beautiful, except when hurricanes come roaring in from the Atlantic. The winds stop the Neuse from flowing toward the sea, the water backs up, and the town starts pretending that it's waiting for Noah's ark. My grandfather had lived through both Fran and Bertha in 1996, but when he spoke about major storms, it was always Hazel he referred to, back in 1954. During the storm, two of the beehives were upended, a catastrophic event in his life. That his roof blew off as well wasn't nearly as important to him as the damage to his pride and joy. However, I'm not sure that Rose felt the same way; she went to stay with her parents until the house was habitable again.

There was a large gazebo in the center of the park, as well as a lovely bricked promenade that ran along the river's edge. I strolled toward an empty bench with a view of the river and took a seat. The sun sparkled off the lazy waters of the Neuse, which was nearly a mile wide at this point, and I watched a boat slowly glide downstream, its sails billowing like a pillow. At a nearby boat launch, I saw a group of paddleboarders getting ready to hit the water. Some were in shorts and T-shirts, others in short wet-suits, and they were clearly discussing their plan of action. At the far end of the park, a few kids were feeding ducks; another pair was playing Frisbee, and still another kid was flying a kite. I appreciated that people around here knew how to enjoy their weekends. In Kandahar — and before that, while in residency — I worked practically every weekend, the days running together in an exhausted blur. But I was getting better at kicking back and relaxing on Saturdays and Sundays. Then again, I was doing pretty much the same thing every other day of the week as well, so I was getting a lot of practice.

After finishing my coffee, I tossed the empty in a nearby garbage can and wandered to the railing. Leaning over, I admitted that small-town life had its charms. I especially thought so a couple of minutes later, when I saw Natalie meandering in my direction, the basket trailing at her side. She seemed to be watching the paddleboarders as they worked their way toward deeper water.

I suppose I could have waved or called out, but considering our recent encounter in the farmers' market, I restrained myself. Instead, I continued to study the slow-moving current until

I heard a voice behind me.

'You again.'

I peeked over my shoulder. Natalie's stance and expression telegraphed that she hadn't expected to find me here.

'Are you talking to me?'

'What are you doing here?'

'I'm enjoying my Saturday morning.'

'Did you know I would be coming here?'

'How would I have known where you were going?'

'I don't know,' she said, suspicion seeping into her voice.

'It's a beautiful morning and a great view. Why wouldn't I come here?'

She opened her mouth to answer, then closed it again before speaking. 'I guess it's none of my business, anyway. I'm sorry for bothering you.'

'You're not bothering me,' I assured her. Then, nodding toward her basket: 'Did you find everything you needed at the market?'

'Why are you asking?'

'Just making conversation. Since you're following me, I mean.'

'I'm not following you!'

I laughed. '*Kidding*. If anything, I have the impression that you're trying to avoid me.'

'I'm not avoiding you. I barely know you.'

'Exactly,' I agreed, and feeling like I was suddenly back in the batter's box, I decided to take another swing. 'And that's a shame.' I gave her a mischievous smile before turning back toward the river.

Natalie studied me, as though uncertain whether to stay or go. Though I thought she

71

would opt to leave, I eventually sensed her presence beside me. Hearing her sigh as she set her basket on the ground, I knew that my third swing at bat had somehow connected.

Finally, she spoke. 'I have a question.'

'Go ahead.'

'Are you always this forward?'

'Never,' I said. 'By nature I'm quiet and reserved. A wallflower, really.'

'I doubt that.'

In the river, the paddleboarders upstream were now hovering in place.

In the silence, I saw her clasp her hands together at the railing. 'About what happened earlier,' she said. 'In the market, when I walked away. If that seemed brusque, I apologize.'

'No apology necessary.'

'Still, I felt bad afterward. But it's just that in small towns, people talk. And Julie . . . '

When she trailed off, I finished for her. 'Talks more than most?'

'I didn't want her to get the wrong idea.'

'I understand,' I said. 'Gossip is the bane of small-town life. Let's just hope she went home to the kids instead of coming to the park, or she might really have something to talk about.'

Though I said it as a joke, Natalie immediately scanned the vicinity and my eyes followed hers. As far as I could tell, no one was paying us any attention at all. Still, it made me wonder what was so terrible about the thought of being seen with someone like me. If she had any idea that she knew what I was thinking, she gave no indication, but I thought I noted an expression of relief.

'How do you make sweet potato pie?'

'Are you asking for the recipe?'

'I don't think I've ever had sweet potato pie. I'm trying to figure out what it tastes like.'

'It's a bit like pumpkin pie. In addition to the potatoes, there's butter, sugar, eggs, vanilla, cinnamon, nutmeg, evaporated milk, and a little bit of salt. But the key is really the crust.'

'Do you make a good crust?'

'I make a great crust. The secret is using butter, not shortening. There are strong feelings on both sides of that debate, by the way. But I've experimented with my mom and we both agree.'

'Does she live in town?'

'No. She's still in La Grange, where I grew up.'

'I'm not sure I know where that is.'

'It's between Kinston and Goldsboro, on the way to Raleigh. My dad was a pharmacist. Still is, in fact. My dad started the business before I was born. There's a store, too, of course. My mom manages that and works the register.'

'When we first met, you said it was a small town.'

'It's only about 2,500 people.'

'And the pharmacy does okay?'

'You'd be surprised. People need their medicines, even in small towns. But you already know that. Since you're a doctor, I mean.'

'Was a doctor. And hope to be a doctor again one day.'

She was quiet for a moment. I studied her profile, but again had no idea what was going through her mind.

73

Finally, she sighed. 'I was thinking about what you said the other night. About you becoming a psychiatrist to help people with PTSD. I think that's a great thing.'

'I appreciate that.'

'How do people even know they have it? How did you know?'

Strangely, I had the impression that she wasn't asking for conversation's sake, or even because she was particularly interested in me. Rather, I had the sense she was asking because she was curious for her own reasons, whatever those might be. In the past, I likely would have tried to change the subject, but regular sessions with Dr. Bowen made talking about my issues easier, no matter who was asking.

'Everyone's different, so the symptoms can vary, but I was pretty much a textbook example of the condition. I alternated between insomnia and nightmares at night, and during the day, I felt on edge almost all the time. Loud noises bothered me, my hands sometimes trembled, I got in ridiculous arguments. I spent almost a year feeling angry at the world, drinking more than I should, and playing way too much *Grand Theft Auto*.'

'And now?'

'I'm managing,' I said. 'Or, at least, I like to think I am. My doctor thinks so, too. We still talk every Monday.'

'So you're cured?'

'It's not something that can really be cured. It's more about managing the condition. Which isn't always easy. Stress tends to make things worse.'

'Isn't stress part of life?'

'No question,' I admitted. 'That's what makes it impossible to cure.'

She was silent for a moment before glancing at me with a wry smile. '*Grand Theft Auto*, huh? For whatever reason, I can't picture you sitting on a couch playing video games all day.'

'I got really good at it. Which wasn't easy, since I'm missing fingers, by the way.'

'Do you still play?'

'No. That was one of the changes I made. Long story short, my therapy is all about changing negative behaviors into positive ones.'

'My brother loves that game. Maybe I should get him to stop.'

'You have a brother?'

'And a sister. Sam is five years older than me, Kristen is three years older. And before you ask, they both live in the Raleigh area. They're married with kids.'

'How did you end up here, then?'

She shifted her weight from one foot to the other, as though debating how best to answer before finally offering a shrug. 'Oh, you know. I met a boy in college. He was from here, and I made the move after I graduated. And here I am.'

'I take it that it didn't work out.'

She closed her eyes before opening them again. 'Not the way I wanted.'

The words came out quietly, but it was hard to read the emotion behind them. Regret? Resentment? Sadness? Figuring it wasn't the time or place to ask, I let the subject drop. Instead, I shifted gears. 'What was it like growing up in a small town? I mean, I thought New Bern was small, but 2,500 is tiny.'

'It was wonderful,' she replied. 'My mom and dad knew just about everyone in town, and we left our doors unlocked. I knew everyone in all my classes, and I'd spend my summers riding my bike and swimming in the pool and catching butterflies. The older I get, the more I marvel at the simplicity of it.'

'Do you think your parents will live there forever?'

She shook her head. 'No. A few years ago, they bought a place in Atlantic Beach. They already spend as much time there as they can, and I'm pretty sure that's where they'll end up when they finally retire. We actually had Thanksgiving there last year, and it's just a matter of time now.' She tucked a loose strand of hair behind her ear.

'How did you end up working for the sheriff's department?'

'You asked me that before.'

'I'm still curious,' I said. 'Because you didn't really answer.'

'There's not much to say about it. It just kind of happened.'

'How so?'

'In college, I majored in sociology, and after I graduated, I realized that unless I wanted to get my master's or a PhD, there weren't a lot of jobs in my field. And when I moved here, it became clear that unless you own a business or have a job at Cherry Point or work for the government or the hospital, you're limited to service jobs. I thought about going back to school to become a nurse, but at the time, it seemed like too much effort. Then, I heard the sheriff's department was hiring and on a whim, I applied. I was as surprised as anyone that I was accepted into the training program. I mean, to that point in my life, I'd never even held a gun. And that's what I thought it would be like — bad guys, dangerous situations, shoot-outs — it's all about the gun, right? That's what they show on television, anyway, and that's all I knew. But once I got in, I quickly figured out that it was more about people skills. It's about defusing situations and calming emotions whenever possible. And, of course, paperwork. Lots of paperwork.'

'Do you enjoy it?'

'It's like any job, I guess. There are parts about it I like, and other parts that I don't. You occasionally experience things that you wish you hadn't. Gut-wrenching things you can't forget.'

'Have you ever shot someone?'

'No. And I've only had to draw my gun once. Like I said, it's not what you see on television. But you know what?'

'Do tell.'

'Even though I'd never held a gun, I ended up being a pretty good shot. Top in my class, in fact. And since then, I've taken up skeet shooting and sporting clays, and I'm pretty good at those, too.'

'Sporting clays?'

'It's like skeet — there are various stands and you use a shotgun — but the clays come from differing angles, with differing speeds and trajectories. It's supposed to more accurately reflect the way birds and small game move in the wild.'

'I've never been hunting.'

'Neither have I. And I don't want to. But if I ever did, I'd probably be pretty good.'

I couldn't help but feel a bit of admiration for her. 'It's actually not that hard to imagine you with a shotgun. Since the first time I saw you, you were armed, I mean.'

'I find it . . . relaxing. When I'm at the range, I'm able to tune everything else out.'

'I hear massages are good for that. Personally, I prefer yoga.'

Her eyebrows shot up. 'You do yoga?'

'My psychiatrist's recommendation. It's helpful. I can now put on my shoes without having to sit down. It makes me popular at parties.'

'I'll bet.' She laughed. 'Where do you do yoga around here?'

'Nowhere yet. I haven't looked for a place.'

'Will you?'

'Maybe. I won't be here that long.'

'Will you ever come back?'

'I don't know. I guess it depends on whether I sell the house. Who knows? Maybe I'll be back at the end of summer for a week to finish harvesting the honey.'

'You know how to do that?'

'Sure,' I said. 'It's actually not that hard. It's sticky and messy, but not hard.'

She shuddered. 'Bees scare me. I mean, not the friendly bumblebees, but the ones that buzz around your face like they're trying to attack you.'

'Guard bees,' I said. 'Some people call them bouncer bees. They're not my favorite, either, but they're important for the hive. They help protect it from predators and keep bees from other colonies out of the hive.'

'Are guard bees different than regular bees?'

'Not really. As a bee goes through its life cycle, it will serve in various jobs at various times: It'll be an undertaker bee, or a bee that cleans the hive, or takes care of the queen, or feeds the larvae, or forages for nectar and pollen. And toward the end of its life, it may become a guard bee.'

'Undertaker bees?' she echoed.

'They remove the dead bees from the hive.'

'Really?'

I nodded. 'My grandfather considered bee-hives to be the world's most perfect community. Of course, the colonies are almost entirely female, so maybe that has something to do with it. In fact, I'd bet that almost every bee you've ever come across has been female.'

'Why?'

'Male bees are called drones, and they only have two functions: They eat, and fertilize the queen, so there's not too many of them.' I grinned. 'It's kind of the perfect job, if you ask me. Eating and sex? I think I would have been a pretty good drone.'

She rolled her eyes, but I could tell she thought it was sort of funny. Score one for Benson.

'So . . . what does a beehive look like?' she asked. 'I mean, the kind that beekeepers maintain, not natural ones?'

'I could describe it, but it would probably be better to actually see one. And I'd be happy to show you my grandfather's, if you'd like to come by sometime.'

She seemed to study me. 'When are you thinking?' she asked.

'Any time tomorrow is fine. Early afternoon? Say one o'clock?'

'Can I think about it?'

'Sure,' I said.

'All right,' she said with a sigh, before bending to retrieve her basket. 'Thanks for the visit.'

'You too. But before you leave, would you like to join me for lunch? I'm getting kind of hungry.'

She tilted her head and I almost thought she'd say yes. Then: 'Thank you, but I really can't. I have some errands I have to run.'

'No worries.' I shrugged. 'I just thought I'd offer.'

She just smiled and started walking, my eyes following her graceful figure.

'Natalie!' I called out.

She turned. 'Yes?'

'If I was a betting man, what kind of odds would you give me that you'll actually show up tomorrow?'

She pursed her lips. 'Fifty-fifty?'

'Is there anything I can do to increase those odds?'

'You know,' she drawled, taking another step backward, 'I really don't think there is. Bye, now.'

I watched her recede into the distance, hoping she would turn to look back at me, but she didn't. I remained at the rail, replaying our conversation, and contrasting it with the way Natalie had reacted when Julie appeared at the farmers' market. I understood Natalie's aversion to being the focus of small-town gossip, and yet the more I considered it, the more I wondered whether that was all of it. Natalie, I suddenly realized, had purposely limited her conversation with Julie not only because of what Julie might say to others, but also because there was something Natalie didn't want me to know about herself.

Now, we all have secrets. Despite what I'd told her about my past, I was still a stranger, so there was no reason to expect her to share whatever hers were. But as I continued to reflect on the situation, I couldn't shake the notion that Natalie was less concerned about what her secrets might reveal than about the guilt her secrets seemed to wield over her.

5

Here's a lesson that was ingrained in me by my mom starting at a very young age: If you're expecting guests, then you'd better clean the house.

I'll admit that when I was a kid, it didn't compute. Why would anyone care whether all my toys had been put away in my bedroom or if I made my bed? It wasn't as though any politicians or lobbyists made their way up the stairs to my bedroom while my parents were throwing their parties. They were too busy sipping wine and downing martinis and feeling *very, very important*. I remember vowing that when I was older, I wouldn't care about such things. But lo and behold, with Natalie's visit looming as a possibility, my mom's directive came roaring back.

Long story short, after I finished my run and other exercises, I tidied up the house, ran the vacuum, wiped the counters and sink, cleaned the bathroom, and finally made the bed. Washed myself, too, while singing in the shower, and then spent the rest of the morning catching up on my reading. The section in the book I was perusing dealt with the effectiveness of music as an adjunct to therapy, and as I worked my way through the material, I remembered the years I'd spent playing the piano. In all candor, I'd always had a bit of an on-again, off-again relationship with the instrument; I played throughout my childhood, ignored it completely while at the Naval Academy, picked it up again while I was in medical school, and then didn't so much as tap a key during my residency. In Pensacola, I played a lot, as I was lucky enough to rent a place with a beautiful 1890 Bösendorfer in the lobby of the building; but Afghanistan was another music-free period, as I doubted whether there was a single piano left in the entire country. Now, with missing fingers, playing like I once did was impossible, which made me suddenly realize how much I missed it.

When I finished studying, I closed the book, got in the car, and made a trip to the grocery store. I stocked up on the essentials and made myself a sandwich when I got home. By the time I rinsed the plate, it was coming up on one o'clock. Still uncertain as to whether Natalie would show up but hoping for the best, I headed out to the honey shed.

Like the house and the barn, it wasn't much from the outside. The tin roof was rusting, the cedar planking had turned gray over the decades, and hinges supporting the large double doors screeched as I pulled them open. After that, however, the similarities ended; inside, the honey shed was like a museum. There was electricity, plumbing, and bright fluorescent lights; the walls and ceiling were insulated, and the concrete floor had a drain in the center. To the left was a stainless-steel sink with a long hose attached to a faucet, as well as shallow supers and queen

83

excluders for the beehives, stacked neatly atop each other. On the right was a plastic garbage can filled with kindling for the smokers, next to deep shelves crammed with dozens of jars of honey. Directly ahead was all the other equipment and gear necessary for an apiarist: five-gallon plastic buckets with honey gates, a plastic wheel-barrow, crates filled with extra jars, and rolls of self-adhesive labels. On the back wall, supported by hooks, were nylon strainers, honey sieves, uncapping knives, two smokers, lighters, a dozen bee suits, and gloves and hoods in various sizes. There were also two extractors, which were used to spin the honey from the combs. I recognized the manual one I used to crank until I could barely move my arm, as well as the newer electric one my grandfather had purchased after his arthritis set in, and both appeared to be in perfect working order.

As for the suits, I knew I'd find ones that would fit both Natalie and me. He had so many because he was always willing to educate people — often groups — who were interested in learning about the bees. Most people weren't comfortable visiting the hives without a bee suit; my grandfather, on the other hand, never bothered to put one on.

'They won't sting me unless I want 'em to,' he would say with a wave. 'They know I take care of 'em.'

Whether that was true or not, I don't remember him ever getting stung while tending the hives. He was, however, a believer in the Southern folklore that bee venom could mitigate the

84

pain of his arthritis, so every day without fail, he'd collect two bees. While holding them by the wings, he'd taunt them into stinging him, once in each knee. The first time I saw him do it, I thought he was crazy; as a physician, I now understand that he was ahead of his time. In controlled clinical studies, bee venom has actually been shown to relieve arthritis pain. If you don't believe me, look it up.

I'd tended to the hives so many times in the past that the next steps were automatic. I filled the smoker with kindling, collected a lighter and an uncapping knife, as well as a pair of suits, hoods, and gloves. On an impulse, I also took down two jars of honey from the shelves and brought everything to the front porch. I shook the dust from the suits and hoods before draping them over the railing, stacking everything else on the small table near the rockers. By then, it was a quarter past one. Things weren't looking good on the Natalie front, but even worse was the idea of her discovering me waiting for her on the porch if she did show up. A man has got to have some pride, after all.

I went back inside and poured myself a glass of sweet tea from the pitcher I had brewed the night before, then wandered to the back porch. As fate would have it, I had taken only a couple of sips before I heard a car pulling up in the drive. I couldn't suppress a smile.

Walking back through the house, I opened the door just as Natalie mounted the porch. She wore jeans and a white button-up shirt that accentuated her olive-colored skin. Her sunglasses hid her eyes and her hair was pulled into a messy ponytail, all of which made her especially alluring.

'Hey there,' I said. 'I'm glad you decided to come.'

She pushed her sunglasses up into her hair. 'Sorry I'm late. I had to take care of some things this morning.'

'Not a problem,' I said. 'My schedule's pretty clear all day.' Then, remembering the jars I'd retrieved from the honey shed, I pointed to the table. 'I pulled those for you,' I said. 'Since you mentioned that you liked my grandfather's honey.'

'Very thoughtful of you,' she murmured. 'But are you sure you have enough?'

'More than enough. Too much, really.'

'You could always get a table at the farmers' market if you want to get rid of it.'

'That probably won't be possible,' I said. 'Saturday mornings are generally when I read to blind orphans. Or rescue kittens from trees.'

'Laying it on a little thick, don't you think?'

'I'm just trying to impress you.'

A smile played about her lips. 'I don't know whether I should be flattered or not.'

'Oh,' I said. 'Definitely flattered.'

'Good to know, but I can't make any promises.'

'I'm not asking you to,' I countered. 'And regarding the honey, Claude over at the Trading Post said he'd take all I could spare, so I'm guessing most of it will end up there.'

'I'll be sure to stock up before the rest of the town finds out.'

86

For a moment, silence descended and her gaze steadied on my own. I cleared my throat, suddenly self-conscious. 'I know you came to visit the hives, but let's sit out back first, so I can tell you what to expect. It'll make things a bit clearer when you get out there.'

'How long will it take?'

'Not long. No more than an hour for everything.'

Pulling a phone from her back pocket, she checked the time. 'That should be okay.' She went on. 'I promised to visit my parents this afternoon. They're at the beach.'

'I thought you had to make pies for your neighbor.'

'I did that yesterday.'

'Very efficient,' I commented. 'Now come on in,' I said, waving her through the doorway.

Her footsteps echoed behind me as we passed from the family room to the kitchen. I paused. 'Can I get you something to drink?'

Eyeing the sweating glass of iced tea in my hand, she nodded and said, 'I'll have one of those, if you don't mind.'

'Good choice — I just brewed it last night, as a matter of fact.'

Retrieving a glass, I added ice cubes and filled it with sweet dark tea from the refrigerator. I handed it to her, then leaned against the counter, watching as she took a sip.

'It's not bad.'

'As good as your pies?'

'No.'

I laughed, watching as she took another sip

and surveyed the house. Despite myself, I was grateful for my mom's training. Natalie, no doubt, now thought of me as tidy, in addition to rather charming. Or maybe not. I knew I was interested in her, but she was still a mystery to me.

'You've made some changes to the place,' she noted.

'Though I loved living in a time capsule, I felt the need to update the decor.'

'It seems more open, too.'

'My grandfather had a lot of stuff. I got rid of it.'

'My parents are like that. On the fireplace mantel back home, there must be fifty framed photographs. Try to dust one, and they topple like dominoes. I don't understand it.'

'Maybe the older people get, the more important the past becomes? Because there's less future ahead?'

'Maybe,' she said, without adding anything else.

Unable to read her, I pushed open the back door. 'Ready?'

I followed her out onto the back porch, watching her settle in the same rocker as she had the first night I'd met her. Unlike me, she didn't lean back; instead, she remained propped on the edge, as if ready to jump up and run away if she had to. After all our banter, I was surprised that she wasn't more relaxed, but I was getting the feeling that Natalie was full of surprises.

I took a sip of my tea, watching as she gazed toward the creek, her profile as perfect as cut glass.

'I think I could stare at this forever.'

'Me too,' I said, looking only at her.

She smirked, but decided to let my remark pass.

'Do you ever swim out there?'

'I did when I was a kid. Right now, the water's still too cold.'

'That might be a good thing. Apparently someone sighted some alligators a little ways upstream.'

'Seriously?'

'It's pretty rare to find them this far north. We get reports of them once or twice a year, but I've never had any luck sighting any. They tend to be in places cars can't reach.'

'If you'd ever like to go out on the water, I've got the boat right out there.'

'That might be fun,' she agreed before folding her hands in her lap, suddenly all business again. 'What did you want to tell me about the bees?'

'Let's start with this,' I said, setting my glass aside. 'How much do you know about bees? And how much do you want to know?'

'I have about an hour, maybe a little more. So tell me whatever you think will be important.'

'Fair enough,' I said. 'Bee colonies have an annual cycle. In the winter, a hive might have five or ten thousand bees. In the spring, once it warms up, the queen begins laying more eggs, and the population begins to grow. During the summer months, a hive might hold up to a hundred thousand bees, which is why an apiarist might add another chamber to the hive. Then, as autumn approaches, the queen begins to lay fewer eggs. The population starts to diminish again, because the colony somehow knows it hasn't stored enough honey to feed all the bees. In the winter, the remaining bees eat the honey to survive. They also cluster together and vibrate to create heat, so the colony doesn't freeze. When it begins to warm, the cycle starts all over again.'

She digested that, then held up a hand. 'Hold on,' she said. 'Before you go on, I want to know how you learned all this stuff. Did your grandfather teach you?'

'We tended the hives together whenever I was down here visiting. But I also heard him give the talk to lots of different people. When I was in high school, I even did a semester-long project on bees for my science class.'

'Just making sure you know what you're talking about. Go on.'

Did I detect a bit of flirting in her tone? I reached for my tea again, trying not to lose track of my thoughts. Her beauty was distracting.

'Every hive also has a single queen. Assuming the queen doesn't get sick, she lives from three to five years. Early on in her life cycle, the queen flies around and gets fertilized by as many male bees as she can before returning to the hive where she'll lay eggs for the rest of her life. The eggs turn to larvae, and then pupae, and when they're mature, the bees are ready to serve the hive. Unlike the queen, these worker bees live only six or seven weeks, and they'll cycle through a variety of different jobs in their short lives. The vast majority are female. The males are called drones.'

90

'And all the drones do is mate with the queen and eat.'

'You remembered.'

'It was hard to forget,' she said. 'What happens if the queen dies?'

'Bee colonies have a fail-safe,' I answered. 'No matter what time of year, when a queen is weakening or not laying enough eggs, the nurse bees will start feeding several of the larvae a substance called royal jelly. This food changes the larvae into queens, and the strongest one will take over. If necessary, that new queen will then replace the older queen. At which point, she'll fly away and mate with as many drones as she can before returning to the hive to spend the rest of her life laying eggs.'

'That isn't much of a life for a queen.'

'Without her, the colony will die. That's why she's called the queen.'

'Still, you'd think she'd get to go shopping or attend a wedding every now and then.'

I smiled, recognizing in her humor something akin to my own. 'Now, yesterday I mentioned a few of the jobs bees do during their life cycle — clean the hive or feed the larvae or whatever. But the majority of bees in any hive collect pollen and nectar. A lot of people might think that pollen and nectar are the same, but they're not. Nectar is the sugary juice in the heart of the flowers. Pollen, on the other hand, are tiny grains that collect on the anthers. Want to guess which one leads to the making of honey?'

She pursed her lips. 'Nectar?'

'Exactly,' I said. 'A bee will fill its nectar sacs,

fly back to the hive, and turn the nectar into honey. A bee also has glands that turn some of the sugar in the honey into beeswax. And little by little, honey is created and stored.'

'How is nectar turned into honey?'

'It's kind of gross.'

'Just tell me.'

'When a bee gets back to the hive with its load of nectar, it passes the nectar mouth-to-mouth to a different bee, who then does the same to another bee, over and over, gradually lowering the moisture content. When it gets concentrated enough, it's called honey.'

She made a face. For a second, I could picture her as a teenager. 'That *is* kind of gross.'

'You asked.'

'What happens with bees who bring in pollen?'

'Pollen is mixed with nectar to make bee bread. That's what they feed the larvae.'

'And the royal jelly?'

'I don't know how that's made,' I admitted. 'I used to know, but I've forgotten.'

'At least you're honest.'

'Always,' I said. 'But that brings us to another important point. Because the bees need to eat the honey to survive the winter, an apiarist has to be careful not to take too much when they harvest.'

'How much is that?'

'My grandfather would only harvest about sixty percent of the honey in any given hive, some in June and the remainder in August. Some of the larger producers will take a higher percentage, but it's generally not a good idea.'

'Is that what happened to the bees?'

'What do you mean?'

'I read some articles saying that bees were dying out. And that if they did, humanity wouldn't survive.'

'The latter part is true. Without bees spreading pollen from one plant to another, many crops simply can't survive. As to the first part, the decline in the bee population probably has less to do with overharvesting than the overuse of chemicals to clear the hive. My grandfather never used chemicals because, really, you don't need them. I'll show you when we get out there, but I think that's it for now.' I set my glass aside. 'Unless there's something else you'd like to know?'

'Yeah, about the guard bees. Why do they buzz around your face?'

'Because it works,' I said with a laugh. 'People don't like it, so they retreat. Keep in mind that in the wild, bears will ravage beehives. The only way a tiny bee can protect the hive from a giant bear is to sting it in the eyes, the nose, or the mouth.'

She hesitated. 'Okay. But I still don't like them.'

'That's why we'll be wearing suits. You ready?'

Natalie stood from her seat and led the way inside before stopping in the kitchen to deposit her glass. Meanwhile, I pulled two spoons from the kitchen drawer, wrapped them in a paper towel, and put them in my pocket. Retracing our steps to the front porch, I handed the smaller suit to her. 'Slip this on over your clothes,' I said. I pulled off my shoes, then put on a suit; Natalie did the same, and I made sure everything was zipped properly. After we put our shoes back on, I handed her the mesh hood — it was connected to a hat with a round brim — and the gloves, then used the lighter to get the smoker going.

'What's that?'

'It's a smoker. It calms the bees.'

'How?'

'The bees interpret smoke as part of a forest fire and they'll begin feeding on the honey in case they have to move the hive somewhere else.'

I collected the rest of the gear and motioned for her to follow. We set off in the direction of the hives, passing clutches of azalea bushes, into an area dense with dogwoods, flowering cherry trees, and magnolias. The air was thick with the sound of buzzing, and bees could be seen clustering on practically every bloom.

At the edge of the property, the vegetation grew denser. Directly ahead I caught sight of one of the hives; though my grandfather had built his own, they were similar to ones that could be purchased as kits or used by commercial farmers, consisting essentially of a stand supporting a stack of wooden chambers, along with lids. As always, I was amazed by the idea that it would be home to more than a hundred thousand bees.

'We should stop here and put on the rest of our gear.'

After donning our gloves, we approached the hive, bees bumping against the mesh of our hoods.

I added air to the smoker and puffed out some smoke near the hive before setting it on the ground.

'That's it?'

'You don't need much smoke,' I explained. 'Bees have an acute sense of smell.' I pointed toward an area beneath the lip of the lid. 'Do you see this? It's how the bees get in and out of the hive.'

She took a cautious step closer. 'How long do we have to wait for the smoke to work?'

'It's working now,' I said. 'They'll be calm for fifteen or twenty minutes.'

'Does the smoke hurt them?'

'Not at all,' I said. 'Let me show you the inside of the hive.'

Lifting off the top lid — or outer cover, in beekeeper-speak — I set it aside. Then, using the uncapping knife, I loosened the inner cover. Always a bit sticky, it was harder than usual to pry off, probably because it hadn't been removed in months.

Once I freed the inner cover, I set it on the ground as well. 'Come take a peek,' I said. 'They're friendly now.'

With obvious trepidation, she peered over my shoulder. I pointed to the top chamber. 'This part of the hive is called the upper deep. It's the food chamber. There are ten hanging frames, and this is where most of the honey is stored.'

Pointing to the chamber beneath it, I went on. 'The one right below is called the lower deep, and it's the brood chamber.'

'Wow,' she murmured. There were hundreds of slow-moving bees crawling on top of and between the frames. Natalie seemed genuinely rapt.

95

'I'm glad you were interested in coming here,'
I said. 'Otherwise I probably would have forgotten to add the shallow super and the queen
excluder. I didn't remember until I saw them in
the honey shed.'

'What are they for?'

'The shallow super adds additional honey
storage to the hive for the larger summer bee
population. It's like the upper deep, only smaller.
The queen excluder ensures that the queen
won't up and fly away.'

'You don't need them year-round?'

I shook my head. 'You'll want a smaller hive in
the winter so it's easier to keep warm.'

On the upper deep, bees continued to crawl
around with unflagging energy and purpose. I
pointed to a large wasplike one. 'See this one?' I
asked. 'That's a drone.'

She peered closer, then eventually pointed to
another. 'That one, too?'

I nodded. 'As I told you, they're greatly
outnumbered by the females, like Hugh Hefner
in the Playboy Mansion.'

'Nice metaphor,' she drawled.

I grinned. 'Let me show you something.'

I removed my gloves, then reached down and
gently picked up one of the worker bees by her
wings. She was still docile from the smoke. Using
the thumbnail on my other hand, I provoked her
until she tried to sting me through the nail.

'What are you doing?' Natalie whispered. 'Are
you trying to make her angry?'

'Bees don't get angry.' I manipulated the bee
again, and again it tried to sting me three, four,

96

and then five times. 'Watch this,' I went on. I put the bee on the back of my hand and let go of the wings. Instead of continuing to try to sting, the bee took a few steps and then flew slowly back toward the upper deep.

'The bee doesn't care about me, or what I just did to her,' I said. 'She was just trying to protect herself. Now that the threat is gone, she doesn't hold a grudge.'

Through the mesh, I read fascination and newfound respect.

'Interesting,' she said. 'Way more complex than I imagined.'

'Bees are extraordinary creatures,' I said, hearing the echo of my grandfather's voice. 'Do you want to see the honey? And the larvae?'

'I'd love to,' she said. Using the uncapping knife, I loosened one of the frames at the top edge, then loosened the other side until I could slowly pull it free. As I did, I watched Natalie's eyes widen; the frame was covered with hundreds of bees on both sides. After checking it over and determining that the cells didn't have the variety I wanted, I slid it back into the hive. 'There should be a better one,' I remarked. 'It's still early in the season.'

It took three frames before I found the one I wanted, and I removed it fully from the hive. Like the others, it was swarmed with bees, and I held it in front of her. 'Do you remember when I told you that big producers use chemicals to clear the hives? So they can harvest the honey?'

'I remember.'

'This is why you don't need chemicals.' I took

a small step back and with a quick motion, jerked the frame up and down. Nearly all the bees flew away and I held up the virtually empty frame in front of her. 'That's all you have to do to clear the bees from the frame so you can get to the honey,' I said. 'Just a single, quick shake.'

'Then why do the big producers use chemicals?'

'I have no idea,' I said. 'I haven't been able to figure that out yet.'

Angling the frame for a better view, I pointed to various cells as I spoke. 'These cells up here in the corner, covered in the beeswax, are filled with honey. These lighter ones down here contain larvae and eggs. And the empty ones will all be filled with honey by the end of the summer.'

More comfortable with the hive now, Natalie moved even closer. There were still a few bees on the frame, and she slowly reached a finger of her gloved hand toward one of them, marveling as it ignored her completely. Another slowly crawled over her gloved finger then onto the frame again. 'They're not mad that you shook off all their friends?'

'Not at all.'

'What about killer bees?'

'They're different,' I said. 'As a colony, they're a lot more aggressive in protecting the hive. These bees might send out ten or fifteen guard bees when they feel the hive is threatened, but killer bees will send out hundreds of guard bees. There are some historical and evolutionary theories as to the reason why, but unless you're really interested, we can save that for another time. Do you want to taste some of the honey?'

'Now?'

'Why not? We're here.'

'Is it . . . ready?'

'It's perfect,' I assured her. Reaching into my pocket, I pulled out the spoons and unwrapped them. I held one out to her. 'Would you mind holding this for a second?'

She took the spoon while I used the other to crush my way through some of the beeswax-coated cells. Raw, pure honey spilled onto the spoon. 'Trade you,' I said.

Natalie took the spoon with honey, while I did the same to mine. 'Hold this one for a second, too, okay?'

She nodded. Her eyes flickered from me to the honey, golden in the sunlight. I reassembled the hive, picked up the smoker and uncapping knife, then took one of the spoons from her. We walked away from the hives, in the direction of the shed. When we were a safe distance away, I motioned to her that it was fine to take off her hood and gloves.

When I could see her face without the mesh, it was glowing with excitement and interest, her skin dewy with a light sheen of perspiration. I held up the spoon, as though making a toast. 'Ready?'

I tapped my spoon against hers, then ate the honey, finding it was sweet enough to make my teeth hurt. After she tasted hers, she closed her eyes and took a long breath. 'It tastes . . . '

'Flowery?'

'And delicious. But yes, there's a very strong floral flavor.'

99

'Honey will taste different depending on where the hive is located, because the nectar the bees collect will be different. That's why some honey is sweeter than others, some have a slightly fruitier flavor, others more flowery. It's kind of like wine.'

'I'm not sure I've noticed a big difference in flavors until now.'

'Most commercial honey is clover honey. Bees love clover, which is why there's a clover patch on the property, too. But honey is also one of the most manipulated and lied-about foods on the planet. A lot of commercial honey is actually honey mixed with flavored corn syrup. You have to be careful where you buy.'

She nodded, but there was something trance-like about her demeanor, as if the combination of the sun, the soothing droning of the bees, and the elixir of honey had relaxed the defenses she usually erected around herself. Her lips were parted and moist, her aquamarine eyes drowsy and translucent. When her gaze drifted from the hive to meet mine, I felt an almost hypnotic pull.

I took a step toward her, the sound of my own breath loud in my ears. She seemed to know how I was feeling and was flattered by it. But just as quickly, she caught herself and picked up the hood and gloves, severing the thread of the moment.

I forced myself to speak. 'Would you like to see how the honey is extracted? It'll only take a couple of minutes.'

'Sure.'

Without another word, we started in the direction of the honey shed. When we got there, she handed me the hood and gloves, then

100

proceeded to take off the bee suit. I did the same and put everything back in place. I moved the manual extractor away from the wall. She came over to inspect the extractor but was careful to keep a safe distance.

'To harvest the honey, you take frames from the hive, shake off the bees, and load them in the wheelbarrow to bring them here,' I began, slowly but surely regaining my equilibrium. 'Then, one at a time, you load the frames into the extractor, between these slots. You turn the crank, and it spins the frame. Centrifugal force will push the honey and beeswax from the combs.' I turned the crank, demonstrating how it worked. 'Once the honey is spun out of the frame, you place one of those nylon bags into a plastic bucket, set it beneath the nozzle on the extractor, open the nozzle, and let the honey drain into the bucket. The nylon bag captures the wax but lets the honey pass through. After that, the honey goes into a jar and it's ready to go.'

Wordlessly, Natalie took in the rest of the shed, wandering idly from one station to the next, finally stopping in front of the plastic garbage can. Lifting the lid, she saw the wood chips and shavings; by her expression, I knew she'd figured out that the contents were for use in the smoker. She examined the back wall, inspecting all the equipment, and waved at the rows of neatly labeled jars of honey.

'It's so organized in here.'

'Always,' I agreed.

'My dad has a work shed like this,' she commented, turning to face me again. 'Where

101

everything has a purpose, everything has a place.'

'Yeah?'

'He buys old transistor radios and phonographs from the 1920s and 1930s and then repairs them in a shed behind our house. I used to love spending time there as a little girl when he was working. He had a high-backed stool and he'd wear these glasses that magnified everything. I can still remember how big his eyes were. Even now, whenever I visit them in La Grange, the shed is usually where the two of us talk about life.'

'That's an unusual hobby.'

'I think he finds it peaceful.' She sounded wistful. 'And he's proud of it, too. There's a whole section in the store with refurbished electronics on display.'

'Does he sell any?'

'Hardly.' She laughed. 'Not everyone shares his fascination with antique electronics. Sometimes he talks about opening a small museum, maybe one that's attached to the store, but he's been talking about it for years, so who knows?'

'What does your mom do while your dad is tinkering?'

'She bakes,' she answered. 'Which is why I know how to make a great piecrust. And she sells what she bakes at the store, unless we eat it first.'

'Your parents sound like good people.'

'They are,' she said. 'They worry about me.'

I stayed quiet, expecting her to go on, but she didn't. I finally offered a gentle prod. 'Because you're a deputy?'

'Partly,' she conceded. Then, as though realizing the conversation had veered in an unintended direction, she shrugged. 'Parents always worry. That's the nature of parenthood. But that reminds me I should get going. They'll be waiting for me.'

'Of course,' I said. 'I'll walk you to your car.'

We left the shed, walking down the pathway toward the drive. She drove an older model, silver Honda, a sensible car she probably intended to keep as long as it still ran. I opened the driver's side door for her; inside, I saw her handbag on the passenger seat, and a small crucifix hanging from the rearview mirror.

'I enjoyed the day so much,' she said. 'Thank you.'

'I did too,' I admitted. 'And you're welcome.'

The sun was at her back, making her face difficult to read, but when she placed her hand lightly on my forearm, I sensed that she, like me, didn't want the day to end just yet.

'How long will you be at your parents'?'

'Not long,' she said. 'I'll visit for a couple of hours and then head back home. I have to work tomorrow morning.'

'How about we meet for dinner later? When you get back?'

She studied me carefully, then hedged. 'I'm not sure what time that will be.'

'Any time is fine,' I said. 'You could shoot me a text when you're leaving and I could meet you somewhere.'

'I . . . um . . .'

She trailed off before reaching into her pocket and pulling out her keys.

'I don't like to go out in New Bern,' she finally said.

Though I could have asked her the reason, I didn't. Instead, I took a step backward, giving her space. 'It's just dinner, not a commitment. Everyone's got to eat.'

She said nothing, but part of me began to suspect that she wanted to say yes. As to why she was holding back, I still wasn't sure.

'I could meet you down at the beach if it's easier,' I offered.

'That's out of the way for you.'

'I haven't been to the beach since I've been back here,' I said. 'I've been meaning to go.'

Well, not really. Not until just now, anyway.

'I don't know of any good restaurants at the beach,' she said.

'Then how about Beaufort? You must have someplace you like there.'

As I waited for her answer, she jingled her keys. 'There is a place . . . ' she began, her voice barely audible.

'Anywhere,' I said.

'The Blue Moon Bistro,' she said in a rush, almost like she was afraid she would change her mind. 'But it can't be too late.'

'Pick the time. I'll meet you there.'

'How about half past six?'

'Perfect.'

'Thank you again for the beekeeping lesson today.'

'Glad to do it,' I said. 'I enjoyed spending time with you.'

She let out a soft exhale as she slipped into the driver's seat. 'Me too.'

I closed her door and she turned the key. The

engine came to life, and glancing over her shoulder, she backed the car out. As the car stopped and then began to roll forward, I reflected on the mystery of Natalie Masterson. By turns confident and vulnerable, revealing and secretive, she seemed to be a woman of complex instincts.

Still, what had begun as a flirty diversion had already begun to morph into something deeper, a desire to connect with and truly understand a woman whom I couldn't figure out. Nor could I shake my desire to connect with the real Natalie — to leap the wall she seemed compelled to build between us — and perhaps form something even deeper and more meaningful. Even to me, it struck me as a romantic notion that bordered on the ridiculous — I reminded myself again that I didn't really know her — but at the same time, I know what my grandfather would have said.

Trust your instincts, just like the bees do.

Walking back to the house, I spotted the jars of honey on the porch table and realized she'd forgotten to take them. I put them in the SUV, then spent the rest of the afternoon on the back porch with a textbook in my lap, trying not to think about Natalie or even my own feelings, but finding it impossible to concentrate. Instead, I replayed our time together over and over again, finally admitting to myself that I was simply counting the minutes until I could see her again.

6

What to wear.

Normally, I wouldn't have thought twice about it, but I found myself googling the restaurant to get a better idea of the dress code. As far as I could tell, the place was tasteful and charming. Built in a historic home, the photos showed heart pine flooring, smaller tables with white tablecloths, and plenty of natural light streaming in through the windows. I could imagine getting away with jeans, but in the end, I went with your basic Annapolis look: tan pants, a white button-up shirt, navy sport jacket, and Top-Siders. All I needed was a scarf, and I could walk around saying things like, *Anyone up for some yachting?*

It would take a little under an hour to get there, but not wanting to be late, I made it across the bridge to Beaufort with at least forty-five minutes to spare. The town was nestled on the Intracoastal, and I parked near the waterfront, just around the corner from the restaurant. I spotted a pair of wild horses across the waterway, grazing on one of the many barrier islands that make up the coastline of North Carolina. My grandfather told me these horses were descended from the mustangs that survived Spanish shipwrecks off the coast, but who knew if that was true?

I decided to use the extra time to browse the art galleries along the waterfront. Most of the work was by local artists, featuring either beach themes or the historic architecture in Beaufort. In one of the galleries, I saw a painting of a house where Blackbeard the Pirate had allegedly lived; I vaguely recalled that the wreck of Blackbeard's ship, the *Queen Anne's Revenge*, had been discovered in the Beaufort Inlet. The gallery owner confirmed my recollection, though he also admitted that there was some uncertainty about the whole thing. The wreck was estimated to be the correct size and the cannons they'd found on the ocean floor were from that period, but there was nothing to specifically indicate the name of the ship. It wasn't as though they'd been able to reach into the glove compartment and check the registration, and the ocean can cause a lot of damage in three hundred years.

Wandering to the waterfront again, I noticed the sun slowly going down, casting a golden prism across the water. Heavenly light, my grandfather used to call it, and I smiled, reminiscing about all the times he'd brought me here for an afternoon at the beach, followed by an ice cream cone in Beaufort. Thinking back, I was amazed by how much time he'd been able to make for me whenever I was in town. I found myself turning again to his strange journey to Easley, my last visit with him, and his final, mystifying words to me.

Go to hell . . .

Not wanting to dwell on it, I shook the thought away. By then, it was coming up on six thirty, and I started toward the restaurant, wondering whether she'd show. Just then, however, I saw Natalie's car pulling into an open space near my SUV. I turned in that direction, reaching her car just as she climbed out.

She'd changed into a flowered, high-necked sleeveless dress that accentuated her figure, and black medium-heeled boots, with a sweater draped over her arm. A thin gold chain around her neck glowed in the waning light. When she reached inside the car for her purse, I noted how graceful her every move was. Her arms and legs were lithe and toned, swishing the thin fabric of her dress around her in a tantalizing motion.

Closing the car door, she turned and startled.

'Oh, hey,' she said. 'I'm not late, am I?'

'You're actually a few minutes early,' I said. 'You look great.'

She adjusted the thin necklace, as though making sure the — locket? medallion? — was hidden from view. 'Thank you,' she said. 'Did you just get here?'

'I came a little early,' I said. 'How did your visit with your parents go?'

'Same as usual.' She sighed. 'When he's at the beach, my dad likes to read on the back porch. My mom has been slowly decorating the place since they bought it, and was dying to show me the redecorated guest room. I love them to bits, but sometimes spending time with them feels like the movie *Groundhog Day*, where every day is the same.'

I nodded in the direction of the restaurant. 'Do you want to head over?'

'Let me put my sweater on. It's a bit chilly, don't you think?' She held out her purse. 'Can you hold this for a second?'

As she slipped the sweater on, I found myself wondering if she felt self-conscious in her lovely, formfitting dress. I wasn't cold in the slightest.

Wrapping it tightly around her, she took her purse back and we crossed the street. There were few other people out and about; the town, I observed, was even sleepier than New Bern.

'When was the last time you ate at the Blue Moon Bistro?'

'It's been a while,' she said. 'A year and a half, maybe?'

'Why so long?'

'Life. Work. Errands. Unless I'm visiting my parents, it's a little out of the way. As a general rule, I tend toward quieter evenings at home.'

'Don't you and your friends ever go out?'

'Not too much, no.'

'Why not?'

'Life. Work. Errands,' she said again. 'Because I'm still low on the totem pole at work, my schedule changes a lot. Sometimes, I work days, other times, it's nights and it changes regularly. It can be a challenge to schedule things with friends.'

'That's inconvenient,' I said.

'It is,' she agreed. 'But it pays the bills. And I'm very responsible.'

'Always?'

'I try to be.'

'That's too bad.'

'No, it's not.'

'I beg to differ,' I said. 'In the end, people generally regret the things they didn't do, not the things they did.'

'Who told you that?' she scoffed.

'Common sense?'

'Try again.'

'My psychiatrist?'

'Did he really say that?'

'No, but I'm sure he would have. He's a very smart guy.'

She laughed, and I noted how different she was from the first night I'd met her. It was almost as though her uniform had the ability to transform her personality. But then I realized that the same was true about me. In a lab coat or scrubs, I was one person; dressed like a yachtsman, I was someone different.

When we reached the restaurant, a teenage girl welcomed us. About half of the tables were occupied. She pulled a pair of menus from the stand and led the way to a small table near one of the many windows. As I walked, I heard the floor creaking with age and history.

I pulled out Natalie's chair for her, then took a seat across from her. Through the window, the view didn't offer much: just another historic house directly across the street. No water view, no potential sunset, no wild horses. As though reading my mind, Natalie leaned across the table.

'It's quaint, but the food is really good,' she said. 'Trust me.'

'Anything I should have in particular?'

'Everything is great,' she assured me.

I nodded and after spreading my napkin in my lap, I perused the menu. 'I've decided to go on the seafood diet,' I announced.

'What's that?'

'See food and eat it.'

She rolled her eyes, but I saw her crack a faint smile. In the silence, I studied the menu again before suddenly remembering what I'd left in the car.

'By the way, you forgot to take the jars of honey I left for you.'

'I remembered as soon as I got home.'

'Well anyway, I brought them for you, so remind me on our way out.'

The waitress arrived and took our drink orders. Both of us ordered iced tea, along with water. When we were alone at the table again, I tried not to stare at her, the burnished halo of her hair in the candlelight framing her delicate features and unusually colored eyes. Instead, I delved into learning more about her, hungry for details about her past and everything that shaped the person she was now.

'So your dad fixes old electronics, your mom bakes and decorates,' I summarized. 'How about your siblings? What can you tell me about them?'

She shrugged. 'They're both in baby hell right now,' she said. 'Or, rather, toddler hell. Both have two kids under three. Even compared to me, they have no life at all.'

'And you?'

'I've already told you about my life.'

Some things, but not really. 'Tell me what you were like as a kid.'

'It's not that exciting. I was pretty shy as a girl, although I loved to sing,' she began. 'But lots of young girls love to sing and it's not as though I did anything with it. I guess I started coming into my own in high school and finally escaped my older siblings' shadows. I won the lead in the high school musical, joined the yearbook committee, even played soccer.'

'We have that in common,' I said. 'Music and soccer.'

'I remember,' she said. 'But I don't think I was as good as you were at either of them. I played soccer mainly so I could spend time with my friends. I didn't even start until I was a senior, and I think I only scored one goal the whole season.'

I quickly chose the fried green tomatoes as an appetizer and tuna for the main course, setting the menu aside.

'Did you go to high school in La Grange?'

'La Grange is too small for a high school, so I ended up going to Salem Academy. Have you heard of it?' When I shook my head, she went on. 'It's an all-girls boarding school in Winston-Salem,' she said. 'My mom went there, and so did my older sister, Kristen. My brother went to Woodberry Forest in Virginia. My parents were big on education, even if it meant shipping us off to boarding schools.'

'Did you like that?'

'Not at first. Even though my sister was there, I was homesick and my grades were terrible. I think I cried myself to sleep every night for months. But I eventually got used to it. By the time I graduated, I loved it, and I still keep in touch with a few of the girls I met there. And I think going away to school helped when I went to NC State. When I moved into the dorms as a freshman, I was used to living without my parents, so the transition to college was super easy. But I'm still not sure I'd go that route with my own kids. If I ever have them, I mean. I think I'd miss them too much.'

'Do you want kids?'

It took her a few beats to answer. 'Maybe,' she finally offered. 'Not right now. And for all I know, it might never happen. The future remains unwritten, right?'

'I suppose.'

She set her menu on top of mine at the edge of the table. I saw her eyes come to rest on my injured hand. Instead of hiding it, I spread my remaining fingers on the table. 'Looks strange, doesn't it?' I commented.

'No.' She shook her head. 'I'm sorry. It was rude of me to stare . . .'

'It's understandable. Even though I'm used to it, I still think it's strange. But losing fingers is better than losing an ear.'

At her puzzled expression, I pointed to the side of my head. 'This isn't real,' I said. 'It's a prosthetic.'

'I wouldn't have known unless you'd told me.'

'I'm not sure why I did.'

But I knew the reason. As much as I wanted to know her, I also wanted her to know the real me,

113

to feel as though I could be completely open with her. She was silent for a moment and I thought she'd change the subject, or even excuse herself to go to the restroom. Instead, she surprised me by reaching out and gently tracing the scarred stumps where my fingers used to be. The touch was electric.

'The explosion must have been . . . horrific,' she said, her fingertip still on my skin. 'I've thought about it since you told me. But you didn't go into any detail. I'd like to hear about it if you're comfortable telling me.'

I offered a condensed version of the story: the random mortar blast after I'd exited the building, a flash of sudden heat and searing, and then nothing at all until I woke after my first surgeries. The flights to Germany and then back to the US, and the series of additional surgeries and rehabilitation at Walter Reed and Johns Hopkins. At some point while I was speaking, she removed her hand from mine, but even after I finished, I could still feel the ghostly remnants of her touch.

'I'm sorry you had to endure all that,' she said.

'If I could go back in time, I'd leave the hospital a few minutes earlier or later. But I can't. As for right now, I'm trying to move forward in positive ways.'

'I'll bet your parents are still proud of you.'

As soon as she said it, I remembered my previous experiences when I'd shared what had happened to them. I knew I should simply offer something ambiguous like, *I hope so*, without going into details, but with the way Natalie was looking at me, I realized I didn't want to keep the words inside me.

'My parents died a month before I graduated from college. They were taking a trip to Martha's Vineyard, some political soiree that probably meant virtually nothing in the long run. A client had chartered a plane, but they never made it. The plane crashed in Virginia less than five minutes after takeoff.'

'Oh my God! That's awful!'

'It was,' I said. 'One day they were there, and the next day they were gone and I was crushed. The whole thing felt surreal — still does sometimes. I was only twenty-two, but I still felt like I was closer to being a teenager than an adult. I can still remember when my commanding officer came into my class and called me to his office so he could tell me.'

I hesitated, the memories still vivid.

'Because I was largely done with my classes, the Academy gave me leave to handle the affairs and that was in some ways even more surreal. My grandfather came up to help, but still . . . I had to find a funeral home and choose caskets and pick out a dress for my mom and a suit for my dad, figure out what they would have wanted for services. I'd just spoken on the phone to them a few days earlier.'

'I'm glad your grandfather was there for you.'

'We needed each other, no question about it. He'd already lost his wife, and had just lost his only child. We ended up driving back to New Bern after the services, and I don't think either of us said a word the entire trip. It wasn't until we got to his house that we could even talk about

115

it at all, and we both shed a lot of tears that week. It was just so sad for me to think of all the things they would never have the chance to do, or what my future would be like without them.'

'I can't imagine losing my parents like that.'

'There are moments when I still can't. It's been a decade now, but sometimes, it still feels like I should be able to pick up the phone and call them.'

'I don't know what to say.'

'No one does. It's hard for people to fathom. I mean, who becomes an orphan at twenty-two? It's not as though there are many people who ever have to deal with something like that.'

She looked away, as though still trying to process what I said, just as the waitress arrived to take our dinner orders. Almost robotically, Natalie ordered a beet salad and red snapper, and I ordered the choices I'd picked earlier. When the waitress retreated, Natalie looked up at me.

'When I was young, my best friend died. I know it's not even close to the same, but I remember how awful it was.'

'What happened?'

'We were both twelve. She lived two doors down, and her birthday was only a week before mine. Her parents were friends with my parents, so we pretty much grew up together. Went to the same school, we were in the same class all the way through, we even both took the same dance lessons. At the time, I think I was closer to Georgianna than I was to either my sister or my brother. Even when we weren't together, we spoke on the phone all the time. But anyway, we'd walked home from school together. I remember we were talking about this boy named Jeff, who she thought was cute, and she was wondering whether he liked her, too. We said goodbye at my house, and I remember hugging her goodbye. We always hugged. Anyway, about an hour after that, she wanted an ice cream sandwich, so she decided to walk to the convenience store, maybe three blocks away. While she was walking, she was hit by a drunk driver and died.'

I could tell by her expression that she was reliving that moment and I stayed silent. When she finally realized I hadn't responded, she shook her head.

'Like I said, it's not the same as losing both your parents.'

'I didn't lose my best friend when I was young, either. I'm sorry for your loss.'

'Thank you,' she said. Then, exhibiting a bit of false cheer, she added: 'But look at us. Could our conversation get any more depressing?'

'I prefer to think of it as the two of us being honest with each other.'

'It's still not the best dinner topic.'

'What would you like to discuss instead?'

'Anything.'

'All right,' I said. 'What else can you tell me about growing up? Good things, I mean.'

'Like what?'

'Did you have any pets?' When she looked skeptical, I added, 'I'm just trying to get an idea of who you were.'

'We had a dog and a cat for most of my childhood. They were named Fred and Barney.'

'From *The Flintstones?*'

'Exactly.'

'How about family vacations?'

'We took them all the time,' she said. 'We went to Disney World every other year, we'd go skiing in West Virginia or Colorado, and we'd rent a house in the Outer Banks for two weeks every summer. One set of grandparents lived in Charlotte, and another near Boone, so we'd visit them, too. There were a lot of long car rides and I used to dread them . . . but now I think it helped us form closer ties as a family.'

'It sounds idyllic.'

'It was,' she said, seemingly growing more comfortable with sharing. 'I have no complaints about our family life.'

'I don't know too many people who can say that. I thought everyone had issues with their parents.'

'I'm not saying they were perfect, but it was easier for me and my siblings because they get along so well. Considering they work together all day and then go home together, you'd think they'd get tired of each other. But my dad is still crazy about my mom, and she dotes on him. There was a lot of laughter and we had dinner together every night as a family.'

I grinned, marveling at how different our childhoods had been. 'What led you to choose NC State? After you finished high school?'

'It's where my dad went to school,' she answered. 'My mom went to Meredith, which is an all-girls college in Raleigh. But after Salem Academy, I wanted a big, public, coed school. I also knew it would make my dad happy. In fact, all of us — my brother and sister — went to NC State. We're all die-hard Wolfpack fans, in case you're wondering. Even my mom has been converted. My dad has season tickets for football and we usually have a family tailgate once or twice a year. My parents go to every home game.'

'And that's where you met the guy you followed to New Bern, right?'

'Mark,' she said, adding nothing else.

'You loved him?' I asked.

'Yes,' she said, her gaze falling. 'But he's not someone I want to talk about.'

'Fair enough,' I said. 'I think I have a pretty good idea of who you are, even without that part of your life.'

'You do, huh?'

'Well, some of it, anyway.'

'What's confusing you?'

'I'm still not sure why you decided to become a deputy. You strike me as more like the teacher or nurse type. Or maybe an accountant.'

'Should I be offended by that?'

'I'm not saying you're not tough enough. I guess it's just that you strike me as intelligent, caring, and thoughtful. It's a good thing.'

She scrutinized me for a beat. 'I already told you,' she answered. 'I sort of fell into it. But to your point about nursing, I get that a lot, actually, although I'm not sure why. To me, hospitals . . . are . . . ' She hesitated. 'They're depressing. I hate hospitals. And besides, I get squeamish at the sight of blood.'

119

'Another reason not to be in your line of work.'

'I think we've established that I'm not engaging in shootouts every shift.'

'But if you were, you'd be fine. Since you're an excellent shot.'

'My nickname is Bull's-eye,' she said with a wink. 'In my own mind, anyway.'

The waitress came by with bread and rolls, apologizing that she hadn't brought them earlier. I took a roll and buttered it, as did Natalie.

While we nibbled, the conversation continued to drift here and there, with an ease typical of people who'd known each other far longer. We talked about the bees and beehives, shared memories of our college experiences, life in a small town versus the city, the Navy, favorite rides at Disney World, a bit about my parents and my grandfather. I even touched on my grandfather's curious journey to Easley and his final words to me.

When the waitress brought our food, it was as delicious as Natalie had promised. Out of town or not, it was a place where I'd gladly eat again. Especially with Natalie.

Though our easy rapport continued throughout dinner, it never crossed into the territory of flirting — whether she felt any real romantic interest in me was hard to tell. That she was enjoying dinner and my company, I had no doubt. As to whether she ever wanted to have dinner again, I honestly had no idea.

And yet, I couldn't recall the last time I'd had such a pleasurable evening. It wasn't just because she'd said the right things when I'd told her about my parents, or that she'd shared with me her own loss from childhood. Instead, I realized that I admired the value she placed on certain things — family, education, friendship, and kindness, among other things — and it was clear that she struggled with some of the things she saw regularly on her job — addiction, domestic violence, bar fights. She confessed that those things sometimes left her feeling agitated and unable to sleep after a shift had ended.

'Why don't you quit?' I finally asked. 'You have a degree and work experience. I'm sure you could find something else.'

'Maybe,' she admitted. 'But for now, I think it's best if I stick with it.'

'Because you want to make a difference?'

She touched the thin gold chain at her neck. 'Sure,' she finally said, 'let's go with that.'

Neither one of us was in the mood for dessert, but we agreed on coffee. A little caffeine would help with the drive back to New Bern. As she stirred her cup, I realized that aside from work and family, she'd told me little about herself since she'd arrived in New Bern a few years back. In fact, she'd said barely anything about her life in New Bern at all.

Maybe to her it wasn't all that interesting. But as I turned these facts over in my mind, Natalie stared out the window. Because of the interior lights of the restaurant, I was treated to her profile as it was reflected back in the glass. And in that moment, I understood that instead of focusing on the evening we'd just spent together, she had something else on her mind.

Something that made her feel sad.

In old-school fashion and because I'd invited her, I paid the check. To her credit, she was content to let me do so with a gracious thank-you.

The night had cooled by the time we began the ambling trek toward our vehicles. It was clear, with a spray of stars overhead and the Milky Way illuminating a path toward the horizon. The streets were empty, but from the restaurants near the water, I could hear the faint murmur of conversation and clinking glasses. Waves gently lapped against the seawall.

It still wasn't late and I thought about suggesting that we sit on the veranda of the restaurant, with its glorious view, but I was nearly certain that she'd decline. To that point, we'd yet to have had so much as a glass of wine when we were together, not that it mattered. It was simply another interesting quality of the time we'd spent together.

'I was thinking about what you told me earlier,' she finally said. 'About your grandfather.'

'Which part?'

'His last trip, and his end at the hospital,' she said. 'You're sure that he'd never mentioned Easley before?'

'Not to me,' I said. 'Claude didn't know anything, either, but I haven't spoken with his father yet.'

'Then for all you know, he could have been on

the way to somewhere else,' she pointed out. By then, we'd reached the waterfront. She paused, her ocean-colored eyes searching mine. A strand of spun-gold hair fell across her face, and I was tempted to tuck it behind her ear. Her voice broke my reverie. 'Have you thought about trying to find his truck?'

'His truck?'

'There might be something in the cab,' she explained. 'Maybe an itinerary, or the name of whomever he was visiting, or even the place he was going. Notes, maps, anything.'

Even before she'd finished speaking, I wondered why I hadn't thought of it before. Then again, I wasn't in law enforcement or a fan of mystery novels, so maybe that had something to do with it.

'You're right,' I mused aloud. 'But how would I find his truck?'

'I'd start with the hospital. Find out who they use for ambulance services. There's probably a record somewhere of where they picked him up. Depending on where he was found, the truck might still be there. Or it may have been towed, but at least you'll have a starting point.'

'That's a great idea,' I said. 'Thank you.'

'You're welcome.' She nodded. 'And let me know what happens. I'm interested, too.'

'I will,' I said. 'Which reminds me — I don't think I have your cell number. In case I need to call.'

Or *wanted* to call, which was far more likely.

'Oh,' she said, and I got the impression that she wasn't sure how she felt about that. Not wanting to give her too much time to think, I reached for my phone and activated the contact list. After a moment, she took it — her reluctance was clear — and typed in her details before handing it back to me.

'I should probably be heading back,' she announced. 'Early day tomorrow, and I still have to finish some laundry.'

'I understand,' I said. 'I have a busy day tomorrow, too.'

'Thank you again for dinner.'

'You're welcome. It was a pleasure getting to know you better.'

'You too. It was nice.'

Nice? Not exactly the description I'd been hoping for.

'Oh, before you go, let me get the honey.'

I retrieved the jars from my SUV and handed them over, feeling a kinetic jolt as our fingers brushed. I was reminded of the way she'd gently touched my scar earlier. I knew I wanted to kiss her, but she must have read my mind and automatically took a small step backward. In the sudden space between us, I detected a lingering energy, as though she'd wanted to kiss me as well. Perhaps I was imagining it, but I thought I detected a trace of regret in her parting smile.

'Thank you for these, too,' she said. 'I'm almost out.'

She turned and slowly made her way to her car. As I watched her go, I thought of something and pulled the phone from my pocket again. The screen was still on the contact page, and I dialed the number. A few seconds later, I heard the faint sound of a phone beginning to ring. She reached into her purse before catching sight of the number and glancing at me over her shoulder.

'Just checking,' I said.

She rolled her eyes before getting into her car. I waved as she drove past and she returned the gesture before reaching the road that would take her back to New Bern.

Alone, I wandered to the railing, watching the ocean sparkle in the moonlight. The breeze had picked up, cooling the air, and I turned my face to it, pondering her reluctance to kiss me. Was it part of her overall hesitation to appear in public with me? Was she really worried about small-town gossip, even this far from New Bern?

Or was it that she was already seeing someone else?

7

I hadn't been lying to Natalie when I'd said I had things to do on Monday. As opposed to most days, when I had time to goof off before taking a break and then goofing off some more, the responsibilities of life sometimes intruded, even if I didn't have to punch a clock or show up at the hospital or office. For starters, it was almost the middle of April, and my taxes were officially due.

The documents had been waiting for weeks in a cardboard box delivered courtesy of UPS. I used the same accounting firm my parents had used, initially because I knew nothing about finance or accounting, and after that because I assumed that switching to another firm would add unnecessary complications to my life, when things were already complicated enough. Frankly, thinking about money bores me, probably because I've never had to really worry about it.

My taxes were complicated because of the various trusts, investments, and portfolios I'd inherited from my parents, some of which had been funded with more life insurance than either of my parents needed. Still, whenever I saw my net worth — my accountants would meticulously prepare a balance sheet for me every February — I would sometimes wonder why I'd been so insistent on becoming a doctor in the first place. It wasn't as though I needed the money. The interest I collected annually was a lot more than I would ever earn as a doctor, but I think something inside me craved my parents' approval, even if they were no longer around. When I graduated from medical school, I imagined them clapping in the audience; in my mind's eye, I saw my mom's eyes welling with tears while my father beamed with pride at a job well done. In that moment, I understood clearly that I'd rather my parents were alive than to have received the generous inheritance they'd left me. When my statements arrive in the mail every year, I'm always reminded of those losses, and there are times when I'm too overwhelmed to even peruse them.

Even though I'd tried to explain it to Natalie while we'd been at dinner, I knew I hadn't been able to find the words to adequately express the loss or grief I really felt. Because I was an only child, I hadn't just lost my parents; I'd lost my entire immediate family as well. Over the years, I'd gradually come to believe that family is like your shadow on a sunny day, always there, just over your shoulder, following you in spirit no matter where you are or what you're doing. They're always with you. Thank God my grandfather was there to carry on part of that role, as he had so many other roles when I was younger. With his passing, however, the days are now endlessly cloudy, and when I glance over my shoulder, there is nothing there at all. I know there are others in my situation, but that doesn't make me feel any better. It just makes me think that no shadows follow them either; that they, like me, often feel entirely alone.

Reflecting on all of this made me wonder whether I would actually sell my grandfather's property. Though I'd told myself that I'd come to New Bern to get the place ready for the realtor, it was also the only remaining link to both my mother and my grandfather. At the same time, if I didn't sell, I wasn't sure what I'd do with it. I couldn't simply lock it up — the vagrant might break in again, right? — but I wasn't sure I wanted to rent it, either, because I didn't want strangers messing with the peculiar charm of the place. In the room where I'd slept as a kid, there were pencil marks on the closet door where my grandfather had duly etched my height next to those he'd marked for my mother; the thought that someone might paint over that history wasn't something I wanted to contemplate. My condo in Pensacola had simply been a place where I lived; this house, my grandfather's house, carried the ghosts of meaningful memory; it was a place where the past continued to whisper, as long as I was willing to hear it.

Knowing I had a lot to do, I went for a halfway decent run, showered, and poured myself a cup of coffee. At the table, I went through the documents from my accountants. As always, there was a cover letter that explained everything I needed to know, and little stickers on various forms indicating where I needed to sign. My eyes began glazing over at the thirty-second mark, which was normal, and I finished two additional cups of coffee before finally sliding the various documents into the appropriate preaddressed envelopes. By midmorning, I stood in line at the post office, making sure everything was postmarked, before heading back to the house and writing an email to my accountants, letting them know the deed was done.

Next on the to-do list were the beehives. After donning the same suit I'd worn the day before, I loaded the wheelbarrow with the equipment I needed, then collected a few shallow supers, along with some queen excluders. I hoped that I wasn't too late. Without the queen excluder, the queen might suddenly fly off in search of a new hive, taking her swarm with her. That was what had happened in Brazil in 1957 after scientists bred Africanized honey bees, aka killer bees, thinking they would thrive in the tropical conditions. A visiting beekeeper, believing the queen excluders were hindering the movement of the bees inside the hives, removed them, and twenty-six queens as well as their swarms escaped, traveling north, eventually reaching the US.

I pushed the wheelbarrow along the same path I'd used the day before, intending to work from left to right. As I got settled in place, I glanced toward the road and saw Callie walking, most likely on her way to the Trading Post. Like the other times I'd seen her walking, her head was bowed and she shuffled along with what seemed to be grim determination.

Wandering toward the edge of the property, I held up a hand in greeting.

'Off to work?'

My sudden appearance must have startled her and she stopped.

'You again.'

They were the same words Natalie had said to me at the park by the river, and I was struck by the notion that Callie was equally mysterious and guarded.

'It's me,' I said. Then, realizing I was wearing the suit, I motioned toward the hives. 'I have to do some work on the hives so the bees stay happy.'

She continued to eye me almost warily. When she crossed her arms, I noticed a bruise near her elbow. 'They're bees. Can't they take care of themselves?'

'You're right,' I admitted. 'They're not like Termite in that you have to feed them, but they still need a little tending now and then.'

'Do they like you?'

'Who? The bees?'

'Yes, the bees.'

'I don't know. They seem okay with me.'

'You're wearing a suit. I never saw your grampa wear a suit. When I walked past here, I mean.'

'He was braver than I am.'

For the first time since I'd seen her, she cracked the slightest of smiles. 'What did you want?'

'Nothing. I saw you walking past and thought I'd say hello.'

'Why?'

Why? I hadn't expected the question and for a moment, I couldn't think of a response. 'Just

130

being neighborly, I suppose.'

She seemed to stare right through me. 'We're not neighbors,' she said. 'I live a ways down the road.'

'You're right,' I said.

'I have to go,' she said. 'I don't want to be late for work.'

'Fair enough. I don't want you to be late, either.'

'Then why did you stop me to talk to you?'

I thought I'd answered that with the whole *being neighborly* thing, but I guess to her mind, I hadn't. But feeling as though she wanted to end the conversation sooner rather than later — again, like Natalie at the farmers' market, which made me think how similar they were in temperament — I took a step backward toward the wheelbarrow.

'No reason,' I said. 'Have a great day.'

She waited until I'd retreated a few steps before starting to walk again. And though I didn't turn around to check, I was certain she didn't cast so much as a single glance my way. Not that it was any of my business.

I put on the hood and gloves, then moved the wheelbarrow closer to the first of the hives. I got the smoker going, puffed enough to calm the hive, and waited another minute before removing both lids. I added the excluder to the top of the upper deep, put the shallow upper super on top of that, and put the lids back on. Same things with the second, third, and fourth hives. I refilled the wheelbarrow multiple times, lost in the routine and remembering my grandfather, until

131

all the hives were done.

Fortunately, all the queens were still in place — eating food and laying eggs, doing their thing — and I was able to finish in under three hours. By then, it was coming up on lunch, and thinking my morning had already been exceedingly productive, I treated myself to a beer with my sandwich.

Sometimes, it just hits the spot. Know what I mean?

After lunch, there were two more things on my agenda, both of which I considered important for my own peace of mind.

Natalie had been right about the possibility of finding answers in my grandfather's truck. She was also smart to suggest that I call the hospital first. For all I knew, my grandfather had been transported from another county. I found the phone number on the internet and spoke to an older lady with an accent so thick it could have been bottled, who had absolutely no idea how to help. After hemming and hawing for a couple of minutes — in addition to her drawl, she spoke incredibly slowly — she finally landed on the name of one of the hospital administrators and offered to connect me. While she was doing so, unfortunately, I was cut off.

I called again, asked for the appropriate name, and then was connected to voicemail. I left my name, number, a brief message, and asked him to return my call.

Maybe because of the experience I'd had with the first lady, I wasn't all that certain I'd receive a call back. Even so, I felt like I'd just taken the first step on a journey to find the answers I needed.

In the various phases of my life — high school, Annapolis, medical school, residency, and the Navy — I became friends with some extraordinary people. In each of those phases, I became particularly close to a small circle of individuals, and I simply assumed that I would remain close with them forever. Because we were hanging out then, my thinking went, we'd hang out forever.

But friendships, I've learned, aren't like that. Things change; people change. Friends mature and move and get married and have children; others become doctors and deploy to Afghanistan and have their careers blown up. Over time, if you're lucky, a few — or maybe just a couple — remain from each of the various phases of your life. I've been fortunate; I have friends who date back to high school, and yet, I sometimes find myself wondering why some people remain in your life while others drift away. I don't have the answer to that, other than to observe that friendship has to flow both ways. Both of you have to be willing to invest in the friendship in order to maintain it.

I mention this because I sometimes wonder whether to consider Dr. Bowen a friend. In some ways, he is. We speak every week and he knows me better than anyone. He's the only person who knows how much I actually used to contemplate suicide after my injuries — daily, if you're curious — and he's the only one who knows that I feel very low every year on the day my parents' plane crashed. He knows how much sleep I get, how many beers I drink in the course of a week, and how hard it used to be for me to control my anger in situations where I should have simply rolled my eyes and gone on with life. Once, about nine months ago, I was standing in the checkout line at Home Depot when the next aisle opened up. The clerk there said he could help the 'next person in line,' which was me, but the man behind me rushed over instead, taking what was rightfully my place. No big deal, right? Maybe an irritation, but what was really at stake? A few minutes? On a day when I wasn't really doing anything at all? The point is that it shouldn't have bothered me, but it did. I was bothered, then angry, and then, as the emotion continued to build, enraged. I stared at the back of his head with death rays, and I ended up walking out the door less than half a minute behind him. Watching him in the parking lot, I had to fight the visceral urge to chase after him and tackle him to the ground. I imagined pummeling him with my fists, even if I could make a fist with only one of my hands; I imagined driving a knee into his kidneys or his stomach; I visualized ripping his ear off, just as I'd lost mine. My jaw was set, my body bracing for confrontation as I began to walk faster when all of a sudden, it dawned on me that I was experiencing a symptom of PTSD, one that Bowen had repeatedly warned me about. I'd been in therapy for a while by then, and like a steady voice of reason amid an orchestra of emotional noise, Bowen was telling me what to do, telling me to change my behavior. *Stop and turn away. Force yourself to smile and relax the muscles. Take five long breaths. Feel the emotion, and then let it go, watching as it dissipates. Weigh the pros and cons regarding the action you want to take. Check the facts and realize that in the broad scheme of things, what really happened doesn't matter at all.*

When my anger finally dissipated to a manageable level, I was able to drive home. Days later, I poured the whole story out to my doctor, but in the following months, I told none of my friends. Nor did I tell my friends about the nightmares and the insomnia or anything else that was making my life a trial. And I wondered: *Why can I tell Dr. Bowen, but not the people I consider friends?*

I suppose it has to do with fear: fear of rejection, fear of disappointing others, fear of their anger or their judgment. This says more about me than it does them, but I don't feel this way when I speak with Dr. Bowen. I'm not sure why. Maybe it has something to do with the simple fact that I pay him. Or maybe it has to do with the idea that, for all our conversations, I know little about him.

In that way, we're not friends at all. Because he wears a wedding ring, I assume he's married, but I have no idea who his wife is, or how long they've been married, or anything else about his wife at all. I don't know whether he has children. From the diplomas on the wall of his office, I know he went to Princeton as an undergraduate and Northwestern for medical school. But I don't know his hobbies, or the kind of house he lives in, the food he likes, or any books or movies that he may have enjoyed. In other words, we're friends, but really, we're not.

He's just my therapist.

Eyeing the clock, I saw it was almost time for our weekly call, so after rinsing my dishes in the sink, I propped open the back door for some fresh air and put the computer on the kitchen table. Dr. Bowen liked to see my eyes when we spoke, so he could tell whether I was lying or hiding something important. On my end, it was a lot easier than meeting him in person, and I had easy access to the bathroom if I had to go. No reason to put the session on hold, no matter what. I could just carry the computer with me while I did my business.

Kidding.

At the top of the hour, I logged into Skype and it automatically dialed the number. When the connection was made, Dr. Bowen popped into view. As usual, he was at his desk in the office, a place I'd visited more times than I could count. Slightly balding with round, wire-rim glasses that made him look more like a professor of mathematics than a psychiatrist, he was, I guessed, about a decade and a half older than I was.

'What's up, Doc?'

'Hello, Trevor.'

'How are you?'

'I'm fine, thank you. How are you?'

When I asked, it was simply part of a greeting. When he asked, he actually meant it.

'I think I'm doing well,' I answered. 'No nightmares, no insomnia, sleeping well. I had one or two beers on four different days last week. I worked out five times. No episodes of anger or anxiety or depression in the last week. Still working the CBT and DBT skills whenever I feel like I need them.'

'Great.' He nodded. 'Sounds very healthy.'

He paused. Bowen did that a lot. Pause, I mean.

'Should we keep talking?' I finally asked.

'Would you like to keep speaking?'

'Are you going to charge me?'

'Yes.'

'Oh, I've got a new joke,' I said. 'How many psychiatrists does it take to change a lightbulb?'

'I don't know.'

'Only one. But the lightbulb has to really *want* to change.'

He laughed, just as I knew he would. Bowen laughs at all my jokes, but then he gets quiet again. He's told me that jokes might be my way of keeping people at a distance.

'Anyway,' I began, and proceeded to catch him up on the basic goings-on in my life in the past week. When I'd first started therapy, I wondered how any of this could possibly be useful; I'd learned over time that it allowed Bowen to have a better idea about the stress I was under at any

137

given time, which was important in my management of PTSD. Add too much stress, remove the skills and healthy behaviors, and it's either *kaboom*, like I felt toward the Home Depot guy, or way too much drinking and *Grand Theft Auto*.

So I talked. I told him that I'd been missing my grandfather and my parents more than usual since I'd last spoken to him. He responded that my feelings were entirely understandable — that checking the hives and fixing the engine on the boat would likely have triggered a mix of nostalgia and feelings of loss for just about anyone. I mentioned that I was nearly certain that someone had broken into the house and had lived there. When he asked if I felt violated or bothered by that, I said that it was more curious than bothersome, since aside from the back door, there'd been no damage and nothing had been stolen. I also mentioned the things Claude had said about my grandfather, and — as we had so often of late — we spoke about my grandfather's last words and my ongoing confusion about them.

'It still troubles you,' he observed.

'Yes,' I admitted. 'It doesn't make sense.'

'Because he told you to go to hell?'

Dr. Bowen, like Natalie, seemed to remember everything.

'It wasn't like him to say something like that,' I insisted.

'Maybe you misunderstood.'

Bowen had suggested this before. As I had in the past, I dismissed it.

'I'm sure he said it.'

'But he also said that he loved you, correct?'

'Yes.'

'And you indicated that he'd had a major stroke? And was on a lot of medication and was quite possibly confused?'

'Yes.'

'And that it took nearly a day for him to be able to speak any words at all?'

'Yes.'

When I said nothing else, he finished with the same question that continued to plague me.

'Yet you still feel he was trying to communicate something important.'

On the monitor, Bowen was watching me. I nodded but said nothing.

'You do realize,' he offered, 'that you may never understand what that might be?'

'He meant the world to me.'

'He sounds like a profoundly decent man.'

I looked away. Through the open door, the creek was black and ancient in the soft Southern light.

'I should have been there,' I muttered. 'I should have gone with him. If I had, maybe he wouldn't have had the stroke. Maybe the drive was too much for him.'

'Maybe,' Bowen said. 'Or maybe not. There's no way to know for sure. And while it may be normal to feel guilty, it's also important to remember that guilt is simply an emotion, and like all emotions, it will eventually pass. Unless you choose to hold on to it.'

'I know,' I said. He'd said this to me before. While I accepted the truth of it, it sometimes struck me that my emotions didn't care. 'Anyway . . . Natalie said that I might find some answers in his truck. As to the reason he was in South Carolina, I mean. So I've begun the process of trying to find out where the truck is.'

'Natalie?' he asked.

'She's a deputy sheriff here in town,' I began, then went on to tell him how we'd met, and a little about our conversations at the park, at the house, and then finally at dinner.

'You've spent quite a bit of time together since we last spoke,' he responded.

'She wanted to see the beehives.'

'Ah,' he said, and because we'd spoken so frequently, I knew exactly what he was thinking.

'Yes,' I said, 'she's attractive. And intelligent. And yes, I enjoyed our time together. However, I'm not sure how Natalie feels about me, which means there's not much else to add.'

'All right,' he said.

'I'm serious,' I insisted. 'And besides, I suspect Natalie might be dating someone else. I'm not sure about that, but there are signs.'

'I understand,' he said.

'Then why does it sound like you don't believe me?'

'I believe you,' he said. 'I simply find it interesting.'

'What's interesting?'

'Natalie is the first woman you've spoken to me about since you broke up with Sandra.'

'That's not true,' I said. 'I told you about Yoga Girl.'

She was a woman I'd gone out with twice the

previous fall, right around the time I'd been accepted into the residency program. We'd had a couple of pleasant evenings, but both of us knew by the end of the second date that it wasn't going to work between us.

I watched as he pushed his glasses up on his nose. 'I remember,' he finally said, his voice coming out with a sigh. 'And do you know what you called her? When you first mentioned her to me?'

'I can't say that I do,' I admitted. I also tried to remember her name. Lisa? Elisa? Elise? Something like that.

'You called her *Yoga Girl*,' he said. 'You didn't use her name.'

'I'm sure I told you her name,' I protested.

'Actually, you didn't,' he said. 'At the time, I found that interesting, too.'

'What are you trying to say? That you think I might be falling for someone in local law enforcement?'

The corners of his mouth turned up slightly as we both noted the fact I'd suddenly avoided her name. 'I have no idea,' he went on. 'And that's not really for me to say one way or the other.'

'I don't even know if I'll see her again.'

The time on my computer showed, amazingly, that nearly an hour had already passed and that our session was about to come to an end.

'Speaking of seeing each other,' he added, 'I wanted to let you know that it's possible we could meet in person next week. Unless you'd prefer to continue communicating electronically.'

'You think I need to travel to Pensacola?'

141

'No, not at all. Perhaps I should have been clearer. There's a conference at Camp Lejeune in Jacksonville concerning PTSD. One of the speakers, unfortunately, had to cancel and I was asked to fill in. It's on Tuesday, but I have to fly up Monday. If you'd like, we could meet in Jacksonville, or I could come to New Bern, if that's easier.'

'That would be great,' I said. 'What time?'

'Same time?' he asked. 'I can catch a morning flight and rent a car.'

'Are you sure it's not too far out of the way?'

'Not at all. I'm looking forward to visiting your grandfather's place. You've painted quite a picture for me.'

I smiled, thinking that even if I had, I still hadn't done it justice.

'I'll see you next week, Doc. Do you need directions?'

'I'm sure I'll be able find it. Take care.'

Two hours later, my cell phone rang. Though I didn't recognize the number, the area code was from upstate South Carolina. The hospital administrator?

'Trevor Benson,' I answered.

'Hi. This is Thomas King from Baptist Easley Hospital. I received your message, but I wasn't exactly sure what information you needed.'

Unlike the receptionist, his accent wasn't nearly as thick or hard to understand.

'Thank you for returning my call,' I started,

before laying out the situation. When I finished, he asked me to hold for a moment.

It was way longer than a moment. I listened to Muzak for at least five minutes before I heard the phone click through to him.

'I apologize that it took so long, but I had to find out who to ask, and then find the information you needed. We generally use two ambulance services,' he explained before giving me their names. As I wrote them down, he went on.

'Unfortunately, we don't have the particulars regarding your grandfather. I suppose your best bet is to call the ambulance services. Perhaps they'll have the information you need. I'm sure they're required to keep records.'

It was just as Natalie had suggested. 'I appreciate your help,' I said. 'This is more than helpful.'

'You're welcome. And my condolences for the passing of your grandfather.'

'Thank you,' I said.

I hung up, thinking that I'd call the ambulance companies in the morning. I wished I had thought about it when my grandfather had been in the hospital; after nearly half a year, who knew how long it might take them to find the answers I needed.

My thoughts turned to Natalie. Since my call with Bowen, images of her kept resurfacing in my mind; I saw her expression of wonder as she watched the bee crawl over her finger, the sensuous swirling of her dress outlining her long legs and the graceful lines of her body as she stepped out of her car in Beaufort. I recalled both our heartfelt discussion and the easy banter between us, and I puzzled over the flash of sadness I thought I'd sensed toward the end of our dinner. I thought about the energy between us and knew exactly why I'd called her by her name when speaking with Bowen.

As much as I'd tried to downplay it with Dr. Bowen, I knew with certainty that I wanted to see her again, sooner rather than later.

After I'd had dinner, I resolved to finally get some reading done on the back porch. But figuring that Natalie would have finished her shift some time ago, I found myself reaching for my cell phone. I debated calling but decided against it. Instead, I typed out a quick text.

I was just thinking about you and hope you had a good day.

Are you free for dinner this weekend?

Though I should have set my phone aside, I waited to see if she was near enough to her phone to read the text right away. Sure enough, I saw the indication that she'd read the text and assumed she would write something back. Instead, there was no response at all.

For the rest of the evening, I continued to check my phone. Childish. Compulsive. Maybe immature. At times, I can be all those things. Like Bowen says, we're all works in progress.

Finally, just as I was getting ready to turn in

for the night, I heard the telltale *ding* of my cell phone.

Thanks. Typical day. Nothing special.

I stared at the screen, thinking it didn't exactly proclaim an undeniable passion and attraction toward me, especially since she hadn't addressed my invitation at all.

I put the phone on the bedside table, feeling . . . confused? hurt? — before reaching for the lamp. I shook those feelings aside, knowing it was way too early to feel either of those things. Besides, if she hadn't wanted to speak with me again, she wouldn't have answered at all. Right?

I turned out the light, then adjusted the covers, when I heard my cell phone suddenly *ding* again. I reached for the phone.

I'll think about it.

Not a yes, but not a no, either. I continued to stare at the screen until it vibrated again with another message from her.

:-)

I smiled. Clasping my hands behind my head, I stared at the ceiling, more curious about her than ever.

8

I didn't hear from Natalie on Tuesday, which disappointed me, but my offer was out there. I knew she was working and busy, and I had things to do as well. Well, sort of. But I didn't text her. It wasn't as though I was thinking about her all the time. Just . . . too much for my own good.

I also spoke to both ambulance companies. As with the hospital, it took a couple of transfers before I was able to reach someone who could help. Yes, I was told, there were records of pickup locations for patients who had been transported to the hospital; no, I was told, they didn't have that information readily available. It would take them a few days to find it, maybe until the end of the week, and if I didn't hear from them to call again.

Hurry up and wait.

Just like so many other things in life.

Hoping for a chance to speak with Claude's father, I decided to visit the Trading Post for lunch. Pulling up, I spotted a bin offering bags of ice, firewood for sale, propane tank refills, an air compressor to fill tires, and an old-fashioned vending machine, which seemed redundant since people could purchase sodas inside. Unfortunately, there was no one out front in the rockers.

Inside, Claude was back at his usual spot behind the register and he raised a hand in greeting as I headed toward the grill. As usual, all the tables were occupied, so I found myself at the counter. A massive man — at least a head taller than me and twice as wide — nodded toward me before handing me a small bowl of boiled peanuts. I assumed this was Frank, the regular grill man. Unlike Claude, he said nothing. Not much of a chatter, which was fine with me.

In honor of my grandfather, I ordered a BLT with fries and a pickle. Behind me, I overheard two guys at one of the tables talking about their fishing trip the weekend before, lamenting their lack of luck, and debating better places to try the following weekend. I peeked over my shoulder. Both were wearing baseball caps; one had the sinewy arms associated with construction, while the other wore a uniform of one of the propane distributors. When one of them mentioned that he'd spotted an alligator recently, my ears perked up.

'Four of 'em actually,' he went on. 'Sunnin' right there on the bank between the trees.'

'Big ones?' his friend asked.

'Nah. Juveniles, probably.'

'Where?'

'You know where the boat launch is? A couple of bends in the river after that, on your right. You remember the bald eagle's nest in the cypress tree? Right around there.'

'What eagle's nest?'

'Same nest as last year.'

'I didn't see it last year.'

'That's because you never take the time to look around.'

'I'm fishing,' he answered, 'not sightseeing.'

'You try the quarry? I've had some luck with bass there lately . . . '

The conversation returned to fishing again and I found myself tuning out. I was, however, interested in the alligators and the bald eagles and wondered if Natalie might want to join me.

By then, my meal was ready, and Frank placed the plate in front of me. I took a bite, confirming that it never tasted as good anywhere else. I finished the sandwich and the pickle, but had only a few of the fries. I could feel my arteries hardening as I sampled them, but my taste buds were happy.

As I was finishing up, I glanced through the windows toward the front of the store and saw a pair of elderly gentlemen sitting in the rockers on the porch. Just what I'd been hoping for. Rising from my seat, I approached the register. Claude, without the apron and shiny face, seemed far more content than he was the last time I'd been here.

'Hey, Claude,' I greeted him. 'Is that your father out front?'

He leaned forward to peek over my shoulder. 'Yeah, that's him. The one with the overalls. The other guy is Jerrold.'

'Do you think your dad would mind if I spoke

with him about my grandfather?'

'Feel free. Can't guarantee he'll know anything. Assuming he even hears what you're asking.'

'Of course.'

'Word of advice? Watch out for Jerrold. Half the time, I have no idea what he's talking about or what he finds so funny.'

I wasn't sure what he meant exactly but I nodded. 'How long do you think your father will be here?'

'They haven't eaten yet, so I reckon he'll be here at least another hour.'

'What does he usually have for lunch?'

'The barbecue sandwich with slaw. And hush puppies.'

'How about I buy that for him?'

'Why? It's not like I can charge him. He still owns a portion of the store.'

'I figure if I'm going to try to get some information from him, it's the least I can do.'

'It's your money.' He shrugged.

I pulled some cash from my wallet and handed it over, watching as he added it to the drawer. He cupped a hand at the corner of his mouth and called across the store. 'Hey, Frank. Get Daddy the usual, okay? And hand it to Trevor here. He'll bring it out.'

The meal didn't take long to prepare and when it was ready, I ferried the plate to the front door. As I passed the register, Claude loosened the cap on a Yoo-hoo, then tightened it slightly before holding it out to me. 'You'll need this, too.'

'Yoo-hoo?'

'It's his favorite. He's been drinking it as long as I can remember.'

I took the bottle and with my hands full, I used my hips to push open the door. As I approached, Jim looked up, his face as gnarled and wrinkled as his hands, all bone and skin and liver spots. He wore glasses and a few of his teeth were missing, but I thought I saw a spark of curiosity in his expression that made me believe he was sharper, and more aware, than Claude's description of him might indicate. Then again, maybe I was just being optimistic.

'Hi, Jim. I thought I'd bring out your lunch,' I started. 'I was hoping to talk to you for a few minutes.'

Jim squinted up at me. 'Huh?'

Jerrold leaned toward Jim. 'Boy here wants to talk to you,' Jerrold shouted.

'Talk about what?' Jim asked.

'How the hell should I know? He just walked out here.'

'Who is he?' Jim asked.

Jerrold swiveled his gaze toward me. He was younger than Jim, but still well past retirement age. I noticed a hearing aid, which might — or might not — make things easier.

He leaned toward Jim again. 'I'm figurin' he's a salesman,' Jerrold shouted. 'Maybe selling them women's panties.'

I blinked, unsure whether to be offended, and suddenly remembered what Claude had told me.

'Tell him to talk to Claude,' Jim said with a wave. 'I'm retired. I don't need nothing from any salesman.'

'The hell you don't,' Jerrold said to him. 'You need a woman and one of them winning lotto tickets, if you ask me.'

'Huh?'

Jerrold leaned back in his seat with mirth in his eyes. 'Women's panties.' He cackled, clearly pleased with himself. 'You sellin' women's panties?'

'No,' I said, 'I'm not a salesman. I just wanted to speak with Jim.'

'About what?'

'About my grandfather,' I said. 'And I brought Jim his lunch.'

'Then don't just stand there.' He waved a bony hand at me. 'Give it to him. Don't be slow, now.'

I leaned down and handed Jim his lunch. As I did, Jerrold frowned, the grooves in his forehead so deep they could hold a pencil.

'Where's my lunch?' Jerrold demanded.

I hadn't expected the question but realized that I probably should have considered the idea they'd want to eat together. 'I'm sorry. I wasn't thinking. What would you like? I'd be happy to get you something.'

'Hmmmm,' Jerrold said, bringing a hand to his chin. 'How about filet mignon with a lobster tail and lots of butter, with some of that rice pilaf?'

He'd pronounced it *pea-laff*.

'Do they serve that here?' I asked.

'Of course they don't. You need to order it special, from one of them fancy places.'

I assumed he meant a different restaurant — a

151

real restaurant — and I was caught off guard.

'Where would I order that?' I asked.

'What's he saying?' Jim asked.

Jerrold leaned toward Jim again. 'He's saying he won't buy me lunch,' Jerrold shouted. 'And he says he'll buy you a Cadillac if you'll talk to him.'

I blinked, wondering how I'd lost control of the conversation. A *Cadillac? Where did that come from?* 'I didn't say that,' I protested. 'And I'd be glad to get you anything the grill offers . . .'

Jerrold slapped his thigh, not letting me finish before suddenly locking eyes with me again. 'Boy, you is dumb as dirt. A Cadillac! What on earth would he do with a Cadillac? He can barely drive as it is.' He shook his head, cackling. 'A Cadillac!' he shouted to Jim.

Standing in place, I could think of nothing to say. Jerrold didn't seem to need me to say anything; he was too happy with himself to care what I might be thinking. Jim, meanwhile, struck me as oblivious. I decided to seize the initiative.

'I was hoping to ask Jim about my grandfather, Carl Haverson.'

Jerrold reached into his pocket and pulled out a bag of snuff. After opening the package, he pinched a few of the leaves together before placing them between his lip and gum. His mouth made a few contortions and he settled back in the chair, looking like he had a tumorous growth in his jaw. 'You're telling me that you're kin to Carl?'

'He was my grandfather,' I said again. 'I'm trying to learn what he was doing in South Carolina. Claude said Jim and my grandfather

152

were close and I was hoping he could answer some questions.'

'Might be hard,' Jerrold said. 'Jim here, he don't hear too well. And he wanders when he talks. Half the time, you don't know what he means.'

I could say the same about you, I thought. 'It's important,' I said instead. 'Maybe you can help?'

'Don't know how.'

'Did you know my grandfather? Did you speak with him before he left?'

'Sure,' he drawled. 'I got out here now and then and we'd talk. Not as much as Jim here, though. But then, one week, he wasn't around, so it was just me and Jim. I was as surprised as anyone when I found out what happened to him. Carl was in good health as far as I knew.'

'How about the trip to South Carolina? Did you know anything about that?'

'He never mentioned anything about it to me.'

'Was he acting differently? Anything like that?'

Jerrold shook his head. 'Not that I could tell.'

I rocked back on my heels, wondering if I was wasting my time. Surprising me, Jerrold slowly rose from the chair. He had to grip both arms and moving into the vertical position seemed both laborious and painful.

'You two go ahead and visit,' he said. 'Maybe Jim knows something I don't. He knew Carl better than I did. But talk loud, toward his right ear. It barely works, but don't even bother trying with the left one.'

'You don't have to leave,' I said.

'You'll need my chair. He won't admit it, but he needs to be able to see your lips moving so he

153

can figure out what you're saying. He'll get about half of what you say, so just keep trying.'

'Where are you going?' Jim said.

'I'm hungry,' Jerrold shouted. 'I want some food.'

'Huh?'

Jerrold waved him off and looked toward me. 'Don't just stand there looking dumb as a tree. Take a seat. I'll be back.'

I watched as Jerrold shuffled toward the door, and when he was safely inside, I sat in the same rocker, then leaned forward as Jerrold had done.

'Hi,' I shouted. 'I'm Trevor Benson.'

'River fencing?'

'Trevor Benson,' I said again. 'I'm Carl's grandkid.'

'Who?'

'Carl!' I said even louder, wondering if I should have kept Jerrold around to translate.

'Oh, Carl,' Jim said. 'He passed on.'

'I know. He was my kin,' I said, hoping Jerrold's phrasing would help.

Jim squinted at me and I could tell he was searching. It took a few beats.

'The Navy doc? You were married to Claire, right?'

'Yes,' I said, even though Claire had been my mother. No reason to make it any more complicated than it already was.

'He sure liked those bees, old Carl,' Jim added. 'Had them a long time. Beehives. For the honey.'

'Yes.' I nodded. 'I wanted to speak to you about Carl.'

154

'I don't much like bees,' he said. 'Never could figure out what he saw in 'em.'

Trying to keep it simple, I opted for the direct approach. 'I have some questions that I was hoping you could answer.'

Jim didn't seem to hear me. 'Carl had a hard time with the honey last summer,' Jim said. 'Arthritis.'

He pronounced it *arthur-itis*.

'He probably did . . . '

'He got help from the girl, though,' Jim added, not hearing me.

'Girl?'

'Yeah,' Jim said. 'The girl. Inside.'

'Okay,' I said, wondering what he was talking about. I hadn't seen any girls in the store today, but Claude had warned me his mind wandered. Leaving that behind, I leaned closer, speaking slowly and replicating Jerrold's volume.

'Do you know why Carl went to South Carolina?'

'Carl died in South Carolina.'

'I know,' I said. 'Do you know why Carl went to South Carolina?' I asked again.

Jim took a bite of his sandwich and chewed slowly before answering. 'I reckon he was going to visit Helen.'

For a second, I wondered if he'd understood my question.

'Helen? He was going to visit Helen?' I shouted.

'Yep. Helen. That's what he told me.'

Or was that what Jim had heard? How much could I trust his hearing? Or the competence of his memory? I wasn't sure.

155

'When did he tell you about Helen?'

'Huh?'

I repeated the question, even louder this time, and Jim reached for a hush puppy. He took a bite and it took him a long time to finally swallow. 'I reckon about a week or so before he left. He was working on the truck.'

To make sure it could get there, no doubt, but . . . who was Helen? How would my grandfather have met a woman from South Carolina? He had neither a computer nor a cell phone, and he rarely left New Bern. It didn't add up . . .

'How did Carl meet Helen?'

'Huh?'

'Helen.'

'I reckon that's what he said.'

'Did Helen live in Easley?'

'What's Easley?'

'The town in South Carolina.'

He picked up another hush puppy. 'Don't know much about South Carolina. I was stationed there during the Korean War, but said good riddance as soon as I got out. Too hot, too far from home. The drill sergeant there . . . oh what was his name . . . R-something . . . like a joke . . .'

As he was searching the past, I tried to figure out what he'd told me, assuming Jim wasn't completely bonkers. A woman named Helen was in Easley and my grandfather had gone to visit her?

'Riddle!' Jim suddenly shouted. 'That's his name. Sergeant Riddle. Meanest, orneriest man there ever was. One time, he made us sleep in the bog. Dank and dirty place, and so many mosquitoes.

156

They bit all night till I swelled up like a tick. Had to go to the infirmary.'

'Did you ever meet Helen?'

'Nope.'

He reached for his Yoo-hoo but even though Claude had loosened the cap, he struggled to open it. I watched as he took a drink, still trying to sort it out, but suspecting he had nothing else to offer.

'Okay,' I said. 'Thank you.'

He lowered the bottle. 'The girl might know more about it.'

It took me a second to recall what he'd said earlier. 'The girl inside?'

He motioned with the bottle toward the window. 'Can't remember her name. He liked her.'

'Helen?'

'No. The one *inside*.'

I'll admit I was completely lost by then and as if on cue, Jerrold pushed out the door, carrying a plate similar to the one I'd brought out to Jim. Eastern North Carolina barbecue, which is flavored with vinegar and red pepper flakes, is different from barbecue anywhere else in the world. When Jerrold was close, I stood from the chair, making room.

'You two about done?' he asked.

I thought about it, wondering what if anything I'd learned, or how much of it was even real.

'Yes,' I said, 'I think we're through.'

'I warned you, he can wander a bit when he talks,' Jerrold admitted. 'Did you get the answers you needed?'

'I'm not sure,' I said. 'He said my grandfather

157

was going to visit Helen. And he mentioned something about a girl inside, but I have no idea what he was talking about.'

'I think I might have part of the answer to that.'

'What part?'

'The girl inside,' Jerrold said. 'He was talking about Callie. She and your grandfather were pretty close.'

Claude was still at the register when I reentered the store. There were a handful of customers in line and I waited until he finished before approaching.

'How'd it go?' he asked.

'Still trying to figure it out,' I said. 'Do you know when Callie will be working again?'

'She's here now,' Claude answered. 'But she's on break. She should be back in a few minutes.'

Which explains why I hadn't noticed her earlier.

'Do you know where she is?'

'If she's not feeding the cat, she usually eats at the picnic table down by the dock,' Claude said.

'Thanks,' I said, pushing back out the door again. Figuring it would be easier to talk while she wasn't on the clock, I rounded the side of the store, to a path that led toward the creek. I knew there was not only a picnic table there, but also some gas pumps near the water's edge where boats could fill their tanks. I'd been there with my grandfather numerous times.

The path wound through some trees and shrubbery, but when the view finally cleared, I saw Callie sitting at the table. As I crossed the grass, I noted the basic lunch she'd clearly brought from home. Peanut butter and jelly sandwich, container of milk, and an apple — most of it nearly finished — in a brown bag. Hearing me approach, she glanced in my direction, then back to the creek again.

'Callie?' I asked when I was close. 'Claude told me that I might find you here.'

She turned her attention back to me, her expression wary. I wondered why she wasn't in school, and noticed another bruise on her arm, close to the one I'd seen when she'd walked past my house. Instead of speaking, she took another bite of her sandwich, nearly finishing it. Remembering her general wariness, I stopped just short of the table, not wanting to crowd her. 'I was hoping to speak with you about my grandfather,' I said. 'I heard that you helped him harvest the honey last summer.'

'Who told you that?'

'Does it matter?'

'I didn't do anything wrong,' she said.

Her comment caught me off guard. 'I'm not implying that you did. I'm just trying to figure out why he went to South Carolina.'

'Why would you think I know anything about that?'

'I was told that the two of you were close.'

Standing from the table, she shoved the last of her sandwich into her mouth and followed it with a final gulp of milk before stuffing the

159

remains of her lunch into the bag. 'I really can't talk right now. I have to get back to work and I can't be late.'

'I understand,' I said. 'And I'm not trying to get you in trouble. Like I said, I'm just trying to figure out what happened to my grandfather.'

'I don't know anything,' she repeated.

'Did you help him harvest the honey?'

'He paid me,' she said, color rising like a stain in her pale cheeks. 'I didn't steal any, if that's what you're asking. I didn't steal anything.'

'I'm sure you didn't. Why didn't you tell me that you knew him as well as you did?'

'I don't know you or anything about you.'

'You knew I was related to him.'

'So?'

'Callie — '

'I didn't do anything wrong!' she cried again, cutting me off. 'I was walking by and he saw me and he asked if I wanted to help him with the honey, so I did. It only took a couple of days and after that, I put the labels on and stacked them on the shelves. Then he paid me. That's it.'

I tried to imagine my grandfather asking her on a whim for help with the harvest, but for whatever reason, I couldn't. And based on the conversations we'd had to this point, I couldn't imagine her agreeing to such a thing, either. At the same time, there *was* some truth there; she had, by her own admission, helped him harvest the honey. What, I wondered, was she not telling me?

'Did he ever mention that he was going to visit Helen?'

160

Her eyes suddenly widened and for the first time, I thought I saw a flash of actual fear. As quickly as it came, however, it vanished with an angry shake of her head. 'I'm sorry about your grandfather, okay? He was a nice old man. And I was happy to help him with the honey. But I don't know anything about why he went to South Carolina, and I'd appreciate it if you just left me alone.'

I said nothing. She lifted her chin defiantly, before finally turning around and heading back toward the store. On her way, she tossed the remains of her lunch into a garbage can without breaking stride.

I watched her leave, wondering what it was that I'd said that had upset her so.

Back at home, I considered what, if anything, I'd actually learned. Could I trust what Jim had told me? Or Jerrold? Had my grandfather gone to Easley because of a woman named Helen? And what was I to make of my conversation with Callie? What had I said to make her believe she was in trouble?

I didn't know. And yet, as I continued to reflect on my encounter with Callie, I had the gnawing sensation that she'd said something — or I'd seen something — important. It was the answer to one of my many questions, but the harder I tried to zero in on it, the hazier my thoughts became. It felt like I was trying to grab a handful of smoke.

9

On Wednesday, while pondering my maybe-but-not-guaranteed date with Natalie, I decided to take my grandfather's boat out to try to find the alligators and bald eagles I'd heard about the day before.

I made a quick inspection before untying the lines and starting the motor. There were no other boats in the vicinity, which was fortunate, because I would need to get used to the steering again. I had no desire to participate in a water-based demolition derby or accidentally run aground, so I gently eased the throttle, turning the wheel as I pulled away from the dock. To my surprise, the boat was a lot easier to maneuver than I remembered, which meant my grandfather must have done some work on it, and I was quickly able to get it headed in the proper direction like the highly skilled Naval Academy graduate that I was supposed to be.

As a kid, I always loved going out with my grandfather on the boat, but unlike most people, who preferred the wider Trent and Neuse Rivers, I always favored Brices Creek. Because the creek wound its way through the Croatan National Forest, it probably hadn't changed since settlers first arrived in the area in the early 1700s. In a way, it felt like traveling back in time, and when my grandfather shut down the engine, we would hear nothing but birdcalls from the trees, while every now and then a fish would jump, making ripples on the otherwise black and silent water.

I settled into the ride, keeping to the middle of the creek. As ugly as it was, the ride itself was surprisingly stable. My grandfather had built the boat the way he had because Rose was afraid of the water. As an epileptic whose seizures grew in frequency and intensity as she'd aged, she'd never learned to swim, so he'd designed something impossible to capsize or sink, with rails to keep her from falling overboard. Even then, it usually took some convincing for Rose to accompany him, so my grandfather often went alone, at least until my mom was old enough to join him. When I began spending my summers with him, we spent almost every afternoon on the water.

Boating always seemed to put my grandfather in a contemplative mood. Sometimes, he would tell stories about his childhood, which was far more interesting than my own, or talk about bees or his work at the mill, or what my mom had been like as a child. Almost always, though, his thoughts would turn to Rose, melancholy settling over him like a familiar shawl. The older he got, the more he repeated himself, and by the time of my last visit, I'd heard all of his stories often enough to recite them by heart. But I would listen without interruption, watching as he lost himself in the memories, because I knew how much she'd meant to him.

I had to admit, their story was charming; it

harkened to a place and time I knew only from black-and-white movies, a world replete with dirt roads and homemade bamboo fishing poles and neighbors who sat on their front porches to beat the heat, waving to passersby. After the war, my grandfather had first spotted Rose having a soda with her friends outside the drugstore, and he'd been so taken with her that he swore to his friends that he'd seen the woman he would one day marry. After that, he saw Rose everywhere, outside Christ Episcopal Church with her mother or strolling through the Piggly Wiggly, and she began to notice him as well. Later in the summer, at the county fair, there was a dance. Rose was there with her friends and though it took him most of the evening to work up the courage to cross the floor to ask her to dance, she told him that she'd been waiting all night for him to do just that.

They married less than six months later. They spent their honeymoon in Charleston before returning to New Bern to settle into their life together. He built the house, and both of them wanted a brood of children. However, perhaps because of Rose's condition, one miscarriage followed another, five in total over an eight-year period. Just when they'd given up hope, my mother was conceived, and the pregnancy went the distance. They considered my mom a gift from God, and my grandfather swore that Rose had never been more beautiful than when he saw mother and daughter together, playing hopscotch or reading or even standing on the porch, shaking dirt from the rugs.

Years later, when my mom went off to college on a full scholarship, my grandfather told me that he and Rose enjoyed a second honeymoon, one that lasted until their very last day together. Every morning, he would head out early to pick Rose a bouquet of flowers; she would make breakfast, and the two of them would eat together on the back porch, while watching the mist rise slowly from the water. He would kiss her before heading off to work and again when he returned at the end of the day; they held hands as they took their evening walk, as though touch could somehow make up for the lost hours they'd spent apart.

My grandfather found her on the kitchen floor on a Saturday, after he'd spent an afternoon building additional hives. He took her lifeless body in his arms and held her. He cried for more than an hour before finally calling the authorities. He was so destroyed that for the first time ever, my mom took a monthlong leave of absence from her practice and came down to stay with him. He spent part of the following year carving her headstone himself, and up until our last phone call, I knew he continued to visit her grave every single week.

There was Rose and only Rose; he'd always sworn no one could ever replace her. There was no reason to doubt him and I never did. Toward the end, my grandfather was more than ninety years old, with arthritis and a dying truck; he led a simple life that included tending to honey bees and tinkering with the boat, all the while cherishing the memories of a wife that he could never forget.

I turned all these things over in my mind while

my thoughts circled back to my conversation with Jim. I tried to reconcile Jim's comments with the grandfather I'd known but simply couldn't do it. Despite what I'd been told, I knew with sudden certainty that my grandfather had never, nor would have ever, gone to South Carolina to visit a woman named Helen.

I continued upstream, motoring from one curve to the next, eventually reaching the public boat ramp in the Croatan National Forest. Interesting tidbit about the forest: It's one of the few places in the world where you can find Venus flytraps and other carnivorous plants growing in the wild. My grandfather used to bring me out to search for them. Somehow, despite constant poaching, they're still relatively common.

The boat ramp was one of the reference points I'd overheard at the Trading Post. Supposedly, the eagles and alligators were a couple of curves farther upstream, but for all I knew, it might be zero or ten curves. The guy's description had been a little vague, so I slowed the boat and scanned the trees on either side of the creek. The problem, I soon realized, was that I had no idea what I was supposed to look for.

Technology, however, is a wonderful thing. Pulling out my phone, I did a quick internet search and was able to find images of bald eagles' nests. To my eye, they looked like regular birds' nests, only much larger, which made me feel foolish for not assuming that in the first place. In the end, I finally spotted it high in the branches of a cypress tree, a feat made even simpler by the fact that mama or papa eagle was sitting in the nest, while the mate perched in the limbs of a nearby tree.

It wasn't two bends in the river past the boat ramp, by the way, but four.

I stopped the boat and scanned the banks for the alligators but had less luck there. I did note a cleared and muddy spot with some telltale burrows, however. Having lived in Florida, I'd seen them before. Unfortunately, no alligators were around, but alligators were territorial, which meant it was likely that they'd return.

In the meantime, my gaze was drawn toward the bald eagles and I snapped some pics with my phone. With brown bodies and white heads, they looked just like the one on the Great Seal of the United States, my first sighting of them in the wild. It soon became rather boring, though. Aside from occasionally turning their heads, they didn't move much, and after a while, they were no more exciting to watch than the trees. I wondered if there were eggs in the nest, but I soon noticed a pair of baby eaglets. Every now and then, one or both of the little ones would poke up their heads and I had the urge to tell someone about it. Reaching for my phone again, I typed out a quick message to Natalie.

Do you have time to chat later?

Again, I found myself watching the phone to see if she'd read it; to my surprise, her response came quickly:

167

I'll probably have some time around 8.

I smiled, thinking that things with Natalie were getting interesting. It wasn't exactly my grandfather and Rose, but definitely interesting.

There was still no word from the ambulance companies, but I figured that I'd give them until Monday before I contacted them again. Despite that, the rest of my afternoon was productive, if you consider taking a long nap after a leisurely boat ride productive.

For dinner, I decided to eat at Morgan's Tavern. Located downtown, it was my kind of place: wood floors, lots of rustic brick, high-beamed ceilings, and an extensive menu. It was bustling, so I ended up sitting at one of the tables in the bar, but the service was quick and the food was tasty. A good place to kill time until I called Natalie.

Not wanting to be too punctual, I dialed seven minutes after the hour. Perhaps not wanting to appear too eager, Natalie answered on the fourth ring. *Oh, the silly games people play . . .*

'Hey there,' I said. 'How was work?'

'Fine, but I'm glad I'm on days for the next few weeks. It's hard for me to sleep when the sun is shining. My body just doesn't like it.'

'You should do a residency. Then you never have to sleep at all.'

She giggled. 'What's going on?'

'You'll never guess where I went today,' I said.

'You called because you want me to guess?'

'No,' I said. 'I went out on the creek today.'

'On your grandfather's boat?'

'I prefer to think of it as a yacht.'

'Ah,' she said, amusement in her voice. 'Why are you telling me this?'

'Because I was hunting for alligators.'

'Don't tell me you found one.'

'I didn't, but I'm pretty sure I know where to find them. I was thinking we might try to find them on Saturday. We could take the boat out, maybe follow that up with dinner at my place. How does that sound?'

A second of silence on the line. Then: 'Won't it be crowded on the water this weekend?'

Your grandfather's boat draws way too much interest from others, she didn't have to add, *and I'd prefer that no one else know I'm spending time with you.*

'Not where we'd be going. We'll be heading up the creek, probably in late afternoon. It's usually pretty quiet. And afterward, we'd eat at my place. I can grill a mean steak.'

'I don't eat red meat.'

Natalie, I was beginning to learn, seldom offered a simple yes or no, but I was growing used to it. 'I can grill seafood if you'd prefer,' I suggested. 'Seafood's okay, right?'

'Yes.'

'Then how about coming by around four thirty? We'll spend a couple of hours on the boat, head back, fire up the grill. Maybe open a bottle of wine. And I promise that even if we don't find the alligators, you'll see something pretty amazing.'

169

'What is it?'

'It's a surprise. What do you think?'

'Four thirty?'

'We could go earlier, but I wouldn't go later or we'll lose the daylight when we're on the water.'

In the silence that followed, I tried and failed to imagine her as she was speaking. Where was she? In her kitchen? The family room? Her bedroom? Finally, I heard her voice again. 'All right,' she said, still sounding hesitant. 'I guess I should drive to your place?'

'If you'd rather, I could pick you up.'

'That won't be necessary,' she said.

Because you don't want me to know where you live? 'Great,' I said, ignoring that internal query. 'A couple of questions . . . are you okay with tuna?'

'That's fine.'

'And my odds that you show are better than fifty-fifty this time?'

'Ha ha,' she said. 'I'll be there at four thirty.'

Maybe I was just imagining it, but I think there was a little part of her that was flattered by my persistence. 'Good night, Trevor.'

'Good night, Natalie.'

On Thursday, I heard from the first of the ambulance companies, who let me know that they hadn't attended to or transported my grandfather.

On Friday, I heard from the second one and struck pay dirt. After a brief conversation, I was emailed a scanned copy of the report.

I read that my grandfather, Carl Haverson, had been picked up near mile marker 7 on Highway 123, and transported to Baptist Easley Hospital. Though light on details, the report showed that he was unconscious, with a thready pulse. Oxygen was administered en route, and he reached the hospital at 8:17 a.m.

It wasn't much information and told me little that I didn't already know, other than the pickup location. A quick search on the internet, including Google Earth, showed a stretch of highway near a dilapidated strip mall, which didn't add any helpful information, primarily because I had no idea of what exactly had led to the call in the first place. He could have been walking to his truck or already driving or heading into a restaurant. I didn't know who'd called the ambulance, or even what *near mile marker 7* actually meant. Perhaps the only way to find the answers to any of these questions was to go there and check it out.

But noting the time of his arrival triggered an additional thought, one that I should have realized before. Easley was at least six hours away by car; in my grandfather's truck, at his age, it might have taken him as long as nine hours to get there. Had he driven through the night? Try as I might, I couldn't imagine that. He was, and always had been, an early riser. In my mind's eye, I could visualize him getting into the truck early in the morning, after sleeping in a hotel or motel . . .

Where, then, had he stayed the night? Near Easley? Farther east?

171

Also, if he'd been found near the truck, I knew there was no way it would still be sitting alongside the highway, not after six months. So how was I going to find it?

I wrestled with the questions on and off the rest of the day, without answers. What I did finally come to accept, however, was that a road trip to Easley was in my very near future. To understand what had happened to my grandfather, I knew I had no choice but to go there.

10

Saturday felt like early summer, at least while I was out for my run. By the time I finished, I was able to wring the perspiration from my shirt before showering, which was kind of gross, but reminded me of the years I'd actually been an athlete, as opposed to a guy who was simply trying to keep his pants from nipping at the waist.

After breakfast, I cleaned the house again, paying special attention to the kitchen and bathrooms, then hauled the small dining room table and chairs out to the back porch. I rearranged the rockers, slid the grill to a new spot, and rifled through the cabinets and closets for a tablecloth and candles, doing my best to create a subtly romantic ambiance.

Getting the boat ready was more of a chore. While I didn't care whether the recliners were ratty or moldy, I figured she might, and I had to run to the store to buy the cleanser I needed. After detouring to the grocery store, I then took the boat to the gas pumps at the Trading Post to fill the tank, but it took longer than expected due to the long line. Three different people whipped out their phones to take photographs of me while I was in the queue, being that I was so handsome and all. Then again, maybe they were more interested in the boat. Who knew?

I set the table, added flowers from the front yard to the vase, put the bottles of wine in the refrigerator to chill, chopped vegetables, and tossed a salad. I loaded the cooler with ice, beer, soda, and bottles of water and ferried it to the boat, along with a snack platter. By that point, it was midafternoon; I tried and failed to remember the last time it had taken me so long to get ready for a date.

I showered for the second time that day and considering the sultry temperature, my instincts told me that shorts and a T-shirt would be most appropriate for the boat. Instead, I opted for jeans, a blue button-up shirt, and Top-Siders. I rolled up my sleeves and hoped the breeze would keep me from sweating through my shirt.

I should have listened to my instincts. Natalie showed up a few minutes later, stepping out of her car in jean shorts, sunglasses, sandals, and a Rolling Stones T-shirt, a casually sexy appearance that registered immediately. I swallowed hard.

After collecting a medium-sized canvas bag from the passenger seat, she turned, stopping in her tracks when she saw me.

'I thought you said we were going on the boat.'

'We are,' I said. 'This is my captain's uniform.'

'You're going to get hot . . .'

Yes, I am, I thought, already feeling the sun beating down on me. 'I'll be fine . . .'

Approaching her car, I was unsure whether to lean in for a hug or stand in place like an idiot. I opted for the latter. She acted equally uncertain, which made me wonder whether she was as nervous as I. I doubted it, but it still made me feel better.

'I wasn't sure if I should bring anything,' she said, motioning to the car. 'But I have a small cooler in the back seat with drinks.'

'I put some in the boat already, but I'm happy to load what you brought just in case.'

Opening the back door, I retrieved the cooler.

'How's your day been?' she asked as we walked toward the house.

'Relaxing,' I lied. 'You?'

'Typical Saturday.'

'Farmers' market?'

'Among other things.' She shrugged. 'Do you really think we'll find an alligator?'

'I hope so,' I said. 'But no guarantees.'

'If we do, it'll still be a first. That's always kind of exciting.'

'What's in your bag?'

'Clothes for later,' she said. 'I didn't want to get cold.'

Frankly, I would have been happy if she stayed in the outfit she was wearing, but I kept quiet.

I pushed the front door open. 'Come on in. Feel free to leave your bag anywhere.'

'How long do you think we'll be on the boat?'

'Hard to say. But we'll definitely be back before dark.'

She dug out some sunscreen from her bag while following me through the house and onto the back porch. When she saw all I'd done, she arched an eyebrow.

'Wow,' she said. 'You've been busy.'

'My parents raised me to make a good impression.'

'You already have,' she said, 'or I wouldn't have agreed to come.'

For the first time in her presence, I was at a loss for words. I think she knew she'd thrown me because she laughed.

'All right,' she went on. 'Let's get on the boat and find some alligators.'

I led the way down to the dock, setting her cooler next to mine as we climbed on board. The boat rocked slightly under our shifting weights.

'I've never been on a yacht before,' she cooed, picking up the thread of my earlier joke. 'I hope it's safe.'

'Don't worry. She's seaworthy.' I hopped back on the dock briefly to untie the ropes, then rejoined her, asking, 'Would you like a beer or glass of wine before we get going?'

'A beer sounds good.'

I reached into my cooler and pulled out a Yuengling. Twisting off the cap, I handed it to her. I opened a beer for myself as well, privately celebrating our first drink together.

I held my bottle toward her. 'Thank you for coming,' I said. 'Cheers.'

She tapped her bottle against mine before taking a small sip. 'This is good,' she commented, inspecting the label.

Wasting no time, I moved to the stern and started the engine with a pull of the cord. Back in the cockpit, I increased the throttle and inched away from the dock. I made my way toward the middle of the creek, grateful for the breeze. I could already feel a thin sheen of perspiration beginning to form, but Natalie seemed more than comfortable. She stood at the railing, watching the scenery with her hair fanning out behind her, gorgeous in the sunlight. I found myself admiring her legs before I turned my attention back to steering the boat. Crashing might mar the good impression I'd made earlier, what with the whole tablecloth-and-candles-on-the-porch thing.

We puttered through one wide turn after the next. Housing on either side of the creek gave way to fishing camps dotting only one bank; and after that, nothing but wilderness. Meanwhile, despite my lack of depth perception, I expertly avoided various hazards and would have pointed out my boating mastery to her, but for the ubiquitous presence of neon-colored buoys alerting boaters to keep a safe distance.

After slathering sunscreen on her arms and legs, Natalie joined me in the cockpit.

'This is the first time I've gone up Brices Creek,' she said. 'It's beautiful.'

'How can you live here and never come up this way?'

'No boat,' she said. 'I mean, I've been on the Trent River and the Neuse River with friends, but we never came up this way.'

'I thought you don't go out much.'

'I don't,' she said. 'Not lately, anyway.'

Though I could have asked her why, I could tell she didn't want me to. 'If you're hungry, there are some snacks on the table.'

'Thanks, but I'm fine for now. I can't

177

remember the last time I had a beer, so I'm kind of enjoying this.'

She stared out at the slow-moving black water, clutching her cold bottle and basking in the sun.

'How did you know where to find the alligators?' she asked.

'I overheard some people talking when I had lunch at the Trading Post, so I decided to check it out.'

'I've never eaten there.'

'Believe it or not, the food is actually pretty good.'

'I've heard that. But it's kind of far from where I live.'

'Nothing is far away in New Bern.'

'I know, but I spend so much time behind the wheel when I'm on duty that I get sick of driving.'

'You drove here and my place isn't far from the Trading Post.'

'The Trading Post doesn't have tablecloths and candles.'

I chuckled. We continued upstream, trees pushing in from the banks, the water ahead as flat as a billiard table. Here and there, we saw the occasional dock, overgrown and rotting, jutting into the creek. Above us, an osprey circled.

Natalie continued to stand beside me, and I had the sense that something had changed between us. Every now and then, she took a sip of her beer and I wondered whether she'd been nervous about our date.

Was she seeing someone else? I still thought it likely, but if that was the case, why had she come today or gone to dinner with me? Because she was bored or unhappy? Or simply lonely? And what was he like? How long had they been going out? It was also possible that she'd just been curious about the alligators and viewed me as a friend, but then why stand so close to me? She knew I was attracted to her. Common sense indicated that asking her to a second dinner in as many weekends meant something more than a desire for simple friendship, yet she'd agreed to meet me again. If she really was dating someone else, how would she explain her absence today? Did he live out of town? Was he in the military and deployed elsewhere? As usual, I had no answers.

The creek continued to narrow until we reached the boat ramp and entered the national forest. On the dock, I saw a father and son fishing; they waved as we motored past. Though I was only half-done with my beer, it was already growing warm. Leaning over the railing, I dumped the remainder and slid the empty bottle into the wastebasket in the cockpit.

'How much longer?' Her voice drifted back to me.

'Almost there,' I answered. 'Another few minutes.'

Rounding the final bend, I began to slow the boat. In the treetop, I spotted one of the eagles sitting in the nest, though its mate wasn't around. Up ahead, on the opposite side of the creek, in the small muddy clearing, were two alligators sunning themselves. They were juveniles, no more than five feet from nose to the tip of their tail, but it still felt like a stroke of luck.

'There they are,' I said, waving her over.

She ran toward the bow, vibrating with excitement.

'I can't believe it,' she offered. 'They're right there!'

Turning the wheel, I tried to angle the boat so we could sit in the recliners and enjoy the wildlife. Satisfied, I shut off the engine, then retreated to the stern to drop anchor, feeling the rope tighten as it caught on the bottom.

By then, Natalie had pulled out her phone and begun to take pictures.

'There's something else, too,' I reminded her. 'The surprise I told you about.'

'What?'

I pointed at the treetop. 'There's an eagle's nest right over there, and there are eaglets, too. They're kind of hard to spot, but keep your eye out.'

Natalie looked from the eagles to the alligators and back again while I removed the plastic cover from the tray of food and grabbed another beer from the cooler. I popped a strawberry into my mouth and settled into one of the recliners. Leaning back, I used the lever to raise the leg support.

'Comfy?' Natalie smirked.

'My grandfather was a wise man when it came to luxury.'

Natalie picked a few grapes from the platter and took a seat, though she didn't fully recline the chair.

'I can't believe I've finally seen an alligator,' she marveled.

'You mention a desire, I make it happen. I'm a bit like a genie in that way.'

She made a face, but I could tell she was warming to my humor. I balanced a piece of cheese on a cracker as Natalie set her beer on the table.

'So . . . is this your thing?' she asked.

'I don't know what you mean.'

'All of this,' she said, spreading her arms wide. 'The setup back at your house, boat rides, surprises. Is this how you generally try to pick up women?'

'Not always.' I took a meek sip of my beer.

'Then why the big show today?'

'Because I thought you'd enjoy it.' I leaned my bottle toward hers. 'To the alligators.'

'And the eagle,' she agreed reluctantly, reaching for her bottle and tapping it against mine. 'But don't try to change the subject.'

'I'm not sure what the subject is.'

'I get the vibe that you're a player. When it comes to women, I mean.'

'Because I'm so clever and charismatic?'

'Because I'm not naïve.'

'Fair enough.' I laughed. 'But it's not just me. You could have declined my invitation.'

She reached for another grape. 'I know,' she finally agreed, her voice dropping an octave.

'Do you regret it?'

'Actually, I don't.'

'You sound surprised.'

'I am,' she said, and for the next few minutes, neither of us said anything. Instead, we took in the view, Natalie finally spotting the eaglets in the nest. She lifted her phone to get some pics, but by that time, they'd ducked below the rim of the nest again. I heard her sigh, squinting at me.

'Have you ever been in love?' she asked.

Though I hadn't expected the question, an unbidden memory of Sandra rose to the surface. 'I think so,' I said.

'You think?'

'When we were together, I thought I was,' I admitted. 'But now, I'm not sure.'

'Why wouldn't you be sure?'

'If I were really in love, I think I'd miss her more than I do. I'd think about her more.'

'Who was she?'

I hesitated. 'She was a trauma nurse — her name was Sandra. She was smart. Beautiful. Passionate about her work. We met in Pensacola and we were happy together at first, but it got complicated after I was deployed to Afghanistan.' I shrugged. 'When I came back, I . . . '

I looked over at her.

'I already told you I wasn't in a good space mentally or emotionally, and I took it out on her. I'm amazed she put up with me for as long as she did.'

'How long were you together?'

'A little more than two years. But you have to remember, I was gone a lot of the time. By the end, I wondered how well we even knew each other. After we broke up, it took me a while to understand that I missed the idea of having someone, as opposed to missing her. I knew I never loved her the way my grandfather loved my grandmother, or even the way my parents loved each other. My grandfather was a true romantic; my parents were partners and friends and they complemented each other perfectly. I didn't feel either of those things with Sandra. I don't know. Maybe I just wasn't ready.'

'Or maybe she wasn't the one.'

'Maybe.'

'Anyone else? When you were younger maybe?'

For whatever reason, my mind flashed to Yoga Girl, but I shook my head. 'I went out with girls in high school and college, but nothing monumental. After my parents died, while in medical school and residency, I told myself that I was too busy for anything serious.'

'You probably were.'

I smiled, appreciating the response, even if we both knew it was an excuse. 'How about you? You said that you've been in love? Are you more the romantic type, or the partner-and-friends type?'

'Both,' she said. 'I wanted it all.'

'Did you get it?'

'Yes,' she said. She held up her bottle, still half-full. 'What should I do with this?'

'I'll take it,' I said, reaching for her bottle. I rose from my seat, emptied the remains into the creek, and put the empty beside my own in the wastebasket. On my way back, I gestured at the cooler. 'Would you like another?'

'Do you have bottled water?'

'Of course. I came prepared.' I handed a water bottle to her before settling in my chair again. We continued to chat while we picked at the snacks, avoiding anything too personal. Our earlier discussion about love seemed to have butted up against some sort of internal personal limit of hers, so we talked about the town, the gun range where Natalie liked to shoot, and some of the more complicated surgeries I'd performed in the past. Eventually she was able to get photos of the eaglets and texted the images to me, something I realized only when I felt my phone vibrate in my pocket and checked the screen.

As we floated in place, a thin layer of clouds had begun to form, turning the sun from yellow to orange, and when the sky began shading toward violet, I knew it was time to start back.

I raised the anchor and started the motor, Natalie covering the snack tray before joining me in the cockpit. I drove faster on the return, making for a shorter trip, but was still amazed at how quickly time had passed. By the time I'd tied up the boat, dusk was settling in, the sky a brilliant palette, and crickets had begun to chirp. I helped Natalie to the dock, then handed the smaller cooler to her. Balancing the platter on the larger cooler, I walked beside her toward the back porch.

Once on the porch, I lifted the cooler lid. 'Would you like another bottle of water?' I asked.

'Do you have any wine?'

'Would you like red or white?'

'White.'

Heading inside, I pulled the wine from the refrigerator and located a corkscrew. Pouring two glasses, I returned to the porch. She was standing near the railing, watching the sunset.

'Here you go,' I said, handing her a glass. 'Sauvignon blanc.'

184

'Thank you.'

We took a sip in tandem, taking in the view.

'I called the hospital, as you suggested,' I said. 'About my grandfather.'

'And?'

'You were right — it was a critical first step.' I went on, filling her in. She listened carefully, her eyes never leaving my face.

'Where do you think he was going? If it wasn't Easley?'

'I don't know.'

'But you don't think he went to see Helen?'

'Unless he'd undergone a radical change, I just can't imagine him being interested in another woman. Not at his age, not so far away, and definitely not with the way he still spoke about my grandmother.'

'He told me about her once,' Natalie mused. 'He said she used to hum to herself in the kitchen when she was cooking and that sometimes, even now, he imagined he could still hear it.'

'When did he tell you that?'

'Last year, maybe? It was at the farmers' market and I can't remember how the subject even came up, but I recall thinking about that story when I got home. I could tell he still loved her.'

'That's what I mean,' I agreed. 'He was a one-woman man.'

She took another sip. 'Do you believe in that? One woman for one man, for all time? The whole soul mate thing?'

'I guess it's possible for some couples — like them or maybe even my parents — but it's probably more the exception than the rule. I

185

think most people fall in love more than once in their life.'

'And yet you're unsure whether you've ever been in love.'

'It's not fair to paraphrase my earlier statements back to me.'

She laughed. 'So what are you going to do about your grandfather?'

'I'm thinking about driving down to Easley on Tuesday. I want to find out where he was picked up and try to locate his truck. Maybe it'll help me figure things out.'

'That's a long way to travel without much to go on,' she pointed out.

'It should only take a couple of days.'

As I spoke, I saw her shiver. She set her wineglass on the railing and rubbed her arms. 'Sorry. I think I'm getting a little cold. Do you have a bathroom where I can change?'

'The bathrooms are tiny, so feel free to use one of the bedrooms if you'd rather. Are you hungry yet? Do you want me to get the grill going?'

She nodded. 'I'm getting hungry, so that would be great. Do you think I could have a little more wine before I go in?'

'Of course.'

In the kitchen, I poured her more wine — she stopped me at half a glass — watching as she retrieved her bag from the family room and disappeared into the bedroom. Uncertain what she wanted for dinner — aside from the tuna — I'd dumped a lot of different options into the grocery cart earlier. There was not only a salad and green bean amandine, but rice pilaf and coleslaw

186

as well. Lest anyone get too impressed, the rice pilaf came in a box with easy-to-prepare directions, and the coleslaw had come from the deli section of the grocery store. Sandra had taught me how to prepare green beans with olive oil, garlic, and slivers of almonds. I set the water boiling on the stove for the rice, scooped the coleslaw into a glass bowl and, along with the green salad and a bottle of dressing, brought all that to the table outside. I started the grill, added salt and pepper to the steak, and poured the rice and seasoning into the pot. After mixing soy sauce and wasabi for a dipping sauce for her tuna, I tossed the steak on the grill and returned to the kitchen for the green beans.

The steak, rice, and beans cooked quickly; I covered them with foil and placed them in the oven to keep warm, but there was still no sign of Natalie. Her tuna would take only a minute or two to sear, so I didn't bother starting it yet. Instead, I moved a speaker out onto the porch, then used my iPhone to play some favorite tunes of mine from the eighties. I took a seat in the rocker, sipped the wine I'd poured earlier, and watched the moon as it rose, glowing just above the trees. It was one of those beautiful crescent-shaped ones — waxing or waning, but I wasn't sure which. At some point in the past year I had downloaded an app that told you everything about the constellations and where to find them in the night sky; it occurred to me that I could fire it up and then try to later impress Natalie with my knowledge of astronomy.

But I dismissed the idea. She'd see right

through me, for starters. Strangely, the more she rolled her eyes, the more I felt like I could simply be myself. I liked that — hell, Natalie was pretty much the entire package as far as I could tell — but what did it matter? I was leaving, so it wasn't as though we had a chance at any kind of lasting relationship. I'd head off on my journey, she'd continue on her way, all of which meant there was no reason to get carried away, right?

It was a familiar exercise for me. In high school, I'd kept an emotional distance from the girls I'd dated, and the same thing had happened in both college and medical school. With Sandra, it might have been different in the beginning, but toward the end, I could barely handle myself, let alone a relationship. While all of those women had their charms, it struck me that I was always thinking about the next phase of my life, one that didn't include them. That might seem shallow and maybe it was, but I firmly believed that everyone should strive to be the best version of themselves that they can possibly be, a belief that sometimes required difficult choices. But Natalie had been wrong in thinking that it made me a player. I was more of a serial dater than a man on the prowl. Yoga Girl (*Lisa? Elisa? Elise?*) was the exception, not the rule.

On the porch, I could feel the pull of my own behavioral history, warning me not to fall for a woman I would soon leave behind. Nothing good could come of that. She would be hurt and I would be hurt, and even if somehow we tried to make a go of it, I'd learned firsthand that distance can put a strain on any relationship. And yet . . .

Something *had* changed between us, and there was no way I could deny it. Nor was I sure exactly when it happened. Maybe it was something as simple as a deeper level of comfort, but I realized that I craved more than a physical relationship with her. I wanted what we'd had when I'd shown her the beehives or ridden on the boat or sipped wine on the back porch. I wanted easy banter and deep communication and long periods when neither of us felt the need to say anything at all. I wanted to wonder what she was thinking, often to be surprised; I wanted her to gently trace the scar on my hand and show her the others that marked my skin. It all felt odd to me, even a bit frightening.

Outside, the moon continued its slow rise, turning the lawn a bluish silver. A warm breeze gently stirred the leaves, like the sound of someone whispering. Stars above were reflected in the waters of the creek, and I suddenly understood why my grandfather had never wanted to leave.

Behind me, I sensed a sudden dimming of light, heralding Natalie's approach from within the house. Turning to greet her, I smiled automatically before fully registering the woman who stood before me in the doorway. For a moment, I could only stare, certain that I'd never seen someone more beautiful.

Natalie was wearing a low-cut, sleeveless burgundy pencil dress that clung to her slender curves. Gone was the chain around her neck I'd never seen her without, and she was wearing wide-hooped earrings and sleek, delicate pumps. But it was her face that mesmerized me. She'd put on mascara, accentuating her thick eyelashes, and her expertly applied makeup gave her skin a luminous quality. I caught the trace of perfume, something that hinted of wildflowers. In her hand, she held her empty wineglass.

My staring must have given her pause, because she wrinkled her nose slightly. 'Too much?'

Her voice was enough to bring me out of my stupor.

'No,' I said. 'You are . . . stunning.'

'Thank you.' She smiled, looking almost shy. 'I know it's not true, but I appreciate it.'

'I mean it,' I said, and all at once, I knew: This is what I wanted; I wanted Natalie, not just for tonight, but for a lifetime of days and nights like the one we were having right now. The feeling was undeniable, and I suddenly understood what my grandfather must have felt when he first saw Rose in front of the drugstore so long ago.

I am in love with her, a voice echoed clearly in my mind. It felt slightly surreal, and yet truer than anything I'd ever known. But I also heard that warning voice again, telling me to end things now, before they became even more serious. To make things easier for both of us. The cautionary voice was only a whisper, though, fading before the surge of my feelings. *This is what it's like*, I thought. *This is what my grandfather was talking about.*

Through it all, Natalie stayed quiet, but for the first time, I knew what she was thinking. I could see in her radiant smile that she was feeling exactly the same way about me.

I forced myself to turn away as Natalie glided onto the porch. Clearing my throat, I asked, 'Would you like another glass? I think I'd like one.'

'Just half,' she murmured.

'I'll be right back.'

In the kitchen, it felt like I was finally able to exhale. I tried to get hold of myself, focusing on the simple act of pouring the wine as a means of slowing things down. I somehow made it to the back porch holding the two glasses, trying desperately to hide my inner turmoil.

I handed her the wine. 'We can eat whenever you're ready. I still have to sear your tuna, but that won't take long.'

'Do you need help?'

'There are a few things in the refrigerator and the oven, but let me start your tuna first, okay?'

At the grill, I unwrapped the tuna, alert to Natalie's approach. She stood close, enveloping me in the smell of her perfume.

'How do you like your tuna?' I asked robotically. 'Rare or medium rare?'

'Rare,' she said.

'I mixed up some soy sauce and wasabi for you.'

'Aren't you something?' she asked in a husky drawl, nudging me slightly, the feeling making me light-headed.

I really, truly have to get hold of myself.

After checking the heat, I put the tuna on the grill. Natalie took that as her cue, returning to the kitchen to bring the other dishes to the table.

I looked over my shoulder. 'Could you bring me your plate? For your tuna?'

'Of course,' she said, sauntering toward me.

I plated the tuna and we walked to the table. As she took her seat, she nodded toward the food.

'You made enough for four people,' she observed. Then, leaning forward, she added, 'I had a really nice time on the boat today. I'm glad you asked me to come.'

'A perfect day,' I agreed.

We served up, passing various sides back and forth with easy familiarity. The conversation roamed from the alligators and the eagles and life in Florida, to the places we wanted to visit one day. Her eyes sparkled with hidden fire, making me feel intensely alive. How had I fallen in love with her so quickly, without even being aware of it?

Afterward, she helped me bring the dishes to the kitchen and put the leftovers away. When we finished, we returned to the porch railing and stared toward the creek, my shoulder nearly touching hers. The music was still playing, a melancholy Fleetwood Mac ballad. Though I wanted to slip my arm around her, I didn't. She cleared her throat before finally raising her eyes to meet mine.

'There's something I should probably tell you,' she said. Her tone was soft but serious, and I felt my stomach contract. I already knew what she was going to say.

'You're seeing someone else,' I said.

She was absolutely still. 'How did you know?'

'I didn't. But I suspected.' I stared at her. 'Does it really matter?'

'I suppose it doesn't.'

'Is it serious?' I asked, hating that I wanted to know.

'Yes,' she said. She turned away, unable to meet my eyes. 'But it's not what you probably think.'

'How long have you been together?'

'A few years,' she answered.

'Do you love him?'

She seemed to struggle with her answer. 'I know I loved him at one time. And until a couple of weeks ago, I thought I still did, but then . . .' She ran her hands through her hair before turning to face me. 'I met you. Even on that first night when we talked right here, I knew that I was attracted to you. Honestly, it terrified me. But as scared as I was, and as wrong as I knew it was, there was part of me that wanted to spend time with you. I tried to pretend the feeling wasn't there; I told myself to ignore it and forget about you. As small a town as New Bern is, I hardly ever go out, so it was unlikely I'd ever see you again. But then . . . you were at the farmers' market. And I knew exactly why you were there. And all those feelings bubbled up again.'

She closed her eyes, something weary in the slump of her shoulders.

'I saw you walking,' she said. 'After you bought a coffee. I just happened to be leaving the market, and there you were. I told myself to let it go. Let you go. But the next thing I knew, I was walking in the same direction and I saw you go into the park.'

'You followed me?'

'It felt like I didn't have a choice. It was like something else — or someone else — was propelling me forward. I . . . I wanted to get to know you even better.'

Despite the seriousness of her words, I smiled. 'Why did you accuse me of following you?'

'Panic,' she admitted. 'Confusion. Shame. Take your pick.'

'You're a good actress.'

'Maybe,' she said. 'I don't know why I couldn't say what I'd hoped to say. We fell so easily into talking about other things . . . and when you offered to show me the beehives, I knew I had to accept. I tried to convince myself that it meant nothing, but deep down, I knew it wasn't true. And it just kept happening . . . with dinner in Beaufort, and the boat, and now this. Every time I'm with you, I tell myself that I shouldn't, that we should stop seeing each other. And every time, the words never come.'

'Until now.'

She nodded, her lips a tight line, and my throat constricted in the silence that followed. Instinctively, I found myself reaching for her hand, felt her fingers stiffen and then, finally, relax. I gently turned her to face me. With my other hand, I reached up and caressed her cheek.

'Look at me,' I whispered. When she slowly lifted her gaze, I went on. 'Do you really want to leave right now?'

At my words, her eyes moistened. Her jaw

194

trembled slightly, but she didn't pull away. 'Yes,' she whispered. And then, with a swallow, she squeezed her eyes shut. 'No.'

In the background, the strains of a song whose name I had forgotten drifted through the air. The porch light cast a golden glow over her sun-kissed skin. I inched forward, placing my other hand on her hip, noting the confusion and fear and love in her expression, then put my arms around her waist. Her eyes were locked on mine as our bodies came together, and I could feel her quiver as I began to caress her back. Beneath the thin fabric of her dress, her skin felt hot, and I was intensely aware of the curves of her body as it pressed against my own.

She felt so good to me — undeniably real, elemental even, as if we had been forged from the same matter. I inhaled the scent of her, unable to stay silent.

'I love you, Natalie,' I whispered. 'And I don't want you to ever leave.'

The words somehow made the feeling even more real, and I suddenly felt the possibility of a lifetime together. I knew I would do anything to make things work between us, even if that meant staying in New Bern. I could switch my residency to East Carolina University, which was less than an hour from my grandfather's home; I could even give up the practice of medicine altogether. The alternative was a future without her in it, and in that instant, there was nothing more important than remaining with this woman, now and forever.

By her expression, I knew she recognized the

intensity of what I was feeling. Though it may have frightened her, she didn't pull away. Instead, she leaned into me and twined her arms around my neck as she rested her head on my shoulder. I could feel her breasts, soft and full, press against me. She inhaled and slowly let out her breath, a kind of release.

'I love you, too, Trevor,' she whispered. 'I shouldn't, and I know I can't, but I do.'

She lifted her head from my shoulder as my lips met her neck. Her skin felt as delicate as silk under the tip of my tongue. With a groan, she pulled me even closer, and I finally moved my lips toward hers.

I kissed her, reveling in the tentative fluttering of her lips as she kissed me back; when my mouth opened, I felt hers open in response and our tongues touched, the feeling as exquisite as anything I'd ever known. My hands began to explore her body, tenderly tracing her stomach, then the side of her breast, trailing down her hip, already memorizing the feel of her body. Through it all, I was conscious of my love for her, coupled with a riptide of desire more powerful than I'd ever felt before. I wanted all of her. When I finally pulled back slightly, our bodies still tight against each other, her eyes were half-closed, her mouth parted in sensual anticipation. Then, in a motion that felt utterly natural, I encircled her hand with my own and took a small step backward. Her eyes stayed on mine, and with a gentle tug, I led her inside, toward the bedroom.

11

'Interesting,' Bowen said to me during our session on Monday.

We were sitting at the dining room table, which I'd moved back into the house, two glasses of iced water between us. He'd arrived almost an hour earlier and I'd walked him around the property and the house. I'd shown him the beehives from a distance (he didn't receive the full song-and-dance I'd offered Natalie) as well as the boat. When our session had begun, I'd started the conversation as I usually did — with an update on various issues associated with PTSD — before finally proceeding to my date with Natalie. I'd told him just about everything, though not with any of the *intimate* details.

'That's all you have to say about it?' I asked. 'That it's interesting?'

'What would you like me to say?'

'I don't know. Something. Anything.'

Bowen brought his hand to his chin. 'Do you really believe you're in love with her?'

'Yes,' I answered. 'Without a doubt.'

'You've known her for less than two weeks.'

'My grandfather fell in love with my grandmother the first time they ever spoke,' I countered. In all fairness, though, I'd been pondering the same question all morning. 'She's . . . unlike anyone I've ever met before,' I went on. 'And I know it's not logical. But yes, I love her.'

'And you'd give up your residency for her?'

'Yes,' I said.

'Interesting,' he repeated. The evasive neuter-speak Bowen used could be frustrating, to say the least.

'You don't believe me?'

'Of course I believe you.'

'But you're concerned about something, aren't you?'

'Aren't you?'

I knew exactly what he was referring to, of course. 'You mean the other guy,' I said.

'It does add potentially challenging implications.'

'I understand that. But her feelings for me are real. And she told me that she loved me.'

He adjusted his glasses. 'Based on what you've described, it sounds like she probably does.'

'You think so?'

'It wouldn't surprise me in the slightest. Sometimes you underestimate how others might perceive you. You're young, intelligent, successful, wealthy, and some would regard you as a hero for your military service.'

'Well, gee. Thanks, Doc.'

'You're welcome. However, my point was that while I can easily imagine a woman falling in love with you, that doesn't necessarily mean that it isn't complicated for her. Nor does it mean your relationship will progress in the way you hope it will. People are complex, life seldom

198

turns out the way you imagine it will, and emotions can be contradictory. From what you said, it seemed she was trying to tell you she was conflicted about the relationship between the two of you. Until she resolves that conflict, it might be a problem.'

I took a sip of my water, processing what Bowen had just said. 'What should I do?' I finally asked.

'About what?'

'About Natalie,' I said, hearing the frustration in my tone. 'What do I do about her relationship with the other guy?'

Bowen raised an eyebrow. He said nothing, waiting for me to answer my own question. He knew me well enough to understand that I'd be able to eventually figure it out, which I did.

'I need to accept that I can't control another person,' I intoned. 'I can only control my own behaviors.'

'That's correct.' Bowen smiled. 'But I suspect it doesn't make you feel any better.'

No, I thought, *it really doesn't*. I took some deep breaths, wishing it weren't the truth, before automatically repeating much of what I'd learned in our previous sessions. 'You'll tell me that for now, I should strive to be the best version of myself that I can be. I need to sleep, exercise, eat healthy, and keep mood-altering substances to a minimum. Practice DBT and CBT skills when I'm feeling on edge. I understand all those things. And I'm doing those things. What I want to know is what I should do with regard to Natalie, so I don't go crazy with worry.'

If Bowen heard the emotion in my voice, he didn't comment on it. Instead, in the calm way he always adopted with me, he shrugged.

'What can you do except to keep doing what you're doing?'

'But I love her.'

'I know you do.'

'I don't even know if she lives with him, or if she's just dating him.'

Bowen appeared almost sad. 'Do you really want to know?'

On the highway the following day, I ruminated on my conversation with Dr. Bowen. I knew what I wanted — I wanted Natalie to dump the guy — but I was only half of that equation. Or maybe only a third of it, which was even worse. I sometimes believe the world would run better if I were put in charge of everything and could indeed control people, but knowing me, I'd probably get tired of the responsibility.

I had the GPS on in the SUV, even though I probably wouldn't need it until I reached the South Carolina border. It was straightforward until then — Highway 70 to Interstate 40 near Raleigh, then Interstate 85 near Greensboro, through Charlotte, and into South Carolina, all the way to Greenville. The computer was calculating that I'd reach my destination somewhere between one and two in the afternoon, which I hoped was enough time to get some answers.

The drive was easy, relatively flat, and

sandwiched between either farmland or forest. Near the cities, the congestion was worse, though nothing like the DC area, where I'd grown up. As I rolled along, I tried to picture my grandfather taking the same route but couldn't. His truck shivered and shook at speeds above forty miles an hour, and driving slowly on the interstates was dangerous. At his age, he would have known that his eyesight and reflexes weren't up to par, either. The more I thought about it, the more I figured he would have opted for rural highways, with a single lane in each direction. It would have added even more time to the journey, and for all I knew, he'd taken two days to reach Easley.

I stopped for lunch south of Charlotte, then hit the road again. According to the GPS, Interstate 85 would intersect with Highway 123 in Greenville, and from there, it was a straight shot to my destination. Before I'd left, I'd learned that Highway 123 also led to Clemson University, which was a bit farther west, which made me wonder if Helen was a coed. My grandfather, the old dog, might have been robbing the cradle.

It was an absurd thought, but after more than six hours in the car, it made me laugh aloud.

I found Highway 123 without a problem, settled in for the final stretch, and when I was five minutes out, I began looking for mile markers. To my mind, had the stroke occurred farther east, he would have been transported to a hospital in Greenville, which was a much larger city and had more hospitals. Reaching the outskirts of Easley brought back memories, but none of the town itself. Nothing seemed familiar, nor could I remember the exact route I'd taken to the hospital, those memories overwhelmed completely by the worries I'd had at the time.

I eventually spotted mile marker 9 and I began to slow the SUV, scanning both sides of the highway. Unlike the majority of the drive, there was more than farmland or forest here; there were houses and pawnshops, used car lots and junkyards, gas stations, and even an antique store. The sight was discouraging; finding someone in any one of those businesses or houses who would remember my grandfather from more than six months ago — much less someone able to offer any helpful advice — might take days, even weeks, and while I was interested in the mystery, I already knew I wouldn't commit to something like that. It made me wonder whether the trip had been worthwhile at all.

And yet, as I finally passed mile marker 8, my heart sped up. On the right was a Waffle House — my grandfather was a fan of their restaurants — and then, about a minute later, another smaller sign on the opposite side of the highway advertising the Evergreen Motel. I remembered from medical school that strokes were most likely to occur during two two-hour windows, one in the morning and one in the evening. Taking into account the normal time he woke, a possible breakfast at Waffle House, and his eventual arrival time at the hospital, I just might have stumbled upon the motel where he'd stayed the night.

My hunch deepened as I approached. I saw the same street scene that I'd spotted on Google

Earth, but in real life, it was more easily understandable. What I thought was a strip mall was actually an old motel located directly behind mile marker 7, the kind of place that might prefer cash, which was a good thing since my grandfather didn't have a credit card. More than that, I could easily imagine my grandfather staying there. It was one story, shaped in a U, with maybe twelve rooms total. The olive-colored exterior had faded to a dull green and there were a few decrepit rocking chairs placed out in front of the rooms, no doubt in an attempt to create a homier feel to the place. It brought to mind a cross between my grandfather's house and the Trading Post, and I could imagine my grandfather breathing a sigh of relief when he'd stumbled across it.

A small sign in a window nearest the highway indicated the lobby, and I pulled to a stop in front of it. There were only three other cars in the lot, but even that struck me as three too many. It was past the normal checkout time, which meant whoever was in the room had decided to stay an additional night here, which was hard to believe. Either that, or they were paying by the hour while enjoying an afternoon fling, which I assumed was far more likely. Not that I was judging them, mind you . . .

I pulled open a squawky screen door, heard a bell jingle, and entered a small, dimly lit room fronted by a chest-high counter. On the wall behind the counter were hooks with actual keys attached to plastic fobs hanging from them. The doorway behind the counter was partially obscured by a beaded curtain, and I could hear a television blaring. The volume was lowered and a short, red-haired woman who could have been anywhere from thirty to fifty emerged from behind the beads. She seemed disappointed, as though my arrival had taken her away from her sole source of enjoyment at work, that being the television.

'Do you need a room?'

'No,' I said, 'but I was hoping you could help me.'

I gave her a brief summary of the information I hoped to learn. As I spoke, her eyes traveled from my injured hand to the scar on my face, her expression openly curious. Instead of answering, she asked, 'You Army?'

'Navy,' I said.

'My brother was in the Army,' she said. 'He was in Iraq three different times.'

'Tough place,' I said. 'I was in Afghanistan.'

'Not so easy there, either.'

'No, it wasn't,' I agreed. 'But at least I wasn't there three times.'

For the first time, she smiled. 'What were you saying? About your grandfather?'

I told her again about my grandfather before adding that the ambulance company indicated that he'd collapsed near the mile marker out front, early in the morning — which made it possible, if not likely, that he'd stayed at the Evergreen. 'I was hoping you could check the register.'

'When was that?'

I told her the date and she shook her head. 'I'm really sorry. As much as I'd like to help, you'll have to ask Beau about that. I'm not supposed to let people see the records unless they have a warrant. I could lose my job.'

'Beau's the owner?'

'The manager,' she answered. 'He runs the place for his uncle in West Virginia.'

'Do you have a number to call him?'

'I do, but I'm not supposed to disturb him. He's sleeping right now. Don't like to be disturbed. He works nights. Eight to eight.'

With hours like that, I wouldn't want to be disturbed, either. 'Would you happen to know anything about my grandfather? Were you working here then? Maybe you heard something?'

Her fingers drummed on the counter. 'I recall hearing about some old guy needing an ambulance right out there in the parking lot. Might've been him. But might not. There's been a few people who've died here in the last couple of years, so they kinda run together. Heart attacks mostly. One time, a suicide.'

I wondered if that was typical of this place or motels and hotels in general. 'Will Beau be working tonight?'

'Yep.' She nodded. 'But don't be put off when you meet him. He looks kind of squirrelly, but he's all right. He's got a good heart.'

'I appreciate your help.'

'I didn't do much,' she said. 'What I can do is leave a note for Beau, telling him to expect you and to help you out if he can.'

'I appreciate that.'

'What's your name again?'

'Trevor Benson.'

'I'm Maggie,' she said. 'Thank you for your service. And sorry I couldn't be more help.'

With hours to kill, I drove back to Greenville and spent some time browsing at Barnes & Noble before having a steak dinner at Ruth's Chris. Figuring I'd need to stay overnight, I arranged for a room at the Marriott. While the Evergreen might have been fine by my grandfather's standards, I preferred a place with a few more amenities.

I returned to the Evergreen Motel at a quarter past eight. By then, it was dark and my headlights illuminated four cars in the parking lot. They weren't the same as the ones that had been there before, the afternoon delights long since over. I parked in the same spot and entered the lobby. Again I heard the television blaring before Beau emerged from the back room.

My first thought was that I understood what Maggie had meant: The man who approached the counter looked exactly like the kind of guy who worked the night shift at a place called the Evergreen Motel on a quiet highway in the middle of nowhere. I suspected he was about the same age as or younger than me; he was rail thin, with a scraggly half beard and hair that probably hadn't been washed in a week. His white T-shirt was stained and he had a small chain hooked from a belt loop to his wallet. His expression flickered between indifference and irritation and I could smell beer on his breath.

'Are you Beau?'

He wiped his chin with the back of his hand and sighed. 'Who's asking?'

'Trevor Benson,' I said. 'I came by earlier and spoke to Maggie.'

'Oh yeah,' he said. 'She left me a note and said that I should help you because you're a veteran. Something about your grandfather.'

I went through the story again. Even before I finished, he was nodding. 'Yeah, I remember him. Old guy — like really old, right? Driving a beater truck?'

'Probably,' I said. 'It sure sounds like him.'

He reached under the counter and pulled out a notebook, the kind you might find at any office supply store. 'What was the date?'

I told him, watching as he began flipping back through the pages. 'Thing is, we only require an ID if they pay with a credit card. With cash and the key deposit, we don't bother checking. There's a lot of John Does in here, so I can't guarantee anything.'

No surprise there. 'I'm sure he would have used his real name.'

He continued thumbing back, finally zeroing in on the appropriate date. 'What was his name again?'

'Carl Haverson.'

'Yep,' he said. 'Paid cash for one night. Returned the key and got his deposit back.'

'Do you remember anything he might have said? Where he might have been going?'

'I can't help you there. Sorry. Guests kind of run together, you know?'

'Can you tell me what you do remember?'

207

'I remember finding him,' he said. 'He was in his truck, with the engine still idling. I don't know how long he was there, but I remember looking out the window and seeing the truck about to turn onto the highway. A couple of minutes later, the truck was still there. I remember because it was belching out a lot of smoke. But anyway, the truck was blocking part of the exit, so I finally went out there and was about to knock on the window when I saw him slumped over the wheel. I opened the door and he didn't look good. I wasn't sure if he was dead or alive, so I went back inside and called 911. The police showed up and an ambulance came and the crew did their thing before loading him into the back. He was still alive at that point, but it was the last I saw of him.'

After he finished, I glanced through the window toward the exit, visualizing the scene. Squirrelly or not, Beau had been helpful.

'Do you know what happened to the truck?'

'Some of it.'

'Just some?'

'I asked the sheriff if I could move it so it wasn't blocking the exit. Like I explained, it was still running. He told me to go ahead, but to put the keys in an envelope, in case the guy came back. So I moved the truck into the lot over by the end and did what he told me to do.'

'Do you still have the keys?'

'No,' he said, shaking his head.

'Why not?'

'I don't want any trouble. I waited a couple of weeks for the guy to come back. Your grandfather, I mean. But he never did and I never heard anything.'

'I'm not angry,' I said, 'and you're not in trouble. I'm just trying to find his truck on the off chance there was something inside that would tell me where he was going.'

He studied me.

'My uncle told me to have it towed,' he finally said. 'I gave the tow truck driver the keys.'

'Do you happen to remember who you called?'

'AJ's,' he said. 'AJ's Towing.'

It was probably too late to pay a visit to AJ's, so I drove back to the Greenville Marriott. I showered and watched an action movie on pay-per-view before crawling in bed. Reaching for my phone, I texted Natalie.

Hey there. It was a long drive, but I'm glad I came. Learned some things, found out the truck was towed. Looking into that tomorrow. Love you.

Too tired to text a second time if she responded, I put the phone on silent and turned out the lamp. I fell asleep within minutes and my last conscious thought was to wonder again where my grandfather had been going.

In the morning, there was no response from Natalie.

After breakfast, I debated whether to call AJ's or swing by, finally deciding on the latter. The GPS guided me to an industrial area of Easley and though I found the address, I saw no sign indicating the name of the business, nor could I find an entrance to any office. Instead, I saw a large, rectangular prefabricated building with three large roll-up doors squatting in the center of a crumbling asphalt yard, all behind tall chain-link fencing. Though there was a gate that led to the property, it was chained and locked. On the opposite side of the yard, I saw three dusty cars parked in a row. No one seemed to be out and about.

It was regular business hours, but once I thought about it, the locked premises seemed logical. Unless someone had their car or truck impounded on the property, there was probably no reason to keep an office staff, or even someone around to answer the phone. Most likely, the phone number for the business went straight to a cell phone.

I dialed it, listened to it ring, and after hearing the gruff recorded voice of AJ, I left a brief message about the information I needed and asked him to call me.

With little to do other than wait, I toured Easley, finding it prettier than I'd expected. I also found the hospital again and though I didn't get out of my vehicle, I sent a silent thanks to the good people who worked there. My grandfather had been well cared for in his final days by conscientious doctors and nurses, people who were thoughtful enough to try to track me down.

210

At noon, I drove back to Greenville and had lunch downtown, at a place that served an exceptional crab melt and appeared to be frequented by women who worked in nearby office buildings. Because I'd checked out of the hotel, I lingered in the restaurant until I finally felt self-conscious, then went for a walk.

Three hours passed without hearing from AJ. Then four and five hours. I debated leaving for New Bern, but felt compelled to speak with AJ face-to-face. Anyway, even if I left then, I wouldn't get home until nearly midnight.

I went back to the Marriott and checked in again. While charging my phone, I kept the ringer on high. I texted Natalie again.

Thinking of you. Probably heading home tomorrow, back in the afternoon.

I opted for Mexican food for dinner, within walking distance of the hotel. As I walked back, I dialed AJ's cell number a second time. This time I got an answer. I identified myself, mentioned that I'd called earlier about my grandfather's truck, and was abruptly cut off. Either AJ had hung up on me or my service had dropped. I dialed again and — as it had earlier that morning — the call went straight to voicemail and I disconnected the call.

In the hotel, I lay in bed thinking about that. It seemed that AJ didn't want to speak with me, though I wasn't sure why. Nor was I sure what to do. Since I couldn't find him at his place of business and didn't know his last name, I was at

211

a loss as to how to reach him. I supposed I could possibly find a business license with a name, or maybe I could call the county offices in the hopes they would provide me with a home address, but would he speak to me then? If I showed up at his front door? Or would he simply shut the door in my face? Based on the way he'd hung up on me, I suspected the latter. I briefly considered calling for a tow, but figured that as soon as he learned why I'd really called, he'd be angry and even less likely to help.

Which left me three options. I could keep leaving messages, I could get an attorney involved, or perhaps I could hire a private investigator. All of those could be done from home, however, and I wanted to evaluate those options in the morning.

I also wanted to think about Natalie because, strangely, I still hadn't heard from her.

12

Leaving Greenville early, I was able to make it home by early afternoon. Because I still hadn't decided what to do about AJ, I went for a longer-than-usual run and followed up with about an hour of stretching. Spending so much time in the car over the last few days had done my back no favors.

In the shower, I wondered whether to text Natalie again. I'd texted twice and had heard nothing, but wasn't sure what to make of that. It was possible she was someone who didn't like to text, or maybe hadn't wanted to bother me when she thought I was busy. It was also possible that her job had kept her on the go — and then, too tired to even peek at her phone. I was certainly guilty of such behavior in the past; I could remember Sandra and I had argued about it. She'd told me how much being ignored bothered her, when even a short response would do. At the time, I thought Sandra was making too big of a deal about it; now, it was easier to understand her frustration.

I made a sandwich at home and ate in front of the television, watching reruns of some cop show set in New York. I was tired from my travels and expected to turn in early. It was already dark, moonlight streaming through the windows. I'd left my phone charging in the kitchen and it was only after I'd washed and dried my plate that I bothered to check it.

Did you make it home?

It was thoughtful, I suppose, for Natalie to check in. However, I confess I was still a bit miffed about the delay and the impersonal nature of the text. Feeling slightly passive-aggressive, I didn't respond right away. I was sure Bowen and I would talk about my decision in our next session, and whether that actually constituted me striving to be the best version of myself.

On the back porch, I read for another half hour, but my concentration kept lapsing and I finally put the book aside. Reaching for the phone, I decided to keep my reply brief and to the point.

Yes

I wondered if she could read the lingering irritation in my terse response. Weren't early-stage relationships supposed to be filled with eagerness and desire? If so, where was hers?

Maybe, I heard the voice inside me whisper, the desire is there, but since you've been away, it's been focused on the *Other Guy*.

I didn't even want to go there and a moment later, Natalie texted me again.

I'm at Green Springs. Can you come and meet me?

A flood of childhood memories surfaced in my mind. Green Springs was known throughout much of Eastern North Carolina as a Water World-type structure, a throwback to the old-fashioned swimming holes common in the South so long ago. Built by a local, it sat on the Neuse River — or more accurately, in the Neuse River — and was constructed of pressure-treated lumber balanced on pilings sunk deep into the mud. Its three sides, each about twenty-five yards long, boasted two levels, except for the tower, which was five stories high, allowing jumpers to test their courage by leaping off the top into the water. There were ropes you could balance on, a zip line, swings, and pilings that kids would hopscotch across like stepping stones. I'd spent many a summer day there swimming, climbing, swinging, and jumping until I was too exhausted to move. My grandfather, who was more than seventy at the time, once joined me on a leap from the second level, triggering a round of spontaneous applause from onlookers.

There was no charge for admission but drinking and drugs were forbidden; nor was anything sexual allowed, even kissing. *No Sex Play* was the actual rule, but strangely, smoking was permitted and I could remember watching young teenagers lighting up while perched in the upper reaches on hot summer days.

I'd never been there at night, however. I didn't think the place was even open at night, but maybe Natalie had special privileges as a deputy. Or maybe the owner of Green Springs had no idea she was even there, despite the fact that it

215

stood in the waters directly behind his property. To get to the structure, you had to walk across his back lawn, to a long pier that extended into the deeper waters of the Neuse.

It didn't take me long to make a decision; despite my prickly pride, I still wanted to see her. In fact, I realized that I'd missed her.

Sure, I texted back. I'll be there in 15 minutes.

Shrugging into a windbreaker — the temperature was dropping again, that yo-yo temperature effect common to spring — I found my keys and wallet and headed to the car.

While I recalled the general area in which Green Springs was located, finding it took longer than I'd anticipated. Google wasn't able to help — there was no listing — so I ended up driving along several roads in James City near the Neuse River, until I finally found the place. I pulled into the graveled parking area, immediately spotting Natalie's car. I wondered if the owner would emerge to check who was pulling in so late, but aside from a small lamp burning in an upstairs window, I saw no evidence that anyone was even awake.

There was enough moonlight to illuminate my path as I eased my way down the gently sloping back lawn toward the water. From the neighbor's house, I heard a dog barking and was again serenaded by crickets as I breathed in the scent of pine and recently cut grass, which always reminded me of summer.

I reached the low pier, noting how, unlike Brices Creek, the Neuse River never stopped flowing. Starlight dappled its wakes and swells, making it seem as though the water was lit from below. My grandfather had told me once that the Neuse was the widest river in the United States when it finally emptied into the Pamlico Sound — wider even than the Mississippi — but here in James City, it was only a mile across. Suppressing a twinge of foreboding, I wondered why Natalie had come here at night.

Halfway down the pier, the structure began to come into focus, bringing a smile to my face. Green Springs was the same as I remembered, the kind of place where kids actually played at their own risk. There were no safety rails or even steps from one level to the next; instead, a person had to scale a series of planks while avoiding popped nails. The owner replaced rotting planks and performed other repairs during the winter months, an ongoing construction project that made Green Springs seem perpetually unfinished.

I finally reached the main structure and searched for Natalie without luck. Finally, I called her name softly in the darkness.

'I'm up here,' she answered, her voice drifting down from above.

It sounded like she was on the second level. When I climbed up to the upper reaches, I saw her sitting at the edge of the platform, her feet dangling. Like me, she was in jeans and wearing a windbreaker; I also clocked the wine bottle beside her.

She turned, offering a smile. 'You came,' she

said, her eyes shining in the moonlight. 'I was beginning to wonder whether you'd changed your mind.'

'I had trouble finding it. It's been a while since I've been here.'

As I took a seat on the edge beside her, Natalie reached for her cup and took a sip; I could smell the wine on her breath and noticed the bottle was nearly empty.

'How was your trip?' she asked in a singsong voice.

'It was fine,' I answered. 'What are you doing out here?'

She ignored my question. 'Did you find your grandfather's truck?'

'Working on it,' I said. 'I know who towed it but I haven't spoken with him yet. How long have you been out here?'

'I don't know. Two hours, maybe? I don't really know. What time is it?'

'It's almost ten.'

'It's getting late,' she declared. I watched as she gulped from her cup again. While she didn't appear to be drunk, it was clear the bottle of wine had been full when she'd arrived and I felt the first flutter of nervousness. Something was going on, something I wasn't sure I was going to like.

'Shouldn't you be heading home? To get some rest for tomorrow?'

'I'm not working tomorrow,' she answered. 'My shifts got moved because another deputy had to testify in court. So I have to work this weekend. Tonight is like my Saturday night.'

'Ah,' I said.

She offered me the cup. 'Do you want some wine?'

'Thank you, but I'm fine.'

She nodded. 'Okay then,' she said. 'I guess I should have brought a Yuengling for you.'

I didn't respond. Instead, I examined her profile, hoping and failing to uncover clues as to why we were here.

She finished her drink, then emptied the rest of the bottle into her cup.

'Are you okay?' I asked. 'Did something happen today?'

'No,' she said. 'Nothing happened today. And no, I'm not okay.'

'Is there something I can do?'

She gave a bitter-sounding laugh but didn't answer. Instead, she focused on her cup. 'Did you know that until last weekend with you, I hadn't had a drop of alcohol in over six months? Now, this is the second time in a week. You must think I have a problem.'

'You don't have a problem, but I do think something's bothering you.'

'You could say that,' she said. 'I used to think that I had things under control, but now I know I was just fooling myself.' Again, she laughed, but the sound was heartbreaking. 'I'm probably not making any sense.'

No, I thought, *you're not*. But I understood emotional turmoil and from experience I knew that talking about it would help only if she was the one who did most of the talking. My role was simply to listen and to empathize, even if I didn't fully understand what was going on.

'Do you believe in God?' she finally asked me.

'Most of the time,' I answered. 'But not always.'

I noticed a flicker of sadness in her expression.

'I do,' she said. 'I always have. Growing up, I went to church every Sunday and Wednesday nights. Good Baptist. I used to enjoy it, and I thought that I understood the way things were supposed to work. But as I grew older, I realized that I didn't. I know that God created us with free will, but I've never understood why there's so much suffering in the world. Why would God, who's supposed to be all good and loving, allow innocent people to suffer? I remember searching for the explanation in the Bible, but it's not in there. It's the biggest question there is, but there's no answer. And I see it all the time in my work. I see it everywhere. But . . . why?'

'I don't know. And I can't say that I know much about the Bible, either. My favorite part of church was staring at the girls.'

'Ha,' she snickered, clutching her cup with both hands. Then, in a subdued voice, 'Do you know why I came out here?'

'I have no idea.'

'Because this was one of the last places I can remember being truly happy. I'd never heard of this place before I moved here, but I remember coming out here late in the summer. The water was perfect, and I spread out a towel to get some sun. And as I lay there, I thought about how wonderful everything was. My life was everything I wanted it to be, and I was just . . . absolutely content. I wanted to feel that way again, even for an instant.'

'And?'

'And what?'

'Did you feel it?'

'No,' she said. 'That's why I brought the wine. Because if I couldn't feel happy, then I didn't want to feel anything at all.'

I didn't like what she was saying, my worry for her growing more pervasive. Perhaps she sensed my concern, because she moved the bottle behind us, then scooted closer to me. Instinctively, I put my arm around her shoulder and neither of us said anything. Instead, we stared toward the river, watching as the celestial light made the water flicker hypnotically.

'It's nice, isn't it?' she said, sighing. 'Being out here at night?'

'Yes,' I agreed. 'I didn't think it was allowed.'

'It's not. But I didn't care.'

'Obviously.'

'You know what else I was thinking about while I was out here? Before you came?'

'I have no idea.'

'I was thinking about the bees. And the alligators and the eagles and the dinner on the porch. I was happy then, too. Maybe not perfectly content, but . . . happy. For the first time in a long time, I kind of felt like myself again and while I was sitting out here, I realized how much I miss that. But . . .'

She trailed off. When she didn't finish her thought, I asked the obvious.

'But what?'

'I realized that I'm not supposed to be happy.'

Her comment jolted me. 'Why would you say

221

that? Of course you are. Why would you think that?'

Instead of answering, she took another swallow from her cup. 'We should probably get going. Or at least, I should go. It's getting late.'

'Please don't change the subject. Why wouldn't you think you're supposed to be happy?'

'You wouldn't understand.'

'Maybe I would, if I knew what you were talking about.'

In the silence, I heard the soft sound of her breaths, could feel the subtle movement beneath my arm. 'Sometimes, in life, you're confronted with an impossible decision, with no happy ending, no matter what you choose. Like . . . imagine you're married with three kids, and you're rock climbing with your wife, and something goes wrong. You're dangling from the cliff, with no rope; one hand is on the rock, and the other hand is holding your wife, and you're getting weaker and you know that there's no way you can save both your wife and yourself. So you either have to let go of your wife — and live with her death — or you both have to die and allow your children to be orphaned. In that situation, neither decision will make you happy. That sort of thing.'

I thought about what she was trying hard not to say.

'You're talking about choosing between me and the other guy.'

She nodded, her mouth a tight line. 'But I don't want to talk about it right now, okay? It's all I've been thinking about since I last saw you, and I'm so tired and I've been drinking. It's not the right time. I'm not ready.'

'Okay,' I said, with difficulty. I loved her. I longed to talk about us, about our future. I wanted to convince her that she could be happy with me, that I'd do everything possible to show her she'd made the right decision by choosing me. 'What would you like to talk about?'

'Nothing,' she said. 'But can you just sit here and hold me for a while?'

I pulled her closer, and we sat in silence on that cool and dark spring evening. In the distance, I saw cars passing over the bridge; lights were glowing in the houses across the river. The air was growing moist, thickening, and I predicted there would be a heavy layer of fog in the morning, blurring the verdant landscape into a world of shadows.

Natalie dumped the remainder of her wine into the water, barely making a splash; I focused on the heat of her skin and the way her body curved into mine. I thought back on our date, and the softness of her lips the first time we kissed. Closing my eyes, I knew that I loved her, no matter what.

We would get past this, I told myself. It would be hard for her — perhaps even excruciating — but I was willing to give her the time and space that she needed. I knew that she loved me the same way that I loved her. It might take a while, but I felt she would reach the same conclusion, and that we would find a way to be together.

And yet, as hard as I tried to convince myself of those things, I feared that I might be wrong about all of it.

But I said nothing. Nor did she, and we sat together, on a night that should have belonged to us but somehow didn't feel that way. Finally, I heard her exhale.

'We should probably be going,' she said again. 'I've got some errands to run first thing in the morning, since I won't have time this weekend.'

I nodded reluctantly. Rising, I offered my hand to help her up, then grabbed the wine bottle and cup. I walked to the spot where I'd climbed up, and while I was worried that the wine would make her unsteady, she climbed down easily. I followed, discarding the wine bottle and cup into the garbage can on the first level, and we started down the pier. As we walked, Natalie reached for my hand, and a wave of relief washed through me. I knew she'd made her decision and I felt suddenly lighter than I had all night.

We walked across the lawn toward our cars. When we reached hers, I cleared my throat.

'I don't think it's a good idea for you to drive.'

'No,' she agreed, 'it isn't. I need to get my bag, but can you bring me home?'

'I'd be happy to,' I said.

She pulled her handbag from the passenger seat while I unlocked my car. Opening the door for her, I waited until she was settled, then rounded the car and slipped behind the wheel. Pulling out into the street, I turned to her.

'Which way?'

'Head back to the highway toward New Bern. I live in the Ghent area. Do you know where that is?'

'I haven't the faintest idea.'

'Take the first exit after the bridge and turn right.'

After only a few minutes, Natalie directed me to turn on Spencer Avenue. It was a pretty street, with mature trees and houses dating from the first half of the previous century. Natalie eventually had me pull into the driveway of a charming two-story home.

Turning off the engine, I got out. Natalie did as well and together we made our way toward the front door.

'So this is where you live, huh?'

'For now,' she said. She began digging around in her purse.

'Are you thinking of moving?'

'Maybe,' she said, fishing out her keys. 'I haven't decided. It's a little too big, and I might want something with a single story.'

'Are you trying to find anything?'

'Not yet,' she said.

'Too many errands?'

'Sure,' she said. 'Let's go with that.'

By then, we were standing on her doorstep. I hesitated, trying to read her expression in the darkened doorway. 'I'm glad you texted.'

'Why? I was a hot mess tonight.'

'I didn't notice.'

'Liar.'

I grinned before leaning in to kiss her. She seemed reluctant but finally kissed me back and we separated. 'I'm glad you're in my life, Natalie. I hope you know that.'

'I know.'

Not wanting to sound desperate, I pretended

not to notice that she hadn't reciprocated my feeling. 'Would you like me to pick you up in the morning so we could go get your car?'

'No,' she answered. 'I'll figure it out.'

'You sure?'

'I'll have someone from work take care of it. It's out of your way, and there's another deputy who lives just down the street. It's not a big deal.'

Using her key, she unlocked the door, pushing it open a crack.

'I know you're working this weekend, but maybe we could get dinner tomorrow?'

She seemed to search the quiet, leafy street before coming back to me. 'I don't think I can make it. After tonight, I'll probably just stay in.'

'All right,' I said, wanting to know the reason, but knowing enough not to ask. 'No worries. We'll try for next week, okay?'

Her hand moved to the chain around her neck, which I knew to be a nervous response. When she spoke, her voice was soft, almost a whisper.

'I know you love me, Trevor, but do you care about me, too? I mean, really and truly care about me?'

'Of course I care about you.'

'Then if I asked you to do something, even if it was something that you didn't want to do, would you do it? If it was the most important thing in the world to me?'

I could see the naked plea in her expression. 'Yes.'

'Then, because you love me, and because you care for me, I want you to do something for me. I want you to promise me that you'll do it.'

'Sure, okay,' I answered, tension rising in me like flood-waters. 'Anything,' I said. 'I promise.'

She smiled, sorrowful, before leaning toward me. We kissed a second time, her body tight against me. I felt her shoulders shudder and heard her fight to steady her breath before she finally pulled back. Her eyes were moist as she reached up, touching the scar on my face.

'We need to stop,' she said. 'I need to stop.'

'Stop what?'

'This. You and me. All of it. We need to stop.'

My stomach did a flip. 'What are you saying?'

She swiped at a tear, her eyes never leaving my own. It took a long time for her to get the words out.

'Please never, ever try to contact me again.'

Shock left me unable to speak, but she seemed to have expected it. With a sad smile, she stepped through the opening, closing the door behind her, leaving me wondering how my world had just come crashing down around me.

13

Friday was spent in a daze, the weekend much the same. Though I forced myself to work out, I couldn't manage much more. My stomach was in knots, the idea of food nausea-inducing, and while part of me longed to drink to oblivion, I was careful not to touch so much as a single beer. I didn't study or clean the house or do laundry; instead, I took long walks in the afternoons, rehashing every moment that Natalie and I had spent together, trying to figure out where things had gone wrong. Where I'd gone wrong.

All signs pointed to the *Other Guy*, but I still couldn't fully accept that. Less than a week had passed since we'd spent that unforgettable day and night together; even if she'd decided to rekindle that other relationship instead of making a go of it with me, why hadn't she said anything? Why the flat request never to contact her again? Was this some kind of game to her? While I granted that she played things close to the vest, she didn't strike me as inherently manipulative. Part of me was certain that Natalie would come around. She'd call and blame her words on the fact that she'd been drinking; she'd admit that she hadn't been thinking clearly.

She'd apologize and we'd talk about what was really going on. We'd work things out, and sooner rather than later, everything would go back to normal.

I carried my phone with me wherever I went, but my phone remained silent. Nor did I attempt to contact her. She'd asked me not to and I honored my promise, even as it simultaneously angered and confused me, even as my heart was breaking.

Gradually, my appetite returned, but I didn't sleep well. In my waking hours, I felt more on edge than I had in a long time, and I was thankful that I'd be speaking with Bowen on Monday. For the first time in a long time, I felt like I really needed his help.

'It's clear that you're upset,' Bowen said. 'Anyone in your situation would feel the same.'

I was in the kitchen, staring at Bowen on the computer screen. I had told him briefly about my trip to Easley before plunging into the events involving Natalie and me. I spoke in circles, repeated myself more than once, continually posing the same questions without really expecting an answer. On his end, Bowen waited for me to finally talk myself out before offering any response.

'I'm more hurt and confused than anything,' I said, running my hand through my hair. 'I just don't understand what happened, Doc. She told me she loves me. What do you think happened?'

'I don't know that I can answer that question,'

he said. 'All I know for certain is that — according to you — she made her wishes known.'

'Do you think it's because of the other man?'

'Don't you?'

Of course I do. Why else would you end a relationship with someone you loved?

When I didn't respond, Bowen cleared his throat. 'How are you sleeping?'

'Not well, the last few days. Maybe three or four hours, with a lot of tossing and turning.'

'Bad dreams?'

'I doubt I'm sleeping enough to dream.'

'And during the day?'

'On edge. Tense. But I'm not drinking and I'm working out. Even though I'm not hungry, I'm still making sure that I eat.'

'How about your hands? Any trembling?'

'Why? Did you expect me to become a total wreck?' I snapped.

'I just asked the question,' he said. 'I take it the answer is no.'

I pinched the bridge of my nose. 'Of course it's a no. Believe me, I know my situation and understand the things I have to do to stay healthy. I'm under stress at the present time, but I'm doing my best, okay? I just want to know what to do about Natalie.'

I could feel him staring at me through the screen before he finally said in a neutral voice, 'If it's so important to you to understand, I suppose you could always go to her house and try to speak with her.'

'Are you suggesting that I do that?'

'No,' he said. 'If you were asking my opinion, I

230

wouldn't recommend it. Not right now, anyway. Based on the way you described the situation, she seemed unequivocal in her decision. To try to revisit it against her wishes would likely backfire and make things even worse.'

'I don't think they can get any worse.'

'Oddly, things can almost always get worse.'

I rolled my shoulders a couple of times before forcing myself to take a deep breath. 'I just want . . .'

When I trailed off, Bowen's eyes were empathetic. 'I know what you want,' he said. 'You want Natalie to feel the same way about you as you do about her. You want your love reciprocated, and you want a future with her.'

'Exactly.'

'And yet you also suspected that she was seeing someone else and was perhaps even in a serious relationship, prior to her actually admitting it. In other words, you were never sure what to expect. Now, couples' counseling is not necessarily my area of expertise except in the context of PTSD, but one thing I've learned in the course of my own life is that you can't force a romantic interest with someone who doesn't want one with you.'

'But that's the thing. I have the sense that she actually *does* want one with me.'

'Despite making it clear she wanted to end it?'

He had me there. Bowen went on. 'Then the best you can do is wait until she changes her mind. In the meantime, it's critical to take care of yourself and continue to move forward in your own life. It's important not to dwell, since it's likely to make you feel even worse.'

'How am I supposed to not think about it?'

'One thing you can do is stay busy. Stay focused on the things you need to do. Remember the lessons of CBT and DBT — that positive behaviors can help lessen the emotional turmoil you're feeling. For instance, have you found a place in Baltimore to live yet? Tomorrow is the first of May.'

'Not yet,' I said. 'I still have to figure that out.'

'It might help you feel better to get out of town. New environments, especially when combined with a specific, important purpose for the visit, can help distract from the emotions you're experiencing.'

I knew that was true, but I nonetheless wondered if my trip to South Carolina had made Natalie's decision to end it that much easier. Had I spent time with her earlier in the week, perhaps none of this would have happened. But who really knew for sure?

'You're right, Doc. I'll get on that.'

'You still have friends there, right?'

'A couple of guys from my residency are still in the area.'

'Maybe go to a ball game, or set up a lunch. Reconnecting with old friends is always good for the soul.'

Bowen, I knew, was a believer in any form of healthy distraction.

'I'll think about it.'

'You also said that you wanted to speak with the owner of the towing company?'

Speaking with AJ had become a low, if not

232

nonexistent, priority over the last few days. It had been all I could do to hold myself together.

'I'll do that, too,' I mumbled.

'Good,' he said. 'Keep in mind that as hard as things are, it is possible to find things to enjoy and to be grateful for the opportunities that life presents.'

Bowen used that expression frequently and while I recognized how important enjoyment and gratitude were when it came to good mental health, there were times it annoyed me. Like right now.

'Any other advice you can offer?'

'Concerning what?'

'What I should do about Natalie.'

'I think,' he said slowly, 'you're handling everything as well as can be expected at the present time. But I'm wondering if it might be a good idea for me to prescribe something that will help you sleep better. Extended periods without quality sleep can greatly affect how PTSD can manifest. Do you have any thoughts on it?'

I'd used sleep aids before, along with antidepressants. I understood well the benefits they could offer, but I preferred to avoid them.

'I think I'm okay, Doc. Let's see how it goes.'

'Let me know if you change your mind. Remember that I'm around if you feel like you need to talk before our next session.'

'Will do.'

Despite my conversation with Bowen, I wasn't inclined to find things to enjoy or to look for

233

ways to be grateful.

Instead, I continued to dwell on the situation while pacing from one end of the property to the other. I tried to reflect on what Bowen had recommended; I did my best to accept the idea that Natalie had to make the decision that was right for her. Through it all, my emotions remained leaden and I could feel the tightness in my jaw coil into an ache.

To my chagrin, Bowen had been proven right again. He was like your parents when they told you to eat your vegetables as a kid: You might not like it, but it was indisputably good for you.

I knew enough not to risk going out in public in case someone cut in front of me in line or otherwise challenged my shaky equilibrium. I was self-aware enough to understand that it was sometimes better to hunker down and avoid human contact altogether.

Which is exactly what I did.

In the morning, I woke feeling more irritated at myself than Natalie. Though I hadn't slept well, I knew it was time for the four-day pity party to end. That didn't mean I was grateful — far from it. But I'd learned over time that CBT and DBT work. In other words, I had to stay busy and knock items off my to-do list.

After my workout and breakfast, I dived into the internet, reviewing descriptions and photographs of furnished rentals in the vicinity of

Johns Hopkins. Because I'd lived there before, I knew the neighborhoods well and was able to find eight different units that piqued my interest.

Thinking Bowen was also right about leaving town, I called various brokers to set up times for viewings through the end of the week. Next, I booked a hotel, then finally emailed with an orthopedic surgeon who still lived in Baltimore and agreed to meet me for dinner Saturday night. I looked into catching an Orioles game as well, but they were playing away. Instead, I reserved tickets to the National Aquarium. I could practically feel Bowen patting me on the back for a job well done.

Toward the end of the day, I called AJ's Towing again and left a slightly different message. I told him that after my grandfather's passing, I had inherited the truck and asked point-blank for its return. If he didn't comply, I would assume that it was stolen and alert the appropriate law enforcement authorities. I left my phone number and address, and gave him until the following Monday to get back to me, suggesting that he contact me sooner rather than later.

Leaving such an aggressive message might not have been the wisest thing to do. People generally don't respond well to threats, though in my current mood it nonetheless felt good to lash out at something.

On Wednesday, I packed a bag, tossed it in the back of the SUV, and was out the door by seven.

The drive, which has a tendency to put one in a reflective mood, naturally brought Natalie to mind, making the inevitable traffic in DC a challenge in my hair-trigger state. I became convinced that certain drivers were purposely trying to annoy me.

Fortunately, and despite myself, I reached Baltimore without incident and drove to my first appointment, where the broker was waiting for me. Functional place, halfway decent building, and while it would have sufficed, that was all the excitement it generated. The decor was dated and the furnishings worn, not to mention the view from the tiny porch was of a garbage-strewn alley. It was basically the same situation with the second unit, though the view was better if one was fond of staring into the neighbor's place and wanted to lean out the window to borrow a cup of sugar. I struck both apartments off my list.

Stiff and out of sorts, I paced the hallways of the hotel for an hour before finally ordering room service. Though I fell asleep early, I woke in the middle of the night and finished an extra-long workout in the gym before anyone else even arrived. I splurged on breakfast, saw three more units for rent on Thursday, of which the second appealed to me. After indicating a strong interest in it, I promised to let the broker know by the end of the day on Friday.

On Friday, two of the three units were also promising, but I was still sold on the one I'd seen on Thursday. I called the broker again, set up a late-afternoon appointment, then signed the lease. Glad that I'd made a decision and taken care of it, I decided to celebrate by eating at the bar instead of ordering room service. I struck up a conversation with a woman who sold veterinary products. Attractive, an engaging conversationalist, and definitely flirty, she made it clear she'd be interested in whatever I happened to propose for later that night. But I wasn't in the mood, and after I finished my second drink, I said my goodbyes. In my room, I lay on the bed with my hands clasped behind my head, wondering if Natalie was experiencing any regrets.

The aquarium was well worth my time despite the crowd; dinner with my friend and his wife was even more fun. Joe and Laurie had been married three years and had a young daughter at home. Laurie spent part of the evening trying to convince me that she had a friend that I really should meet. 'You two would hit it off,' she said. 'She's just your type.' I demurred — I was leaving the following morning, I reminded them — but to Laurie, that made no difference. 'You'll be living here soon,' she said. 'We'll all get together then.'

Who knew? Maybe by then, I might be in a frame of mind to take them up on that.

Right now, I couldn't conceive of it.

I made the drive home on Sunday. After tossing my dirty clothes in the laundry, I collected the mail that had built up in my absence. Generally, there wasn't much — assorted bills and junk mail — but I was surprised to find a letter from an attorney named Marvin Kerman in South Carolina, addressed to me.

After tearing open the envelope, I read the

letter while I walked, finishing it on the front porch. The attorney, who represented AJ's Towing, had written to inform me that my grandfather's truck had been auctioned off for nonpayment of the tow and automobile storage, in accordance with South Carolina law. I was further informed that a letter had been sent to my grandfather's home the previous December, explaining that unless remittance was made, the truck would be considered abandoned and the towing company would take appropriate action. Toward the end, the attorney stated that unless I stopped harassing the owner, criminal or civil charges would be pursued against me.

More than likely, the original notice had been in the mail that I'd carelessly thrown away when I'd first moved in, and as my instincts had predicted, it had been a stupid idea to threaten AJ whatever-his-last-name-was. Which left me largely at a dead end.

But not entirely.

With the letter, there was one more angle I could pursue, even if I wasn't sure it would lead anywhere. I had the name and number of the attorney, after all.

With my apartment secured, the move to Baltimore felt imminent, even though I still had a month or more before I had to go. Feeling nostalgic, I decided to spend some time with the bees before my session with Bowen.

I suited up, collected everything I needed, and

picked four of the hives at random. Pulling out the frames, I noted that honey collection was well underway; the bees had been busy in recent weeks. Though my residency would be in full swing, I made the decision to return to New Bern in early August to harvest the honey. I could do it over the weekend and figured that it was something my grandfather would have wanted me to do. Claude, I assumed, would be thrilled.

In making that decision, I realized that I had no intention of either selling or renting the property. There were too many memories for me to reconcile and while I wasn't sure what that meant for me in the future, I simply couldn't imagine someone else living here. I wondered whether my decision was some sort of subconscious desire to be near Natalie but dismissed the idea.

I was keeping the house because of my grandfather, not her. Which also meant that I needed to hire a contractor because the house was in serious need of repairs. It was one thing to stay for a few months; it was entirely another to make the house permanently livable. It still needed a new roof and kitchen floor, I assumed there was termite and water damage affecting the foundation, and if I ever wanted to spend any time here in the future, the house was in dire need of a larger master bathroom while the kitchen needed work, too. For all I knew, there might be plumbing or electrical issues as well, all of which would keep the contractor busy for months. I'd need a property manager, someone to watch over the place and keep the contractor on task while sending me photos of the progress.

I wondered then whether Callie would help watch over the hives, adding the queen excluders and shallow supers in early spring. Since she passed the property on her way to work, it wouldn't be out of the way, and I'd offer to pay her more than the work was probably worth. I was sure she could use the extra money, but I wanted to speak with Claude about her work habits first. Even if she had helped my grandfather once, I still wanted someone dependable.

My to-do list — which I thought had been completed — was suddenly up and running again. Contractor, property manager, Callie and Claude . . . people to speak with, responsibilities to arrange. Today was as good a day as any to get things started; aside from my session with Bowen, I had only one other item on my agenda.

I made the call to Marvin Kerman, the attorney for AJ's Towing, immediately after finishing with the hives. His receptionist said that he was in court but would likely return my call later that afternoon.

I set up an appointment with the same general contractor I'd used months earlier, and he told me he'd be able to come by the following week. He also recommended that I get a home inspection beforehand, offering me the name of someone he trusted. The inspector, fortunately, was less busy, and said that he could inspect the home on Thursday. I was also able to find three potential property managers, and I set up times to have them come by, so I could interview them. My session with Bowen went well. He was a bit concerned that I still wasn't sleeping well, but was pleased to hear I'd secured a new place to live in Baltimore. We discussed my continued agitation over Natalie, and he urged me to give myself time to heal, reminding me that it wasn't possible to rush through what he described as a period of grief. I tried to deny my angst, but speaking about her made my emotions rise to the surface again in a way that they hadn't in days. I was shaky by the time I hung up.

And for the first time since she'd ended things, I broke down and wept.

Marvin Kerman returned my call later that afternoon. It was half past five and I suspected I was the last call of his day. When he identified himself, he nearly barked his name into the receiver.

'Thank you for returning my call, Mr. Kerman,' I responded. 'I was hoping that you might be able to help me.'

'Unfortunately the truck has already been auctioned,' he said. 'As my letter indicated, the process was an entirely legal form of recompense for services rendered.'

'I understand,' I said in a conciliatory tone. 'I'm not upset about the truck, nor do I have an issue with the fact that it's been sold. I'm calling to ask if you might be able to contact your client about something else.'

'I'm not sure what you mean.'

Again, I recounted the story of what had happened to my grandfather and my nagging questions about it. 'I wonder if AJ or someone else may have cleaned the truck and put the personal items in a box or in storage somewhere,' I added. 'I was hoping I could get those things back.'

'You're interested in his personal effects, but not the truck or the money?'

'I'm just trying to figure out what happened to him.'

'I don't know if any personal effects were saved.'

'Would you be willing to ask your client?'

'I suppose. And if there aren't any personal effects?'

'Then that will be the end of it. I can't chase clues if there aren't any.'

Kerman sighed. 'I suppose that I can ask him, but again, I can't guarantee anything.'

'I would appreciate it. Thank you.'

Drained by my tears on Monday and wanting to avoid a recurrence, I spent the rest of the week on autopilot while trying to stay as busy as possible. With the principles of CBT and DBT ringing through my head, I exercised longer and harder than usual, avoided alcohol, and ate as healthy as possible. I pressed forward with the things I needed to do. The inspector came and promised me that he'd have the report ready by Monday, so that the contractor would be able to use the information to put together an estimate.

I interviewed property managers and settled on a woman who also worked as a realtor and whose husband was a contractor. She assured me that she had the ability to oversee a construction crew and promised to walk the property at least once a week while I was in Baltimore. I still hadn't spoken to Claude or Callie, but I figured I could do that any time.

On Friday night, while sitting on the porch, I realized that it had been fifteen days since I'd last spoken with Natalie. Again, I had trouble sleeping, and when I woke in the middle of the night, I decided I was tired of staring at the darkened ceiling for hours. Crawling out of bed, I dressed and noted that it was a little past two in the morning. After a quick trip to the honey shed, I hopped in my SUV and drove to Spencer Avenue. Parking down the block, I walked to Natalie's property. As I approached, I wondered if she was with the *Other Guy* right now; I wondered if they were in bed, or if they were out on the town. I wondered whether she was staring at him in the same way she'd stared at me. All of it made it difficult to swallow as I set two jars of honey on her doorstep.

There was no doubt she'd know who had left them, and I wondered what would happen if the *Other Guy* found them. What story would she tell him? Had she mentioned me at all? Had she even thought about me in the last couple of weeks, or had I already become a half-remembered memory, colored with regret?

Trudging back to the SUV, I heard only the echo of my unanswered questions.

14

Another weekend passed, another session with Bowen. I received the inspection report, met with the contractor on Tuesday, and he promised to get me a bid as soon as possible.

Because I hadn't paid attention to the outside world in days, I had no idea a storm was imminent until heavy clouds and wind began rolling in, shortly after the contractor had departed. My first thought was that it would be a typical late-spring downpour, but after tuning in to the local news, I wondered how concerned I should actually be. Heavy rain and gusting winds were expected, with local schools canceling classes for the next two days. Live reports from Raleigh showed flooded roads, with numerous rescues already underway.

The first drops of rain fell within the hour; by the time I went to bed, it was coming down so hard that it sounded as though I were sleeping in a train station. When I woke the following morning, the storm had intensified to almost hurricane levels. The sky boiled with dark clouds and wind rattled the windows, the far side of the creek reduced to a mere shadow, obscured by the downpour.

For a while, I watched from the back porch,

the splashing rain wetting my face. Finally retreating to the kitchen, I used a hand towel to dry off. I was just starting some coffee when I heard steady plinking sounds echoing throughout the house. Sure enough, I found a leak in the living room, two more in the guest room, and still another in one of the bathrooms. There were large circular stains in the ceilings and pieces of drywall were hanging in strips, indicating that the leaks had probably started overnight. How I'd missed them earlier was beyond me, but I backtracked to the pantry and kitchen to grab the mop bucket and three pots. I used the mop to dry the floor after putting the rain catchers in place, but the drips seemed to be increasing in speed.

I sighed. The roof needed a tarp, which meant I was going to end up outside in the deluge, probably for *hours*. I'd need bricks, too, to hold the tarp in place.

The day was just getting better and better.

Not.

I decided not to do a thing until after coffee. I tossed on an old T-shirt and sweatshirt, returned to the kitchen, and poured myself a cup of coffee. As I took a sip, I saw that my hands were trembling. Putting the cup down, I stared at my hands in fascination. Was it the thought of having to work outside in the rain? The journey upon which I was about to embark at Johns Hopkins? Or was it Natalie?

The answer seemed obvious, but as I stared, I was thankful that the trembling wasn't as severe as it once had been. Still, it surprised me. Yes, I hadn't been sleeping well and I'd recently cried for the first time in years. I admitted that I'd also been feeling edgy, but it was hard to remember the last time my hands went bonkers. They hadn't trembled after my grandfather passed away, nor when I'd moved to New Bern. So why now? Natalie had ended things almost three weeks ago. How could the passage of time make things even worse?

Upon reflection, I knew the answer. My hands hadn't trembled in the immediate aftermath of my wounds, either — it wasn't until after all my surgeries that I began to notice various symptoms and that realization brought with it a ray of clarity. The explosion in Afghanistan blew up my future, and on some subconscious level, Natalie's rejection — which blew up a different sort of future — was manifesting in the same sort of delayed reaction. I had no doubt that Bowen would assure me that I was right on the money. Hadn't he asked me about it? Almost as if he'd expected them to begin trembling? Of course he had. He knew me so well. As hurt as I was, I still loved and missed Natalie.

I took a few deep breaths, made a series of fists, and little by little, the trembling subsided. Caffeine probably wasn't a good idea, but so what? I liked coffee and drank two cups anyway. Then I grabbed a rain jacket on the way out the door. If anything, the storm had grown even stronger. The wind had picked up and opaque sheets of rain were blowing diagonally. In the SUV, I wiped water from my face and noted the puddle on the seat I made after getting in.

Water was already six inches deep in parts of the driveway, and the road was only slightly better. Even with my wipers on high, I had to lean over the steering wheel and I kept my speed well below the limit. When a truck passed heading in the opposite direction, it sent a wave over the windshield and I had to hit the brakes so I wouldn't veer off the road. It was like driving through a blustery car wash, and with gusts shaking the car, I knew that even bricks wouldn't be enough to keep the tarp from flying to Oz. I'd need cinder blocks, making each trip up the ladder that much more exciting.

Lucky me.

I didn't spot her until the very last second, a lone figure walking at the edge of the road. I jerked the wheel slightly while my brain processed what I'd seen; I simply couldn't imagine anyone voluntarily venturing outside in weather like this. To my amazement, I recognized her. Bringing the SUV to a stop, I rolled down the passenger window.

'Hey, Callie. It's me, Trevor!' I shouted above the din of the storm. 'Do you need a ride to work?'

Though she had the hood up, her jacket didn't appear to be waterproof. Over her shoulder, she had slung a plastic garbage bag, no doubt loaded with dry clothes.

'I'm fine,' she said, shaking her head. 'I don't need a ride.'

'Are you sure?' I asked. 'I'm heading in that direction anyway, and it's dangerous on the road. Drivers can barely see you. Come on. Hop in.'

She seemed to debate for a moment before

reluctantly reaching for the handle and pulling open the door. She crawled up to the seat, drenched and bedraggled, her skin the bluish tint of porcelain. She clutched the plastic bag in her lap as I slowly pulled back onto the road.

'Aside from the weather, are you doing okay?'

'I'm fine.' Then in an almost begrudging tone, she added, 'Thanks for stopping.'

'You're welcome. You can put the bag on the back seat if you'd like.'

'I'm already wet. It doesn't matter.'

'I'm glad I saw you. It's terrible out here.'

'It's just water.'

'I take it you have dry clothes in the bag?'

She eyed me with suspicion. 'How did you know that?'

'Common sense.'

'Oh.'

I debated asking her whether she'd be interested in watching over the hives, but I still wanted to speak with Claude first. I decided to keep things light.

'How are things going at the Trading Post?'

'Fine.'

'That's good to hear. Do you enjoy it?'

'Why do you want to know?'

'Just making conversation.'

'Why?'

'Why not?'

She didn't seem to have an answer for that. Glancing over at her, I again thought she looked too young to be working full-time instead of going to school, but I had the sense that she'd shut down if I asked her about it. In that

248

moment, a gust of wind buffeted the car, making it shimmy. I slowed the car to a crawl, navigating the flooded road.

'Have you ever seen a storm with rain and wind like this? It's like a mini hurricane out here.'

'I've never been in a hurricane.'

'I thought you grew up here.'

'No,' she said.

'Your parents don't live here?'

'No.'

'Then what brought you to New Bern?'

'I don't want to talk about it.'

Because she wasn't in school and a job at the Trading Post wasn't exactly a profession, I wondered if — like Natalie — she'd come here because she was in a relationship with a local. But she seemed too young for that, or any of those things, for that matter. Which, to me, suggested family problems.

'Obviously it's none of my business,' I offered. 'I'm sorry for asking. But I hope things get better for you with your parents.'

Her head swiveled in my direction. 'Why would you say that?' she demanded. 'You don't know anything about me or my parents,' she snapped. 'Just stop the car. I want to get out. I can walk the rest of the way.'

'Are you sure? We're almost there,' I protested. The Trading Post was less than a hundred yards away.

'Stop the car!'

Clearly I'd hit a nerve. Not wanting to make things worse, I pulled over, bringing the SUV to

249

a stop. Without a backward glance, she swung open the car door and got out, slamming it shut.

I watched her for a moment, trudging through the puddles. When there was enough space between her and the SUV, I inched back onto the road, feeling bad that I'd upset her. It hadn't been any of my business, but I thought again about her overreaction. It reminded me of my attempted conversation during her lunch. She struck me as secretive and wary, and I wondered how my grandfather had been able to overcome her defenses. From what I'd seen of her, I couldn't imagine her volunteering to help with the hives; I felt sure my grandfather's request would have been rejected immediately unless they'd somehow known each other. She must have trusted him even before he'd asked.

But how had that come about?

I wasn't sure, but I still intended to speak with her, if only to apologize. Depending on how that went — and what Claude had to say about her — I was still hoping to offer her the job.

Who knew? Maybe she'd eventually decide that she could trust me, too.

The hardware store was already running low on tarps, but because the house was small and rect-angular, I got lucky and found one that would suffice. From there, I found a metal trolley and loaded it up with cinder blocks. There was a line at the cashier, but no one cut in front of me, which was good news for all those involved.

I loaded the car, drove home, and backed the SUV as close to the house as possible. Inside, I emptied the buckets and the pots, then retrieved a ladder from the barn. After that, I began the long process of climbing up and down the ladder, carrying the tarp and cinder blocks to the roof, and then putting it all in place while being lashed by driving rain and wind. There were better ways to spend a morning.

By the end, I was starved and freezing and after a long hot shower, I decided to eat lunch at the Trading Post. The parking lot was fuller than I anticipated, but I figured if I wasn't in the mood to make a sandwich, it was no surprise that others weren't, either.

Inside, Claude nodded from the register and I spotted Callie on a stepladder in the back of the store, hanging fishing waders on pegs mounted high on the wall. Frank was in his usual spot behind the grill and there were several men eating at the tables. The seats at the counter were full, so I squeezed between customers while I waited to order a cheeseburger and fries. Rain continued to sheet against the windows and I overheard people discussing the storm. Supposedly, the downtown area and other neighborhoods were already flooding.

After Frank took my order, I pulled a Snapple from the refrigerator and went to the register. Claude nodded toward the windows.

'Can you believe this? It's spitting serious water out there.'

'Crazy weather,' I agreed.

'What did you order?'

I told him and he rang me up; after receiving my change, I went on. 'Do you have a minute? I'd like to ask you a couple of questions about Callie.'

'She's right over there if you want to speak with her yourself.'

'I was hoping for a reference,' I began, and after I explained what I was thinking, he nodded.

'She's a great worker,' he said. 'She doesn't complain, doesn't mind staying late, and she's never missed a shift, even when she was going through some hard times. She's really good at cleaning, too — almost OCD about it. I think she'd do a great job for you, but keep in mind she's a strange one.'

'In what way?'

'She's worked here for . . . I don't know. Ten or eleven months? She came on at the end of last summer, but aside from the fact that she still lives in the trailer park up the road, I swear I don't know the first thing about her. No one knows much about her.'

No surprise there, I thought. 'She told me she wasn't from New Bern.'

'I don't doubt it. Until Carl recommended her, I'd never seen her before. It's like she dropped in out of the sky one day.'

I tilted my head, wondering if I'd heard him correctly. 'My grandfather recommended her?'

'That he did,' Claude said. 'He drove her here, in fact, and walked her in the door. Asked me to take a chance on her and said he'd vouch for her personally. It was the end of summer and a couple of the college kids that had worked for me over the summer were heading back to school, so I had an opening. I took a chance and I'm glad I did. But it's a shame you'll be leaving.'

'I'm sure I'll be back,' I said. 'Thanks for the info.'

'She should be going on break in a little while if you want to talk to her about the hives. Because of the weather, she'll probably eat in the back instead of by the creek.'

'I imagine so. It's miserable out there.'

'She was soaking wet when she arrived. Felt bad for her. If her lunch got wet, I'll probably try to get her something from the grill. If she'll take it, which she might not. She isn't real good at accepting favors. But I can't imagine eating a soggy peanut butter and jelly sandwich.'

I felt the clicking of a memory, like a bubble slowly rising to the surface, when Claude mentioned the sandwich. Strangely, I felt certain it had something to do with my grandfather, but I couldn't yet put my finger on it.

'That's what she was eating when I talked to her before.'

'It's what she eats every day.'

I raised my gaze. Finished with the waders, Callie was still high on the stepladder, now hanging fluorescent hunting vests. I was wondering again how she'd come to know my grandfather when I heard Frank call out my order.

'You should grab your burger before it gets cold,' Claude said. 'A quick question, though. I've heard rumors that you're going to sell the place, so why worry about the hives?'

'I've decided I'm going to keep it.'

'Yeah?'

'It's what my grandfather would have wanted.'

Claude smiled. 'No doubt about it.'

The burger was cooked and seasoned perfectly, and I devoured my lunch in minutes. While tossing the remains in the waste-basket, I heard a sudden crash from the back of the store and saw Claude rush out from behind the register. Other diners jumped up as well, everyone moving in the same direction, and I followed. When I spotted the toppled ladder and Callie's crumpled form on the floor, instincts kicked in, and I began pushing past people.

'Let me through!' I shouted. 'I'm a doctor.'

Claude was already squatting beside her body, his face strained with worry, and by the time I reached her side I was already taking in the scene, the information coming quickly.

Patient on her side . . . not moving . . . pallor almost a grayish white . . . possible internal bleeding? . . . blood in her hair and beginning to pool on the floor beneath her head . . . arm bent at an unnatural angle beneath her body, indicating likely fractures of the radius and ulna . . .

I gently reached for her carotid while others crowded around; I vaguely heard Claude telling people that he saw her fall from the ladder. Her pulse was thready and weak.

'Everyone step back!' I shouted. 'Claude . . . I need you to call 911!'

It took a second for him to register that I was shouting at him.

Claude dug into his back pocket for his phone and I returned my attention to Callie. Though it had been years since I did a rotation in emergency medicine, I'd seen numerous head wounds, and the blood from her ear was a dangerous sign. While I suspected a possible subdural hematoma, she'd need a CT scan before anything was definitive. I gently repositioned Callie's body onto her back, while keeping her neck as steady as possible. Her breathing was shallow, the compound fractures visible. Her arm was already swelling and beginning to turn black and purple. She remained unconscious. Pulling my phone from my pocket, I turned on the flashlight and checked her pupils. Thankfully, they dilated with the light, but head wounds always needed to be treated with caution . . .

I heard Claude on the phone, panic in his voice as he explained the situation before growing silent.

'They're saying that an ambulance might be a while. There was flooding at one of the nursing homes and emergency services are swamped. They're also uncertain whether an ambulance can make it here because the roads are so bad.'

In front of my eyes, Callie's pallor seemed to grow even more ashen, another serious complication. I saw numerous bruises on her undamaged arm; most appeared to be days or weeks old. Gently lifting her shirt, I looked for evidence of internal bleeding but strangely didn't find anything that would explain her worsening color.

255

She needed to be at the hospital, sooner rather than later. I calculated the odds, knowing that while there was risk in transporting her, there was more risk in waiting for an ambulance that might not be able to make it here at all.

'My SUV can make it, but you'll have to drive so I can stay in the back with her. Do you have something we can carry her on? A stretcher? A cot? Anything?'

'We have cots in the back. A shipment of camping gear just came in. Will that work?'

'Yes,' I said. 'Go get one!'

Claude rushed off. Around me, men watched with wide eyes. I pulled the keys from my pocket and held them up.

'I need one of you to go out to my SUV. It's parked to the left of the entrance, the big black one. Fold down the seats and make room for the cot. Leave the back hatch open. For the rest of you, I'm going to need some help getting her on the cot, and then carrying her. Does anyone have an umbrella? I want to keep her as dry as possible.'

They stared at me, unmoving, until Frank suddenly lunged forward and grabbed my keys before racing toward the door. At the same time, Claude burst from the back carrying a bulky cardboard box.

'Get out of the way! I need room!' he shouted before practically dropping it on the floor. He began ripping it open.

'Is she going to be okay?' he asked.

'I hope so,' I said. 'Listen to me. I need you to call the emergency room at the hospital. They

256

need to know that the patient has a serious head injury, possible internal bleeding, and compound fractures of the radius and ulna. Can you do that?'

By then, he'd freed the cot, revealing heavy plastic straps locking it into the closed position.

'Does anyone have scissors or a knife?' Claude shouted.

'Did you hear me, Claude? You need to call the emergency room. They need to be ready for her.'

'I got it. I have to call the hospital. She's going to be okay, right?'

I repeated to him what I needed him to say.

'Yeah, okay.' He nodded. 'I don't know what happened.'

'For now let's just take care of her, okay?'

Claude shouted to the others while pointing toward the cot. Again, I saw him reaching for his phone. 'I need scissors or a knife to cut these straps.'

Someone I didn't recognize stepped forward while whipping out a knife. With the press of a button, the blade flicked open; it wasn't just a knife but a weapon, but who really cared? He used the blade to cut the plastic straps, and pushed the cot open, snapping it into place. He began to unfold the legs and I waved him off.

'It'll be too tall if you open the legs. Just move the cot next to her, okay? I'm going to need some help gently moving her onto the cot, and then more help carrying her out to the car. I need as many hands as possible, so get close.'

People react in various ways during life-and-death moments. I'd seen people rise to the occasion or freeze in place, but the men at the Trading Post seemed to have collected their wits enough to know what needed to be done. The knife owner inched the cot into position; several others moved around her body.

'I'm going to keep her neck as steady as I can, in case there's a spinal injury. The rest of you slide your hands under her. I doubt she weighs a hundred pounds, so she's not going to be heavy. I'll count down from three, and when I say lift, use a smooth, gentle motion while we move her onto the cot. The whole thing should take only a few seconds, okay? Does everyone understand?'

I made eye contact with each of them and saw them nod. 'Once she's on the cot, we'll carry her out to the car. There aren't good handles, so it might be kind of awkward, but she doesn't weigh much, and there's a lot of us. All right?'

Again, I saw them nod.

I called out the countdown and instructed them to lift. I kept her neck steady, and she was moved onto the cot without incident. A moment later, we began carrying her through the store. At the door, another man was waiting with an open umbrella, which he used to shield Callie from the downpour. The back hatch stood open.

With the downpour continuing, I had to shout to be heard. 'I need someone to get inside the SUV and be ready to grab the cot as we load it, so there's no extra jostling!'

A young man in his twenties hopped in, wedging between the driver and passenger seat, facing the rear. As a cohesive unit, we gently loaded the cot into the back, more smoothly than I'd imagined possible. I hopped up, kneeling, and hunched over beside her body. 'Claude? Can you drive?'

Claude jumped behind the wheel as someone closed the back hatch. The cot had only inches to spare between the rear hatch and the seats up front. Callie remained unconscious, her breathing still shallow. Blood continued to drip from her ear. I checked her pupils again, and they were still reactive. I prayed we would get to the hospital on time.

'Do your best to keep the ride as smooth as possible,' I said to Claude as he started the engine.

A moment later, we were on the rain-drenched roads, but I barely noticed the drive. I kept my attention on Callie, wishing she'd wake, wishing she would move. Her arm continued to swell. I wanted Claude to drive faster, but in these conditions it was impossible. The SUV shook in the gusts; at times we slowed to a crawl while rolling through water that nearly reached the floorboards and splashed against the windows. I prayed that a neurologist would be waiting in the emergency room, and I wished that the local hospital were a trauma center. The nearest one — Vidant, in Greenville — was at least another hour distant in good weather; today, I doubted an ambulance could make it there at all. A helicopter was out of the question.

Claude shouted back to me, letting me know when detours were required or when he was about to turn, all while continuing to inquire about Callie. In time — it seemed like too much

259

time — we turned into the hospital parking lot, heading for the emergency room. Callie's condition seemed to have deteriorated even more. To Claude, I barked an order.

'Tell them we're going to need a stretcher and a lot of hands to move her.'

Claude jumped out and raced inside; almost instantly, a stretcher appeared, surrounded by half a dozen nurses and a physician. I climbed out from the rear hatch and recited what I knew about her condition. Callie was moved to the stretcher and then wheeled inside with the nurses and physician surrounding her before vanishing into the back. Claude and I trailed behind, finally stopping in the waiting room. I could still feel the surge of adrenaline coursing through my body. I felt strangely disassociated, almost as though I were an observer of my own life.

In the waiting room, half the chairs were empty. There was a mother and a couple of younger children, another small group of elderly people, a lady who was clearly pregnant, and a man in a makeshift sling. It was busy but not chaotically so, which I hoped would allow Callie to get the attention she needed.

A single glance at Claude revealed how shaken he remained by what had occurred.

'Nice job getting us here. You did well.'

'Thanks. In another hour, we might not have been able to make it. It's flooded everywhere. Do you think she'll be all right?'

'I hope so.'

'You don't think she'll die, do you?'

'I don't know,' I answered, unwilling to lie to

260

him. 'I'm worried that she didn't regain conscious-ness. That's never a good sign.'

'Jesus,' he said. 'The poor thing. You'd think she'd finally catch a break. First the fire and now this.'

'What fire?'

'Her trailer burned down last November, not long after Thanksgiving. She barely got out and lost pretty much everything except the clothes she was wearing. It took her some time to get a new trailer. When she finally did, I let her have some old furniture I had in the garage. Despite all that, she never missed a shift. Makes me wish the store offered health insurance. Do you think the hospital here will still take care of her? I don't think she has any.'

'Legally, they have to take care of her. And a lot of hospitals have programs to help those who can't pay. I don't know what they do here, but I'm sure they'll figure something out.'

'I hope so,' he said. 'Damn. I still can't believe it. I keep seeing the whole thing over and over in my mind.'

'Did she lose her balance and slip?'

'No,' he said. 'That's what was so crazy about it.'

'What do you mean?'

'She was on the top step, hanging another vest. She was using an extender and stretching out so she could reach the peg, and then . . . all of a sudden, her eyes closed and she just kind of . . . *folded*. Like she fainted.'

Little alarm bells suddenly rang as I processed Claude's words.

'Are you saying she was unconscious *before* she fell and hit her head?'

'That's what it looked like to me. Right before it happened, I remember watching her and thinking that her coordination was off, like she was off-balance or something. A customer in the store fainted one time and she looked just like he did.'

He sounded believable, and I wondered what that meant. Fainting could be due to something as simple as dehydration or low blood pressure but it was occasionally a sign of something more serious. It was regarded as its own medical emergency until the cause was known. I thought about her pallor, and wondered if somehow the two were connected.

'Hold on,' I said. 'I need to let the doctor know about this.'

I walked to the registration desk. As I did, the woman behind the desk handed me a sheaf of papers. 'We need to get her checked in,' she said. 'Are you family?'

'No,' I said. 'I'm not sure she has any family in town and I don't know much about her. But she works for Claude, and he might be able to get the paperwork started,' I said. I motioned for Claude to join me before I explained that I might have additional information for the physician and asked her for a piece of paper. I scrawled out a note, repeating what Claude had told me, and watched as the woman behind the desk passed it on to a nurse before returning to the desk. Meanwhile, Claude sat down and scanned the forms.

'I don't know how much of this I can answer,' he muttered.

'Just do what you can for now,' the woman responded. 'We can get the rest from her later.'

I hope so was all I could think.

Claude called Frank at the store to pull her personal file for some of the information; while he was doing that, I sat in the waiting room. Little by little, the adrenaline was receding from my system, leaving me drained. In silence, I continued to think about Callie, hoping for the best but feeling unsettled by the strange and sudden notion that the worst was still to come.

I dropped Claude back off at the store, still fighting the storm and multiple flooded roads before finally making it back to my house. A quick run-through left me pleasantly surprised that the tarp seemed to be working and all the leaks had stopped. Soaking wet again, I threw my clothes in the dryer, put on some sweats, and made another pot of coffee.

While it was brewing, I fired up my laptop and did a little digging on medical sites on possible causes of fainting, then other conditions that might explain her poor color and assorted bruising. There were too many possibilities to consider, some even life-threatening, but nothing definitive until tests were done. Even then, the primary worry right now was the head trauma. I hoped she'd had her CT scan, and that they were already figuring out next steps.

Not that it was any of my business. We were strangers and if getting out of the car earlier that morning was any indication, she might prefer to keep it that way. I wondered again why mentioning her parents had provoked such a violent reaction. Until that moment, she'd been distant; it was only then that Callie had panicked.

Except . . .

I suddenly remembered that she'd seemed to panic when I'd spoken to her at lunch as well. I tried to remember what I'd specifically said that had upset her then, but could only recall generalities and was too tired to think about it any further.

After pouring myself a cup of coffee, I surfed some news sites and checked my email. Most of it was junk that I deleted quickly, but toward the bottom, I opened an email from Marvin Kerman. Though I'd expected a negative reply, I learned that AJ had indeed saved my grandfather's effects and would send them along. He asked for my shipping address and requested a waiver of any legal claims against his client. Attached to the letter was a form I was asked to sign, which I printed, scanned, and faxed back to Kerman. Depending on how quickly the items were sent, it was possible that I'd have them sometime next week.

Hungry again and deciding on a sandwich, I fished some turkey from the refrigerator, then went to the cupboard for a loaf of bread. Like my grandfather, I generally didn't keep a lot of food in the house, but as I pulled down the bread, I suddenly remembered cleaning out all the old food when I'd first moved in. And, like a key turning in a lock, I had a strong hunch as to the identity of the person who'd squatted in my grandfather's house after he'd passed away.

I wasn't absolutely certain, but I felt it had to have been Callie. I'd thrown away a nearly empty jar of peanut butter, something my grandfather wouldn't have had in the house because he was allergic to peanuts, but something Callie ate every day. Claude had also mentioned Callie was almost OCD about cleanliness and aside from the broken back door, the house had been in nearly perfect order when Natalie had walked through. Those things could be written off as coincidences, but given her friendship with my grandfather and no family in the area, where else would she have gone when her trailer burned down? It also explained why she'd been so insistent that she'd done nothing wrong when I'd tried to speak with her at lunch; those adamant and fearful denials made a bit more sense if she'd actually broken into the house, since she knew she'd been guilty.

Added all together, it was convincing if not absolute proof, but over the next few days, I grew even more certain I was right, even as I continued to wonder about her condition. Then, on the following Monday, right after my session with Bowen, I received unexpected confirmation that Callie had indeed been inside my grandfather's house.

A woman identifying herself as Susan Hudson, an administrator in the billing department of the hospital, called the house, asking for my grandfather. I informed her that he'd passed away but that I was the next of kin, and after a bit of hemming and hawing, she finally revealed the real reason for her call.

'Callie,' she told me, 'is using your late grandmother's social security number.'

15

I met with Susan Hudson the following morning. She was a dark-haired, dark-eyed woman in her fifties who seemed to navigate an incredibly difficult job with relatively good cheer. Spending most of the day on the phone arguing with insurance companies, speaking to patients about various past-due accounts, or letting people know that one procedure or another wasn't covered by their health plans would have made me absolutely miserable. She was nonetheless friendly and apparently relieved that I'd come in, which I hadn't anticipated. Motioning for me to take a seat in one of the chairs in front of her desk, she made a quick call, telling someone that I'd arrived. Less than a minute later, a physician entered the office.

'Dr. Adrian Manville,' he said to me, offering his hand. 'I'm the chief medical officer here,' he said.

'Dr. Trevor Benson,' I replied, wondering why he had decided to join us.

'You're a physician?' he asked.

'Orthopedic surgeon,' I said. 'Retired. I hope I didn't do anything wrong by transporting Callie to the hospital myself.'

'Not at all,' Manville responded, taking a seat.

267

'We appreciate you coming in today.'

'I'm still a little confused as to why you needed me.' I met Manville's gaze. 'Or why you're here. I thought this was just about my late grandmother's social security number.'

Susan reached for a file beside her computer. 'We weren't sure what else to do. I understand you're not family, but we were hoping you'd be able to shed some light on the situation.'

'We?'

'The billing department,' she said. 'The hospital. No one here is exactly clear on how we should proceed.'

'I doubt I can be helpful. I don't know anything. I've only met Callie a couple of times and I don't even know her last name.'

'Well, we don't, either.'

'Excuse me?'

'She doesn't have any identification, and we're having trouble verifying anything about her.'

My eyes flashed toward Manville, then back to her. 'Maybe you should start from the beginning? Tell me what you do know.'

'Of course,' Susan said. 'As I mentioned on the phone, Callie is using your grandmother's social security number. Frankly, we were fortunate to catch it. Your grandmother was last here as a patient a long time ago, before all the records were computerized. We've been catching up, but it takes time and we got lucky. Do you have any idea how the patient could have gotten it?'

'I'd be guessing, but I'm assuming that either she found it, or my grandfather gave it to her.'

Susan's pen hovered in place over the file.

'Why would your grandfather have given it to her?'

'Because he always had a fondness for strays. I think she does, too, by the way.'

'Excuse me?'

'He would feed stray animals if they happened to enter his property,' I explained. 'Maybe Callie showed up and he thought she needed his help, too.'

'It's illegal to knowingly let someone use another person's social security number.'

'It'll be hard to press charges,' I said. 'As I mentioned on the phone, my grandfather passed away last fall.'

She scrutinized the file and made some notes before setting her pen aside. 'It's complicated, but because Callie's treatment falls under a charity program we have at the hospital, we're going to need her to be truthful on her admittance forms. There are reporting requirements and paperwork, and the documents need to be accurate.'

'Have you tried asking her?'

'I have,' she said. 'So has Dr. Manville and some other administrators. That's in addition to her regular physicians. At first, we thought the head trauma might have left her confused, but when we spoke to her employer, he verified that was the same social security number she'd given him when she'd been hired. Further, the previous address she listed on the form doesn't exist. After we pointed those things out to her, she stopped answering our questions about it.'

Dr. Manville cleared his throat. 'She's also begun asking when she can be discharged, and that's concerning, too, but for entirely different reasons. Are you sure there's nothing you can tell us about her?'

I shook my head, realizing that everything I'd heard seemed consistent with what I knew of Callie. 'Her name is Callie. She told me she wasn't from New Bern, but I don't have any idea where she lived before. Currently she lives in a trailer park near my house and she works at Slow Jim's Trading Post.' I paused, looking over at Dr. Manville. 'But this is less about a billing issue than something else, right? I'm guessing you think there's a possibility that there might be something seriously wrong with her beyond her head injury. Maybe because she fainted before falling off the ladder, or because of her pallor, or maybe because of something the tests have shown. Maybe even all three. That's why you're worried about her insisting that she be discharged.'

I offered it as a statement, not a question, and Manville straightened slightly in his seat.

'As you know, there are issues regarding medical privacy,' Manville hedged. 'We can't divulge a patient's medical information without their consent.'

That was true, but I could tell by his expression as he spoke that my assumption was correct.

Susan cleared her throat. 'We were hoping you would speak with her, so that at the very least, she'll stay in the hospital long enough to receive the care she needs. And so that we can have accurate information on file and there are no remaining financial obligations for which she might be responsible.'

'Wouldn't either of you be more appropriate for that?'

'We've been trying our best, but she still insists on being discharged,' Susan said. 'She says that she feels fine.'

'You should speak with Claude,' I said. 'Callie works for him, and he knows her a lot better than I do.'

'He came in yesterday,' Susan said. 'He was the one who'd initially filled out the forms and he left his contact information, so we reached out to him. He didn't have any luck with her — she wouldn't answer his questions, either — so he suggested that we ask you. He says that because she knew and liked your grandfather, you might be able to get through to her.'

He obviously didn't know that she'd practically screamed at me the day she collapsed. 'I highly doubt she'll be willing to open up to me.'

'Could you at least try?' Manville said. 'It's important medically. For Callie's sake. We understand you're under no obligation to help, but . . .'

After he trailed off, it was a few seconds before I finally nodded. My grandfather would have wanted me to help her, whatever that meant. Because she'd been important to him, he would have wanted me to treat her that way, too.

'I can't make any promises that she'll cooperate, but I'd be happy to speak with her.'

'Thank you.'

'I do have one condition, though.'

'Yes?'

'Can you get me a HIPAA form? So I can review her case and speak with her physicians?'

'Yes, but you'd still have to convince her to sign it.'

'Let me worry about that.'

Susan pulled out a HIPAA form and after borrowing a pen, I was on my way to Callie's room on the third floor.

The hospital, like every hospital, flooded me with a sense of déjà vu. As soon as I stepped out of the elevator, I saw the same fluorescent lights, the same speckled tile flooring, the same off-white paint on the walls that I remembered from my residency, in Pensacola, and even Kandahar. I followed a sign indicating room numbers, turning down a hallway as I debated which approach to take when I came face-to-face with Callie. I had no doubt that both Susan and Claude had tried the friendly, *we're here to help you* approach, while Manville and her other physicians had probably leaned toward the *we're the professionals here and you should listen to us* style of communication. And yet, Callie still insisted on being discharged, despite her illness. But why?

Because she was angry they were taking away her independence?

Possible, I thought. More likely was the notion that Callie was afraid and possibly on the run. Maybe from her family, from a boyfriend, or from the law, but it was definitely something. I guessed that as soon as she exited, she'd vanish within hours. She'd hit the road and start over somewhere else. It was also possible she'd use my grandmother's social security number again. I didn't personally care whether she did or not, though I had little doubt it would eventually land her in trouble again. I was more concerned that she'd end up in another hospital, maybe when it was too late to help her, if her condition was as dire as Dr. Manville's presence suggested. At the same time, she was old enough to make her own decisions . . .

Or was she?

Was she truly old enough to be on her own? Or was she a minor who'd run away from home?

I walked past the nurses' station, making for Callie's room. Outside, I hesitated only briefly before pushing my way inside with a brisk step. The television was tuned to a daytime talk show, the volume low. Callie was lying in bed, her arm in a cast and her head wrapped in gauze; I surmised she'd had a craniotomy to drain a subdural hematoma. She was hooked up to monitors and her vitals seemed fine. Seeing me, she pointedly turned away, focusing on the television again. I waited for her to speak, but she said nothing.

I walked toward the window and stared out at the view, noting the cars in the lot and the heavily clouded sky. Though the rain had finally stopped yesterday, it had remained gloomy, with more rain in the forecast. After a moment I turned from the window and took a seat in the chair nearest the bed. Callie continued to ignore me, so I figured I'd treat her like any other patient and go straight into it.

'Hi, Callie,' I said. 'I've been told you're not answering important questions and that you want to leave the hospital. Is that right?'

Her lips compressed but otherwise she gave no sign of having heard me.

'People here are on your side and it's not a good idea to ignore what they're telling you. I assume that in addition to your broken arm, you had some buildup of fluid around your brain, which meant you had to have it drained. How are you feeling now?'

She blinked but said nothing.

'It was a very nasty fall. I don't know if you're aware, but I was the one who brought you to the hospital. Is there anything you can remember about it? I was told that you might have fainted or passed out beforehand.'

She finally turned to face me but ignored my question. 'When can I get out of here?'

'It takes time to heal,' I said. 'And head wounds should never be taken lightly.'

'The doctor said that I would only have to stay for a couple of days. I've been here longer than that.'

That was before he knew how sick you are.

'Have you considered answering their questions?'

'I did.' Her voice was truculent.

'Not all of them. And you're not telling the truth.'

Her eyes narrowed. 'Go away. I don't want to talk to you.'

I continued to hold her gaze. Following a hunch, I asked, 'Have they done a bone marrow biopsy yet?'

One of her hands moved reflexively toward her

274

hip. It was the most common spot for a bone marrow biopsy, so I took that as a yes, even though she hadn't answered. Whether she'd received the results was a different question, but not one that I needed answered right now. On her bedside table was a magazine and I reached for it. I laid the form on top of it along with the pen and leaned forward, setting it next to her on the bed.

'I'm going to need you to sign this form,' I said. 'It's a HIPAA form, and it gives me the right to speak with your doctors, review your charts, and discuss your case. You can consider me your advocate if you'd like. Believe it or not, I'm here to help you.'

'I don't need your help.'

'You don't know that. I can answer questions, explain your diagnosis, discuss treatment options with your doctors. You need to be truthful and answer their questions. And for now, you need to stay here.'

'You can't tell me what to do.'

'I think I can.' I leaned back, keeping my tone conversational. 'If you leave the hospital, one of two things is going to happen. Either you're going to end up in another hospital, or you're going to end up in jail.'

'I fell!' she snapped. 'And I didn't ask to come here — you dragged me here. I would have told them that I can't pay.'

'It's not about your bill,' I said. 'You're using my late grandmother's social security number,' I said. 'That's a federal crime. You also broke my back door, so you could stay at my house after

275

your trailer burned down. That's breaking and entering, as well as trespassing. I might even tell them that you're both a minor and a runaway.' I paused. 'Unless, of course, we can make a deal.'

Frankly, I had no idea whether the police would even be interested in any of it, except for her being a possible runaway, and I wasn't even sure about that. But if *nice* or *professional concern* hadn't worked to get her to be more cooperative, then maybe threatening her would. I pulled my cell phone from my pocket, making sure she saw it. 'I'll call the police from here,' I said. 'You can listen in, if you'd like.'

When she focused on the television again, I went on. 'It wasn't that hard to figure out. The only thing I'm not sure about is how you met my grandfather in the first place. Were you walking by the house late one night? Maybe it was raining or you were just worn out and you spotted the barn? You snuck in there, saw the cot — the same one I saw — and crashed for the night. Maybe you stayed a few nights, but I'm guessing my grandfather eventually found you. And instead of running you out once he found you, he probably gave you something to eat. Maybe even let you stay a night or two in the guest room. That's the kind of guy he was. After that, you began to trust him. But you found the social security card in a box beneath the bed. After you helped him with the honey, he suggested to Claude that he hire you, and you used my grandmother's social security number. After that, he passed away. When your place burned down, you broke into the house through the back door and stayed until you were able to rent another trailer. You ate peanut butter and jelly sandwiches and apples while you were there, kept the place clean, and used candles since the power was out. Have I about summed it up?'

Though she didn't answer, her wide-eyed stare confirmed that I was more right than wrong about all of it.

'I also know what you're thinking right now — that you'll bolt from the hospital as soon as I walk out of here. In your condition, I'm guessing you won't get far. Especially since I'll let the nurses know what you're thinking, and I'll be waiting downstairs for the police to arrive.' I paused, letting all of that sink in before leaning forward and tapping the form. 'Your other option is to sign this form, be more cooperative with the people here, and agree to stay in the hospital until you're better. If you do those things, I won't contact the police.' When she made no move toward the form, I held up my cell phone. 'I'm losing patience,' I said, fixing her with a look that let her know I was serious.

Finally, reluctantly, she reached for the form and scribbled her name at the bottom.

'I didn't steal your grandmother's social security number,' she said, putting the pen down. 'He gave it to me.'

Maybe, I thought. *Maybe not.* 'Where are you from, Callie?'

'Florida,' she answered, almost too quickly. Wherever she was from, it wasn't Florida.

'How old are you?'

'Nineteen.'

Not a chance, I thought. I remembered the way she'd reacted when I'd asked about her parents. 'Do you have any family you need me to contact?'

She turned away.

'No,' she said, 'there's no one.'

Again, I didn't believe her.

I brought the signed HIPAA form to the nurses' station, where they promised to enter it into Callie's medical records. I learned the names of her other doctors — one was an oncologist, which further raised my concerns — and when they would be making rounds. I let them know I'd be returning to the hospital later to speak with the oncologist, if she was available. After that, I went back to Callie's room and sat with her awhile. I asked her about favorite books and movies, trying to make small talk, but I could tell she wanted nothing to do with me and I eventually left her room.

By then, the clouds had opened up again and I splashed my way to my SUV. Back at home, I made a late lunch, read about bone marrow biopsies and transplants, and then — killing time — called the contractor I'd hired. I told him that I wanted work started on the roof as soon as I moved to Baltimore, which would hopefully give him enough time to make the arrangements. The tarp, after all, would only last so long.

I thought about the lies Callie had told me,

especially the last one. There had to be someone in her life. I suspected either one or both parents were still alive, but even if she didn't want to speak to them, wasn't there someone else? Brothers or sisters, aunts or uncles, grandparents? Even a favorite teacher or friend? *Anyone?* When people were in the hospital, they almost always wanted support from those they cared about; when faced with something possibly life-threatening, that desire became almost universal. It seemed almost hardwired into human nature, which made me think something awful had happened to her to make her disavow them.

It was possible, of course, that they had a terrible relationship, even abusive. In that case, I supposed I could understand her reluctance to see or speak to them, but depending on what I learned from the oncologist, she might be risking her life by not bringing them here no matter what.

The hours moved slowly throughout the rest of the day, but eventually it was time to go back to the hospital. I swung by the Trading Post for a coffee and talked with Claude a bit. Like me, he hadn't a clue what was going on with Callie or why she wouldn't answer questions. He mentioned nothing about the false social security number that Callie had been using and I wondered if he'd been told about that, guessing that he probably hadn't.

Later, as I pushed through the hospital doors, I realized something else: Since Callie had fallen from the ladder, my hands hadn't trembled, nor had I felt on edge. I'd had no difficulty sleeping and was even feeling more like my old self again. It seemed that in trying to save Callie, I'd somehow ended up saving myself.

I was early for rounds and settled in to wait. Most of the physicians had offices in town and wouldn't leave for the hospital until after their last patient had departed. The nurses on duty described Dr. Mollie Nobles, Callie's oncologist, as having short blond hair cut in a bob and blue eyes, making her nearly impossible to miss. The neurologist, I was told, may or may not be coming, since he'd already been by earlier in the morning.

I took a seat in the lobby near the elevator on Callie's floor, watching people stride past me in both directions, while also noting the quiet efficiency of the nurses as they darted in and out of rooms. I'd always believed nurses were under-appreciated. Half an hour passed, then an hour, but after a couple of years of doing not much of anything, I'd become good at waiting. One by one, physicians began exiting the elevator, but the first four were not the ones I needed. Excellent detective that I am, I noticed that all of them had been males.

The blue-eyed blonde with a bob cut arrived a few minutes after that, looking harried as she exited the elevator, files in hand.

'Dr. Nobles?' I asked, rising from my seat.

She turned. 'Yes?'

'I was hoping I could speak with you about

Callie.' I introduced myself, indicating that there was a HIPAA form on file. 'I know you're busy and probably have a lot of patients to visit, but I'd really love a few minutes of your time.'

'You're with Callie?'

'Kind of,' I hedged. 'For now, anyway.'

'How well do you know her?'

'Not well. I spent some time with her this afternoon, but I'm not family. I'm not sure she'd even consider me a friend. But it's important that I speak with you about her situation.'

'Who are you?'

I explained my relationship, adding that I was also a physician, and we went through the same song and dance that I had with Dr. Manville.

When I finished, she looked down the hall toward Callie's room, then back to me again. 'Yeah,' she finally said. 'Okay. You said the form is on file?'

When I nodded, she went on. 'I'll need to check on that, but do you want to meet in her room in a few minutes?'

'Is there any way we could speak someplace more private?'

She glanced at her watch and did a quick mental calculation. 'All right. But it can't be long. I've got a full house tonight,' she said. 'Let's go to the lounge.'

After she checked the computer in the nurses' station, we took the elevator down to the lounge and found a seat at a small table.

'What can I do for you?' she asked.

'I was wondering if you had the results of the bone marrow biopsy yet.'

'If you don't know her that well, how do you know she had a bone marrow biopsy? And why did she give you permission to speak with me in the first place?'

'I blackmailed her.'

'Excuse me?'

'I threatened to call the police. It's a long story, but hopefully, she'll stick around until she's better. And for now, you're free to speak with me.'

'Blackmailing her might have invalidated the form.'

'Or it might not. I'm not a lawyer. However, the form is on file, so you're technically in the clear.'

She still didn't look persuaded but finally shook her head. 'Frankly, it might make things easier to be able to speak with you. She's been a difficult patient so far and I'm uncertain what to make of all of it.'

'In what way?'

'I don't get the feeling that anything she's told me is true.'

Likewise, I thought. 'I can't help you there. I was more interested in her medical condition.'

'What do you want to know?'

'Can you give me a quick run-through about her case? Just the highlights.'

'For some of this, you might want to speak with the neurologist or the orthopedist.'

'I will if I need to,' I said.

She nodded. 'As you know, she was admitted with a head injury and compound fractures to her arm. The head CT indicated a subdural

282

hematoma. She drifted in and out of conscious-
ness, and we kept her under close evaluation
while we waited for the storm to break. The
hospital here doesn't normally operate on heads,
so we transfer those out. But the helicopters were
grounded, roads were still flooded, and there was
concern that the transport would further increase
her risk. Meanwhile, the fluid continued to build,
and her condition grew steadily worse. We finally
made the decision to perform the craniotomy
at our hospital, and fortunately, a neurosurgeon
from Vidant was able to make it down here
despite the storm. The operation went well. Callie's confusion and dizziness almost immediately
subsided and she's been conscious ever since.
She's no longer slurring her words and has full
motor function, too.'

'She seemed okay when I spoke to her.'

'I thought the same thing yesterday. But you
should speak to the neurologist if you need more
information on those issues. My impression is
that he's pretty confident about her recovery.'

'How about her arm?'

'The ortho was finally able to get to that on
Sunday and it ended up being rather complex
and it took longer than he'd anticipated. Again,
though, he said it went well and he's confident.
You'd have to ask him more about that, though.'

When she didn't add more, I asked, 'And?'

'As you can imagine, there've been a lot of
physicians and specialties involved in her care.
Emergency, neurology, orthopedics, and now
oncology.'

'When were you brought in?'

'Sunday evening,' she said. 'Prior to undergoing treatment for her injuries, she had the usual battery of tests and there were some problems with her blood work. She had low red blood cell, low white blood cell, and low platelet counts, and she needed a transfusion. Because we couldn't find any internal bleeding, there were worries she might have leukemia, so here I am.'

'Which explains the bone marrow biopsy.'

'It's been a very hectic few days with all the doctors and procedures, and we've all spent some time with her. And that's the other problem.'

'Why is that?'

'Because she told us different stories,' Nobles said, 'and no one knows the truth. For starters, she said she was nineteen, but I don't believe that for a minute. She looks like she's fifteen or sixteen. She also told me that her parents had died in an automobile accident last year, that she doesn't have any other family, and has been on her own ever since. On the other hand, she told the orthopedist that they'd died in a house fire. It didn't add up.'

'Maybe she was confused.'

'Maybe early on, but not by Sunday. She was fine — she could add, knew who the president was, knew the day of the week, and everything else. During that round of questioning, she also mentioned that she was from Tallahassee.'

'She told me she was from Florida, too.'

'*I'm* from Tallahassee,' Nobles emphasized. 'I grew up there, went to Florida State, and lived most of my life there. When I asked her what

284

high school she attended — just chatting, you know — she said George Washington High. I'd never heard of it, so I checked my phone and realized it doesn't exist. I asked about a couple of other places — the Alfred Maclay Gardens Park or St. Marks Wildlife Refuge — and though she acted like she'd heard of them, I could tell she hadn't. So I asked if she really was from Tallahassee and after that, she stopped answering my questions. I need to know whether she has family, though, and she won't tell me anything. But she's going to need a bone marrow transplant sooner rather than later, or there's not going to be anything we can do for her. We need to find her family.'

'How bad is the leukemia?'

'I'm sorry,' she said, quickly shaking her head. 'I wasn't clear. Callie doesn't have leukemia. The biopsy shows that she has aplastic anemia.'

'Is that better or worse than leukemia?'

'Six of one, half dozen of the other. Basically, aplastic anemia means she's not producing enough new blood cells, and in her case, the disease is very advanced, so it's a crisis situation. But let's back up a second. How much do you know about bone marrow transplants?'

'Not as much as you do, I'm sure.'

She smiled. 'It can be an arduous process to find an appropriate donor, but basically, in the first step, we try to find donors with matching human leukocyte antigens, or HLAs. There are six major antigens, and with the best donors, all six of the antigens match. Five is less good, four is a possibility but riskier, et cetera. Anyway, after

285

I got the results of the biopsy, I ran Callie's HLAs through the marrow registry, and the best matches we have now are a couple of threes. She needs a better match, which usually means family.'

'Does Callie know yet?'

'No,' she said. 'The results came in earlier this afternoon. She knows that a transplant is a possibility, though. After I leave here, I'm going to share the results with her and hopefully, she'll tell me something about her family. I mean . . . how can she not have any family? She's too young not to have anyone, right?'

Though I agreed with her, I remembered my earlier experience with Callie. 'What if she doesn't tell you anything about them? Or denies their existence again?'

'Then all we can do is pray that another donor shows up in the registry.'

'How long does she have?'

'Hard to know for sure. There's medication and we can keep her alive with the transfusions, but she'll have to remain in treatment and be consistent with it. She doesn't have insurance for that kind of long-term care. She needs a transplant. She needs to be honest, too, so she can be transferred to Vidant in Greenville. They won't take her if she keeps playing games.'

'Why does she need to be transferred?'

'We don't do irradiation at this hospital,' she said, 'but it's not a big deal. I'm already in touch with Felicia Watkins, an oncologist at Vidant, and she's reviewing Callie's files now. I've worked with her before and she's terrific. If we do find a donor, Callie will be in excellent hands.'

'Good to know. Let me know what Callie says.'
'Will you be around?'
'Yeah,' I said. 'I'll be here.'

Nobles took down my number and said she'd be in touch shortly. I decided to wait in the cafeteria, where I ordered a cup of coffee, preoccupied with Callie.

How old was she? Where was she from? What exactly was her relationship with my grandfather, and why had he taken her in? More importantly, were her parents alive and did she have siblings? And why was she alternately lying or stonewalling, when her family might be the only way to possibly save her life?

Of course, she hadn't known the results of the biopsy yet, nor did she know that there were no good matches in the registry. To this point, she might have been stubborn because she'd believed she'd recover, but if she remained silent, then what?

What could be worse than dying?

When the answer didn't come, I reframed the question from Callie's perspective, with a slight variation. *I'd rather die than live with . . .*

There were more possibilities with that option. *My father*, or *my parents*. *My abusive uncle*, and the list could go on from there, any of which would explain her reticence.

But . . . would it really?

Even if she wasn't nineteen and still a minor in an abusive situation, did she realize she could go to a judge and make a request to become emancipated? She'd already been on her own for almost a year, had a job, had a place to live, paid her bills. She was more functional than many actual adults. She didn't have to live with anyone, I reasoned.

Unable to wrap my mind around an answer, I finished my coffee, then went back to the counter to buy an apple. As I munched, I took a break from thinking and watched people in the cafeteria come and go. Eventually, I received a text from Dr. Nobles, asking if I was still at the hospital. When I texted that I was in the cafeteria, she told me to wait, and that she'd be there in a few minutes.

In the silence, I suddenly realized I knew some of the answer to my earlier, rephrased question. I didn't know all of it, however — or the why — and it left me feeling like I was caught in a powerful current, bearing me to an unknown destination.

Nobles joined me at the table a few minutes later.

'What happened?' I asked.

'I explained the results and the reality of the situation, and all the medical options to her,' she said, sounding tired. 'All of it — the risks, what the procedure required, outcomes. Everything. I also asked her where and when her parents died, so I could possibly search for relatives, and again, she got very agitated, like she knew she'd

288

been caught in a lie. She insisted again that she was old enough to make her own decisions and the more I pressed, the more adamant she became about waiting for a better donor in the registry. I'm hoping you'll have better luck.'

'If she wouldn't tell you, why do you think she'd tell me?'

'I don't know,' Nobles answered, massaging her temples. 'Maybe you can blackmail her again.'

Visiting hours were nearly over by the time I reached Callie's room. This time, the door was open, the television still blaring, and Callie pointedly kept her eyes focused on the screen. She was a predictable thing.

I sat in the chair again and leaned forward, bringing my hands together. I decided to go all in, guns blazing, with a gamble.

'So,' I said, 'you're a liar. Your parents are alive.'

She flinched before turning toward me and I knew I was right.

'Go away.'

'I should have guessed,' I said, ignoring her. 'Anyone who breaks the law like you have isn't generally an honest person in the first place. But why lie about your parents being dead? Why lie when you told me that there was no one I could contact?'

Knowing she wouldn't answer, I went on. 'I got to thinking about the possible reasons for telling your doctor that they were dead, none of which make a lot of sense to me. Even if my dad had been the most awful man in the world, I'd want him to be tested if he could save me. Just so I could make sure I'd be alive and well and able to spit in his face afterward. But if he wasn't an awful guy, how do you think he'll feel if you die and he finds out that he could have helped you?'

She said nothing.

'And what about your mom? Is she a monster, too? If so, why sacrifice yourself? Isn't that giving her exactly what she wants? But if she's not all bad, then don't you think she'll care if you live or die?'

She blinked and I took my hunch a step further.

'And let's talk about your brothers and sisters. How about them? Don't you think they might feel guilty? If any of them could have saved you?'

'They won't care,' she insisted, her voice a hoarse growl.

Bingo. She had siblings, which made her response that much more interesting. 'How about you? Do you care if you live or die?'

'I won't die.'

'You need a bone marrow transplant.'

'I know. Dr. Nobles told me.'

'Do you have any questions about it?'

'No.'

'So you understand that unless they find a matching donor quickly, there might not be anything they can do to save you.'

'They'll find a donor.'

'What if they don't? What then?'

This time, she didn't answer.

'I know you're scared,' I said, softening. 'But no matter what happened with your family, it's not worth dying over. But that's what's going on, isn't it? You'd rather die than live with . . . *yourself*. For something *you* did.'

I clocked her sharp inhale, before I went on. 'Whatever it is, it can't be that bad. I'm sure they don't want you to die.'

Her eyes started to glisten.

'Or how about this? If you don't want to see them, I'm sure the hospital can make arrangements so that you don't have to. We just need to get them tested, and they don't have to come here to do that. All you have to do is tell me how I can contact them.'

She remained silent, her knees drawn up to her body, and in that moment, I caught sight of the lonely stray that my grandfather must have noticed when he'd found her in the barn.

'I'm not going to let you die,' I said.

Strangely, I realized that I meant it. But Callie simply turned away.

As far as I could tell, I only had two options to help Callie: I could get the police involved, or I could try to find her family myself. But could the police do anything if she refused to answer their questions? Unless her fingerprints were on file somewhere, she wouldn't necessarily be in any of the databases; if she insisted to them that she was an adult, they might not be interested at all.

What, after all, was the crime she was committing? I supposed I could tell them about the social security number and the break-in, but I didn't want to get her into any trouble if I didn't have to. Like her doctors, I simply wanted her to get better. If it came to that, I'd make the call, but by the time I woke the following morning, I wanted to try something else first.

Not long after the sun had risen, I hopped in the SUV. No one was on the roads, and thankfully the sky had finally cleared. As I rolled past the trailer park, I studied the trailers. Six were in livable condition and of those, four had vehicles parked in front of them. Because Callie walked everywhere, I assumed she lived in one of the other two. Thankfully, the evil, angry dog with teeth the size of bacon was nowhere to be seen.

I went back to the house, waited until midmorning, then drove past the trailer park again. Of the four vehicles that were there earlier, three of them had left, which I took as a good sign that I might be able to poke around without being noticed. If questioned by anyone who lived there, I'd tell them that Callie had asked me to bring some of her things to the hospital.

I inched the car onto an old logging track up the road and started walking back toward the trailer park. It was already getting warm, the crazy late-spring weather suddenly acting like summer. The humidity was oppressive and I could feel the sweat beginning to tack the shirt to my back. At the trailer park, I made my way toward the first of the two trailers I'd noticed earlier, trying to avoid the occasional chicken. It sat toward the back, close to the charred remains of Callie's former residence, and I saw no lights blazing from inside. When I got closer, I spotted a grill out front, a pair of roller skates on the porch, and a child's wagon filled with plastic toys. Unless Callie had children — which I doubted — this one wasn't hers.

I changed direction, heading to the other one. As I reversed course, I saw a figure emerge from one of the other trailers, the one with the car parked out front. He was an older man wearing overalls and I could feel his eyes on me as I walked past him. I raised a hand in greeting, trying to make it seem like I belonged. Instead of waving back, he scowled.

As I approached what I thought to be Callie's trailer, I began to get a good feeling. There were no curtains in the windows, no toys in the yard, no flowerpots or wind chimes or engine parts, which were typical of the others. It looked like the kind of place a girl would live who had barely enough money to pay her bills and hadn't accumulated much of anything.

Peeking over my shoulder, I noticed the man who'd stepped outside earlier was gone, probably back inside. I hoped he wasn't watching as I sidled toward one of the windows and peered inside, taking in a small, functional, and exceedingly clean kitchen. There were no dishes or silverware in the sink or on the counters, nor any spills on the floor. In one of the corners, I saw jars of peanut butter and jelly lined up neatly next to a loaf of bread.

I scooted to another window and peered in, noting a couch futon and a pair of small mismatching tables, maybe the ones that Claude had given her. There was a lamp, too, but otherwise it was about as spartan as a place could get.

I paced around the trailer, searching for more windows, but there weren't any. On a whim, I tried the doorknob and was surprised when it turned in my hand. When she'd left for work, Callie hadn't locked the door. Then again, there didn't seem to be much worth stealing.

I hesitated. It was one thing to peek in her windows; it was another thing to enter her home. I reminded myself that Callie had broken into my grandfather's house and that I still needed answers, so I pushed open the door and entered.

It didn't take long to go through the trailer. There was no chest of drawers; instead, she had stacked her folded clothes against a wall. In the closet, I found a few blouses and pants on hangers, and two pairs of shoes. A worn University of Georgia Bulldogs sweatshirt sat on the top shelf, but most everything else looked like thrift store finds.

There were no photographs, diaries, or journals, though on the wall in the kitchen, I noted a hanging calendar featuring picturesque Georgia sites, including Tallulah Gorge and Raven Cliff Falls, with her work schedule neatly outlined, and a few dates throughout the year marked in red marker. M's birthday in June, R's birthday in August, T and H's birthday in October, and D's birthday in December. The first initial of someone she knew, but nothing that would tell me anything more than that.

But it made me wonder . . .

Why, unless she was fond of or drawn to Georgia, would she have purchased this particular calendar? Or have a Georgia Bulldogs sweatshirt separated from her other clothing?

I rifled through the drawers and cupboards in the kitchen, then did the same in the bathroom. Again, the stark absence of belongings yielded few clues. I looked for a phone, hoping for an answering machine, but there was none.

I have no idea how long I was in the house, and I gazed warily through the kitchen window in the direction of where I'd spotted the old man earlier. I didn't want him to see me leaving, but luckily he hadn't reappeared.

I exited the front door quickly, hoping to make a clean getaway, but instantly registered the maroon car emblazoned with the word SHERIFF across the doors. I felt my stomach drop.

A moment later, it dropped even further when I spotted Natalie emerging from the car, and for a long time, all I could do was stare at her.

16

If I was stunned to see her, she seemed equally taken aback. When she finally stepped out from behind the open car door, I was reminded of how she looked the first time I'd ever met her. As I stood before her, it seemed like a lifetime ago.

'Trevor?' she ventured, closing the door.

'Natalie,' I said, finding my voice.

'What are you doing here? I got a call about a possible burglary in progress.'

The old man. 'You mean this?' I waved at Callie's trailer. 'I didn't take anything.'

'Did you just break into someone's house? I saw you walking out.'

'The door was unlocked.'

'And you went inside?'

'It's good to see you, by the way.'

'This is not a social call.'

'I know.' I sighed. 'I guess I should explain what I was doing.'

Over her shoulder, I spotted the older man stepping out onto the porch. Part of me wanted to thank him for being so conscientious.

'Well?' she asked.

'The girl who lives here is named Callie. She's in the hospital right now. So I came by to check on some things.'

'Does she know you're here?'

'Not exactly.'

'Not exactly?' She frowned. 'What kind of things were you checking?'

'I'm trying to help her and it was the only thing I could think to do.'

'Are you being purposely evasive?'

Behind her, the old man had climbed down from his porch and was inching closer, no doubt as curious as Natalie was.

'Is there someplace we can speak in private?'

For the first time, her gaze faltered.

'I don't think that's such a good idea. First, I need to understand what's going on here.'

Clearly she anticipated that in addition to explaining about Callie, I'd try to speak with her about the way we'd said goodbye. Which was exactly what I intended, if given the chance.

'I've told you what I'm doing. There's a girl in the hospital and she needs my help. I came here to do just that.'

'How can you help her if she doesn't know you're here?'

'Please,' I said. 'I don't want to speak in front of an audience.' I nodded at the neighbor, who now stood only several feet away.

'Did you remove anything from the premises?'

'No.'

'Damage anything?'

'No,' I insisted. 'Feel free to go inside and check. The door's unlocked.'

'It's still trespassing,' she pointed out.

'I highly doubt that she'll press charges.'

'Is that so?'

I moved closer, keeping my voice low. 'She was the one who broke into my grandfather's house. She also stole my grandmother's social security number. And she's very sick. Having to deal with a sheriff is probably the last thing she wants.'

'You know I'm going to have to speak with her about this, don't you?'

'Good luck,' I said. 'She may not speak to you at all.'

'And why is that?'

By then, the older man was nearly within hearing distance. Another neighbor, too, had appeared and was heading our way. When I saw a third door open and yet another woman emerge, I leaned in.

'Please,' I pleaded. 'It's no one else's business. I'm saying this for Callie's sake, not mine.'

'I can't just let you walk away. People saw you trespassing.'

'Then put me in your car. You can bring me to mine.'

'Where's yours?'

'Up the road. You can't miss it. I think the folks around here would be happier if I got in. Like I was in trouble.'

'You are in trouble.'

'I don't think so.' When she didn't respond, I turned toward her car, noting that all three neighbors had congregated a short distance away and were casting wary glances at me. 'If you'd like, we can speak at the station.'

I walked past her and slid into the back seat of the cruiser before Natalie could stop me. For a few seconds, she continued to stand outside the car before finally approaching the gathered neighbors. I watched as the old man began motioning toward me, clearly exercised. Natalie nodded, saying little as the man went on, and after a few minutes, she returned to the car and got in.

As Natalie started the engine and pulled onto the main road, her eyes flashed to the rearview mirror. I could see her irritation at being put in a situation she clearly wished she could have avoided. 'Which way to your vehicle?'

'To the left,' I said. 'A couple hundred yards.'

'I should just bring you to the station.'

'Then how would I get my SUV?'

I heard her sigh. It took less than a minute for her to reach the spot where I'd parked. When I tried to get out, I realized that the door was locked. Natalie graciously stepped out and opened the door for me.

'Thank you,' I said.

'What's going on?' she asked, crossing her arms. 'I want the full story.'

'I'm thirsty,' I said. 'Let's go to my house.'

'Not a chance.'

'It's getting warm out here and it's going to take a while.'

'What's the girl's name again?'

'Callie.'

'I know that much,' she said. 'What's her last name?'

'That's what I was trying to find out.'

Natalie followed me back to the house and turned up the drive, eventually coming to a stop beside me. I got out of the car first but waited for her and we approached the house together. I remembered doing the same thing after we'd visited the beehives and I felt a sudden stab of loss. We had been drawn to each other and fallen in love, only to have her end it. What had I done wrong? Why hadn't she given us a chance?

I led the way inside to the kitchen, taking down two glasses from the cupboard and turning to her. 'Tea or water?'

Her eyes flickered to the porch, which looked different than it had the night of our dinner. 'Homemade sweet tea?'

'What else?'

'Yes, please.'

I filled our glasses, then added ice. Handing her a glass, I motioned at the porch.

'Can't you just tell me what's going on without making an event out of it?' she demanded, clearly exasperated.

'I just want to sit down,' I said. 'Don't make it into something that it isn't.'

On the back porch and thankful for the shade, I waited for her to join me. After a few beats, she reluctantly took her place in the other rocker. 'Well?' she asked. 'This better be good.'

I related everything from the very beginning, finishing with the hospital and an attempt to locate Callie's family by looking for clues in the trailer. Through it all, Natalie remained quiet but attentive.

'You really think she might die?'

'She *will* die,' I said. 'Medicine and transfusions can help in the short run, but in her case, it

300

will eventually be fatal. It's actually the same disease that killed Eleanor Roosevelt.'

'Why didn't you call the police?'

'I didn't want to get her in any trouble and for now, she has to remain in the hospital no matter what. Besides, if she won't speak to the doctors, she probably won't speak to the police, either.'

She considered that. 'Did you find any clues in the house?'

'Not much,' I said. 'Probably because of the fire, there wasn't a lot there. I did find a Georgia Bulldogs sweatshirt and a calendar with scenes of Georgia, though.'

'Do you think that's where she's from?'

'I don't know. Maybe.'

'That's not much.'

'No,' I admitted. 'It isn't. And Georgia's a big state. I wouldn't even know where to begin.'

She squinted at me. 'Why do you care so much?'

'I'm not just handsome and rich. I'm also a good guy.'

For the first time, Natalie cracked a wry smile. I remembered that smile and was struck by how much I'd missed it, how much I still wanted it to be part of my life. I think she knew what I was thinking because she turned away. Finally, she went on.

'Do you want me to try to talk to her?'

'I think it would make her clam up even more.'

'I could try for fingerprints.'

'Do you think that would help? If she's never been arrested?'

'Probably not.'

'What should I do, then?'

'I don't know. Maybe she'll start talking when she starts feeling worse.'

'Maybe.' I hesitated before going on. 'Can I ask you a question?'

She seemed to sense what was coming. 'Trevor . . . please don't.'

'I just want to know what happened between us. What did I do wrong?'

'You didn't do anything wrong.'

'Then what was it?'

'It had nothing to do with you and everything to do with me.'

'What does that mean?'

'It means that I was scared,' she said in a low voice.

'Of me?'

'You. Me. Us.'

'What was so frightening?'

'All of it,' she said. Her gaze took in the creek, anguish etched in the lines of her face. 'I loved every moment with you,' she admitted. 'At the park, tending the beehives, our dinner in Beaufort. The boat ride and dinner here. Everything was . . . just the way I hoped it would be. It was perfect. But . . .'

She trailed off.

'But what?'

'You're leaving,' she said. 'Soon, right?'

'I told you that I didn't have to move to Baltimore. I would have stayed. I can make other arrangements. It's not a big deal.'

'But it *is* a big deal. It's your next career. It's Johns Hopkins and you can't put that on hold for me.'

302

'You do realize I'm old enough to make my own decisions, right?'

Wearily, she stood from her chair and walked to the railing. After a moment, I rose and joined her. Across the river, cypress trees stretched their whitewashed trunks from the ancient waters. Her profile was as lovely as ever. I waited for her to say something, anything, but she continued to avoid my gaze.

'I know this is hard for you,' I said, 'but if you put yourself in my situation, can you understand how baffling this feels to me?'

'I do understand. And I know I'm not really answering your questions, but please know how heartbreaking that is to me.'

As she spoke, I had the feeling that not only were we speaking entirely different languages, but that translation was impossible.

'Did you even love me, Natalie?'

'Yes,' she said, turning to look at me for the first time. Her voice was ragged. 'I did. And I still do. Saying goodbye to you was one of the hardest things I've ever had to do.'

'If I meant so much to you, then why did it have to end?'

'Because sometimes, that's just the way things have to be.'

I was about to respond when I heard the sound of a vehicle pulling onto the property and crackling over the gravel driveway. I heard a door slam, followed by a rapping at the door. I had no idea who it could be; other than Natalie, visitors to the house were practically nonexistent. I desperately wanted to continue the conversation with Natalie — or begin a conversation that I understood — but Natalie nodded toward the house.

'Someone's at the door,' she said.

'I know. But . . . '

'You should probably answer it. And I need to get back to work.'

Though I could have asked if we could continue the conversation, I already knew what her answer would be and retreated into the house.

At the door, I recognized the brown uniform of a UPS delivery driver. He was about my age, thin and wiry, and he handed me a medium-sized box. For a moment, I tried to recall if I'd ordered something, but came up empty. He held out an electronic clipboard, along with the attached pen.

'Could you please sign for this?'

I set the box down, scribbled my name, then closed the door behind me. On the return label, I saw the address of a law firm in South Carolina, and it all came rushing back.

My grandfather's things.

I brought the box to the kitchen. Natalie came in from the porch as I placed it on the table. I hesitated, torn. I wanted to open the box immediately; I also longed to keep Natalie here, to continue to try to reach her and persuade her that she was making a mistake for both of us.

'New pots and pans?'

'No,' I said. Pulling out a penknife, I began to cut through the tape. 'It's from the lawyer for the tow truck guy. He had my grandfather's things.'

'After all this time?'

'Lucky break,' I said.

304

'I'll let you get to it.'

'If you wouldn't mind, could you wait? There might be something in here that I need help figuring out.'

I flipped open the lids and removed some crumpled newspaper. On top was a baseball cap, one I recognized from many long-ago summers. It was worn and stained, but I greeted the sight of it like an old and beloved friend. I wondered whether he'd been wearing it when he'd had his stroke and it had fallen off, or whether it had been in the passenger seat beside him. I didn't know; all I knew was that it was coming with me, wherever I ended up in life.

I found his wallet next, bent and molded, the leather creased. Whatever cash had been in it had been taken, but I was far more interested in the photographs. There were a couple of Rose, a photo of me when I was a child, and a family portrait that my mother must have sent him when I was in high school. There was a photo of my mom and dad as well. In a ziplock baggie, I found his car registration, along with some pens and a pencil with bite marks in it, all of which were probably taken from the glove compartment. Beneath that was a small duffel bag, and I pulled it out. Inside were socks and underwear, pants and two shirts, along with a toothbrush, toothpaste, and deodorant. Wherever he was going, he didn't intend to stay long, but nothing I'd found got me any closer to knowing where that might be.

The answer came at the bottom of the box, in the form of two highway maps that had been paper-clipped together. They were at least thirty years old, yellowed and thin, and when I unfolded them, I noticed routes highlighted in yellow. One route led north toward Alexandria, where he'd gone for my parents' funeral, but the route he'd traced avoided the interstate, following smaller, more rural highways.

I could feel Natalie at my shoulder and watched as she traced the other highlighted route, leading west on other rural highways toward Charlotte, then across the border into South Carolina. *Easley?* Though it was impossible to know for sure, the highlighter ink looked fresh, more vivid than the other highlighted route on the map.

The second map showed the states of South Carolina and Georgia. For an instant, I was afraid that my grandfather hadn't marked it. But I quickly realized that he had. It picked up where the other map had left off. He'd circumvented Greenville — the detour kept him north of the city — but then caught the highway that led directly to Easley.

And then kept going.

Through South Carolina and into Georgia, where the route ended in a small town northeast of Atlanta, right on the edge of the Chatta-hoochee National Forest. From Easley, it wasn't that far — I'd guess less than two hours, even at speeds my grandfather drove — and as I saw the name of the town, I felt crucial pieces of the puzzle begin to lock together.

The name of the town was Helen.

17

Even as I stared in shock, I felt my mind flashing back to the conversation with the old men on the porch at the Trading Post, and I thought about the ride I'd taken in the boat, when I knew in my heart that my grandfather wouldn't have gone to visit a woman named Helen. It hadn't made sense to me, because my grandfather had still been in love with the same woman he'd always loved, even though she had long since passed away.

Natalie, too, was staring at the name. She was standing close to me, close enough to touch, and I remembered the night I'd taken her in my arms. She'd felt so perfect and I thought we were perfect together, but she wasn't willing to tell me the truth of what was really going on with her. Now, as I caught the faint sounds of her exhales, I noticed she was studying the map in the same way I was. I sensed that pieces were beginning to fall into place for her as well, even if I was no closer to understanding how she felt about me.

Instead of speaking, I scanned the maps again, making sure there were no other clues, no other possible destinations. I ran the timeline in my head — just as I'd done before — and felt again that my grandfather must have known the trip might be risky for him because of the distance, as well as his age. Whatever the reason, it had been important, and I could think of only a single possible reason.

When I glanced at Natalie, I suspected I was further along in my suspicion than she was. Which made sense, because it was my mystery, not hers. As she continued to ponder, her brow was furrowed slightly, and as always, I thought she was beautiful.

'Helen, Georgia?' Natalie finally asked.

'So it seems.'

'Did he know anyone there?'

That was the question, wasn't it? I tried to remember whether I'd ever heard him mention the town, or even whether he'd mentioned a friend from anywhere in Georgia. Someone from the war, or a work buddy who'd moved away, perhaps, or maybe even a fellow beekeeper. But it didn't take long for me to realize that my grandfather's life had always been about New Bern, while Callie had both a sweatshirt and a calendar from Georgia.

'I doubt it,' I finally said. 'But I think he knew someone *from* there.'

It took her a few moments to intuit what I was thinking. 'You mean Callie?'

I nodded. 'I think he went to find her family.'

'Why? She didn't get sick until last week.'

'I don't know. But if we assume Callie was from Georgia and he was traveling to Helen, Georgia, it makes sense.'

'That's a little thin, don't you think? And if she's so secretive, how would he have even known she was from Helen?'

'I don't have all the answers yet. But they did know each other. He cared about her enough to help her get a job. He was going to Helen for a reason. Like me, maybe he thought she was a runaway and wanted to help her.'

'Are you going to ask Callie about it?'

I didn't answer right away, another recovered memory suddenly leaping to mind. When I'd approached Callie during her lunch, she hadn't become upset until I'd asked specifically whether my grandfather had ever mentioned Helen. At which point, she'd panicked.

I said as much to Natalie, though she still looked doubtful.

'I know I'm right,' I added. 'Can't you see how it all fits?'

Natalie exhaled. 'Gimme a few minutes, okay? I need to make a phone call. I'll be right back.'

Without further explanation, Natalie walked out the front door. I watched through the window as she tapped some numbers into her phone, then a couple more. It was more than a few minutes — closer to ten — before she finally came back inside.

'I called the police department in Helen.'

'And?'

'I asked them to check on any runaways named Callie. No one with that name is missing.'

'Are they sure?'

'It's a small town,' she explained. 'Super small. Like six hundred people. He would know. There are only a few runaways in the books at all in the last five years.'

Despite her findings, I still knew I was right. I could feel it and knew I had to check it out. Though I could drive, flying would be easier. I took a seat at the kitchen table and booted up my computer.

'What are you doing?' she asked.

'I'm checking on flights to Atlanta.'

'You're going to Helen after what I just told you? To do what? Knock on doors? Ask people on street corners?'

'If I have to,' I said.

'What if she lived in the country somewhere? Or in the next town over?'

'It doesn't matter,' I said.

'You're doing all this for a girl you barely know?'

'I told her that I wasn't going to let her die.'

'And you mean that?' Her tone verged on disbelief.

'Yes.'

She was quiet for a moment and when she spoke again, her voice was softer.

'Assuming you're right and she ran away from home . . . why would she rather die than contact them?'

'That's what I'm trying to find out, and it's the reason I'm going. I'd like to ask a favor, though.'

'What's that?'

'Call the police department again. Maybe the sheriff, too, while you're at it, to let them know I'm coming. I'm sure I'll need to speak with them. Maybe you can help make that part a little easier.'

'When do you think you'll be there?'

'Tomorrow,' I said. 'There's a flight leaving around eleven. If I rent a car, I should be in Helen by early afternoon.'

'How long are you planning to stay there?'

'A day or two. If I can't find any answers there, I'll have to try to convince Callie to speak to me again.'

She considered my request. 'I can make the calls, but I don't know if it will do any good. You're not in law enforcement and you're not her family.'

'Any recommendations?'

'How about if I come with you?' she said.

For a moment, I wasn't sure if I'd heard her correctly. 'You'd like to come?'

'If she's technically a missing person, law enforcement does have a bit of responsibility.'

I tried not to smile. 'I'll need your date of birth so I can book the tickets.'

'I can take care of it.'

'It'll be easier to do both reservations at once.'

She gave me the information and as I began to type, she suddenly interrupted me.

'Wait.' Her expression was serious. 'Before I go, I have one condition.'

I already knew that she was going to tell me to book separate hotel rooms, and that she was only accompanying me in a law enforcement capacity. In other words, I wasn't to attempt to rekindle things between us.

'I want you to do something tonight. I can pick you up after work.'

'Yes?'
Her exhale was one of surrender.
'I want you to meet my husband.'

18

I was too stunned to respond. Suddenly, everything fell into place: why she'd been so uncomfortable at the farmers' market when the dentist had seen us together, why she preferred to meet at out-of-the-way locations. Why she'd suddenly ended our relationship . . .

But not everything added up . . .

Before I could summon anything to say, she hurriedly moved to the front door and opened it, pausing on the threshold.

'I know you have questions,' she said without turning to face me, 'but you'll understand everything later. I'll pick you up at six.'

I finished booking the tickets, made hotel reservations, read the reviews for some restaurants in Helen, then spent the rest of the day trying to figure out the nature of Natalie's marriage. Were they separated but now trying to work things out? Did they have an open marriage? I even flirted with the idea that the husband had passed away and we'd be making a trip to the cemetery, but none of those answers seemed to fit with the woman I'd come to know. And why did she want me to meet him?

Was that what married people did these days when another person was interested in their spouse? *Hey, let's all meet so we can talk this through?*

What was I supposed to say to him? Should I avow my ignorance at the fact that she'd been married? Admit that I'd begged her to start a new life with me but that she'd nonetheless chosen him?

I spent the rest of the afternoon spinning through questions and possible answers. In the meantime, I packed a duffel bag for my trip to Helen and went through my grandfather's box again, searching for more clues without luck.

When Natalie pulled into my drive, I stepped out of the house before she'd even had a chance to turn off the engine. As I got in, she offered a mysterious, unreadable look at me before directing the car back onto the road. Because she remained quiet, I did too.

My first surprise was that instead of driving to her house, we took the highway heading east, toward the coast. No longer in uniform, she was wearing jeans and a cream-colored blouse, more casual than dressy. Around her neck hung the gold chain she was never without. 'Do you and your husband live together?' I finally asked.

She adjusted her hands on the wheel. 'Not anymore,' she responded without elaborating further.

My mind flashed to the idea that he'd passed away and again, we settled into silence. After ten or fifteen minutes, Natalie slowed the car and left the highway, turning onto a commercial road I'd passed countless times but had never really seen. There was a shopping center to the right;

on the left, fronted by a cheerful, tree-shaded parking lot, was a single-story brick building that looked as though it had been constructed sometime in the last five years. As soon as I saw the name of the place, I felt my heart sink.

It wasn't the cemetery.

It was worse.

We parked out front near the entrance, in the near-empty visitors' lot. After exiting the car, Natalie pulled a small bag from the back seat, and we headed toward the double glass doors of the entrance. At the sign-in desk, a woman in a uniform smiled as we approached.

'Hi, Mrs. Masterson. How are you?'

'I'm fine, Sophia,' Natalie said. She signed her name into the visitors' log, chatting with the woman like an old friend. 'How are you? How's Brian?'

'The usual. He's driving me crazy. The way he reacts, you'd think that cleaning your room is worse than scrubbing septic tanks.'

'He's still a teenager. How's he doing in school?'

'No complaints there, thank goodness. It's just me he seems to hate.'

'He doesn't hate you, I'm sure,' Natalie said with a sympathetic smile.

'Easy for you to say.'

Natalie turned to me. 'This is Trevor Benson. He's a friend of mine and he'll be visiting, too.'

Sophia directed her attention to me. 'Nice to meet you, Mr. Benson. Would you mind signing in, too?'

'Of course.'

315

As I signed in, Sophia asked, 'Do you want me to walk with you?'

'No,' Natalie answered. 'I know the way.'

We left the desk and proceeded down the corridor. It was well-lit and clean, with wood-laminate flooring and wrought iron benches between the doors. Here and there were artificial ficus trees in large pots, no doubt intended to provide a soothing environment for visitors.

Eventually we reached our destination, and Natalie paused before pushing open the door. My heart contracted as I watched her steel herself before walking into the room.

'Hi, Mark,' she said. 'It's me again. Surprise.'

Mark lay in the bed with his eyes closed, hooked up to what I knew to be feeding tubes. He was thin, his face partially sunken, but it was still possible to glimpse the handsome man he once had been. I guessed that he was a few years younger than I was, which made everything even worse. Natalie went on, her tone almost conversational. 'Trevor, this is Mark, my husband. Mark, I'd like you to meet Trevor.'

When she gestured at me, I cleared my throat. 'Hi, Mark,' I said.

Mark could not answer. As I stared at him, Natalie's voice seemed to float toward me from afar. 'He's been in a persistent vegetative state for almost fourteen months now,' she offered. 'He had a resistant strain of bacterial meningitis.'

I nodded, my stomach in knots as Natalie approached the bed. After setting her bag beside him, she used her fingers to part his hair, and spoke to him as though I wasn't in the room.

316

'How are you feeling?' she asked. 'I know it's been a few days since I've visited, but I've been super busy at work. I saw on the sign-in sheet that your mom came by earlier. I'm sure she was happy to see you. You know how much she worries about you.'

I stood in place, feeling like an intruder. When she realized I hadn't moved, she motioned toward the chair. 'Make yourself comfortable,' she said to me before turning her attention back to Mark.

'The research isn't clear on how much patients really experience when in a vegetative state.' Even though she remained focused on Mark, I knew the words were meant for me. 'Some patients wake up and remember certain things, others wake up and don't remember anything at all, so I try to visit a few times a week just in case.'

I nearly collapsed in the seat and leaned forward, propping my forearms on my thighs, watching.

'Trevor's an orthopedist,' she said to Mark, 'so he might not know exactly what a persistent vegetative state is or how it differs from a coma.' She continued in a gentle yet matter-of-fact tone. 'I know we've talked about all this before, but humor me, okay, sweetheart? You know your lower brain stem is still working so you can breathe on your own, and sometimes, you even open your eyes and blink. Your reflexes still work, too. Of course, you still can't eat on your own yet, but you have the hospital for that, right, honey? You also get physical therapy so your muscles don't atrophy. That way, when you wake up, you'll be able to walk or use a fork or go fishing like you used to.'

There was none of the excruciating sadness in her demeanor that I felt in witnessing the scene play out before me. Maybe she was used to the experience, as numb to it all as I was heartsick about it. Natalie went on.

'I know they shave you here at the hospital, but you know how much I still like to do that for you when I visit. And it looks like your hair needs a bit of a trim, too. Do you remember when I used to cut your hair in the kitchen? I don't know how you ever talked me into that. It's not like I was any good, but you always insisted. I think you just liked me standing so close to you.'

She pulled out a washcloth and can of shaving cream, as well as a razor. To me, she asked, 'Would you mind putting some warm water on the washcloth? The sink is in the bathroom.'

I did as she asked, making sure it was the right temperature before bringing it back to her. She smiled with an expression of gratitude, then gently dabbed the washcloth to his cheeks.

'Trevor is moving to Baltimore soon,' she said, beginning to lather his face. 'He's going to become a psychiatrist. I'm not sure if I mentioned that to you before. He told me that he struggled with PTSD after he was injured and he's hoping to help veterans who have the same issue. He's the one with the beehives, remember? And the one who brought me to see the alligators? I told you about that. Like I mentioned, he's been a good friend to me. I'm sure the two of you would get along well.'

When ready, she began to shave him, the movements graceful. 'Oh, I forgot to tell you. I saw your father last week at the dealership. He seems to be doing okay. He stopped losing weight, at least. I know he doesn't visit as much as your mom does, but it's hard for him since the two of you worked together, too. I hope you always knew how much he loved you. I know he wasn't great at saying it when you were little, but he does. Did I tell you that your parents invited me on their boat for the Fourth of July? The problem is, my family's going to be at the beach, and they want me there. I hate when that happens . . . I guess I could split the time, but I haven't decided yet. And all of that's even assuming I'll get the day off, which I probably won't. It's no fun being the low man on the totem pole.'

When she was finished with the shave, she wiped his face with the washcloth again, then ran her finger over his cheeks.

'Feels better, I'll bet. You never were the scruffy type. But let me trim some of your hair, too, while I'm here.'

She took out a pair of scissors and went to work; because Mark was prone, she was careful to put the trimmings in the bag. 'I used to make such a mess when I did this, so be patient with me, okay? I don't want you to get itchy. Oh, I heard from your sister Isabelle this week. She's expecting her first child in August. Can you believe that? She used to swear that she never wanted kids, and now she's singing an entirely different song. I don't know if I'll be able to make it up there for the birth, but I'm sure I'll get there before the end of the year. I want to give her a chance to settle in first.'

Her patter continued while she finished cutting his hair. Afterward, she gently lifted his head and slid out the pillow. She removed the pillowcase, shook it a couple of times, and examined it to make sure it was clean before reversing the process, putting the pillow back in place. She adjusted the sheet and kissed his lips with a tenderness that nearly brought a tear to my eye.

'I miss you, sweetheart,' she whispered. 'Please try to get better soon, okay? I love you.'

She reached for her bag, then stood from the bed and motioned toward the door. I led the way out into the corridor, and we retraced our footsteps to the car. When we arrived, she pulled out the keys. 'I could use a glass of wine,' she said. 'Are you up for that?'

'Without a doubt.'

We went to a bar in Havelock called Everly's. It wasn't too far from the hospital and I had the sense when we walked in that it wasn't Natalie's first visit to the place. After ordering our drinks, we found a quiet booth, partially sheltered from the noise.

'Now you know,' she said.

'I'm very sorry for what you're going through. It must be awful.'

'It is,' she admitted. 'It's like nothing I ever imagined.'

'What do the physicians say?'

320

'After three months, the chances for recovery are very slight.'

'What happened? If you don't want to talk about it, I'll understand.'

'It's all right. You're not the first to ask. A year ago last April, for our third anniversary, we spent a long weekend in Charleston. As crazy as it sounds, neither of us had ever been there before and we'd heard so much about it. We left Thursday night. He told me that he felt tired and he had a headache, but who doesn't toward the end of a workweek? Anyway, we had a nice day on Friday despite his headache, and then on Saturday, he got a fever. It got worse as the day went on, so we went to the emergency room and he was diagnosed with the flu. We were supposed to be heading home on Sunday anyway, so neither of us was too worried about it. But in the car the next day, his fever kept getting higher and higher. I wanted to stop in Wilmington, but he told me to just keep going. By the time we got back to New Bern, his temperature was a hundred and four. We went straight to the hospital, but they didn't figure out what was wrong with him until the next day. By then, his fever was over a hundred and six, and even with all the antibiotics, the fever just didn't break. It was a nasty virulent strain. After the seventh day of sky-high fevers, he went into a coma. After that, once the fever finally broke, he was able to open his eyes. I thought that meant we were past the worst, but he didn't seem to know who I was and . . . '

She took a sip of wine before going on. 'He

stayed in the hospital for another month, but after that, it was pretty clear he was in a vegetative state. We eventually found a really good place for him — where we just were — and he's been there ever since.'

'That's terrible,' I said, grasping for words. 'I can't imagine how hard that must have been — must still be.'

'It was worse last year,' she said. 'Because I still had hope. But these days, I don't have a lot of hope.'

With my stomach in knots, I couldn't fathom taking a drink. 'Was he the one you met in college?'

She nodded. 'Just such a sweet guy. He was shy and handsome, but wasn't arrogant in the slightest, which surprised me, especially considering how wealthy his family is. They own one of the car dealerships here in town, and two or three others in other parts of the state. Anyway, he was on the lacrosse team, and I used to watch him play. He wasn't quite good enough for a scholarship, but he was a recruited walk-on and played in almost every game his last two years. He could run like a gazelle and score from almost anywhere.'

'Was it love at first sight?'

'Not quite. We actually met at a formal. I was there with another guy, he had a date, and after his date ditched him and my date had wandered off, we started talking. I must have given him my number because he started texting me. Nothing weird, nothing stalker-like . . . after a month or so, we met for pizza. We dated the last two and a half years of college, got engaged a year after we graduated, and we married a year after that.'

'And you were happy together?'

'We were both happy,' she said. 'You would have liked him. He was such a genuine person, so loving and energetic.' She caught herself. 'I'm sorry. *Is* a genuine person.' She took another sip of wine before looking at my glass. 'You're not having any?'

'In a minute,' I said. 'I'm still processing.'

'I guess I owe you an apology. For not telling you straightaway.'

'Even if you had, I'm not sure it would have stopped me from going to the farmers' market or inviting you over to see the bees.'

'I'll take that as a compliment, I guess. But . . . you should be aware that it's not a secret. A lot of people in town know the situation. Mark grew up in New Bern; his family is well-known here. Had you asked around, it wouldn't have taken you long to find out.'

'It never occurred to me to ask anyone about you. Honestly, I don't know enough people in town well enough to ask. But I am curious as to why you don't wear a wedding ring.'

'I do,' she said. 'I wear it around my neck.'

When she pulled out her chain, I saw a lovely rose gold wedding band that looked like something from Cartier.

'Why not on your finger?'

'I never wore rings growing up and when I was in college, I began working out at the gym. Nothing too strenuous, but I do try to do sets on a few of the machines. After I got engaged, the

323

ring would pinch and I was afraid to scratch it. I just got into the habit of wearing it around my neck. Once I became a sheriff's deputy, I didn't want people knowing anything about me.'

'Didn't that bother Mark?'

'Not at all. He wasn't the jealous type. I used to tell him that the ring was closer to my heart. I meant that and he knew it.'

I took a small sip of water, moistening my tight throat. Humoring her, I chased that with a swallow of wine, which tasted way too sour. 'What do your mom and dad think?'

'They adored Mark. But they're my parents. I told you they worry about me.'

Because of her job in law enforcement, I remembered thinking at the time. I couldn't have been more wrong.

'It seems like they take good care of him here.'

'It's a top-notch facility for those who can afford it. Insurance only covers so much, but his parents make up the difference. It's important to them. It's important to me, too.'

'What happens . . . '

When I didn't finish, she nodded. 'What happens if we decide to pull the plug? I don't think that's going to happen.'

'Ever?'

'It's not my decision. It's up to his parents.'

'But you're his wife.'

'They have medical power of attorney. They make those decisions, not me. When he turned eighteen, Mark got access to a trust. He had to sign all sorts of documents, including the ones that gave them the right to make end-of-life

324

decisions for him. I doubt he even thought about it afterward and after we were married, it never came up. Before the marriage, he was way more upset that his parents insisted on a prenup. He didn't have a choice and I really didn't care. I thought we'd be married forever and have kids and grow old together.'

'Have you spoken to his parents about Mark's future?'

'Once or twice, but it didn't go well. His mom is very religious and to her, ending the feeding tube is the same thing as murder. The last time I tried to talk to her about it, she told me that the week before, Mark had opened his eyes and stared at her, and she read that as a sign he's getting better. She's convinced that if she prays enough, Mark will just suddenly blink and be back to normal one day. As for his dad, I think he just wants to keep peace in his own house.'

'So you're left in a kind of limbo.'

'For now,' she agreed.

'You could get a divorce.'

'I can't do that.'

'Why not?'

'Because even if there's less than a one percent chance that Mark will get better, it's a chance I'm willing to take. I made a vow to stay married in sickness and in health. Health is the easy part; it's remaining faithful in sickness where love really shines.'

Perhaps she was right, but I wondered if it smacked a little of martyrdom. Then again, who was I to judge?

'I understand,' I said.

'I also want to apologize about the night at your house. After the boat ride and dinner — '

I held up my hand to stop her.

'Natalie . . .'

'Please,' she said. 'I need to explain. While we were at dinner, I sensed that we were going to sleep together, and then when we kissed, I knew it for certain. And I wanted to. Because I really had fallen in love with you, and at that moment, it felt like it was just the two of us in the world. It was easy for me to pretend that I wasn't married, or that my husband wasn't being taken care of around the clock by nurses, or even that I could have the best of both worlds. I could stay married and still have you. I could move to Baltimore and get a job there while you did your residency and we'd start a new life together. I was fantasizing about all those things, even as we moved to the bedroom . . .'

When she paused, memories flooded my senses. I remembered pulling her close and the tautness of her body against my own. The wildflower scent of her perfume, light and exotic, as I buried my face in her neck. I could feel her breasts pressed against my chest and her fingers clutching my back. When our lips came together, the flicker of her tongue triggered a wave of pleasure.

I helped her untuck my shirt and watched her unbutton it; within a moment, we both had our shirts off and our heated skin came together. And yet, when I began to kiss the tops of her breasts, I heard what sounded like a muffled sob. Pulling back, she seemed frozen except for a tear drifting down her cheek. Alarmed, I pulled back.

'I can't,' she whispered. 'I'm so sorry, but I can't. Please forgive me.'

Now, as I sat across from her in the bar, I watched as she swallowed, her gaze fixed on the tabletop.

'That night . . . you kissed me right below my collarbone. That was a thing Mark always used to do, and I suddenly saw him in my mind — lying in bed, surrounded by tubes in that sterile room. And I couldn't get his image out of my head and I hated myself for that. For doing that to you. I wanted you and I wanted to make love to you, but I couldn't. It felt . . . wrong, somehow. Like I was about to do something I would regret, even though I wanted it more than anything in the world.' She drew a long breath. 'I just wanted to tell you again that I was sorry.'

'I told you that night that you didn't have to apologize.'

'I know you did, and somehow, that made me feel even worse. Because you were so kind about the whole thing.'

Gently, I laid my hand over hers. 'For what it's worth, I'd do it all over again.'

'You fell in love with a dishonest woman.'

'You weren't dishonest,' I offered. 'You just . . . omitted some things. We all do that. For instance, I didn't tell you that in addition to being rich and handsome, I'm very skilled when it comes to putting tarps on roofs as well.'

For the first time since we'd arrived, she cracked a smile. She gave my hand a quick squeeze before withdrawing her own.

Lifting her glass of wine, she held it up in toast. 'You're a good man, Trevor Benson.'

I knew it was yet another ending for us, but I reached for my glass of wine anyway. Tapping it against hers, I forced myself to smile.

'I think,' I answered, 'you're pretty great, too.'

19

Natalie dropped me off and though I didn't sleep well, I felt all right in the morning. No trembling in my hands and my mood was steady enough for me to feel confident with a third cup of coffee after my run. Though I'd offered to pick her up on the way to the airport, she thought it better to meet me there.

No doubt because she didn't want people to see us arrive together or be seen jetting off as a couple.

I arrived at the airport before she did and checked in. Natalie arrived ten minutes after that while I was in line for security. Once I reached the gate, I took a seat and though there was a spot next to me, she chose a seat three rows away. It wasn't until we were on the plane that we finally had the chance to speak.

'Hi,' I said as she squeezed past me to the window seat, 'I'm Trevor Benson.'

'Oh, shut up.'

I thought we'd visit a bit, but she closed her eyes while tucking up her legs and promptly went to sleep. I wondered how many people she recognized on the plane.

The flight was slightly more than an hour, and after exiting the plane, we made our way to the rental counter. I'd requested my usual SUV and it was ready when we arrived. Not long after that, we were on our way to Helen.

'Seems like you had a good nap on the plane,' I observed.

'I was tired,' she said. 'I didn't sleep well last night. I did, however, have a chance yesterday to speak with the police again, as well as the sheriff. Before I picked you up, I mean.'

'And?'

'Like the police, the sheriff didn't have any information on a runaway named Callie. I don't know how much help they'll be.'

'I still have confidence that we'll get to the bottom of this,' I said.

'I also wanted to explain about earlier,' she said. 'At the airport.'

'Don't worry about it. I was able to figure out your reasons for avoiding me.'

'No hard feelings?'

'Not at all,' I said. 'You still have to live in New Bern.'

'And you're leaving soon.'

'My new life awaits.'

I could feel her eyes on me as I said it, and wondered whether she would tell me that she was going to miss me. But she didn't. Nor did I tell her that I would miss her. We both already knew that. Instead, we didn't speak much the rest of the way, both of us content to ride in silence, alone with our thoughts, wherever they would lead us.

330

Natalie was right; Helen was a very small town but remarkably scenic and beautiful in a way I hadn't expected. It looked as though it had taken its inspiration from alpine villages in Bavaria; the buildings were sandwiched together, with red-tiled roofs and painted a variety of colors, some featuring decorative trim and even the occasional turret. I imagined it was popular with tourists in search of hiking or zip-lining adventures, or tubing on the Chattahoochee River before retiring for the night in a setting that felt exotic for north-eastern Georgia.

Since neither of us had eaten, we had lunch at a small sandwich shop downtown. We discussed our game plan, which didn't consist of much other than stops at the police station and sheriff's office. I'd been hoping that I'd come up with a better idea than the one Natalie had quizzed me about — knocking on doors or talking to people on street corners — but so far, I had nothing. I wished I had had the foresight to snap a photograph of Callie in the hospital to see if her face would jog anyone's memory, but I doubted whether she would have consented to it if I'd tried.

Our first stop was the police station, quartered in a building that looked more like a house than a municipal office complex and that blended well into the community. The chief, Harvey Robertson, who'd been expecting us, met us out front. He was tall and thin with white receding hair and spoke with a thick Georgia accent. He led us inside, seating us in his office. After introductions, he handed over a manila envelope.

'As I mentioned on the phone, these are the only three runaways that I know about with any certainty,' he explained. 'One from last year, and two of them from two years ago.'

I opened the manila envelope and pulled out three flyers with the word MISSING emblazoned across the top, bearing photos of the girls, descriptions, and information as to their last known whereabouts. They looked handmade — like something the families had put together — not official police bulletins. A quick scan of the pictures confirmed that none of them was Callie.

'How about missing persons in general?'

'Again, there's no one named Callie. Now, if the family or other acquaintances didn't report her missing for whatever reason, we'd have no way of knowing. But because it's a small community, I think I have a pretty good handle on who's around and who's not.'

'I know it's not my business, but do you have any idea what happened to these other girls?'

'Two of them had boyfriends and we can't find them, either, so my hunch is that they ran off together. As to the third young lady, we have no idea what happened to her. She wasn't a minor and she was reported missing by her landlord, but for all we know, she could have moved away.'

'I'm sorry to hear that.'

'You said on the phone that this girl Callie you're looking for . . . she's sick? And that you need to find her family?'

'If we can.'

'Why did you think you might find her here?'

I told him the whole story, watching as he

seemed to soak in every word. I had the sense that he was the kind of person who could surprise you with his intuition.

'That's not much to go on,' he commented when I was finished.

'That's what Natalie said, too.'

He looked to her then back to me again. 'She's a smart one. You should think about keeping her.'

If only, I thought.

If only I could.

The sheriff's department was in Cleveland, Georgia, about twenty minutes from Helen. It was a much more imposing building than the police department in Helen, which made sense since it was responsible for a larger geographic area. We were ushered into the office of a deputy sheriff, who had likewise compiled the information we'd requested.

In total, nine people were missing, which included the three from Helen. Of the remaining six, two were males. Of the remaining four, only three were Caucasian, and only one was a girl in her teens, though it wasn't Callie.

On our way out, Natalie turned to me. 'Now what?'

'I'm working on it.'

'What does that mean?'

'I'm missing something. I'm not sure what it is, but it's there.'

'Do you still think she's from around here?'

'I don't know,' I admitted. 'But the answer is here somehow.'

We climbed into our rental before Natalie spoke again. 'I have an idea,' she finally offered.

'What's that?'

'If Callie is from here, she probably went to school, right? And you think she might be sixteen? Or seventeen?'

'That would be my guess.'

'High schools have yearbooks. Some middle schools do, too. I have no idea how many high schools there are in the county, but there can't be that many and I'd bet that none of them are very big. Assuming there are yearbooks in the school libraries, maybe we could find a name.'

I wondered why I hadn't thought of it. 'That's brilliant.'

'We'll see,' she said. 'It'll be after five before we get back to Helen, so it's probably too late to start today. So first thing tomorrow?'

'Sounds like a plan. How did you think of that?'

'I don't know. It just came to me.'

'Impressive.'

'Aren't you glad I'm here?'

Yes, I thought, *absolutely. But perhaps not for the reason you meant.*

Back in Helen, we checked into our hotel. As I spoke to the clerk at the front desk, I sensed Natalie's relief at the fact I'd reserved two rooms, even if they were adjacent. The clerk handed us magnetic key cards and we headed for the elevators.

Though sunset was still more than an hour away, I was tired. As much as I'd enjoyed spending time with Natalie, it was a strain to keep things entirely professional and pretend I wasn't in love with her. I told myself to simply accept what she was offering, without expectation — but some things are easier in theory than in reality.

In the elevator, I pressed the button for the third floor.

'How do you want to do this?' she asked. 'Do you want to look up the schools or should I?'

'I can do that. As you pointed out, there can't be too many.'

'What time tomorrow?'

'Breakfast at seven here at the hotel, and maybe hit the road by eight?'

'Sounds like a plan.'

By then, we'd reached the third floor and we stepped into the corridor. Our rooms were on the left, not too far down.

'What are you doing for dinner tonight?' she asked as I unlocked my door.

'I was thinking the Bodensee. 'Authentic German cuisine.' I saw a review when I was finding hotels. Seems pretty good.'

'I don't think I've ever had authentic German cuisine.'

Was that a hint?

'How about I get reservations at eight for the two of us? I'm pretty sure we can walk, so meet downstairs at a quarter till?'

'Perfect.' She smiled. 'See you then.'

In my room, after making the reservation, I took a quick nap, showered, and spent some time googling schools in the area on my phone. Through it all, I tried not to think about Natalie.

I couldn't do it. The heart wants what it wants.

At a quarter till, she was waiting for me in the lobby looking as dazzling as ever in a red blouse, jeans, and pumps. As I approached, I wondered whether she'd been obsessing about me in the same way I had been about her, but as usual I couldn't tell.

'You ready?' I asked.

'I was waiting on you.'

The Bodensee was only a short walk away and the evening was pleasant, with a gentle breeze that carried the scent of conifers. We were the only ones on the sidewalk and I could hear her shoes tapping against the concrete, my own steps falling in unison with hers.

'I have a question,' she finally asked.

'Go ahead.'

'What are you going to do if we actually find Callie's family? What do you plan to tell them?'

'I'm not sure,' I said. 'I guess that depends on what we learn.'

'If she is a minor, I have a duty to inform law enforcement.'

'Even if she was abused?'

'Yes, but that's where it might get complicated,' she said. 'It's also tricky if she ran away at seventeen or whatever, but is now technically an adult. Frankly, I'm not sure what my obligations

336

would be in that situation.'

'How about we cross that bridge when we get to it?'

The Bodensee, like the police station, looked more like a house than a commercial building, and I felt at home as soon as we arrived. The servers were dressed in Bavarian fashion in tight-waisted frocks, short-sleeved blouses, and colorful aprons; a bustling bar offered a variety of German beer. We were led to a table in the corner that seemed to promise a modicum of privacy in an otherwise crowded room. As we sat, I could hear faint strains of conversation drifting toward us.

Natalie glanced around, taking in the environment, a smile on her face.

'I can't believe we're in Georgia,' she said, coming back to me. 'This place is amazing.'

'It does have its charms.'

We reached for our menus. The choices were more extensive than I imagined they would be, but given my lack of familiarity with German cuisine, I wasn't sure how the dishes would taste, despite the descriptions.

'Are you going with the Wiener schnitzel?'

'Probably,' I said. 'You?'

'I'm not a very adventurous eater,' she confessed. 'I think I'll go with the grilled salmon.'

'I'm sure it'll be fine.'

When the waitress came by, I ordered a lager; Natalie opted for a glass of wine and we told her our selections. Making conversation, Natalie asked her how long she'd lived in Helen.

'Only two years,' she said. 'My husband works for the parks department and he got transferred here.'

'Is that typical, you think? Or did most of the residents grow up in the area?'

'I'd guess it's a bit of both. Why?'

'Just curious.'

When she was gone, I leaned across the table. 'What was that about?'

'Just collecting information. Who knows? It might end up being helpful.'

I put my napkin in my lap. 'I want you to know that I appreciate you coming here with me and laying the ground-work with the police and the sheriff.'

'My pleasure.'

'I'm surprised you didn't have to work.'

'I took a couple of vacation days.' She shrugged. 'It's not like I really need them anymore. It's hard for me to go anywhere other than my parents' beach house. As much as I enjoy spending time with them, I can only stay there so long before I start going crazy.' She shook her head. 'I'm sorry. That probably sounds selfish.'

'Not at all.'

'It is compared to you. Since you lost your parents, I mean.'

'We all have our challenges, don't we?'

The waitress reappeared with our drinks and dropped them at our table. I took a drink of the lager and found it delicious.

Natalie toyed with her glass, seemingly lost in thought, before finally realizing she'd gone quiet.

338

'Sorry,' she said. 'I sort of drifted off there.'

'Care to share?'

'I was thinking about life. It's not important.'

'I'd love to hear it.' When she still seemed hesitant, I added, 'Really.'

She took a sip of her wine. 'During our first year of marriage, Mark and I visited Blowing Rock. We spent the weekend at a charming bed-and-breakfast, hiking and antiquing. I remember thinking the whole weekend that my life was exactly what I wanted it to be.'

I studied her. 'What are you going to do?'

'About what? Mark?' When I nodded, she went on. 'I'll just keep taking it day by day.'

'Is that fair to you?'

She gave a half-hearted laugh, but I caught the sadness in it. 'Tell me, Trevor. When is life ever fair?'

Our conversation drifted to easier topics as we tucked into our dinners. We mused about Callie, wondering again why she seemed intent on keeping her family secret, and caught up on almost everything I'd been doing since I'd last seen her. I told her about my decision not to sell my grandfather's house and the repairs I wanted to do; I showed her some pics I'd snapped of my new apartment in Baltimore. I described my psychiatric residency program, but I didn't mention the struggles I'd experienced after she'd broken things off. Bringing it up, I felt, would have only piled on useless guilt.

After we finished our meals, neither of us was in the mood for dessert, so I paid the bill and we sauntered back into the evening air. It had cooled slightly but the stars were out in full, glowing in the ebony sky. The streets were quiet and empty; I could hear the hushed stirring of leaves in the trees, and it brought to mind the sound of a mother soothing her child to sleep.

'I didn't really answer your question,' Natalie said into the silence.

'What question?'

'When you asked if putting my life on hold was fair to me. I didn't give you a real answer.'

'I think I understood what you meant.'

She smiled, looking almost sad. 'I should have said that there are moments when it's not so bad. When I'm with my family, there are times when I can actually forget about the reality of my situation. Like when one of them tells a super funny story and we're all laughing, it's easy to pretend I lead a normal life. Then, in the next minute, it all comes rushing back. The truth is that the reality is always there, even if it is temporarily cloaked . . . but then it emerges again and I suddenly feel like I shouldn't be laughing or smiling because that feels wrong somehow. Because it seems like I don't care about him. I spend too much time thinking that I'm not allowed to be happy, and that I shouldn't even try to be happy. I know that sounds crazy, but I can't help it.'

'Do you think Mark would have wanted you to feel that way?'

'No,' she said. 'I know he wouldn't. We even talked about things like this. Well, not about this

340

situation exactly, but what we wanted if the other person were to die in a car accident or whatever. Pillow talk, you know? We played those silly hypothetical games — like if either of us died — and he always told me that he'd want me to move on, to find someone new and start a family. Of course, right after that, he'd add that I'd better not love the new guy as much as I loved him.'

'At least he was honest,' I said with a smile.

'Yeah,' she said. 'He was. But I don't know what any of it really means anymore. There's a part of me that says I should spend as much time with Mark as I can, that I should quit my job and visit him every day. Because that's what you're supposed to do when someone is sick, right? But the truth is that's the last thing I want to do. Because every time I go, a little part of me dies inside. But then I feel guilty about feeling that way, so I steel myself and do what I'm supposed to do. Even though I know he wouldn't have wanted that for me.'

She seemed to be studying the pavement in front of us.

'It's so hard not knowing when, or even if, any of this will ever end. People in vegetative states can live decades. What do I do, knowing that? I know I still have time to have children, but do I have to give that up? And what about all the other little things that make life worthwhile? Like being held by someone who loves you, or even being kissed. Do I give those things up forever, too? Do I have to live in New Bern until either he or I die? Don't get me wrong — I love New

Bern. But there's a part of me that sometimes imagines a different life — living in New York or Miami or Chicago or Los Angeles. I've lived in small North Carolina towns my entire life. Don't I deserve the chance to make that choice for myself?'

By then, we'd reached the hotel, but she paused outside the entrance.

'You want to know what the worst part is? There's no one I can talk to about this. No one really gets it. My parents are heartsick about all of it, so when I'm with them, I'm constantly reassuring them that I'm okay. His parents and I are on different wavelengths. My friends talk about work or their spouses or their kids, and I don't even know what to do. It's just . . . lonely. I know people sympathize and care about me, but I don't think they can truly empathize since this is so entirely foreign to the way anyone imagines that their life will turn out. And . . . '

I waited.

'Do you know when people ask you what your dreams or goals are? Like in a year or three years or five years? I think about that sometimes, and I realize that not only do I not know, I don't even know how to go about trying to find the answer. Because so much of it is out of my control and there's nothing I can do.'

I reached out, taking her hand. 'I wish there was something I could say to make things easier for you.'

'I know you do,' she said, squeezing my hand. 'Just like I know that tomorrow will be just another day.'

A few minutes later, we were each in our separate rooms. Natalie's confession had left me feeling both sad for her and disappointed in myself. As empathetic as I imagined myself to be, it was — as she'd said — difficult for me to put myself in exactly her position or to fully imagine what her life was like on a daily basis. I understood it, I sympathized with it, I felt terrible for her, but when I was honest with myself, I knew that I couldn't fully empathize. Everyone has inner lives to which no one else can be privy.

Turning on the television, I settled on ESPN, not because I cared who won the latest baseball game or golf tournament, but because I was too tired to concentrate on anything that might have any kind of story or plot. I kicked off my shoes, took off my shirt, and lay back on the bed, alternately listening to the announcers and puzzling over Callie, while simultaneously reliving the last couple of days I'd spent with Natalie.

I wondered whether I would ever meet anyone like her again. Even if I were to fall in love again, wouldn't I consciously and subconsciously compare the new woman to the woman I loved right now?

Here, in this moment, we were together, except that we weren't. She was in the room next door, with a wall and an entire world between us. Could it be that she, like me, was dwelling on the impossible and wishing there were some world made just for the two of us?

I didn't know. All I knew for sure was that as exhausted as I felt, I wouldn't have traded the last two days for anything.

I woke to the sound of someone knocking on my door.

Squinting at the clock, I saw it was coming up on midnight; both the lamp and the television were on and I fumbled for the remote control, only half-aware of my surroundings.

I turned off the television, wondering if I'd imagined it, when I heard a tentative knock. It was coupled with a voice I recognized.

'Trevor? Are you awake?'

I crawled out of bed and did a sleepy stagger across the room, thankful I had my pants on. Opening the door, I saw Natalie, still dressed in her dinner attire, her expression one of wary desperation, her eyes rimmed in red.

'What's going on? Are you okay?'

'No,' she said, 'I'm not okay. Can I come in?'

'Yeah, of course,' I said, making room for Natalie as she entered. She paused in the middle of the room as though looking for a place to sit. I pulled out the desk chair for her and took a seat on the bed facing her.

'I heard the television, so I figured you were still awake,' she said, taking in my still sleep-ridden state for the first time.

'I am now,' I said. 'I'm glad you're here.'

For a moment, she twisted her hands in her lap, her eyes framed in anguish. 'I don't want to be alone right now.'

'Do you want to see if there's someplace open in Helen?' I asked. 'Maybe get a drink or some decaf?'

'I don't want to go out.' Then, looking up at me, hesitantly: 'Can I sleep here? With you? I don't want to have sex . . . ' She closed her eyes, her voice tight. 'But aside from you, I haven't slept in bed with someone since Mark got sick, and I just want someone next to me tonight. I know it's wrong and that I should go back to my room — '

'Of course you can sleep here,' I interrupted.

'Trevor . . . '

'Come here.' I stood from the bed, and rising slowly, she went into my arms. I held her for a long time before we both got into the bed. As I reached for the lamp to turn it out, I hesitated.

'Can I turn the light off, or do you want to talk some more?'

'You can turn it out,' she murmured.

I hit the switch and the room went dark. I rolled to face her, and saw only a vague shadow, but I caught the faintest whiff of perfume.

'I'm glad it's dark,' she whispered. 'I look terrible.'

'You've never been anything but beautiful.'

I felt her hand on my chest, then as it brushed my cheek. 'I do love you, Trevor Benson. I want you to know that.'

'I know,' I said. 'I love you, too.'

'Will you hold me?'

At her words, I drew my arms around her, letting her rest her head on my shoulder where I

345

could feel the heat of her breath on my skin. As much as I longed to kiss her, I didn't. More than anything, I wanted to ease the tiniest bit of her sadness and confusion, if only for a few hours.

She relaxed into me, her body molding itself to mine, a position both new and familiar at exactly the same time. Eventually I heard her breaths begin to slow, and I realized that she was sleeping.

But I stayed awake, knowing that this was the last time I would hold her this way. I wanted to savor the feeling, to make it last forever. I ached at the thought that I might never experience this particular bliss again.

20

I woke as the early-dawn light began to seep under the curtains. Natalie was still asleep, and I slipped from the bed, trying not to wake her.

After pulling a clean shirt from my duffel bag, I put on my shoes and found my wallet, then crept from the room. The light from the hallway brightened the room momentarily as I opened the door, but Natalie didn't stir. More sleep was exactly what she needed; I, on the other hand, needed coffee.

Breakfast would be served in an alcove just off the lobby. It was still too early for the food to be laid out, but luckily there was plenty of coffee available. I filled a foam cup and took a seat at one of the empty tables, my mind filled with bittersweet thoughts of Natalie.

I sipped my coffee, slowly coming back to life, and on a whim, pulled out my wallet and unfolded the note I'd written, transcribing my grandfather's final words. Studying it once again, I was unable to escape the gnawing sensation that I was missing something important, something that had to do with Callie.

Trevor . . . help care . . . and . . . if you can . . . collapsed . . . sick . . . like Rose . . . find

*family . . . go to hell . . . and run away . . . love
you . . . you came . . . now go . . . please*

Rising from the table, I approached the front desk and asked if I could borrow a pen and pad of paper. Taking my seat again, I remembered the long pauses between words, and started with the assumption that he'd been trying to tell me something about Callie.

The instruction to *run away*, in hindsight, was clearly meant to describe Callie, as in *runaway*. *Find family* made sense as well. Since he'd spent time with Callie, *sick like Rose* and *collapsed* were also relatively easy to understand, especially if he'd seen something concerning.

But *go to hell* still made no sense. Neither did the word *and* before *runaway*. What if, however, the pauses were out of place? I whispered the phrases, sounding it out. Instead of *go to hell
. . . and run away*, how about:

Go to Helen? Runaway?

My heart suddenly started to pound as I rewrote the last half of the note.

Collapsed. Sick like Rose. Find family. Go to Helen. Runaway. Love you. You came. Now go. Please.

Though it was impossible to know whether I was correct, it *felt* right. Despite what the police and sheriff had told me about runaways — or missing persons in general from the area — I knew my grandfather had been talking about Callie.

348

Why, then, hadn't he mentioned her by name?

I continued to drink my coffee, turning my focus to the first part of the note, trying different reinterpretations. I finished one cup and poured myself another, running through the words, reordering the pauses, but never once could I come up with Callie, or anything even close. I'd think about it, then let my thoughts drift to Natalie again, then return my concentration to the task at hand.

Halfway through my third cup of coffee, I felt the emergence of a new idea and if I was correct, then everything in the note was startlingly clear.

While admitting that I might be wrong, I suddenly felt confident that I would have the answer before the morning was out.

'Hey,' Natalie said.

Lost in thought, I hadn't seen her enter the alcove. Unlike me, she'd already showered, the ends of her hair still wet. Her eyes were bright, with none of the weariness I'd expected.

'Good morning.'

'You were up early. I didn't hear you leave.'

'I'm like a mouse when I sneak away.'

'I'm going to get some yogurt. Do you want anything?'

'I can go with you.'

Good to her word, she selected a container of yogurt and prepared a cup of tea. I opted for eggs and bacon with a side of toast, giving myself a pass on my healthy diet.

Back at the table, we sat across from each other.

'Did you sleep well?' I asked.

'Like a baby,' she said with a sheepish air. 'That was nice, last night. Thank you.'

'Please don't thank me. That might ruin it.'

'Deal,' she said. 'Did you find the schools in the area?'

'I did,' I said. 'Before dinner.'

'Me too,' she said. 'There aren't too many, but they're spread through the county. We'll do a lot of driving today.'

'I want to go to the police station first. What time do you think the chief will be there?'

'Hard to say. Probably around eight. Why?'

'I'd rather not say until I know for sure. But it might make for less driving if I'm right.'

Having eaten, I went back to the room, showered, and packed up my things. After meeting in the lobby, we were in the car before the top of the hour.

At the station, we were again ushered into Robertson's office. Because I hadn't shared my thinking with Natalie, she was as curious about the visit as he was.

'I'm sure you're not here for a social visit,' he began, 'so what can I do for you?'

'I'm wondering how missing persons are categorized in Georgia,' I said. 'Is there a statewide database?'

'There is and there isn't. Missing persons

350

reports are generally handled locally, so every police department has its own list. Sometimes, the GBI might be involved as well, and they do operate statewide.'

'GBI?'

'Georgia Bureau of Investigation,' he said. 'Small communities can't necessarily afford to have full-time detectives or investigators on staff, so when crimes are committed or people go missing outside of major cities, the GBI steps in. They have their own missing persons list.'

'So if you had a name, you could check if someone is missing?'

'Of course,' he said. 'Missing persons are usually listed alphabetically, but some departments list them chronologically. Depending on the department, some of those lists are public.'

'What if you only have a first name?'

'That's obviously a slower process, but it's still possible. You'd have to look over the various lists yourself. Keep in mind that there are missing people in the books that go back more than ten years.'

'Would you be willing to check for us?'

'You want me to look for Callie's name? Neither of you are even certain that she went missing from Georgia.'

'She's a kid and she's dying.'

It took him a second before he finally nodded. 'All right. I don't have any idea how long this might take, though.'

'There's something else, too.'

'Yes?'

'In addition to Callie, can you look for the

name Karen as well?'

'Karen?'

I nodded. 'A Caucasian teenage girl, missing since last spring or summer.'

Even as I said it, I could feel Natalie's questioning gaze on me.

Robertson told us to wait in a coffee shop down the street. Though we'd both eaten, I ordered another cup of coffee and Natalie ordered tea again. I left a 500 percent tip on the table in open view, in case we had to stay at the table for a while.

'Karen?' Natalie asked.

I handed her the original note. Natalie read through it. When she finished, I went through the latter part of it.

> Trevor . . . help care . . . and . . . if you can
> . . . collapsed . . . sick . . . like Rose . . . find
> family . . . go to hell . . . and run away . . . love
> you . . . you came . . . now go . . . please

'It seems clear that he was talking about her.'

'He doesn't mention the name Callie.'

'No, he doesn't. But if you combine the words *care* and *and* while changing some of the pauses, you come up with this.' I handed over the reinterpretation I'd scribbled earlier.

> Trevor . . . help Karen if you can. Collapsed.
> Sick like Rose. Find family. Go to Helen.

352

Runaway. Love you. You came. Now go. Please.

She read it before looking at me. 'How did you come up with this?'

'I guess I must have been inspired.'

It took less time than either of us anticipated. Forty-five minutes later, Robertson entered the coffee shop holding a manila file. There were extra seats at the table and he took one of them. Without prompting, the waitress returned to the table with a cup of coffee for him. I guessed he was a regular. In the meantime, he slid the file across to me.

'I think I might have found her.'

'Already?'

'Karen Anne-Marie Johnson,' he said. 'From Decatur. Age sixteen. Ran off at age fifteen last May, which means she's been missing a little more than a year. That sounds like your girl, doesn't it? I wanted you to check it out before I keep going.'

I opened the thin file and my eyes settled on a copied photograph of Callie. For a moment, I didn't believe it. Though I'd been hopeful, the sense of relief I felt was overwhelming.

'It's her.'

'Are you sure?'

'No question,' I said. Natalie leaned toward me, her eyes examining the photograph as well. I had to remind myself that — other than the

353

hectic night of the trailer fire, and maybe not even then — Natalie had never seen her.

'I can't believe how quickly you found her,' I said.

'It wasn't that difficult. She was on the GBI missing persons list, which was the first one I checked. It took me less than ten minutes. It's on their website, photos and all, so you really didn't need my help. You could have stayed in North Carolina and done your own search.'

Except I hadn't known the GBI had a website. Until that morning, I'd never heard of the GBI at all.

'I appreciate your help.'

'It's what we do. I'm hoping there will be a happy ending to all this.'

'Is there anything else you can tell us?'

Robertson nodded. 'I spoke to the people in Decatur and they pulled the file. You have the copy in the folder there, but it's a typical story. She'd told her parents she was going to spend the night at a friend's house. When they hadn't heard from her by the following evening, the parents contacted the friend and learned that Karen had never gone there in the first place. As far as the parents knew, she didn't have a boyfriend, so it wasn't about that. You'll note in there, too, that she has two younger sisters.'

Which meant possible bone marrow matches.

'If she's from Decatur, how did Helen come into the equation?' Natalie asked.

'I don't know,' I said. 'But I have a hunch that I'm going to find out.'

'As for me,' Robertson said, 'I'm going to have

354

to contact the GBI and let them know Karen's whereabouts. Decatur police, too. I'm sure the parents will be relieved.'

I thought about that. 'Would it be possible to hold off on that until tomorrow?'

'Why would I do that?' Robertson frowned.

'Because I want to talk to her first.'

'That's not the way we do things in Georgia.'

'I know. But I'd like to know why she ran off in the first place. If it was because she was being abused, I want her to be prepared.'

'My gut is telling me that her running off had nothing to do with abuse.'

'Why would you say that?'

'Take a peek at the last page,' he said. 'After talking to the Decatur folks, I printed out a news article that I was able to find. You might want to peruse that.'

Originally printed in the *Atlanta Journal-Constitution*, the news article was short, only a couple of paragraphs long, and as I read it, I found myself agreeing with Robertson's hunch.

To me, it explained just about everything.

With a bit of pleading from both Natalie and me, Robertson agreed to give me twenty-four hours before he contacted the GBI and the Decatur police. He also swore to hold me personally responsible if any aspect of my plan went sideways.

My first call was to Dr. Nobles. After a long hold, she let me know that Callie was still in the hospital, and that her condition had deteriorated slightly overnight. I told her that I'd found her family and planned to speak with Callie that afternoon. After that, I rebooked our flight so I could be at the hospital by midafternoon. Natalie and I discussed the best way to handle the situation as we made the drive back to Atlanta. We dropped off the rental car, checked in, and eventually made our way to the gate.

Once aboard, Natalie grew quiet, as did I. Both of us knew our time together was almost over, but neither of us wanted to talk about it. I noticed Natalie had been surreptitiously studying the other passengers as they arrived at the gate, no doubt concerned again that someone might recognize her. I understood her rationale, but it still left me feeling empty inside.

In the terminal back in New Bern, as we were walking through we both heard someone call out her name. Another woman, roughly her age, was approaching and clearly wanted to chat. I was torn between waiting for her or simply walking on, but I could see the plea in Natalie's eyes, begging me to go.

I continued toward the parking area alone, fighting the urge to glance over my shoulder, and wondering if that was the final memory I would have of her.

Fifteen minutes later, I was at the hospital, walking toward Callie's room.

Her door was open and I entered, noticing

that the bandage around her head had been removed, leaving her hair a tangled mess. As usual, the television was on and after Callie noted my presence, she turned her attention back to it. I scooted the chair closer to the bed and took a seat.

'How are you feeling?'

'I want to go home.'

'I spoke with Dr. Nobles earlier.'

'She was here this morning,' Callie said. 'She said they're still trying to find donors.'

I watched her, trying to picture how hard the last year must have been for her. 'I was in Georgia this morning,' I finally said.

She turned toward me, wary. 'So?'

'I know who you are.'

'No, you don't.'

'Your name is Karen Johnson, and you're sixteen years old. You ran away from your home in Decatur, Georgia, last May, when you were fifteen. Your parents are named Curtis and Louise, and you have twin sisters named Heather and Tammy.'

After the shock passed, her eyes narrowed. 'I suppose you've already called my parents? And they're on their way?'

'No,' I said. 'I didn't. Not yet, anyway.'

'Why not? Because you plan to have me arrested?'

'No. Because I'd like you to contact your parents before the police do.'

'I don't want to talk to them,' she said, her voice rising. 'I've already told you that.'

'You told me a lot of things,' I continued,

357

remaining calm. 'But you're a minor and technically a missing person. The police will contact your parents no later than tomorrow, so all of this is over no matter what you decide. They'll find out where you are and I'm sure they'll come to see you. I just think it would be better if they heard everything from you first. I'm sure they've been really worried about you and they miss you.'

'You don't know anything!'

'What don't I know?'

'They hate me.' Her voice was half sob, half cry of rage.

I stared at her, thinking about the news clipping I'd read. 'Because of what happened to Roger?'

She flinched at the name and I knew I'd unleashed a tidal wave of painful emotions. Instead of answering, she drew her legs up, her knees to her chest, and began to rock. I wished that I could somehow help her, but I knew from experience that guilt is an individual battle, always waged alone. I watched as she began to cry before swiping angrily at her tears with the back of her hand.

'Do you want to talk about it?' I asked.

'Why? It won't change what happened.'

'You're right,' I admitted. 'But talking about sadness or guilt can help let out some of the pain, and sometimes, that leaves more room in your heart to remember what you loved about someone.'

After a long silence, she finally spoke, her voice ragged. 'It's my fault that he died. I was supposed to be watching him.'

'What happened to Roger was a terrible, terrible accident. I'm sure you loved your little brother very much.'

She rested her chin on her knees, looking absolutely drained. I waited in silence, allowing her to make her own decision. I'd learned in my own therapy how powerful silence can be; it gives people time to figure out how they want to tell the story, or whether they want to tell it at all. When she finally began, she almost sounded as though she were talking to herself.

'We all loved Roger. My parents always wanted a son, but after Heather and Tammy were born, my mom had trouble getting pregnant again. So when Roger finally came along, it was like a miracle. When he was a baby, me and Tammy and Heather treated him like a doll. We'd change his outfits and take pictures of each one. He was always so happy, one of those babies that always smiled, and as soon as he could walk, he would follow us everywhere. It never bothered me when I had to watch him. My parents didn't go out all that much, but that night it was their anniversary. Tammy and Heather were staying over at a friend's house, so it was just me and Rog. We were playing with his Thomas the Tank Engine set and when he got hungry, I brought him to the kitchen to make him a hot dog. They were his favorite. He ate them all the time and I cut it into small pieces, so when my friend Maddie called, I thought it would be okay to talk to her on the porch outside. She was upset because her boyfriend had just broken up with her. I didn't think we talked that long, but when I came inside again, Roger was on the floor and his lips were blue and I didn't know what to do . . . ' She trailed off, as if caught up in the paralyzing moment all over again. When she continued, her expression was dazed. 'He was only four years old . . . I started screaming and eventually one of the neighbors heard me and came over. She called 911 and then my parents and the ambulance came, but by then . . . '

She took a long, uneven breath.

'At the funeral, he wore a blue suit that my parents had to buy for him. We each got to put a toy in the casket with him, and I picked Thomas. But . . . it was like this horrible dream. He didn't even look like Rog. His hair was parted on the wrong side and I can remember thinking that if his hair had been parted the right way, then I would wake up and everything would be back to normal again. But of course everything was different after that. It was like this blackness settled over us. My mom cried and my dad spent all his time in the garage and Heather and Tammy fought all the time. No one was allowed in Roger's room and it stayed exactly the same as when I'd been playing Thomas the Tank Engine with him. I had to walk by that room every time I went to my room, or to the bathroom, and all I could think was that if we'd stayed in the room a few minutes longer, then Maddie wouldn't have called while he was eating and nothing bad would have happened. And my mom and dad . . . they could barely look at me because they blamed me for what happened. And it happened on their anniversary, so I killed that, too.'

I hesitated, wondering how to make sense of such a terrible tragedy. Finally, I said, 'Callie, I'm sure they know it wasn't your fault.'

'You're wrong,' she said, her tone suddenly rising. 'You weren't there. I heard them talking one night, and they were saying that if I hadn't been on the phone, then Roger would be alive. Or that maybe if I'd called 911 right away, they might have been able to save him.'

I tried to imagine how devastating it must have been to overhear those words.

'That doesn't mean they stopped loving you,' I offered.

'But it was my fault!' she cried. 'I'm the one who went outside to talk on the phone and left him alone and every time they looked at me, I knew what they were really thinking. And then . . . everything started going bad. My dad got laid off, my mom got skin cancer, and even though they caught it in time, it was just one more thing. Finally, my dad found another job, but we had to sell our house and Tammy and Heather were really upset because they had to leave all their friends. All I could think was that I set it all in motion and suddenly I knew I had to leave. If I left, then things would eventually return to normal.'

I wanted to tell her that layoffs happen and that anyone can get cancer; I wanted to explain that in stressful situations, arguments are far more likely. But Callie wasn't ready to hear any of those things just yet, because blaming herself allowed her to feel some control over all of it.

'So you decided to run away.'

'I had to. I went to the bus station and caught the first one that was leaving. I went to Charlotte first, then Raleigh, and after that, I caught a ride with a man who was heading toward the coast. I ended up in New Bern.'

'Where you slept in my grandfather's barn and he found you.'

'I didn't have any money and I was so tired and dirty by then,' she said, sounding impossibly old for her age. 'I hadn't showered in days. He found me the following morning.'

'My guess is he probably offered you breakfast.'

For the first time since I'd been in the room, she cracked the weariest of smiles. 'He did. He didn't seem angry at all. He just asked who I was and I accidentally told him my real name, but then Callie popped in my head, so I told him it was my middle name and asked that he call me that instead. So, he said, 'Okay, Callie, I'll bet you're hungry. Let's get you some grub and get your clothes cleaned up.' He didn't ask me a lot of questions. Mostly he talked about the bees.'

'That sounds like him.'

'When I finished eating, he asked me where I was going. I didn't know, so he told me he'd get clean sheets on the bed in the guest room and that I could stay until I figured it out. It was almost like he'd expected me to show up. I can remember that one morning, after he'd given me breakfast, he asked me to help him with the bees. He put me in one of the suits but he wouldn't wear one himself. He told me they were his

362

friends and they trusted him. I thought he should have said it the other way around — that *he* trusted *them*, but he didn't. I still think that's kind of funny, don't you?'

I smiled. 'I do. But he used to say the same thing to me.'

She nodded. 'Anyway, after a couple of weeks, he told me about the Trading Post. When I said that I'd never worked in a store before, he said it wouldn't matter. So we got in his truck and he walked in with me, and pretty much convinced Claude to give me a job. Then, after I'd saved a little bit, he kicked in some more money so I could move into the trailer. Helped me move in, too, not that I had a whole lot to move. But he had some extra furniture, just like Claude did later after the trailer burned down.'

She'd told me a lot that I hadn't known, though none of it surprised me.

'Did he really give you my grandmother's social security number?'

After a moment, she shook her head. 'No. I found the card in a box under the bed the first night I was there. I'm sorry for taking it, but I didn't know what else to do. I knew my parents might find me if I used mine.'

'How did you learn that?'

'TV,' she said with a shrug. 'Movies. That was also the reason I didn't bring my phone, and rode the bus, and changed my name.'

'Pretty smart,' I said with a touch of admiration.

'It worked,' she said. 'Until you figured it out.'

'Can I ask a couple more questions?'

'Why not?' She seemed resigned. 'You'll probably find out everything anyway.'

'Why did you pick the name Callie?'

'Because I'm originally from California.'

'No kidding?'

'I was born in San Diego. My dad was in the Navy.'

Another detail I didn't know, but one that probably wasn't important.

'How did my grandfather know you were sick?'

'Oh, yeah. I'm not even sure I was sick then. Or maybe I was. I don't know. Anyway, I fainted when I was helping him harvest the honey. When I came to, he told me I'd scared him practically to death. He tried to get me to go to a doctor, but I wouldn't. I thought they would ask too many questions. Which turned out to be right, you know.'

I raised an eyebrow, thinking she was savvier than I'd imagined. I doubted I would have been able to do everything she'd done at her age. With all of that, however, only a couple of obvious questions remained.

'I'm assuming that after your family sold the house, your dad found a job in Helen, right?'

'I ran away before they actually moved, but that was the plan. My dad got a job as a hotel manager up there.'

I wondered if it was the same hotel where I'd stayed; I wondered if it was the same man who'd handed me the pen earlier in the morning. 'How did my grandfather know your family was in Helen?'

'One night, I was really homesick. Heather

and Tammy are twins and it was their birthday, and I was crying because I missed them. Somehow, I think I mentioned that I wished I were with them in Helen now. I didn't think he'd even heard me or knew what I was saying, but I guess he did.' Her eyes shifted off to the side, and I knew she had more to say. I brought my hands together, listening as she sighed.

'I really liked your grampa,' she offered. 'He always watched out for me, you know? Like he truly cared about me, even though he had no reason to. When he died, I was so upset. It kind of felt like I lost the one person in this town who I really trusted. I went to the funeral, you know.'

'You did? I don't remember seeing you.'

'I stood in the back,' she said. 'But after everyone left, I stayed around. I told him thank you, and I said I'd watch out for the bees for him.'

I smiled. 'I know he cared about you, too.'

When she stayed silent, I finally reached into my pocket. I pulled out my phone and set it on the bed beside her. Callie stared at it without reaching for it.

'What do you think about calling your parents?' I said.

'Do I have to?' she asked in a small voice.

'No. I'm not going to make you do that. But it's either you speak to them on the phone, or the police are going to show up at their door, which might be frightening for them.'

'And the police will tell them for sure? Even if I don't want them to?'

'Yes.'

'In other words, I don't have a choice.'

'Of course you have a choice. But even if you don't call them, they'll show up here. You're going to see them whether you want to or not.'

She picked at one of her fingernails. 'What if they still hate me?'

'I don't think they ever hated you. I think they were just struggling with grief, like you were. People do that in different ways.'

'Will you stay here with me? So they can speak to you if they need to? Or if I need you to talk to them because they start yelling or going crazy? And maybe be here tomorrow, too?'

'Of course,' I said.

She chewed her lip. 'Do you think you could do me another favor, too?' She touched her matted hair subconsciously. 'Could you pick up some things for me from the drugstore? I look like hell.'

'What do you need?'

'You know . . . makeup. A hairbrush, some cleanser, and lotion for my hands.' She stared at her cracked cuticles in disgust.

I nodded, making notes on my phone as she rattled off a list of products. 'Anything else?'

'No,' she said. 'I guess I should call, huh?'

'Probably. But I want you to know something first.'

'What's that?'

'I'm proud of you.'

21

I stayed with Callie as she made the call. Naturally, her parents were both shocked and elated to hear from their daughter. After gasps of disbelief and joyful sobs, they had a barrage of questions, many of which Callie promised to answer more fully when they arrived. But when Callie handed the phone to me, their initial relief was gutted by fear as I explained who I was and walked them through Callie's diagnosis and prognosis. I promised them that Callie's doctors would fill them in on all of her treatment options when they reached New Bern, and that it was imperative that they come as soon as possible in order for Callie to explore all of her medical alternatives.

I also updated Chief Robertson by phone, letting him know he could contact the GBI and Decatur police with the news that Callie had been located and had already contacted her parents. At the end of the call, he asked that I keep him apprised of Callie's condition, and — with Callie's permission — I promised to do so.

For the rest of the afternoon I continued to sit with her, listening as she spontaneously lapsed into memories of her life before Roger had died, sharing details of an ordinary teenage existence.

It was as if the dam imposed by the past year's isolation and secrecy had suddenly burst, releasing a flood of nostalgia for the life she had been grieving all this time. From her regional volleyball tournaments to the habits of her Labrador retriever, the names of her favorite high school teachers and the boy she'd briefly dated, the particulars of her personal life tumbled out randomly over the next several hours, painting a picture almost startling in its normalcy. I found myself marveling at the courage and independence she'd developed since running away, as nothing in the placid, relatively tame existence she described could have prepared her for the hardships she would face as a runaway.

I was with her when Dr. Nobles came by during rounds and watched silently as Callie finally related the truth about herself. Avoiding the doctor's gaze and twisting a section of her bedsheet into a tight corkscrew, she apologized for lying. When she finished, Dr. Nobles squeezed Callie's hand.

'Let's just try to get you better, okay?' she said.

I knew Callie's family was planning to drive through the night and would be at the hospital first thing in the morning. Callie made me promise again to be there, and I assured her that I would stay as long as she needed. As darkness fell over the parking lot outside her window, I asked her whether she wanted me to stay on until visiting hours were over. She shook her head.

'I'm tired,' she said, slumping back against her pillows. 'I'll be all right now.' Somehow, I believed her.

By the time I got home, I was utterly spent. I called Natalie but the call went to voicemail. I kept the message short, letting her know that Callie's family would arrive in the morning in case she wanted to meet them, and that I'd already spoken to Robertson. After that, I collapsed on top of my bed and didn't wake until the following morning.

On my way to the hospital the next day, I stopped at the drug-store. With the help of one of the employees, I spent a small fortune on beauty products, a hairbrush, and a hand mirror. Handing the bag to Callie, I could see the strain on her face. I watched as she picked ceaselessly at her hair, the skin on her forearms, the bedsheets.

'How did you sleep?' I asked, taking a seat next to her bed.

'I didn't,' she said. 'I felt like I stared at the ceiling all night.'

'It's a big day. For everyone.'

'What do I do if they're angry, and start yelling?'

'If I have to, I'll mediate, okay? If things get out of hand, I mean. But they were happy to hear from you yesterday, right? I don't think they'll yell at you.'

'Even if they're happy I'm alive . . . ' She paused to swallow, her face wooden. 'Deep down, they still blame me for killing Roger.'

I wasn't sure what to say to that, so I stayed

369

quiet. In the silence, Callie rifled through the bag with her good hand, inspecting the items I'd purchased.

'Do you need me to hold the hand mirror?'

'You wouldn't mind?'

'Not at all,' I said, reaching for the mirror. When Callie saw herself in the reflection, she winced.

'I look horrible.'

'No, you don't,' I said. 'You're a very pretty girl, Callie.'

She grimaced as she ran the brush through her hair, then started applying the makeup. Though I doubted her grooming would matter to her family, it seemed to make Callie feel better about herself, and that was all that mattered.

She seemed to know what she was doing, and in the end I was surprised by her transformation. When she was satisfied, she put the items back in the bag and set it on the bedside table.

'How do I look?' she asked, skeptical.

'Beautiful. And now, you actually do look nineteen.'

She frowned. 'I'm so pale . . . '

'You're too critical.'

She gazed toward the window. 'I'm not worried about my mom or my sisters,' she said. 'But I'm a little afraid of how my dad will react.'

'Why?'

'I didn't tell you this, but even before Roger died, we weren't getting along very well. He's really quiet and usually doesn't show a lot of emotion, until he gets angry. And he was angry a lot even before Roger died. He didn't like the people I hung around with, he thought I could be doing better in school, he didn't like what I wore. Half the time, I was grounded. I hated that.'

'Most teens would.'

'I'm not sure I want to go back,' she confessed, dread coloring her voice. 'What if things are just as bad as before?'

'I think,' I said, 'your best bet is to just take things one step at a time. You don't need to make that decision right now.'

'Do you think they'll be mad at me? For running away and not calling?'

Because I didn't want to lie to her, I nodded. 'Yes. Part of them will be angry. But another part will be excited to see you. Still another part will be worried because you're sick. I think they're going to be feeling a lot of different things all at once. My hunch is that they'll feel kind of overwhelmed, which is something to bear in mind when you talk to them. But the more important question right now is, How are you feeling?'

She weighed her response. 'I'm excited to see them, but at the same time, I'm scared.'

'I'd be scared, too,' I said. 'That's normal.'

'I just want . . .'

She trailed off, but she didn't need to finish. I could see in her expression what she wanted, for it was the same thing every child wanted. She wanted to be loved by her parents. Accepted. Forgiven.

'There's something else you might want to consider,' I added after a moment.

'What's that?'

'If you want your parents to forgive you, then

371

you're also going to have to forgive yourself.'

'How?' she demanded. 'After what I did?'

'Forgiveness doesn't mean you forget, or you stop wishing that you can change the past. Mainly it means that you accept the idea that you're not perfect, because no one is perfect. And terrible things can happen to anyone.'

She lowered her gaze, and in the silence I could see her struggling with the idea. It would take time — and probably a lot of counseling — for her to get there, but it was a journey she was going to have to take in order to heal and move on with her life. I didn't continue to press the issue, though; right now, she had more immediate challenges to face.

To keep her from dwelling on the obvious, I moved the conversation to easier ground. I shared instead my impressions of Helen and pulled up some photos on my phone so she could more easily visualize the town; I suggested that if she got the chance, she should try the Wiener schnitzel at the Bodensee. And for the first time, I told her about Natalie, not everything, but enough for her to know how much she meant to me.

During a pause in the conversation, I heard voices rising from down the corridor; I heard the name Karen Johnson and the sound of footsteps approaching. I stood and moved my chair back to the other side of the room and caught sight of Callie. Her eyes were frantic.

'I'm scared,' she said, panic in her tone. 'They're going to hate me.'

'They never hated you,' I soothed. 'I'm sure of it.'

'I don't even know what to say — '

'It'll come to you. But a word of advice? Tell them the truth about everything.'

'They don't want the truth.'

'Maybe not,' I said. 'But it's the best you can do.'

I was standing as one of the nurses led Callie's family into the room, where they suddenly came to a stop, as if unable to process what they were seeing. Louise was in front, flanked by Tammy and Heather; I felt four sets of eyes skim over me before they focused on the girl who'd run away from home more than a year earlier. As they grappled with their surging emotions, I noticed how much Callie resembled her mother, Louise. They had the same color hair and eyes, the same petite frame and pale skin. I doubted whether she was much older than I. Curtis, too, looked to be in his thirties, but he was taller and wider than I'd expected, with a rough beard and dark hollows under his eyes. He looked at me quizzically, as though wondering whether I was someone official whom he needed to address, but I shook my head.

Callie's voice was soft. 'Hi, Mommy.'

The words were enough to break the spell, and Louise suddenly rushed toward the bed, tears already flooding her eyes. Heather and Tammy were close behind, emitting a collective wail of excitement. They were fraternal twins, not identical, and didn't resemble each other in the slightest. Like overjoyed puppies, they practically climbed into Callie's bed as they leaned in to hug and paw at Callie. From where I was standing, I could hear Louise repeating *I can't believe it* and *We've been so worried* over and over as she stroked Callie's hair and gripped her daughter's hands, tears running unchecked down her face. Curtis, meanwhile, remained unmoving, as though paralyzed.

Finally, I heard Callie's voice again. 'Hi, Daddy,' she said, from beneath a swarm of arms. Curtis finally gave a small nod and approached the bed. The girls moved aside, making room for their father and turning to him expectantly. Hesitating, he leaned forward.

Callie sat up straighter and put her good arm around his neck.

'I'm sorry for running away and not calling,' she said in a broken whisper. 'I missed all of you so much. I love you.'

'I missed you, too, sweetheart,' he said, his words choked with emotion. 'And I love you, too.'

I stayed with Callie, remaining quiet as she told her story and answered their unending stream of questions. Some were big (*Why did you run away?*) and some were mundane (*What did you eat for lunch every day?*). Curtis asked more than once why she'd never tried to contact them, if only to let them know she was still alive. Though Callie was honest, it wasn't always an easy conversation. Their pain, and Callie's, was tangible and still fresh, even amid the joy of reunion. I could see that the real work of their healing as a family lay ahead of them, assuming Callie was even able to recover fully from her illness. She wasn't the girl she was when she ran away a year ago, yet their lives remained bound up in a tragedy that none of them had really come to terms with — least of all, Callie.

As I left the room to allow them to continue their conversation in privacy, I sent up a silent prayer that they would have the courage to navigate the months and years ahead. Walking down the hallway of this now-familiar hospital, I couldn't help thinking how strange it was that I had become so deeply enmeshed in the life of a girl I had never heard of until two months ago.

And yet, the oddest part of the entire experience was hearing her family use the name Karen over and over, which didn't seem to fit the girl I'd come to know.

To me, after all, she would always be Callie.

The next day, Dr. Nobles told me that she spent nearly an hour with the family after I left, trying to explain Callie's condition to them in a way they could easily understand. Both parents, as well as Callie's sisters, agreed to have their bone marrow tested. Because of the seriousness of Callie's condition, the lab had already promised to rush the results; they would likely know within a day or two whether any of them had a close enough HLA match, which would set the stage for additional testing. If a match was found, Callie would have to be transported to

Greenville for the remainder of her treatment. Nobles also connected them with Dr. Felicia Watkins, the oncologist at Vidant, and assured them that the hospital there would be ready for her arrival. To that end, after speaking with Nobles, I reserved and paid for rooms in New Bern for the family for the week, as well as an additional two weeks for a hotel in Greenville. It was the least I could do in light of their all-consuming worries about Callie, and the challenges of being so far from home.

Having heard my name mentioned often in the course of their talk with Callie, Curtis and Louise were naturally curious to know more about me. When I stopped by Callie's room after meeting with Dr. Nobles, I was happy to give them a brief rundown of how I'd ended up living in New Bern these past few months, while omitting the more complicated aspects of my military service and ongoing recovery. I was also able to share what I'd learned about Callie's friendship with my grandfather and the kind of man he was. It made me sad that he was not there to finally meet Callie's parents, but in some way, I felt that he was watching over this reunion, pleased that I had seen his efforts through to the end.

Natalie had responded to my text the night before, and when she later came by the hospital, I introduced her to Callie and the family. She conferred with them privately for twenty minutes, ensuring that she had all the details right for the report she would eventually have to file. On the way out, she sought me out in the waiting area, asking if I had time for a cup of coffee.

In the cafeteria, she sat across from me at the table, looking official in her uniform and as beautiful as ever. As we nursed our cups of weak coffee, I described the long hours I had spent with Callie, piecing together the shape of her story and witnessing her fraught reunion with her family.

'All in all, I guess it was a happy ending,' she said.

'So far. Now it depends on the testing.'

'It would be tragic for the parents to find her, only to lose her again.'

'Yes,' I said. 'But I have faith that it will work out.'

Natalie smiled. 'I can understand why you were so intent on helping her. She's . . . compelling. It's hard to believe she's only sixteen. She's more mature than a lot of the adults I know. I wonder how she'll adapt to living with her family again and going to high school and doing things normal teenagers do.'

'It'll be an adjustment for sure. It might take some getting used to, but I have a feeling she's going to be okay.'

'I think so, too. Oh, on another note, your grandfather was a very clever man.'

'In what way?'

'Had he said the name Callie in the hospital room, we might never have found out who she really was. We never would have tried to find a Karen.'

I considered that, realizing she was right. My

grandfather never ceased to amaze me.

'Robertson was right, too,' she went on. 'When he told us that we could have found the information ourselves. I visited the website for the GBI, and it took all of five minutes to find her once I had her real first name and knew what she looked like. We didn't have to travel to Georgia.'

'I'm still glad we went,' I said. 'Otherwise, I might not have seen you again.'

She stared down at her coffee cup. 'I'm going to miss you.'

Me too. More than you'll ever know. 'I think I'm going to harvest some of the honey before I go. Do you want to come over and help? I'll show you how to spin and filter the combs, and if you're lucky, I might let you take a few jars home.'

She hesitated, then said, 'I don't think that's such a good idea. Knowing that you're leaving is already hard enough.'

'So this is it? Our last goodbye?'

'I don't want to think of it like that.'

'How do you want to think about it?'

She paused, reflecting. 'I want to remember our time together as if it were a beautiful dream,' she finally said. 'In the moment, it was powerful and real and completely transporting.'

But then you have to wake up, I thought. 'I'll probably have to come back to New Bern from time to time to check on the house and the hives. Would you like me to let you know when I'm in town? Maybe we could meet for the occasional lunch or dinner?'

378

'Maybe . . . ' But even as she said it, I had the sense that she would prefer that I didn't. Still, I played along.

'I'll let you know.'

'Thanks. When do you think you'll be leaving?'

'In a couple of weeks, probably. I want to have time to get settled in before the program starts.'

'Of course,' she said.

'And you? Any summer plans?'

'The usual,' she said. 'I'll probably spend a few weekends here and there with my parents at the beach.'

It pained me to hear how stilted our conversation was and I wondered why talking had seemed so much easier only days earlier. This wasn't the way I imagined saying goodbye, but like her, I didn't know how to change it.

'If you ever make it up to Baltimore or DC, let me know. I'll be happy to show you around. We could visit the Smithsonian.'

'I'll do that,' she promised, even though both of us knew she wouldn't. As she said it, her lips trembled.

'Natalie . . . '

'I should probably go,' she said, suddenly standing. 'I have to get back to work.'

'I know.'

'I'll swing by your grandfather's house while you're away. Make sure no vagrants break in.'

'I'd appreciate that.'

We left the cafeteria and I walked her to the main entrance, even though I wasn't sure she wanted me to.

Reaching the doors, I followed her outside,

thinking that all of this was happening too fast. Unable to stop myself, I suddenly took her hand in mine. She paused, turning toward me, and the sight of the tears beginning to spill over her lashes brought a hard knot to my throat. Though I knew I shouldn't, I leaned in, my lips gently touching hers, before wrapping my arms around her. I kissed the top of her head and pulled her close.

'I understand, Natalie,' I murmured into her hair. 'I do.'

'I'm so sorry,' she whispered back, her body trembling against mine.

'I love you, and I'll never forget you.'

'I love you, too.'

The sun was high and bright, the air sultry with humidity and heat. I was vaguely aware of a man strolling past us holding a bouquet of flowers; an elderly woman in a wheelchair was rolled outside a few seconds later. Inside the hospital, women were giving birth to children who had their whole lives ahead of them while other patients were reaching the ends of theirs. It was an ordinary day but nothing was ordinary for me, and as tears pricked my eyes, I wanted nothing more than to make this moment last forever.

Within a couple of days, Dr. Nobles informed me that Heather's bone marrow was a six-out-of-six HLA match for Callie; Tammy's was five out of six. Additional screening and testing were already underway, but Dr. Nobles was confident that the match was a successful one.

Later in the week, Nobles confirmed it, and that both the transfer and the transplant were scheduled for a date the following week, when I would already be in Baltimore. Though there were certainly risks on the horizon and Callie would remain on medication for years, Dr. Nobles was optimistic that in the long run, she would be able to lead a normal life.

I continued to spend time with Callie and her family at the hospital right up until my departure; when I wasn't there, I was packing and getting the house ready for its impending vacancy. On my last full day there, a cleaning crew scoured the house from top to bottom and linens were stored in plastic bags to prevent mold and dust from forming. I met again with the property manager and the contractor, supervising the delivery of the roofing and flooring materials and their storage in the barn.

I also harvested the honey. I kept several jars for myself, sold much of the remainder to Claude, and also left some on Natalie's doorstep. However, I didn't knock at the door nor did I call.

I thought about her constantly; I awakened to memories of her scent and her smile; she was the last image I saw before closing my eyes at night. Throughout my remaining days in New Bern, I wondered what she was doing at any given moment and where she was. I no longer felt complete, as if part of me had been hollowed out, leaving only an aching void. Before Natalie, I used to believe that with love, anything was possible. Now I understand that sometimes love isn't enough.

It wasn't until I'd been living in Baltimore for three days that I found the letter Natalie had left for me, tucked into one of the boxes of books that had been in the back of my SUV. At first, I couldn't identify the envelope and considered throwing it away. When I realized that it was sealed, however, curiosity won out. Recognizing her signature at the bottom of the letter, I suddenly couldn't catch my breath.

I walked like a zombie to the living room and sat on the couch. It was still daylight, with light pouring through the French doors, and in the silence of my new apartment, I finally began to read.

Dear Trevor,

I'm writing this letter because I'm not sure what else to do. I don't know when you'll find it, since I had to sneak it into one of the boxes you'd packed. On the other hand, since you've now left jars of honey on my doorstep twice without letting me know you were at my house, I figured you might even appreciate the idea that you'd had a secret visitor.

I wanted to tell you that for the first time in my life, I truly understand what people mean when they say, 'I fell in love.' Because when I fell in love with you, I didn't drift into it, it didn't happen over time, it wasn't anything that I even thought I wanted. In hindsight it's like I had spent the last fourteen months standing on a building ledge. I was balanced precariously and doing everything I could to stay rooted in place. If I didn't move, if I was somehow able to remain perfectly focused, then I'd somehow be okay. But then out of the blue, you showed up. You called to me from the ground and I stepped from the ledge . . . and then I was falling, right up until the moment you caught me in your arms.

Trevor, falling in love with you has been one of the most exalted experiences of my life. As hard as it is for me now — and I torment myself constantly over whether I made the right decision — I wouldn't have traded it for anything. You made me feel more fully alive than I have in what seems like forever. Until you came along, I wasn't sure I would ever feel that way — and more — again.

My desire for you feels unquenchable, unbounded. But the truth is that desire comes at a terrible price. I can't allow myself to wish that my husband was dead, nor could I live with myself if I divorced him, if only because he isn't capable of trying to change my mind. If I did either of those things, I wouldn't be the same woman you fell in love with; to do either of those things would change me forever. It would transform me into a villain, a person I couldn't recognize and have no desire to be. And of course, I couldn't do that to you, either.

This was the reason I couldn't see you again after saying goodbye at the hospital; this is the reason it would be best if we didn't meet when you come back to town. I know how much I love you, and if you asked me again to come with you, I don't think I would be able to resist. If you ask again, I'll come to you; if you as much as hint toward that end, I'll show up at your door. But please — please, please, please — don't ever let me become the villain of my own story. I'm begging you to never put me in that position. Instead, let me be the woman you came to know and love, the same woman who fell deeply in love with you.

While I don't know what the future holds for either of us, I want you to know that I'll always treasure our time together, however brief. In a way, I want you to know that I'll always believe that you saved me. Had you not come along, I think a vital, precious part of myself would have simply dried up and withered away; now, with our memories to sustain me — with my memories of you — I finally feel as if I can go on. Thank you for that. Thank you for everything.

I already miss you. I miss your teasing and your terrible jokes, and your slightly crooked smile, even your silly attempts to get me to roll my eyes. Most of all, I miss your friendship, and the way you always made me feel as though I were the most desirable woman in the world. I do love *you, and if I were living a different life, I would follow you anywhere.*

I love you,
Natalie

When I finished reading the letter, I rose from my spot on the couch and wandered to the kitchen on unsteady legs. Opening the refrigerator, I found a beer and twisted off the cap before taking a long pull. Then, returning to the living room, I stared out the French doors, imagining where Natalie might be in this very moment — perhaps visiting her parents at the beach and taking a long and quiet stroll on the shore. Every now and then, she would examine a seashell, or maybe stop to follow the flight of some pelicans as they skimmed low over the breakers. Perhaps, I wanted to believe, she was remembering me in that very same instant, holding our love close like a comforting secret in her otherwise merciless world.

I was glad she'd written me the letter and wondered whether she wanted a letter in return. Maybe I'd write one, or because it might make things even more difficult for her, maybe I wouldn't. I didn't have the energy to make that decision.

Instead, returning to the couch, I set the beer on the table. And with a sigh, I began to read the letter again.

Epilogue

Though I began many letters to Natalie, in the end I never sent them. Nor, during my regular but infrequent visits to New Bern, did I seek out or call her. Occasionally I would overhear things, usually people talking in low whispers about how hard it must be for her, or whether she should somehow find a way to move on. Whenever I heard those comments, I felt a deep ache at the thought that her life remained on permanent hold.

For me, moving on meant five years of residency, long hours, and completing enough clinical practice to finish the program. Though I'd originally thought that my interest would lie almost exclusively in the treatment of PTSD, I quickly came to discover that patients with PTSD often presented with other issues as well. They might be concurrently struggling with drug or alcohol addiction or suffering from depression; still others had bipolar disorder or various personality disorders. I learned that the treatment of every patient was unique, and though I tried, I couldn't help everyone. While I was in Baltimore, two patients committed suicide, and another was arrested after an argument in a bar led to a charge of second-degree murder. That patient is currently behind bars for a minimum of nine years. Every now and then, he'll send me a letter complaining that he isn't receiving the treatment he needs, and I have no doubt that he is correct.

I have found the work deeply interesting, perhaps more than I expected. In its own way, it is more of an intellectual challenge than orthopedic surgery had ever been and I can honestly say that I look forward to my work every day. Unlike some of the other residents, I have little trouble separating myself from my patients at the end of the day; to carry the cumulative psychological burdens of others is too much for anyone to bear. Still, there are times when it isn't possible to simply walk away; even when some patients can't afford to pay for treatment, I often make myself available to them.

I have continued my own sessions with Dr. Bowen as well, though over time, the sessions have become more infrequent. Now I speak with him about once a month and only rarely do I experience any physical symptoms associated with PTSD. I sleep well and my hands haven't trembled since my time in New Bern, but every now and then, I still feel an ache of sadness for Natalie and the life I imagined we would have made together.

As for Callie, there were regular calls in the beginning, but those eventually faded to the occasional text, usually around the holidays. The transplant was successful, her health was as stable as it could be considering her situation, and she had moved back in with her family. She graduated from high school and became a dental hygienist. I have no idea how or when she met Jeff McCorkle — she hinted that it was a story in and of itself — and as I wait in the church for Callie to walk down the aisle, the cynical side of me wonders whether the two of them are too young to be getting married. Both of them are only twenty-one, and the statistics don't paint an entirely rosy scenario for their marriage in the long run. On the other hand, Callie has always been a person of extraordinary maturity and determination.

Most important, she — like me — fully understands that life's twists and turns are impossible to predict.

When I drove through Helen on my way to the church, I was overwhelmed with déjà vu. The town looked exactly the same as it had the last time I'd been here. I passed the police station and the Bodensee restaurant, and despite running late, I idled in front of the hotel where Natalie had asked me to hold her on our last night together.

I like to think that I've moved forward since then, and in many ways, I know that I have. My residency and training complete, I have multiple offers in three different states. I have a favorite, but whether I choose that position depends to a degree on what happens later today.

From my seat, I can hear murmuring and whispers from people in the pews all around me; despite myself, I can't help turning around to scrutinize every new arrival. When Natalie finally arrives, I feel my heart skip a beat. She is wearing a lovely peach-colored sundress and although she's allowed her hair to grow out, she doesn't appear to have aged in the five years since I last saw her. I watch as she scans the church, trying to locate an open seat, and is eventually escorted to a spot three rows in front of me. As I stare at the back of her head, I offer a silent thank-you to Callie, who had agreed to extend a special invitation to Natalie at my request.

Jeff eventually takes his place at the front of the church near the minister, with three groomsmen and a best man beside him. The music begins, Wagner's *Lohengrin*, and Callie appears at the back of the church. Standing beside her is her clean-shaven father, Curtis, dressed in a dark blue suit. Both of them are beaming and we all stand as they proceed down the aisle. Curtis kisses his daughter on the cheek and takes his seat beside Louise, who is already dabbing at her eyes. Tammy and Heather are both bridesmaids, wearing matching pink dresses.

The ceremony is as traditional as I'd expected, and Callie and Jeff are pronounced husband and wife in short order. The guests applaud, and I smile when I hear a few whistles as well.

At the reception under an expansive white tent, I am seated with some of Callie's cousins and their spouses, and grin every time guests gently tap their wineglasses with spoons, prompting yet another kiss by Callie and Jeff.

Callie dances with her husband and then her father, before others join in. I even manage to snag a dance with Callie, after which she introduces me to her new husband. He comes across as an earnest young man, and they are enviably, obviously in love. As I part from them, I hear Jeff ask Callie in a puzzled whisper, 'Why does he call you Callie?'

I wonder how much she's told him about the time she spent in New Bern, or whether she's simply glossed over the details. In the long run, I suppose it won't matter. Jeff, I suspect, will probably learn everything, as secrets are almost always impossible to keep.

Not long after the dancing began, I had seen Natalie step out of the tent. I follow and spot her standing near an ancient magnolia tree. As I approach, the music from the reception dwindles, leaving only the two of us in the still summer afternoon. I marvel again at how ageless and beautiful she is.

I remind myself not to expect much. Five years is a long time, and there is no doubt in my mind that it has changed both of us. Part of me wonders whether she will recognize me right away or whether I will notice a split-second hesitation while she tries to locate me in her memories. Nor am I exactly sure what to say to her, but as I draw near, Natalie turns to face me with a knowing smile.

'Hello, Trevor,' she says. 'I was wondering how long it would take you to come find me.'

'You knew I was here?'

'I saw you in the church,' she says. 'I thought about sitting beside you, but I didn't want to make it too easy for you.'

With that, she moves closer, and as though our time apart had collapsed in the blink of an eye, she steps into my arms. I pull her close, absorbing the feel of her body with reverence. I catch her familiar scent, something I hadn't realized how much I'd missed.

'It's good to see you,' she whispers in my ear.

'You too. You look beautiful.'

We separate and for the first time, I am able to study her up close. Except for the tiniest of lines at the corners of her eyes and her lusciously long hair, she is the same woman who has visited me in my dreams for the last five years. Though I'd dated a few different women, each of those relationships had ended even before they'd had a chance to begin. At the time, I'd told myself that I simply didn't have the energy for a new relationship; as I stand with Natalie, I know that I'd really been waiting for her.

'So? Are you a psychiatrist now?'

'I passed my boards last month,' I say. 'It's official. How about you? Are you still working for the sheriff's department?'

'Not anymore,' she says. 'Believe it or not, I own a flower shop now.'

'You're kidding.'

'I'm not. It's in downtown New Bern.'

'How did that happen?'

'I saw a listing that the shop was for sale. The owner was retiring so he didn't want much for the business, and by then, I knew that I didn't want to remain a sheriff's deputy. So the owner and I worked something out.'

'When was this?'

'About eighteen months ago.'

I smile. 'I'm so happy for you.'

'Me too.'

'How's your family?'

'Other than my parents retiring to the beach, not much has changed.'

'Do you still visit them regularly?'

'I get to the coast every other weekend. They spend all their time there now. They sold their business and the house in La Grange. How about you? Still living in Baltimore?'

'For the time being. Just trying to figure out where I want to settle down.'

'Are you thinking anyplace in particular?'

'Maybe,' I say. 'Still working through my options.'

'I've heard there's a shortage of psychiatrists in Eastern North Carolina.'

'Is that so?' I say. 'Where would you have heard something like that?'

'I can't really remember. Oh, by the way, I kept an eye on your grandfather's house for you. Back when I was a sheriff's deputy, I mean. But even now, I still look in on the place from time to time.'

'Did you check out the beehives?'

'I didn't,' she says, with a touch of regret. 'You?'

'A couple of times a year. They don't need much tending.'

'I should have known. They had the honey at

the Trading Post the last few years. Only place in town you can get it.'

'I'm glad you remembered.'

Using both hands, she pulls her hair back into a ponytail, then releases it. 'Callie sure looked pretty. I loved her dress. And it seems like she's still getting along with her family, too.'

'It was a lovely ceremony. I'm happy for her. How about you, though? How long are you staying in Helen?'

'Just overnight. I flew and rented a car this morning.'

'And then you're heading back to New Bern?'

'Of course,' she says. 'My mom is standing in for me at the shop, but I'm pretty sure she'd like to get back to the beach.'

For the first time, I notice she isn't wearing the chain around her neck, the one with the wedding band. Nor is the band on her finger. 'Where's your ring?'

'I don't wear it any longer.'

'Why not?'

'Mark passed away,' she says, meeting my gaze. 'Ten months ago. They think it was a pulmonary embolism.'

'I'm sorry.'

'He was a good man,' she says. 'My first love.' She flashes a wistful smile. 'And I guess you'll be heading back to Baltimore after this, huh?'

'In time,' I say. 'I'll need to pack my things eventually. But actually, I'm heading to New Bern, too. It's time to harvest the honey, and I figure I'll stick around for a little while. I'm meeting with a couple of practices in the area.'

'In New Bern?'

'One in New Bern, the other in Greenville. I have offers from both, but I want to make sure I'm making the right decision.'

She stares at me before finally beginning to smile.

'You might end up in New Bern?'

'Maybe,' I say. 'Hey, by the way, are you dating anyone right now?'

'No,' she says with a coy smile. 'I mean, I've been on a few dates, but they didn't stick. How about you?'

'Same,' I say. 'I've been pretty busy the last few years.'

'I can imagine,' she says, her smile widening.

At that, my heart begins to lift and I thumb toward the tent. 'Would you care to dance?'

'I'd love to.' Surprising me just a little, she loops her arm through mine and we start back toward the reception.

'Oh, and one more thing,' I say. 'If you'd like to help me harvest the honey once I'm back in New Bern, I'd love to show you the process. Maybe the timing is better this time.'

'How much does it pay?'

I laugh. 'How much do you want?'

She pretends to think about it before turning her gaze to me again. 'How about dinner on the back porch afterward?'

'Dinner?'

'I'm sure I'll work up an appetite.'

'That sounds like a fair trade.' I pause, suddenly serious. 'I've missed you, Natalie.'

At the entrance to the tent, she pulls me to a